The Bridge

Trip Tressler

Table of Contents

Acknowledgements..4
Prologue...9
Chapter 1..16
Chapter 2..36
Chapter 3..43
Chapter 4..52
Chapter 5..58
Chapter 6..73
Chapter 7..81
Chapter 8..86
Chapter 9..91
Chapter 10...102
Chapter 11...107
Chapter 12...110
Chapter 13...115
Chapter 14...122
Chapter 15...128
Chapter 16...136
Chapter 17...148
Chapter 18...160
Chapter 19...167
Chapter 20...172
Chapter 21...182
Chapter 22...198
Chapter 23...207
Chapter 24...214
Chapter 25...229
Chapter 26...239
Chapter 27...247
Chapter 28...255
Chapter 29...269
Chapter 30...291
Chapter 31...301
Chapter 32...311
Chapter 33...316
Chapter 34...337
Chapter 35...345
Chapter 36...352
Chapter 37...357
Chapter 38...366
Chapter 39...379
Chapter 40...386
Chapter 41...395
Chapter 42...402
Chapter 43...411
Chapter 44...432
Chapter 45...444
Chapter 46...460
Chapter 47...484
Epilogue..497

Acknowledgements

For my parents and family, who have supported me in this long journey in so many unbelievable ways.

For my friends, who continue spending time with me even when I won't stop talking about all my completely wacky ideas. You all rock!

For my fans, who without who I wouldn't be able to continue my pursuit of being an author! If my work touches the heart of even one of you, then I consider the entire project a victory.

For You

For my friend

"The greatest stories build the strongest bridges."

I stood upon the edge of the shore and looked

Upon the water of the sea

There I saw myself,

My reflection cold

Hoping it would change

That I could change for the better

And make it right.

A girl appeared on the shore

She came to me

As I stood there, weeping

She held my hand, and smiled

And the sun burned away the clouds

Shining light

On my fears, my doubt.

"Come, my friend.

I will show you the way

Walk down this path with me

It's the hardest one around

I know

But I'd rather not walk it

Alone."

My friend let go of my hand

And smiled

She walked into the sea

Her feet floating on its surface

Before I knew it, she was far away

So I took a deep breath and walked across the bridge

She had made on top of the water.

Whether I sink or swim

I have decided

I will tread this path

That I will walk forever

With her by my side.

"Welcome to Arthridall."

Prologue

Tall trees whizzed by Jamey's head as she ran along the somewhat worn dirt path, her small feet pounding against the ground in the anticipation of getting caught. Fading flecks of light flashed on her face through the canopy above, creating an even greater sense of urgency. She only had thirty seconds before the chase began.

She turned around the corner and leaned against the tree bark to catch her breath before making another break for it. Jehu was going to catch her if she ran out of energy too soon and getting caught meant bedtime. And bedtime was only for people who got caught.

"Ten, nine… I've got to find a spot!"

Jamey could still hear his countdown. She wasn't far enough into the woods to get to the biggest trees with the best branches; she would need to find a spot to hide in on the ground. Besides, she didn't have time to climb.

"READY OR NOT, HERE I COME!" Jehu called from the camp.

"What?! He totally didn't count ten seconds!" she angrily whispered, snapping to the nearest bush in the underbrush and crawling under it for cover.

She dared not move. Her great grandpa had the best hearing ever, even for someone his age. And he was fast. There were times she was actually inclined to believe the tale of when he taught a pack of cheetahs how to hunt.

"WHEEERE ARRRE YOUUU?"

It was a ploy. A tactic meant to get her to reveal herself so he could pinpoint his target with his god-like echolocation. She would not be fooled. Jamey's nose quivered as she felt her pent-up breath run down to her lip before she cut the flow off altogether. He couldn't win again. Sleep was for the weak.

Her ears perked up at the sound of his footsteps crunching a cluster of sticks and leaves some distance away. She still had a bit of time yet. Jamey slowly began to breathe again, but she could still feel her lungs shaking. It was going to give her away if she didn't start controlling herself soon. Her foot slid on the dirt slightly as she adjusted to get more comfortable.

The footsteps stopped. Jamey was instantly on high alert again, not daring to make a move for fear of being spotted. The woods were eerily quiet, save for the slight noise of the wind pushing the leaves around up above. She was almost free; if she stayed hidden until sunset she'd be allowed to go to bed on her own time.

Jehu knew where she was hiding but decided to play along for a bit. It was for the best. If he didn't spoil his kid every so often while her parents weren't around, who would? But he also wanted to have some fun with it.

He pulled out his walking staff and began tapping around the underbrush with it. The reality was he was only ten feet away from Jamey's hiding spot, but he knew all this extra searching in the nearby area would only make the finale that much more fun.

"She's getting better at this," he muttered loud enough for her to hear. "If I don't get her soon I might not even able to get a piece of pie back at camp once she's done with it."

Jamey giggled quietly despite herself. She loved pie.

"AHAH! I FOUND YOU!"

Jamey's entire body tensed up. He still had to actually find and catch her before sunset for it to count. She looked up to the sky through the bush; she only needed to last another thirty seconds. She was going to make it. Finally going to beat him at his own game.

Jehu grinned mischievously and lifted his staff into the air, pointing it toward Jamey's hiding spot. She looked quizzically at him from her spot through the brush, not knowing what he meant by it.

And then a blindingly bright fireball erupted out the end of it and launched towards her, instantly vaporizing the bush above her and turning what was left into ash. Her piercing scream only stopped once she found herself in the middle of his hug as he crouched next to her.

"Time for bed, kiddo."

Jamey collapsed in defeat. She'd been so incredibly close for once this time. It wasn't fair. But rules were rules and she'd agreed to them. Anything was better than just simply going to sleep. Jamey stood and began walking back towards camp to get ready for bed. Jehu followed, draping his hand on her shoulder to console her.

"You'll get it next time, I'm sure. You almost had me there. Had to pull out my trump card."

Jamey moped.

"I didn't even know you could shoot fireballs..."

Jehu laughed heartily.

"There's a lot of things I can do... Tell ya what, once you finish getting ready I'll tell you a story about your parents. You're... you're still working on writing it all down, right?"

Jamey shrugged, still disappointed by her loss.

"Yeah, I guess so..."

"Then you're going to love this one. Hurry up though, this one might take some time."

"Okay..."

She couldn't complain. Nothing was better than listening to his stories about her parents, not even hide and seek. Jamey decided to make a game out of how quickly she could get ready for bed too, so she ran back to the edge of camp where the other adults were cleaning up after supper. She'd always wanted to join them for the fireside chats after the sunset, but for now she wasn't allowed. Something about being too rambunctious, whatever that meant.

Jamey crawled into her tent on her hands and knees, untying the bow she'd put in her hair that morning. She still wasn't used to dressing up like a girl, but she was starting to like it. Other than the times her dresses got stuck on the tree branches of course.

"The price for being pretty, I suppose."

Jehu finished walking back to camp and immediately sat down on the stump next to the fire pit. No one dared ask him to help finish cleaning up; tiring Jamey out was easily one of the hardest chores they had, and no one did it better than him.

Jamey crawled out of her tent, her nightgown snagging on a stick by the entrance. She stumbled upright after untangling herself and waltzed over to her grandpa as if nothing had happened. Jehu wisely made no indication that he'd seen it, instead motioning to her to come over and sit.

"Did you brush your teeth?"

Jamey groaned, but said she did. He smiled. Kids would be kids. The rest of the group filtered in as they finished their chores. Jamey wasn't the only one who enjoyed listening to Jehu's stories.

"Alright, tonight is a special night, so listen closely. It is a tale of love and adventure and mystery. It is perhaps even the very reason we gathered together to fight back and take back our land. James and Amy, as you now know are Jamey's parents, weren't always residents of Arthridall. But they might've just saved it."

Jehu coughed lightly and pulled out his pipe to begin smoking it.

"Before they were Arthrindians, they were inhabitants of Earth. And after they became Arthrindians, they went back to Earth to save it. James you see, was a writer. Excuse me," he said apologetically while looking at his child, "Is a writer. You see, Arthridall was not always the land we know it to be today. Back in those days people still had hope. Or, more specifically, they didn't have a reason to fear. We were simple folk: farmers, blacksmiths, carpenters, masons and home-makers. I'd be lying to say everything was perfect, but what our people had was nice."

Jehu took a deep breath from his pipe to steady himself. All eyes were on him, save Jamey's. He'd done a better job at tiring her out than he'd thought.

"This is the story of how James and Amy, friends of the High-King, discovered the grand vizier's intentions to overthrow his rule and cast this land into the abyss."

Jehu looked each one of them in the eye in turn.

"I shudder to think what may have befallen us had they not uncovered his plot and escaped with their lives to bring us what we know now as self-evident."

Jehu allowed himself a small smile as he looked down at his granddaughter. Even in slumber she still held her simple and worn brown leather book. She'd inscribed a carving into the front, filling the lines in with some metallic ink so it had the same shape and color as the necklace around her neck.

"This is the story of how James and Amy outwitted Thorne and saved their daughter by fleeing to Earth."

1

James looked at his computer blankly, unsure of the outcome from his undertaking. It was a dangerous thing to write one's self into a book, and yet he felt like it was still genius. His genius. He enjoyed the feeling of putting pen to paper; writing on a computer was an interesting experience after all this time. Not that he didn't enjoy it, because he really did like the fact that he could save his work and it would be safe from those sudden and pesky thunderstorms that always seemed to occur whenever he began a new story.

His thoughts were never not with him. They were his friends, in a way. He didn't have too many people he counted as friends. Earth was relatively boring in that respect.

"But Arthridall... now that's a different story," he thought.

He still couldn't believe he was still alive, or how he'd managed to come back. Here of all places. Earth. The memories were still hazy, but his gut told him if he was ever going to make it back home he would need to keep writing. As he'd always had. And to be fair, it could've been worse.

There were far worse places to end up than Earth. It was familiar at least.

James looked at his computer screen again. It'd been a while since worked on it. Getting used to routine again had been tedious at best. He sometimes couldn't remember where he'd come from to get to this place and time. The memories he searched for danced just outside his reach, tempting him with the promise of adventure, other mundane events threatening to steal precious creativity and override his sense of belonging.

"The answers are in there somewhere. Arthridall needs me... right?" he asked.

He closed his laptop and began packing his bags. There were still pieces missing and it bothered him. He was here for a reason, that he was sure about. He needed to keep writing, that he knew. What that reason was, he wasn't sure. But he'd been here for months now and nothing had changed. But something had happened and now he was here.

"I was in Arthridall. That I'm sure about," he said, walking out the door and towards home. "I think... I was writing about Arthridall. Well duh, of course I'd be writing. Hmm... Maybe I'm here because I need to write about Earth for a bit. King did say he was working on expanding the system. If that's the case..."

James walked in the front door and started getting ready for bed. His bed. His big, oh so fluffy bed. It was one of the few perks Earth had that Arthridall tended to lack in. Big, soft beds.

"If that's the case maybe I'm here to help him build one of them."

He climbed into bed and flipped off his lamp. It was the best thought he'd had all night.

"Building another portal. As if we didn't already have enough of them. Wonder what we're going to call this one," he said.

James closed his eyes and smiled for the first time that day. Finally, a part of his confusion solved. Maybe he'd get going on the book after all.

***

Amy knew she'd heard a noise somewhere further inside the cavern. Whether that noise was born from her imagination or from another source was yet to be determined. Caverns were by nature secret echo chambers, meant to be places to hide in. But what was hidden there always revealed the hider's intent.

"Secrets? Or hiding from something?" She thought.

Large stone columns braced the low-ceilinged entrance to the temple, providing a sense of anxiety and adventure. For all she knew it could've been her friend inside, hiding behind a random rock just deep enough in to where she'd get scared, but not so far in as to lose her friendship.

The columns continued to line the walkway as she walked further in; the torches mounted on each alternate pillar looked like they'd either been recently lit or had never been snuffed. It was eerily quiet, save the occasional flicker of light as a stray spiderweb ventured a little too close.

"James?" she whispered. "Are you here? I heard a noise coming from outside... If it's you? You better show yourself!"

She felt a chill creep up her spine as she neared the staircase and still saw no sign of him. If he was really hiding he was doing a really good job of it. Amy tentatively took a few steps up, tempted to hold onto the torch bases on the left wall. Whoever had mounted them had done a phenomenal job of making sure they could never be stolen.

She stifled a tiny shriek as her foot briefly slipped on the corner of the stair and a bit of the corner broke off, falling into the pitch-black abyss on her right. But she'd already made it this far, and her curiosity had already been piqued. There was something or someone up there. She could see the shadows bouncing off the boulder of a wall as it curved around the opening up ahead on her left.

"I swear, if this is another one of those over-the-top surprise parties he's always planning I'm actually going to throttle him this time." she grimaced.

Amy allowed herself a moment to lean against the top and look behind her. She was getting better at this. She'd never had an issue with heights, but she had her reasons for hating the dark. Falling down into it because of a cheap scare wasn't exactly high on her bucket list.

She quietly approached the opening. Roughly chiseled, low hanging arches ran around the upper edge of a massive auditorium-esque chamber, a single torch mounted on the backside of each pillar. Amy could barely stand without bumping her head, so she decided to stay crouched until she could stretch out fully. She heard a few familiar voices down below but couldn't quite make out what they were saying. Something about caverns being an echo chamber whether one wanted them to be or not. But something in her gut told her they weren't planning a surprise party.

Amy approached the edge of one of the arches to peek over ever so slightly. If it wasn't a surprise party she was going to be disappointed. A series of large columns similar in shape to the ones she'd encountered at the entrance lined each side of the center of the room. They were much taller than the others and thicker around, but weren't attached to the ceiling. She found it odd to look down and see the squared-shaped tops of the columns rather than supporting a box shaped space she imagined would house the control room if this stone auditorium were a play-house.

What they did denote however, were the edges of the room down below. A relatively long path with a set of tall, carved doors to her relative left marked the real entrance. The path led into the rectangular space the columns boxed in. She couldn't see the far end of the chamber thanks to the pillar blocking her angle on the right, but she supposed that was where the large, singular stone chair with demented carvings inscribed in it would be.

"That's where the voices are coming from..." she whispered. "But I can't even see the space around the room. It's like it's a peninsula where you can die on all sides."

She shuddered to think about being pushed over the side into the abyss like that. Or slipping on one of the massive ingrained tiles and do herself in. For all she knew, the abyss could really just be an unlit area. It could've actually been the same height as the rest of the chamber, as the torches below were situated on the inside of the pillars, but she wasn't just about to test that theory.

"But I do need to move..." she thought. "I must've come in the technician's entrance."

The good news was she hadn't given herself away yet, on the off-chance that it was not actually a surprise party. But she did feel like she knew those voices from somewhere, and it was driving her nuts that she couldn't quite place them.

Amy inched on her hands and knees to the right, hoping her shadow would be well hidden by brightness of the torches and the fact that no one should be climbing up there in the first place. As far as she could tell she was succeeding. But it was aggravating that she still couldn't see who they were, as the next pillar over also blocked her line of sight.

"I guess it also means they can't see me." she whispered.

She jumped in her boots, almost hitting her head on the curved ceiling as she heard the slight shuffle of a pair of shoes coming from the opening she'd entered in from. She froze in place, hoping the new intruder hadn't seen her intrusion. The shoes crunched lightly on the clay dust for a few moments and stopped right behind her. A hand gently rested itself on her shoulder and she braced herself for the worst until it turned her around.

"James?"

A slightly shaggy brown-haired boy about her age nodded, putting a finger to his lips to let her know to keep quiet.

"What are you doing here?" he whispered.

Amy combed her hair a little to brush off the dust from the ceiling. At least he was one person she could cross off her list.

"I heard a noise coming from the cavern and I thought it was you trying to scare me. Why are you here?"

"I followed you in after I couldn't find you around outside. How on earth did you find this place?"

She sat on her butt and tied her hair back into a ponytail.

"I wouldn't have found it if I hadn't heard it coming from the woods... but there's people down there. I've got to figure out what's going on."

He grabbed her shoulder as she started standing.

"What are you doing?"

"I'm going to find out who's down there and why they're in such a weird secret lair."

He let her go.

"And how do you think you're going to do that? Are you trying to let them know we're here? Let me do it."

Amy shook her head. She was tired of always relying on him to finish everything.

"No. I have an idea."

James tried to convince her but she was past convincing.

"You aren't going to try jumping on those pillars, are you? I can't even see the bottom if you miss."

Amy grinned impishly.

"Don't remind me. Besides, I've done jumps way harder than this. Remember…?"

He shushed her.

"Oh, oh, oh I remember. I still don't think it's a good idea. You could be walking into a trap."

Amy planted her feet on the edge and prepared to take the leap.

"Just be ready to save me, then!"

James watched on in horror as his friend almost slipped off the edge into what was almost certainly an abyss. Her hair flipped to the side as she steadied herself again. She hated the dark but when he was with her it was different somehow.

"I'll probably need it..."

He felt his heart drop in his chest as she leaped, a small whoosh of air brushing his cheek as if to say goodbye. Amy's makeshift hair tie flew off mid-flight, her dirty-blonde hair streaming like a waterfall over a cliff.

"Amy..." he whispered.

Amy clambered onto the edge of the pillar with a gut-wrenching groan as it knocked the air out of her. She looked over at him with a huge grin and stood up after a moment to peer over the edge.

James decided to take the safer route along the wall. No reason for both of them to get caught. They might be able to see his shadow but he was willing to take that trade if it came to it. Someone had to plan the escape route.

Unfortunately for Amy she still couldn't make out what the voices were saying. But she was able to distinguish that there were only two of them. Her hunch had been right. She had a knack for sniffing out plot devices. She knew James wouldn't approve but she needed to see who they were.

"Don't...!"

James caught himself. He'd almost given her away. She had a handle on the pillars now and he needed to trust her. He needed to focus on his task.

Amy darted along the string of pillars like a game of hop-scotch, quietly dodging one of the bats that'd decided to nest in the area. She peered over the corner, finally able to make out their faces. She'd been right about the stone chair.

"Cifer? What's he doing in a place like this?" she thought.

She looked backed to where she'd come from to let her friend know and panicked until she looked back over to her right. James was directly across the gap in the alcove she'd jumped across. She shook her head.

"Leave it to him to take the most obvious route sometimes." she shrugged.

James waved and she meekly waved back. He still wasn't able to see from his vantage. They mouthed the words.

"It's Cifer!" Amy said.

"Cifer?"

"Yes!"

"What's Cifer doing in a place like this?"

"Why are you asking me?!"

"Why else would you jump?"

"You're asking me now?"

"Yes."

Amy didn't really have an answer. She lifted her hands as if to give up and they both snickered knowingly. Still, it was an interesting question.

"I'm going to sneak down this column and get closer."

"What?!"

"And yes it's empty space down there. I can feel a draft."

"Are you out of your mind?"

"Hmmm... Probably?"

Amy assumed the position. James knew he wasn't going to change her mind at this point, but he was going to help. He spotted another small opening at the far end of the pass behind the back wall. He motioned to her.

"I think there's another staircase over there," he motioned, pointing behind the throne. "Sit tight until I get down."

"Gotcha."

Amy slowly slid down the column, using its large ridges to pivot her hands and feet into it and create some resistance. Things weren't adding up. Why was Cifer hiding in an abandoned throne room? And why didn't she just crawl along the edge with James?

"Just had to show off..." she thought, landing on the ground with a soft thud. "Still, that was pretty amazing."

The voices immediately stopped talking. Amy immediately crouched and froze in her tracks, hoping the torch on her left hadn't revealed her.

"Totally plotting something…"

They started talking again. Amy took a deep breath and walked out from her hiding spot.

"Cifer!" she shouted, pointing.

Two pairs of eyes turned to meet her gaze. A voluptuous lady in red looked down at her from the second highest step, her gaze snarling at her like a caged animal waiting for its meal. Cifer sat in the chair, his chin leaned against his fist.

"Well, well, well." He said slowly. "I thought I'd heard something crawling around in the attic."

Amy felt shivers crawl up her spine, but she couldn't quite place it.

"Where have you been?" Amy asked. "The whole city's been searching for you for weeks!"

Cifer slowly stood, pushing up off the throne with an odd grimace.

"Oh, you know… Amy." He said, pacing around as if he was about to fall asleep. "I had to… slay some dragons. They… were stronger than I anticipated…"

"Dragons?" Amy asked, watching the lady suggestively brush against his shoulder and sit in the chair behind him.

"Dragons!" he said, his eyes lighting up.

Her skin crawled again. His eyes were a different color from the last time she'd seen him.

"Do... you know... why... I had to slay... dragons?"

"No?"

Cifer took a step down, leaning into the conversation. The lady smiled maliciously.

"I... needed something of theirs..."

It clicked for her.

"You didn't... you performed the...?"

Cipher swooped to her spot in an instant. It was all Amy could do to not fall from the impact of his presence.

"Ki...King wouldn't have you do tha... that... would he?"

"OH NO, my sweet child... I drank dragon's blood so I could kill King. Look..." he said, eyes flaring.

Amy took a step back as Cifer unfurled a pair of large, leathery, venomous looking wings and the wind punched her in the face. She was distraught.

"Why... Why would you do... that? Why would you want to kill King? Cife...?"

"MY NAME... IS THORNE! AND I... WILL RULE THIS WORLD."

He leaned in and she fell backwards.

"But… He must not know I am coming…" he said. "It might… ruin me…"

Amy watched in horror as his legs turned into the claws of nightmares. It was all she could do not to vomit. The lady laughed wickedly. She needed to think fast.

"Wai… Wait!" Amy shouted, catching them by surprise. "I… I have something you need!"

Thorne put his leg down, suddenly interested by her proposal. Power was the only thing on his mind now, fractured and splintered as it was.

Amy reached under her shirt and gingerly pulled it out to show them. His face lit up.

"That's…"

"That's right… Thorne! It's a key. But you already know what it goes to, right?"

"Give it to me!" he screeched, reaching for it like his life depended on it.

Amy smiled inwardly despite her intense fear.

"Got him," she thought.

"Wait!" she shouted. "It won't work for you if I don't give it willingly!"

Amy desperately searched for James' outline. Nowhere to be seen. But Thorne noticed her hesitation.

"You're… not alone… Are you? That simply… won't do."

She had to believe he was still there somewhere. But she needed to buy time. Something told her Thorne wasn't about to let her go willingly.

"You're... you're right! I'm not alone! But... you probably wouldn't want to kill me, right? If... If you did, you'd never find my t... team, right?"

Thorne froze as Amy's bizarrely obvious logic drove a stake through his power-hungry brain. Amy's teeth were starting to chatter. The room was definitely growing colder. Not exactly the warm welcome she was hoping for.

A loud whinnying outside the main entrance startled everyone and caused them to look away from her. Thankfully, Amy was facing the right direction to see her friend quietly clambering down the stone face behind the lady after removing his hand from his mouth. Amy took the moment press her ruse.

"See?" she said. "He's right outside waiting for me! He even brought my horse... Stanford! If... If you took me now you'd never get him!"

The lady took a step towards her cohort and put a hand on his shoulder. Thorne slapped it away, his mind riddled with the ramifications if Amy's travel partner were to escape after seeing her head severed from her body by his claw.

"Stanford... why... does that name sound... Familiar? You said... that's your steed's name?"

Amy jerked her gaze away from James to protect his approach.

"Uh... I... Yeah! That's my horse's name!" Amy replied, pretending to pout and wagging a finger at him. "So don't you go doing anything that'd make him mad!"

James was close to the ground now, blending himself into the shadow of the steep-backed throne like a chameleon. He needed just a little more time. She still didn't know what he was going to do when he got there but him being there was better than nothing.

"I'd already be dead if I'd come alone..." she thought.

James slid down the rest of the wall and landed with a small thud. The lady started walking across the marble moat, obviously pissed that Thorne would shrug her away so easily.

"Oh, of course!" Thorne said, his raspy throat dripping with sarcasm. "Of course I wouldn't want to make ol'... Stanford uncomfortable! That would be... a horrid conclusion!"

Amy would've rolled her eyes had she not been on the lookout for her friend's cue. Instead, the tiniest of pebbles bounced off the back of the chair, presumably broken off the column James had jumped from. But the damage had been done. The evil pair snapped to attention. Thorne grinned wickedly as he turned around and Amy's shoulder's slumped.

James's shaggy frame materialized from the shadows. Thorne started cackling maniacally, casually thrusting a claw over Amy's body and knocking the wind out of her. But she couldn't tell if it was the leg's impact or the look on James' face that startled her more. It gave her goosebumps.

"Let. Her. Go." he said.

Thorne kept cackling.

"Or... what?" he said, leaning into his body-weight. "You'll... Whinny?"

James stood his ground even as Thorne continued to crush his friend.

"I said. Let her go. I won't let anyone hurt her ever again."

He began to laugh even more but the atmosphere began to ripple. Amy had never seen James this angry. She almost felt sorry for the pair.

The laughter cut short to briefly reveal an emotion she hadn't seen on his face before. Fear. And just enough of it for Thorne to loosen his grip on her long enough to free her arm and rip the necklace off its chain.

"James!" she shouted. "Catch!"

The key flew through the air, spinning a few times before he caught it mid-flight without batting an eye. Thorne's fear immediately transformed into anger. The pulsating atmosphere intensified as James began to activate it and

Thorne let go of Amy completely as he turned to face the bigger threat.

"I heard everything too." James said, pulling the medallion to his chest. "And we're going to make sure everyone finds out. King will crush you."

Amy shakily stood up in agreement. Thorne needed to be stopped before he caused more destruction. The key James held began glowing brightly, and the entire amphitheater began resonating with its energy. Thorne fumed.

"King? KING? King will die. YOU! WILL DIE! I WILL RULE! I will hunt you… down."

Thorne whipped around and began rising into the air to punch Amy in the face. She barely managed to avoid immediate decapitation.

"Hurry James!" she shouted.

The demon swiped at Amy again and she rolled to the side. The intensity of the pendant was blindingly bright now, the columns crumbling under their newfound weight. Even James struggled to hold onto it.

"Amy!" he screamed. "If we don't make it out of here! Remember! I love you!"

Tears streamed down her face as she reached out for him. Thorne whizzed through the sky, chunks of the roof breaking away and revealing the sunshine above.

"I WILL HAVE YOU!" he shrieked, dodging a massive boulder. "You will die!"

Time stood still. James looked to his friend one last time and smiled genuinely. He winked.

"See you on the other side."

The air around him exploded into light, Thorne's arm inches from his throat. The shockwave sent the demon flying back, his wings flailing about as he fell into the abyss and his artificial throne crumbled behind him. Amy finally smiled through her tears as the light enveloped her and she disappeared too.

"On the other side..."

***

James shot awake in a cold sweat screaming breathlessly, his brain racing, grasping at anything he could to center himself. The dull light from the alarm clock finally drew his attention and he began to breathe again. Nightmares were no joke.

He looked down and wiped his palms on the sheets, squeezing them briefly. At least it was quiet outside at this hour.

"He... He tried to kill us... That's right."

Cifer. No, it was Thorne now. Why had he forgotten about him? Of all his adventures until that point, that was one he wanted to forget.

"It was so dream-like…" James whispered. "Did that all happen or was it just my imagination?"

James eased back into his cocoon and rolled to his side to gaze at the window.

"Come to think of it… I don't remember her name. But she was scared of losing me, I know that much." he thought, his eyes slowly sliding shut.

He rolled back over and adjusted his pillow under his neck. A small metallic object plopped down near his head and a small speckle of light flashed across his face. James smiled as his heavy eyes finally closed.

"History always repeats itself. I'll need to find her again and we'll need to fight back."

2

James Pensworth woke up. Sunday. He knew he should be up and doing productive things like anybody else in the world called Earth in which he was supposed to exist. It didn't stop him from wondering what might happen to him if he were to lay down and stay there. Possibly forever. He didn't want to die; he wanted to, somehow, gain the power to feel comfortable forever, in a sort of never ending story one experiences right before waking and once upright wishes they could remember just a bit better. Those times were always among his favorites; neither fully awake nor asleep, or fully awake and fully asleep at once, and therein laid impossibility. James always dreamed. He wondered if his entire life consisted of dreaming in an ordinary sort like so many others, or if life here had always seemed too boring and monotonous for his tastes.

Granted, it never appeared to anyone else that he ever actually accomplished anything of value. And it definitely appeared as such on the surface, so their sentiment was probably true. But only to an extent. It wasn't as if they cared enough to peer into his introverted life either. He wasn't not accomplishing something. More like he was accomplishing something that happened to only involve him and his dreams.

It was, in his experience, that very few people cared to listen to him or what he had to say. To listen to events and places that technically, in their minds, had never happened or ever existed, at least as far as they were concerned. The world of dreams was unfamiliar and foreign to almost everyone, at best a pseudoscience rooted in mysticism and occult.

Or worse, many had given up on their dreams altogether. James felt most sorry for those people; they were no more than shells of their childhood, long since replaced by paper-pushers hating their cubicle neighbors and who's greatest half-assed hope was that they would be noticed just long enough to win that four day vacation to Hawaii.

Dreams weren't concrete, or scientific. They were childish; fairytales meant to entertain children during the times their parent's television sets could not reach. Most scientists believed dreams were no more than a tool, a single tool among many in humanity's wide array of subconscious diagnostics designed to help process and rationalize the day's events. This morbid hypothesis, in James' mind, backed by a host of their research and their papers, was no more than an adult attempt to rationalize and rule over a phenomenon that was simply bigger than them. Dreams were by definition infinite and impossible to explain other than simply 'getting it'.

James woke up. He'd worked himself up again last night, and he was a little angry because he knew what was coming. There were zero reasons for why his own inward debating should manage to get under his skin, and yet here he was, beating himself up for literally no reason whatsoever. Most likely it was because he wanted to keep dreaming. His body had other plans in mind.

The ever-present brain had sent the signal down to his arms and his legs to somehow miraculously, magically, mysteriously, pull off the covers. The disagreeable venture arrived sometime between his mild morning groan and his half-hearted rolling between pillow and face to gain appropriate leverage.

He didn't get it. Why would he possibly ever want to move a muscle when it was so nice and warm here in his bed, and the air in his house was so icy he'd find snowmen trying to stab him as soon as he opened his eyes? That cursed, gloriously terrible period of deciding to move before his joints had creaked to life like an old hand powered motor! James knew it was still Fall, but when one wasn't prepared for the brutal ice demon of death and one's only comforter in life doubled as an impenetrable shield of warmth, the decision suddenly became much more strenuous.

James did the only true logical thing he'd done the entire morning; that is, rolling from floor to bed with a soft thud, protecting himself from the world by means of his fluffy shield of solidarity. The struggle was too real, both as he tried to stand upright, and as he tried to stay wrapped within his blanket's Eskimo embrace.

Once James felt he'd drunk in as much tender warmth his body could handle for the time being he threw the flowing cape off majestically onto his bed, ready to recharge its magical powers for the next evening. James shrugged; it was the little things on Earth that kept him coming back.

He looked at the clock; it was already ten-thirty. James knew he was slacking. He should have been by all accounts be waking up no earlier than twelve. After all, only professionals stayed up till four AM, pounding out another few pages of literary gold and heartfelt enthusiasm for Arthridall.

James looked into his full-length mirror, quickly deciding he needed to start exercising. Who knew when he might need to actually impress someone?

"At least I'm not a ghost," James thought. "Too tan."

Who was he kidding? He rarely interacted with anybody, let alone anyone he could be interested in spending a considerable amount of time with. He wasn't shy, or at least he didn't see himself as being a shy person. He didn't know because no one had ever taken the time to tell him that he was, indeed, beyond shy. At least he knew he wasn't ugly, or un-agreeably stinky, or anything else horrid like that. He was either not talking at all or talking entirely too much about his dreams to a few fabled heroes.

James wasn't bitter about his life being quiet in the least; in fact, he preferred to be left to his own devices. He was free to dream about anything he could possibly ever want to, and without interruptions. In a way, James never left his dreams; it was just when he got out of bed in the morning he was in a different dream. A boring one.

Finally opening his bedroom door to jump in the shower, James walked down the hallway. It was already quiet, just the way he liked it. James was an only child, already sixteen and wishing he could stay in Arthridall all the time. James sighed a little.

"They must've gone to brunch. They always go to brunch. It's how they stay connected. God help them they're always so busy."

James flipped the shower on but didn't immediately jump in, knowing it would take exactly one minute and forty-seven seconds for the artic water to jettison and drain from the piping downstairs. He didn't have a phone, so soap bottle labels and odd quirks were a must.

"This is exactly what I needed," James thought.

It was as if he'd worked outside all day and was cold and stinky and had jumped into a perfectly beautiful slice of heaven, except that he hadn't worked all day and he didn't stink. He was, however, quite cold. The steaming water hit the back of his head and shoulders.

"Glorious."

It felt like he hadn't been alive for ages, even though he'd only been waiting for a whopping two minutes. James glanced down his arms, briefly wishing he wasn't so selectively lazy when it came to physical fitness. He grabbed a random bottle of some sort of soap something rather from the corner, haphazardly spreading it over his hair and deciding to spend an exorbitant amount of time massaging the skull and temples in an attempt to avoid the inevitable chill of stepping out.

"Well," he said finally as he turned the knob, "no time like the present."

James dried himself off with a towel. His family had always had the best towels in the world for as long as he could remember. They were warm, and so soft. Not that his parents had noticed or cared about the quality of their towels like he did.

"No matter."

He tucked the towel into itself, walking back to put on what he hoped was clean clothing.

"Blue-jeans and white tee-shirt? The two button one? Scratch that... long-sleeved green shirt and the grey hoodie."

It was chilly outside, but it didn't mean he couldn't continue being stylish. James pushed a strand of hair out of his face, using the mirror to adjust the rest in an attempt to prevent his stray hair from crowing like a rooster, and grabbed his wallet off the top of the dresser, sliding it into his pocket so he wouldn't forget it later. When he needed to pay for food and stuff.

James wasn't hungry right then, but decided a warm cup of coffee would really hit the spot for the poor, humble night-owl. James put on a pair of boots and a black and white beanie, finally walking out the door. Coffee would be swell.

"Swell? Yep. Swell is the best word for sure," James thought.

The word reminded him of the ocean. He wanted to go back to how it was in that moment, for he couldn't help but feel he'd made a mistake back then somehow. There was a reason they'd moved here, he was sure of it. But time stood still for no one, not even him, and those lovely images from childhood ebbed ever more further away, the ghost of a dream from memories long gone by.

"It was my choice... I can't forget that. I gave that up for now... but I wouldn't say that I've given up completely."

3

James looked at his watch, quickly shoving his hand back into his pocket to keep it warm.

"It's actually freezing out here," he thought more than once in the half-minute he'd been standing outside.

The sunshine hadn't yet burned off the chill of the previous night and he found it a bit windy. James refused to wear mittens; not because he didn't appreciate their warmth, but because they always managed to look dorky no matter how he wore them. Besides, his pockets were warm enough. The chill autumn breeze teased at James' sandy-blonde and brown hair as he walked down the road, the cold whipping up and down his face over and over, making him wish he'd stayed in the shower a wee-bit longer.

"I hate cold."

He owned a bicycle he'd won in a Christmas costume party a few years ago if he wanted it. It was a good bike, but he didn't feel like riding it.

"Too windy. Not worth it. I'm complaining too much as it is."

The local coffee shop was James' second most favorite place in the world to spend his time. His first love had always been the downtown library, as he was an avid book reader. So much so that he'd tried his hand at writing some of his own stories the past few years, and finding he'd developed quite a talent for it. The coffee house was situated about four blocks away from his house, right on the end of one of the most popular places in town to go shopping and sightseeing, but the local coffee house and its neighboring shops were by no means tourist attractions. But the strip, as the locals called it, was a place the city's local artisans and craftsmen liked frequently setting up shop, drawing avid craft-hunters and patrons from all over the city and the surrounding areas.

It was not one of those days today however, and for that James was grateful. He liked the locale best when it wasn't too overcrowded by middle-aged ladies wearing too much makeup and trying to exude an air of somehow being very elegant and refined because they liked to look at 'artwork' from time to time. James would take the alluring smell of a hot cup of coffee over potent old lady perfumes any day of the week.

James rounded the corner, entering the warm haven that'd quickly become his secondary base of operations.

"Local shops do brew it best though," he thought. "The hipsters know what's up with their coffee."

The smells of various foreign and fancy flavors gently wafted across James' palate, and he smiled inwardly.

"Worth it."

A new smell in the building drew his curiosity; it was sweet and chocolaty, with a hint of infused peppermint. James' hopes rose.

"Is it… Is it finally back?"

It was, and it was his absolute favorite.

He walked to the counter and ordered the largest white-chocolate peppermint mocha physically offered in a cup. A few minutes later he received his concoction and was about drink it when he weighed it in his hand and realized exactly how much sugar he was about to consume.

"I regret nothing," he thought, grabbing a comfortable seat in the corner to indulge himself.

James was a man of simple pleasures, and unlike many people his age who'd immediately hop on their phone and catch up with the latest gossip, he was content to watch the world as it unfolded around him. And maybe change it for the better. He took another sip of his drink, smiling.

"Some things are worth living for."

Leaning over, James started pushing the morning paper out of the way when an article caught his eye. He set his drink down on the open space and picked it up.

Six different companies' stock had risen by thirty-two percent in less than two and a half weeks. The authorities didn't believe it was coincidence; none of the companies listed had made any significant leaps in growth during the period, and none of the companies were related, as they were all in completely different fields of expertise.

The largest company under scrutiny was an oil company by the name of Overan. This company was getting the most attention because the company had been known to shoot up their prices for a day or two every so often to apparently squeeze every penny they could from the public. Most people allowed for it because the rest of the time the company guaranteed their gas would be five to ten cents cheaper than anyone else in the area. So far, they'd stuck to their word. On public media, Overan referred to their policy as a 'new alternative to the crushing pressure of rising gas prices'. They believed if they kept their prices consistently low, only raising them for brief, scheduled periods of time, they'd be able to benefit the community and still make a profit. The system sparked countless debates on all the major news networks, and it made for an interesting conversation topic for politicians and home-makers alike. There were, of course, many strong advocates for and against the policy. For Overan it was free publicity and therefore more profits.

Many questioned the policy against the Constitution and other such documents, and rabble-rousers liked to accuse the company of being in cahoots with middle-easterners or the like. The majority of the population continued to give the company their business because they were cheaper, even going to them when they briefly raised their prices. Much of the populace believed that it was how the company was able to continue surviving. James figured that, in reality, the company was probably doing even better for itself than if they were to join the rest of the crowd and stick with the normal price ranges.

"It's all based on perception."

The article went on to explain the rest of the companies whose stocks had been affected by this 'miraculous' chain of events, but James only glazed over the names. He wanted to get to the part of the article that'd caught his attention in the first place. A computer hacker who referred to himself as Soggy had recently spread word that the artificial spikes were his doing, even going so far as to taunt the authorities by mandating they try changing the system back to normal. Obviously enough, it was what authorities had been trying to accomplish ever since they realized the errors in the system. Much to the delight of Soggy's fans, every time authorities tried fixing the system it would magically raise the worth of the companies' stocks even higher.

It was a catch twenty-two, and the authorities' only possible lead was they believed the hacker had shares of the six different companies' stock and he was raking in ridiculous amounts profit from them. At least, that's what they thought, but the internet community had come to a different consensus. Soggy had become internet famous for previously hacking into some of the toughest systems the world had ever offered. Some considered him a modern day Robin Hood, however, no one had ever been able to confirm he'd ever given any money to charity in his life. Soggy had never stolen anything of value from any of the systems he'd cracked, which led the world to believe that the man simply did it for fame and glory.

The government didn't see it that way. Soggy was a threat, and they were doing everything in their power to catch the criminal as soon as possible. He was a thorn in their side that needed to be pulled out, and quickly. The world cheered him on; it made for lots of fun debates about his identity, and why he consistently antagonized so many powerful people in the first place.

James smiled, setting the paper down and picking up his coffee. He secretly cheered for Soggy's exploits. It sounded like something out of a comic book or a movie.

"Perhaps the guy simply wants to entertain people," he thought.

After all, Soggy had never done any serious harm to anyone, and it was a lot more fun to fantasize about his work rather than the wars happening overseas. James had tremendous respect for the armed forces to be sure, but he hated how the media and the government treated the wars as a political game, instead of honoring the brave men and women risking their lives every single day to protect their country.

"God bless them."

James took another swig of coffee, deciding to start watching the café's current crowd. A man in a black suit and tie was ordering a tall non-fat latte; James thought that he'd either just gotten away from a wedding ceremony, or he was running late for an important meeting with his boss.

"Either way, he looks stressed out. He needs a cookie," James thought.

James laughed aloud a little. The man locked eyes with James almost instinctively, and suddenly James' drink was the most interesting thing James had ever looked at.

"That man's glare could cause newborn puppies to burst into flames."

James decided he didn't like the angry puppy murderer very much. Good riddance.

Soon afterwards Mrs. Tamburton walked in, saw him, and smiled. She was an old family friend, and James had taken a liking to her even though he hadn't talked with her much. She'd been a widow for a while now, but unlike many people her age she wasn't bitter about it. Her children had long left her house, and had moved to all parts of the country to raise families. At least, that was as much as he remembered from their last chat.

He recalled that one of her children had moved overseas, while the other daughter had stayed behind to raise her own family about an hour away from town.

"If I remember correctly, that daughter passed away though," James thought.

Mrs. Tamburton's grandchildren called her Gram-Gram, or sometimes Nana, and she was visited by them on all the major holidays and sometimes over the summers when their parents wanted to have some alone time.

Mrs. Tamburton made her purchase and waited for her drink at the counter. James knew she had good taste: a medium pumpkin spice latte with extra cream and a hint of vanilla.

"She sure has a sweet-tooth," James thought. "Maybe even more than I do."

She walked over to him without a word, handing him one of the rich chocolate cream chocolates he was so fond of.

"Say hi to the folks for me okay?" she said with a gleam in her eye.

She walked away. The little bell above the exit tinged, and James nodded his appreciation. He liked her.

James finished the other half of his drink and walked over to the trashcan to throw it out. He'd decided he'd done enough people watching; he should go to the park, or at the very least do something productive with his life. Like getting back to work on his book portal. Or exercising.

"Maybe."

He hadn't been outside for a while, so being cold was still a possibility. James turned to walk out of the shop but stopped. A blonde-haired girl was running towards the shop, her friend close in tow. She won, surprisingly, as her friend appeared to be in much better shape. She waited.

"They're laughing way too hard for something this simple," James thought. "Girls are weird... Then again I was just laughing at that penguin."

James opened the door for them, standing behind it. The loser ran inside to place her order, almost slamming the door into his face in the process. He brushed it off.

"They're girls," he thought.

It didn't hurt their case that they were very pretty. The blonde-haired girl, realizing what her friend had done to him, apologized on her behalf. James nodded, assuring her it wasn't a problem.

"Thank you." she said.

The girl went on to catch her friend. She was very pretty.

"She's very pretty," James thought.

He paused at the door for a moment, if only to view the backs of their heads, noticing the girl who'd thanked him had a light brown color in her hair.

"Sandy-blonde, more like..."

James felt like at least one of them went to his school. For all he knew maybe they both did; he didn't really pay much attention to anything outside his daydreams. And for now, he was okay with that. His kingdom awaited him.

4

James plucked his books from the table and packed his belongings. He'd been at the library for over six hours and probably needed to get home and eat. James wasn't worried whether his parents would be impatiently waiting for him; they knew he went to the library all the time to read fantasy novels or finish homework. They trusted him and allowed him to do as he saw fit. Unusual, but true.

***

For the longest time James' father strongly believed that his son's hanging out in the library all day was merely an excuse for staying out late to party with girls and hooligans. There was no way that his quiet guy routine wasn't an act at least some of the time. One day, acting on his hunch, Mr. Pensworth followed James all the way there in his car, only to find himself sitting still for the next eight and a half hours across the street, bored to death. James' father thought he'd done his job in absolute secrecy. He thought he'd won somehow, being as tenacious as he'd been and the like. It was one of the first times he'd been sorely mistaken.

James was extremely perceptive about a lot of things, which is why he enjoyed writing. Even when he quite often wasn't perceptive of others, his undeniable gift of perception allowed him to realize that his father had been trailing him all day long. James decided to ignore the thought because he wanted to read the new book the library had recently acquired. Priorities.

It wasn't until dinner that evening when James brought it up to his parents that he knew his father's schemes. He assured him he was up to nothing wrong or evil. James' bold statement put his father's mind through a plethora of thoughts pertaining to his son's elaborate conspiracy; one thought being that James had simply gone to the library to throw him off the trail of his real life. So, when James specifically told them he was going to the library again that upcoming weekend, Mr. Pensworth felt obligated to accompany his son along on his travels from a distance once again. After all, from a parent's point of view, it was very strange for a boy his age to want to go to such a boring place as the library as often as his son apparently did. And on a Saturday evening no less. Either that, or James really was an odd child.

It was exactly what he wanted his dad to think. James did want to go back to the library to finish the book he'd started, but he figured he might as well throw his father for a loop in the process. James wasn't a malicious child by any stretch of the imagination, but that wasn't to say he didn't like to have his fun every now and then. Especially when his father had handed it to him on a silver platter.

That Saturday, James went to the library just as he said he would, ending up staying for a full ten hours. The book he'd finished was over four hundred pages long, and, as any avid book reader ought to, he'd finished the thing as fast as possible. The library had a policy of not loaning out books that'd been in stock for under a month in order to prevent theft. After all, it was far more difficult to steal and resell a book that looked like an old library book rather than something brand new and still flying off the shelves. Because of the rule, James had to stay at the library to read it in its entirety. The policy didn't bother James in the slightest; he found he always gleaned more from the books he read in his special chair on the fourth floor more than anywhere else because it reminded him of his study back in Arthridall.

Meanwhile, his father once again sat obstinately in the cramped family vehicle parked across the street, this time with a pair of binoculars in hand so he'd have a perfect view of his son if tried to pull a fast one on him. The real catch James pulled that day was the fact that he'd convinced his father he was going to be up to no good. So much so that his father had waited ten hours in a hot and cramped car for a mere possibility he'd concocted himself.

James' mother had a much better method of gaining proof. Instead of creating an uncomfortable stake-out, she simply asked him at the dinner table how the book he'd supposedly been reading was. James knew right away that she'd called his bluff and he was happy to oblige. He immediately went into extraordinary detail on the book; the characters, the plot, and all the locations and twists that would be practically impossible to make up on the spot if he were lying.

The only way his father could react as James explained the story was start blushing a deep shade of beet-red. It was as if the two of them ganged up on him in a sort of giant practical joke without any prior communication. Only after he'd finished his report did James and his mother look at him and pause for a second before laughing hysterically.

Mr. Pensworth couldn't help but eventually join in; he'd been thoroughly and triumphantly duped by his two very important clowns. It goes without saying that his dad never questioned him about his intentions ever again.

***

James felt hungry. He knew that waking up at six-thirty wasn't going to be fun, so he took the books he'd picked out and returned them to their rightful places, praying there would be at least some meager sustenance in the fridge when he arrived.

It was an easy feat for him, considering he knew the library better than all the employees combined and spent more time in the place than they did on any given day. James had considered getting a job here in the past, but decided against it due to his busy school schedule, as well as his severe allergy to manual labor. After all, most librarians are not high-school kids with a penchant for adventure. On the other hand, most sixteen-year old boys don't spend ten hours of their Saturday finishing up a novel.

After a twenty minutes walking in the dark, James was cold once again.

"I need some food!" he thought aggressively.

James didn't like how it got seasonably darker as the year progressed. He comforted himself with the fact that the wind had finally died down. James opened the front door after fumbling with the keys with his numb noodles, stepped inside, and unzipped his hoodie. James felt pride in how his house had a home-like feel to it; characterized by its simple but warm tastes and its quiet but inviting inhabitants. He heard his mom's call from the couch; his food was indeed in the fridge. The lights emanating from living room television flashed as some sort of gunfight from one of his parents' favorite action films as they cuddled together on the sofa. The kitchen was almost dark when he walked in, save for a small blue cone shaped glass fixture above the sink, which always brought a surprising amount of comfort whenever he came home on these late nights. It was just enough to make out everything in the room without becoming obtrusive or annoying.

James leaned down and opened the refrigerator, allowing the artificial brightness of it to mingle with the rest of the room. After some searching, he finally spotted his familial rations behind a half-empty gallon of milk. One of his favorites; half a homemade chicken-pot-pie large enough to feed a family of eight if need be, or in this case a married couple and their resident high-school freshman. Even better. The pie was still warm.

"They must've just started," James thought as he scooped a heaping portion into an equally massive bowl and popped it in the microwave.

James plopped down into his favorite lounge chair and watched the rest of the movie with them, only getting up once or twice to serve himself more pie and later, ice-cream. After the film ended, James decided he needed to be alert enough to catch the bus in the morning, so he bid his parents goodnight. His mother caught him before he made his way up the stairs to remind him to put his dirty dishes 'where they belong'. Moms. Mrs. Pensworth gave her son a kiss on the forehead. Dreamland called.

5

"Six-thirty shouldn't exist," James thought as he agonizingly rolled out of bed in a big fluffy heap.

It was habitual. James showered and returned to his room, putting on the same pair of jeans from the day before and the white tee-shirt that he'd been planning on wearing then too. James was a creature of habit. He looked closely at himself in the mirror and brushed his hair to the side. He noticed a red pimple peering back at him on the left side of his forehead.

"No matter, he thought.

At his age, zits were inevitable. James gazed at his deep-blue eyes for a second, reassuring himself that the monstrosity would remove itself from his otherwise cheerful face within the next day or two. They never tended to last longer than that. He adjusted his hair to cover it up. He was indeed, still human. But not an embarrassed one.

"After all, stress only makes matters like acne worse."

James realized he finally had a chance to empathize with his classmates. He rarely got acne and was quite thankful for the fact.

"Popping them hurts like crazy, though."

James finished getting ready. His mother handed him his lunchbox as he walked out the door for the seven-sharp bus. It was a vintage looking metal lunchbox that depicted some of his favorite super-heroes in comic book style. Some might consider it a dorky thing to cherish, but he didn't care. He liked the box and that's all that mattered.

"Haters gonna' hate," James thought with a grin, carrying himself to the stop-sign at the end of the street. "Insert copyrighted catch phrase here."

A few other people at the bus-stop were waiting with him. For some reason this day, out of all days, was the first time he realized that the neighborhood the bus serviced was actually quite large. Thirty or more kids about his age were waiting, trampling the innocent grass and dirt like an African stampede. James had nothing better to do so he started watching them. It was the first time, for whatever reason, that he realized it was more fun watching people his own age than all of the adults at the coffee shop.

"I'll be old and crochety myself one day. I can watch old people when I get there," James thought.

Two of the girls present in the crowd were watching him, giggling. James snapped to the present.

"Wait... Have I been staring?"

The laughter in their eyes and smiles answered him immediately. James, feeling both incredibly embarrassed and exhilarated, looked away like his life depended on it. Because it did. His embarrassment didn't leave as he averted his gaze, so he walked to the back of the crowd to gain some extra distance. His ears, finally starting to cool down, allowed him to be curious again, and he went back to watching them.

"Thank God they aren't staring. It was probably just embarrassing for them too. That's all. Yeah, they must've been as weirded out as me," James thought.

His face returned to normal as he had the chance to watch them from afar, and it struck him. They must've been the same people from yesterday.

The bus arrived and the crowd started to form a line of sorts. James filed in after the first few groups of threes and fours, finally settling in with a window seat in one of the first few rows. He watched the rest of the kids walk up the patterned metal steps; those two hadn't entered yet. He had to confirm it; he needed an alibi in case he needed to explain himself. It was just his luck they were among the last to enter. The first rushed past her friend to get the last window seat at the very back of bus, her curly, raven hair bouncing up and down in pace with her step. The other took her time. She wore a light blue, almost white, knee length dress with a coat wrapped around her shoulders.

"Fairy..." James thought. "I've met her before... haven't I?"

She'd completed her outfit with some sort of super comfortable looking shoe that he had no idea as to its name.

Fairy-girl met his awestruck gaze and blushed, hurrying past him to meet up with her friend. James hadn't realized he'd been creeping the entire time. Again. It was only after she'd settled down in the back that the realization struck him, yet again, his face cascading into an even deeper shade of cherry-tomato. James reached into his back-pack and grabbed his jacket. He might as well be crying too.

"There's not enough camouflage in the world," he thought, disintegrating into the corner seat next to the window.

He was grateful that the bus wasn't so crowded up front that someone had to sit next to him.

James recognized her. There was no doubt about it. He could never forget the look in her eyes in the few times he'd seen her, nor did he want to. She was that girl from yesterday. The fact she was on the same bus as him meant she and her friend lived in the same neighborhood and went to the same school as him.

"And the dream I had... Gah... too much social interaction. Hiss..."

James wasn't actually mad. He sure liked to pretend from time to time though. More often than not he would burst out laughing after a moment because he refused to take himself seriously. James readjusted himself, keeping his hood down to protect his zit and looking out the window. The deep green of the trees and the occasional vehicle helped calm his nerves.

"She's only human," he assured himself. "Same neighborhood doesn't mean anything."

He decided he wouldn't think about it anymore. But the resemblance was uncanny.

The bus pulled into the loop outside the school grounds and the students filed out one crowded cluster at a time. James made sure he was the first one off. He didn't want any more confrontation for the day, fully aware he had an important test after lunch and needed to retain his focus. They could wait for some other time.

***

The front of the school wasn't nearly as dilapidated as some of the others in town; certainly not as rough as the middle school James had moved away from a few months before. Unfortunately, the same people that'd made his middle school so rough since graduating had transferred to this building, meaning they'd also attend the same high school.

"Different building, same people."

And now these same people had gone through changes that gave them significant advantages over him in almost every front possible.

"Except for book-smarts perhaps," he reminded himself.

The most notorious of the kids in the high school had formed a gang created for the sole purposes destroying people's social lives. They called themselves the Un'darbrids.

The Un'darbrids' leader, Astwin Panickle, claimed the groups' name was foreign in origin. The reality of it was it was a dumb and completely made up word intended to strike fear into the hearts of those who dared stand up to their utterly childish playground style supremacy.

Most kids referred to the gang as the U.N. They never said it to the gang's face, as those involved with the organization hated the nickname with a passion, going particularly out of their way to punish any who dared defile such a foreign sounding title. Out of a school of five thousand students, a mere thirty man-sized teenagers ruined it for everyone. At least half of them were seniors and many of whom were legal drinking age, or at least knew someone who was. The upper classmen were easily the most dangerous ones, as the other half of the group was much less intimidating in both physical size and experience. They acted mostly as spies and grunts for the bigger people, feeding them information about their classes and their juicy secrets. It was in this way the organization could ensure they maintained their share of profit, if indeed there was profit to be made.

Astwin considered his gang to be a sort of high school mafia. He liked to consider himself as a relatively average sized person with no significant or ugly features besides the company he kept. Reality said he was short and fat. Incredibly fat. If it weren't for the gang he'd paid off with booze using his fake I.D card he'd be the laughing stock of the entire population.

Astwin always looked seedy, up to no good, and as majestic as a cow-pie being shot with a paintball gun. Whether by unfortunate happenstance, or just ill-timing on his part James would never know, but it was into this obese man-child that James bumped shoulders with or, more like Astwin's shoulder into his ribcage, as he walked down the only obvious route to the front entrance.

Astwin's bear of a bodyguard took notice of the 'assault', shoving James so violently that he fell into the torn-up grass on the side of the grounds, muddying the entire left side of his body. James almost stood up to fight back but caught himself, letting his anger from the blatant bullying pass.

"It's just what they want. They just want a reason to keep going. Any excuse to tell the teacher when we fight back."

There was no reason to start a fight, especially not one he couldn't win. Astwin's bodyguard could hold his own against a bear if he felt like it.

Not a single person came to help.

"And why would they? I'm the only one who angered them. They're not about to get on their bad side just because they were helping me."

No one knew James in any capacity other than his name on the roll call at the beginning of class. James knew he wasn't unattractive. It wasn't because he seemed un-helpable. In fact, he hoped most of the girls at school might place him in the upper echelon of their attractiveness scale. Well, at least one of them.

"The one they like to think is kept top secret…"

The real issue was James refused to be anyone other than himself and society didn't know how to deal with it. So they ignored him.

The girl from the coffee shop had seen him fall though. She and her friend had taken some time to get off the bus, still trapped behind the centipede cluster of school-kids crowding the bus exit. She'd watched the scene unfold as the gang loafed around the school's large oak tree, tormenting more of the new arrivals as James fell to the ground.

She watched one of the Un'darbrids checkmate the couple of chess club kids playing on the main stairway; pawns and rooks and knights scattering across the lawn like a spray of bullets during a snowstorm. One of the boys' shoulders slumped; it was a handmade set his grandfather had built for him and given to him as his final Christmas gift before he'd passed away. Irreplaceable. And the bully knew about it thanks to one of his underling's tips.

One of the beefy steroid-pumped Un'darbrid chicks harassed a girl because she'd decided to wear a ponytail and tacky pink and green striped socks at the same time. Others threw slurs completely inappropriate and unquestionably racist at each other in order to determine their rank. No one escaped their evil eye, save the jocks and the cheerleaders; they were the only ones on the totem pole that carried more weight and influence than them, as they represented the school's pride and joy. That, and the fact they were the only ones the administration ever gave second thought about protecting.

She knew the boy was different though. He was the only one the bullies physically injured this morning, as if his antisocial traits made him an automatic magnet for personal abuse. She knew she couldn't stand up to them any more than he could, and because of that notion she was in the same boat he was. It made her sick to her stomach. She stayed close in tow to her more popular, raven-haired friend as they disembarked the bus and began to cross through the badlands. They'd done the same routine hundreds of times during middle school, always escaping to class with hardly any less than they'd started with. She chalked it up to the fact that her friend was an intimidating sports player, thus falling under the popular crowd's unspoken protection.

She still didn't know how they'd ever become friends in the first place. They were nothing alike; no common interests, or skills, or similar personalities, or anything really. But somehow, they enjoyed each other's company and, for whatever reason, they were able to find a bit of solace in each other when they caught a glimpse of the other's personal life. It worked somehow.

The girl found herself watching the boy, stifling her surprise at his reaction to being bullied. He didn't look like he was in pain. She'd seen him fall and get scraped up. She knew the fall had hurt. So why on God's green earth did he not show it? The girl found herself cheering him on and, for whatever reason, he simply picked himself up and started to shake off the mud's hold on his clothing as if he'd planned the entire scene from the start. It was almost unnatural.

"And badass," she thought.

The girl kept her binder close to her face as she passed the tree, thinking she'd make it through the day again unscathed by the trouble stewing around the schoolyard pot. The gang was apparently in a particularly rough mood, because it was the fat-man himself who knocked the papers from her hand and into the sky to be swept away by the morning breeze.

She almost screamed at the suddenness of the action but caught herself when she realized the source of the fright. Astwin wanted to see her scream etch itself into her face and she knew it. She felt exposed, his seedy eyes searching up and down her, knowing she was more unprotected than ever. It was as if he had pervert vision and was planning to destroy her very soul with it.

She brought her arm up to protect her face out of instinct. Her instincts betrayed her, as it was the very thing they'd wanted her to do in the first place. A scream would be a mere bonus. The bear-eater of a bodyguard caught her wrist with ease from behind, forcing both arms down behind her. Her skin crawled violently as if she'd been injected with hatching spider eggs.

"So this is what it's like," she thought. "But where the hell did Susan go?"

She felt her gut sink as she caught sight of the back of Susan's head as she comingled on the main steps with a bunch of the football team.

"Crap..." she thought. "That's what I get for standing still."

"Well, well, well, you sure are pretty!" Astwin said with a sinister smirk. "Are you new here?"

The rest of the Un'darbrids laughed with him. They were dead if they didn't laugh.

"But how pretty are you really, snowflake? Here, let me help you find out!"

Astwin laughed maniacally as she struggled to pull her arms away and protect herself. Her efforts were wasted against the bodyguard, who refused to let her budge lest she escape his majesty's just punishments. Another girl was already on the ground sobbing nearby; one of the man-eater girls had slapped her for being better looking than her, leaving a large red mark on her cheek. She found herself wanting to do the impossible to help her, but was pinned mercilessly.

"Run!" she shouted at the girl on the ground, thrashing wildly as she tried to squirm out of the bear-man's grasp and create a distraction.

She knew it was hopeless for her. Her protector was off smacking lips and high-fives with the cool kids, but she tried to kick Astwin in the face anyway, trying to at least buy the other girl on the ground enough time to retreat into the building. Astwin simply stepped back, laughing even more as he enjoyed the spectacle of her light blue dress as it blew about in the breeze.

"You look cold! Let me help you warm up!" he shouted to his crowd, rubbing his hands together.

The rest of the gang followed their leader's example and grinned; this particular form of degradation had become a tradition over the years, and it was their absolute favorite way to humiliate schoolgirls who'd done nothing wrong. The practice had a horrendous nickname much too unmentionable to name in polite company.

"Not that these people are polite company."

She knew it was coming, and, despite her resolution to save the other girl first, began to panic. She'd seen where their exercises led to before, and she'd heard the girls crying in the bathroom stalls who had received it. It grieved her every time she'd heard them sobbing, but now she was about to join them.

Astwin separated his hands, walking closer and closer, spreading them into the horribly inappropriate groping gesture. She started to scream, but her voice was instantly muffled by the beefy chick's mitten from behind.

She'd lost. The girl's body slumped. She resigned herself to the fact that she was about to be horribly groped and there was nothing she could do about it. She lowered her head and closed her eyes, expecting the worst.

"At least she's escaped their attention now," she consoled herself. "I did something good for once… I hope."

WHAM!!!

The girl felt a burst of wind and speed, grimacing as the sickening sound of crunching bone reached her ear. Her arms were thrown loose and she stumbled backwards.

"What happened…?"

She was confused. Astwin lay writhing on the ground, his face bloodied and muddied almost unbelievably so. He looked like he had a smashed and broken nose, screaming bloody murder for the entire world to hear. She also saw a boy about her age layed out on the ground completely unconscious, with a black eye so dark it was almost indistinguishable from the gritty mud that encased it.

The bear-man stood over the kid, growling and cursing like a caged animal, and would've murdered him on the spot had he not been restrained by the only person at the school large enough to stop him, his arms pinned behind him like steel cables.

"At least someone finally had the sense to call the P.E. teacher," she thought.

The school nurse was quickly called. She had a few of the bigger soccer team kids carry the injured on the ground over to her office. No one wanted to help Astwin, but they followed the nurses' orders to a tee as she was scarier than any P.E. teacher in the world when it came to emergencies.

Man-bear was immediately suspended for at least a month without any chance of returning early.

***

"Was that the kid from the coffee house?" she asked herself.

The girl noticed as James was hoisted that one of his hands was bleeding slowly.

"He protected me..."

No one had ever stood up to the Un'darbrids before. Was this really all it'd taken to dethrone the king? A simple punch to the face? The rest of them had scattered like rats as soon as they'd seen the coach running up. She silently thanked the boy and helped the other girl up, hugging her closely and allowing her to cry profusely. Partly for the emotional release, and partly because of the humanity of it all.

"Those jerks are done for," she said finally, wiping a smudge from the smaller girl's cheekbone.

A few friends helped the two of them up the stairs to take them to the counselor, but she assured them she would be just fine in a little while and didn't need counseling. Susan ran up, apologizing to them profusely. She made sure that Susan knew it wasn't her fault.

"Yeah, but you're always saving my butt and when I finally get the chance to save you I wasn't there!" Susan complained.

The other girl shyly interjected, tapping her rescuer on the shoulder. A little rushed, as her friends were calling her in from down the hall.

"Thanks for saving me," the smaller girl said. "What's your name?"

"You would... you would totally do the same. I... I had to. I couldn't get trapped like that and not try to help. Name's... The name's Amy."

"Thank you, Amy."

"You're... very welcome."

Amy watched her scamper off to her group of friends. It was no wonder why she'd been singled out. The girl was small for a junior, and cute as a button. Amy could tell her friends were relieved to see her alive and well. They waved back to them in thanks as they retreated inside.

6

The news of a kid who'd taken on the Un'darbrids by himself spread throughout the entire school faster than wildfire. It wasn't too difficult, considering almost everyone in the school had seen it happen. Only the late arrivals hadn't heard the story yet, but they too would soon hear the news from those who'd been there to see the spectacle.

They cheered James' courage, though almost nobody knew his name or what he looked like. They nicknamed their hero Knockout on account of his overwhelming victory. Ironically or not, no one had seen what he actually looked like before the black eye or the mud besides Amy. Had James been awake he would've probably preferred it to remain that way. He never liked being the center of attention, and he wasn't going to start simply because he'd gotten into a fight. Fights happened all the time in schools without anyone caring. There was no reason this one should be any different.

The school nurses' office would make any hospital bay jealous. It was large, clean, and stocked with almost every kind of bandage and medicine known to mankind. Granted, it was also the neighborhood clinic, and was in a separate building from the school grounds altogether. It didn't make sense for the school to make a separate office for the occasional scrape or bruise, especially since the clinic was right next door to the school's main campus. It didn't hurt that the arrangement had been previously approved by the city council and would require a lot of paperwork to alter or reverse an arrangement that everyone felt was extremely beneficial. No one liked to fill out paperwork in any form or fashion; it was a straight up hassle.

The clinic was divided into two bays, if they were large enough to be called bays. The two sections housed the general public in the larger section on the south side and the student geared facility on the north. There was a host of medical equipment, supplies, and lollipops for the children that did well when they received their shots in a special storage area. When the back storage area was not in use, it was kept under so many locks and key-codes that it would make most bank security systems blush at their inadequacies.

***

Everyone knew it was the head nurse at the clinic who was responsible for making it shine. Ms. Oranorth had been there since she was thirty-seven years old, and been on more battlefields than most men would ever see. She was top of her class in medical school, deciding there that her skills would be best put to use in the place they were needed most. At the incredibly young age of twenty-three, degree in hand, Ms. Oranorth hopped on a plane, sailing overseas into what she would call one of the worst wars in human history. Had she known what awaited her in the field, she would've never gone to medical school. The pain that she'd experienced there was unfathomable. She would've gone into some sort of child psychology practice instead. She was strong, but no one could ever be that strong.

The war was gruesome beyond words. Legs completely blown off from the knee down, shrapnel in shoulders, gouged eyes, knife wounds; the list went on and on. It was into one of these jungle-like nightmares that she'd been thrown, and to this day decrees she would've gone insane had it not been for the love she felt from and returned to Charles Oranorth.

When Charles was carried into her tent he was brutally wounded under his left arm and deep into his ribcage; she claimed it must have been a very sharp knife because of it. It was almost as deep as a stab wound, but stretched far longer. She would tell people later that it was most likely from a saber or a sword, but she never got the chance to ask him.

Charles came into her care, completely unconscious from blood loss. Somehow, miraculously, she was able to get him to a somewhat stable condition by pumping a rudimentary I.V. and binding the wound with the cleanest pillowcase she could find. Her quick thinking saved him from certain doom. The field aid tents had run out of gauze over four days earlier and stitching thread was scarce, so they had to make do until the next shipment could be air-dropped. The pillowcase was the only thing she could find, but it saved his life.

He remained unconscious for three days, finally waking up to the sight of her as she was changing his bandages. Despite her frizzy hair and sleepless eye wrinkles he thought she was beautiful, and foolishly tried to raise himself up to tell her. Thinking he was going into shock at the time, Ms. Oranorth steadied his shoulders to calm him down.

He stopped struggling then, allowing her to mother him once she realized he wasn't in critical condition. In the brief moments he could steal her from her other patients, he'd grab her hand and gently pull her close as she was changing his bandages and, like two doves nesting together, whisper in her ear that he loved her with all his heart, kissing her delicately on the cheek. It was not too many days later they began conversing with their lips.

Perhaps it was the suddenness of it all, or the look in his eyes as he gazed at her, or the slight smell of sweat as she gingerly washed his wounds and stitching, but she soon found that she loved him too.

For some reason, she couldn't bring herself to tell him out loud. She didn't really know why; perhaps it was because he was a beast of a man and she was still very young. Maybe it was because she couldn't bear the thought of losing someone she loved to the machine of war.

Her feelings for Charles swelled within her heart. And, as suddenly as she fell in love with him, she found her job suddenly more palpable. It didn't matter how many tragedies she had to witness every day anymore because she knew she would have him waiting for her at the end of the day, to tend to his wounds as a loved one, not a nurse. To tend his heart as a hopeful bride.

It was on one such day that Ms. Oranorth came to tend to Charles' wounds as she always had. The day she'd tell him she loved him, and accept his proposal to marry. As she walked over to his bedside however, she immediately knew that something had changed. His face was paler than before, and there was a slight wheezing in his voice, not unlike the sound of a lawn-mower threatening to run out of fuel.

She checked the wound on his side; it wasn't infected. It struck her; had she been missing the signs? The wound hadn't been deep enough to puncture his lung, right? It couldn't be.

"No!" she cried, "You can't..."

Charles did everything in his power to calm her down.

His voice soothed her, even as his own bodily fluids gradually leaked into his vitals. To stay in the land of the living. The dusk that had brought the terrible news slipped into the night.

The other nurses knew of Ms. Oranorth's attraction, and graciously covered the rest of her rounds so she could weep upon what was no longer meant to be. Charles told her of his past, and she hers. They spoke of what could have been had there hadn't been a shortage of supplies, as the puncture was originally just deep enough to do hardly any real damage. They could have easily operated if he'd been able to be safely transported from the war zone. The operation that was prevented by his initial blood loss. That blood loss prevented everything.

They spoke of what their lives together might've been like, as a family. One with children. Two adorable twin daughters, and a well-mannered handsome young gentleman. Charles said they'd need to own a dog as well. He liked dogs; big ones with happy demeanors. She agreed with him completely, which made their parting even more difficult.

Sooner than either of them would have liked, Charles H. Oranorth II grew faint, his breath shallow and moist. She could hardly bear to watch his face as it gained a blue tinge she'd seen far too many times. And she still hadn't told him she loved him.

Charles started to struggle and choke as if he were drowning. He was growing weaker and couldn't move very much. Her voice kept catching in her throat.

"I have to say it!"

His weak thrashing increased. He thrashed more, but there was nothing they could do for him now; he was truly dying. Ms. Oranorth tried comforting him through her tears as best she could, but they both knew he had finally won the war.

"I love you." she finally said, and kissed him.

"I... wi..ll... al..ways... love... you..."

Charles' body fell still. She felt his last breath intertwine with hers and mingle within her chest as their lips gently parted for the last time. And she knew she'd never love another the same.

***

Ms. Oranorth was sent home the next morning. They told her she'd done enough to help the war efforts. They told her Charles had passed in truest order, and would receive the highest honors for his valiant sacrifice. They told her he'd passed with a look of peace on his face. She already knew. She'd been there.

It was rare to see any kind of peace in the face of a corpse, but Charles' casket was a miracle. The funeral was small and solemn, but simple and happy in the way he would have liked. At home. Charles' fellow soldiers, the ones he'd died to save, arrived in military fashion to salute him, and paid his widow their humblest respect. Ms. Oranorth received the salutes of the eight hundred saved men that day. She was told after the service by one of the survived that it was unheard of to save that many people in a battle. Most came back with little more than three-hundred, he said.

"Charles only lost eleven men under his command," the soldier said, "and he grieved for every one of them."

She remembered the smile he wore when she'd told him about her younger sister's antics and how she wanted to be a teacher when she grew up. She remembered the exact moment when she realized she loved him back. And she remembered the first time he'd pulled her in to kiss her cheek in spite of how painful moving was, realizing he'd been in love ever since the moment he'd met her.

She cried some more then, but she was happy. She felt honored by those who continued to live. He'd held onto life for as long as he could because he loved her with everything he had. She knew she had to help everyone she could, because that's what he would have done.

Whenever her patients ask about her husband, she swears she still feels the same warmth as if he'd never left, and that's what keeps her strong.

7

James woke up briefly to a very bright light shining in his face. It felt somehow warmer and softer than sunshine, and was one of the strangest sensations he'd felt in a long time. As if he was looking directly at the sun, without the dangers of it.

"King?" James asked. "What are you doing here?"

"Go back James, it's not time for this yet."

"King? What's going on? Is this…?"

King escorted James to the edge of a wide river.

"Perhaps? Am I… Am I dead?"

A rounded tunnel sat quietly nestled into the side of a forested, majestic mountain on the other side of the river. For some reason, James felt like he already knew where it led to, but it didn't feel like he was being forced there against his will. Someone or something was drawing him back.

"James?"

He bolted awake. A kind but firm hand grabbed his shoulders and held him down.

"Calm, easy now. You've taken quite a beating young man."

Those hands helped him steady his nerves. He was back. James looked at the hands' owner. Ms. Oranorth's eyes released some tension and she allowed herself to smile a little. She handed him a little paper cone filled with water.

"Here, drink this."

James propped himself up in the cot he'd been placed on, his left eye throbbing something fierce. The water felt amazing going down his throat, and he realized how thirsty he was. He asked for another one.

"Slow down or you'll make yourself feel sick."

James knew better than to disobey her. She'd known his parents since he was a little kid.

"Is she ok?" James finally managed to say.

Ms. Oranorth handed him an ice-pack wrapped in a paper-towel. He held it up to his face. It felt magical.

"The girl? Your quick thinking saved her. I was told she used the commotion you made to help the other girl too."

"Good."

That was all he needed to know. He'd never held any kind of grudge against the Un'darbrids, contrary to what most of the school now thought of him. He wasn't a hero. He was simply someone who couldn't stand to see innocent people get hurt. Usually, he just left everyone at school to their own devices. So why, of all times, had he suddenly picked a fight he couldn't win?

"Oh, right… fairy girl. Hmm… why is she special?"

Something inside him had risen up. But he hadn't snapped. He wasn't a peace-keeper. He just did it. He looked at Ms. Oranorth.

"Both of the boys you picked a fight with will be expelled once they hear everyone's account, I'd imagine. Right now they're suspended, but I'll make sure that changes," she said. "You've finally given me enough concrete evidence to take it to the principal."

James nodded. He believed her. But he didn't really care about much at the moment. She continued.

"Take that ice off for a minute. You don't want to freeze your brain, do you?"

"I think I might've been in heaven for a minute." he said.

"You weren't out cold for that long, kiddo. They wanted to send you to the hospital along with that chump, but I wouldn't have it. I know when you're faking and you were faking it hard-core. You did break his nose though. Good job."

"I wasn't faking it. I got socked pretty good."

James gingerly touched around his eye. It still hurt something fierce. Ms. Oranorth raised an eyebrow and, after deciding he was sincere, gave him a couple pills and another cup of water.

"I'll have you rest here for the day so I can keep an eye on you just in case you show symptoms of concussion. They suspended you for a week, but only because it's school policy. I don't think you're in trouble."

James thanked her and reclined back into the cot to rest. She was a saint. The most beloved of saints.

His mother arrived that afternoon to pick up her son. She didn't yell at him like he might've been reasonably expected. She was just glad he was safe.

Soon after Mrs. Pensworth arrived Ms. Oranorth explained the entire situation to her, both about his week of suspension, and how not-so-secretly proud she was of him. She gave her instructions for his eye so it wouldn't get infected and handed her some medication.

The car ride home was short and uneventful. James was tired and hungry from his drug induced nap, but at least the nurse's care was doing its job because he was feeling significantly better. His eye wasn't throbbing like it'd been earlier. And it was still numb from ice.

The car pulled into the driveway. Mrs. Pensworth guided her son to the door. The house was quiet until she turned on the television and James was upstairs taking a shower. After making a grocery list, Mrs. Pensworth called upstairs telling him that she'd be back in about forty-five minutes with food. They would eat Chinese tonight. She loved her son and he loved Chinese food. It was a good choice for everyone.

***

James sat down in the tub and let the water splash down on his face. He avoided letting it directly hit his wound like the plague, but the occasional splash felt heavenly. Like liquid sunshine on a thirsty plant. The rest of the mud he hadn't washed off earlier ran down the drain.

"It was totally worth it," he thought.

She was safe. And he could afford to wait to take the test.

Mrs. Pensworth called her husband on her way to the restaurant and told him everything. He too felt incredible pride for his son; he'd known very few people in his lifetime besides himself who'd protect a woman's honor so fiercely. He assured her that they were raising their son just fine. She agreed, only after expressing her concerns about his black-eye.

Mr. Pensworth reassured her that it would heal up as quickly as any other kind of school injury. She laughed, saying something funny about boys and their nonstop fighting, ending the call as she pulled into the parking lot. The line was a lot longer than expected, so she called home to tell James she'd be home a little later than planned. He got the message. James shrugged and put the phone up, letting the towel he'd wrapped around his waist slide off. No one was home yet, which meant more time for a bath.

8

Dinner was fairly uneventful. James' father gave him a pat on the back. They watched a movie together afterwards. James felt his eye already beginning to heal. They decided it'd probably be completely fine within the next few days and convened on the fact that Ms. Oranorth was more magician than nurse. But he was still suspended for the week. James felt this was unfair but understood after his parents explained for the tenth time that it was necessary for the school to understand he wasn't a trouble maker.

"At least I have more time to sleep," he thought. "Maybe even dream up something cool."

James loved the dreams where he was the hero and had to save the princess most. Perhaps his dreams had been pointing him to this day all along.

"No, that's impossible. Those are just dreams," he thought. "But still... It fits somehow. She..."

He didn't know what he wanted to think.

The movie ended almost without his realizing it. He thought it'd been a western flick, but it turned out he was way off mark.

"Not a western, but a sci-fi set on mars…"

"It explains all the lasers," he thought. "Pew pew."

He shook himself out of the trance. The pain medicine wasn't helping his energy levels.

"Night, you two." he said.

James steadied himself with the hand rail and waddled upstairs. Dream land awaited.

***

Images of spacecraft and futuristic swords arced across the visions of his mind as James rolled under the covers. He forgot to brush his teeth. He moaned weakly.

"I'll do it in the morning."

James rolled under the covers before he'd even taken his shirt off. Such mundane habits could wait. A wind chime whispered a gentle song from one of the neighbors' porches and its lullaby was the last thing he heard before passing out, drool and snoring included.

James saw the river and the tunnel again that night, though he didn't know why, or what he was supposed to make of it. He also saw a girl's face, and more weapons, and things; all of them blended together into some weird hodgepodge of daily events.

"Why the random panda chewing on bamboo and smiling at me? Oh right, Chinese food."

It was all very confusing. James' eyes fluttered a little underneath his eyelids. He couldn't get her out of his head. She set his heart at ease, as if he'd been carrying a very heavy burden for a long time and hadn't realized it was there before. He'd never felt lonely, even though he was almost always alone these days.

"So why does it ache whenever I think about them hanging out without me? It feels like she's the key to this."

His thought filter couldn't handle it. If he hadn't been so physically tired and still recovering, he would've kept himself awake all night. It was better that he was wounded for now. It gave him a fighting chance to process all his life choices before they had the chance to slam him in the face again.

***

James woke up in the morning around eleven and remembered it was a weekday.

"Lunch time."

Lunch happened to be his favorite meal since dinner. It didn't matter what it was. James liked food. He stopped himself mid-leftover-chicken-wing.

"Do I really need friends?"

The thought had never occurred to him. Having friends wasn't a foreign concept to him, but he realized that morning he'd never had any. At least, not for quite some time. He didn't need them, really. He had his friends back in Arthridall waiting for him.

"Oh chicken-wing, I'm so glad you understand me."

James dunked the other half of his wing into the sauce, realizing he didn't really like breakfast food that much. And the fact that bacon wasn't restricted to breakfast. He could put it on top of any kind of meat he wanted to, at any time of the day, except for fish. Not that he didn't like fish, he just found that couldn't be easily paired with bacon, and for him that was a definite con. James decided he liked bacon more than fish, and locked the knowledge somewhere in his brain, labeled 'food for thought'.

"But she smiled at me," he thought.

He didn't even know her name. But he had an idea.

"Stop it," he told himself.

The wing sauce tasted good, but not nearly as good as he remembered.

"Nothing makes sense anymore. Dang sauce... letting me down..."

James finished his meal and locked himself away in his room with another icepack. He decided he needed to make friends with people at some point.

"People... do I know people? Maybe I could with those two."

"They make it look so easy."

For some reason, it had entered into his mind that being friends with anybody nowadays was difficult. James buried his face in his pillow along with his icepack and stayed there, unmoving for the entire week, except for the occasional kitchen run now and then. He did, however, manage to reach a restaurant or two with his mother over his hiatus. James never, ever missed food, and would not be deterred in his mission to feed the belly beast, regardless of the 'critical nature' of his injuries.

9

Monday morning rolled around soon enough. James didn't know if he was supposed to dread the approaching day or not; even though all the potential threats from the ranks of the Un'darbrids were currently a bunch of hot fluff thanks to last week's heroism, he still had the test to worry about. The one he'd so conveniently missed.

James searched deep down inside himself, trying to decide if he may have punched the Astwin simply because he didn't want to take that evil, evil test. He wasn't a hundred percent sure.

"Maybe five percent."

Saving fairy girl had definitely been the main reason. But he also really, really, really did not like his math teacher.

"Strongly dislike is too polite... more like she's a snot garbler... gross..."

She was one of those people whose only source of joy was in her students' collective and utter despair. The funny part was James wasn't doing poorly in her class; he just hated how her nasally voice somehow always managed to penetrate his well-bred daydreaming imagination at the most inopportune moments.

He still remembered the time last month, when she'd interrupted his train of thought concerning a unique idea for a movie franchise starring a man and his pet sloth named Joffrey. James' inner voice of reason kicked in before he could pass it off as a fluke.

"Seriously?! She's inhuman."

He always struggled to forget the sound of his teacher coughing fluidly and spitting the phlegm she'd hacked up into her handkerchief. James could've sworn she did it on purpose.

"Maybe ten percent of the reason."

It didn't help her case that her class was the first one of the day three times a week, and the second to last on the other two.

"Those times are prime real estate for daydreaming. Anyone worth their salt knows that."

James had been fighting the good fight for some time now; despite the constant bombardments to his defenses, he'd still managed to determine the perfect fruit punch mix to water ratio, the perfect size and shape of the swimming pool he was going to build in the back of his modern castle, and the true nature of the Higgs Boson particle that'd recently been discovered and released to the public.

"It'll be a natural pool. Shaped like an octopus."

James decided the eight legs would have the freedom to twist and turn a bit before eventually reaching a dead end, the other two or three legs stretching further and eventually connecting to the lazy river on the outer ring. Standard pools were simply too mainstream.

James laughed a little at his pool pun as he towel dried his hair and wrapped himself in it like some sort of half mummy.

"School days begin way too early."

His father had already left for work, so James consoled himself with the fact that he didn't have the shortest end of the stick. Yet. He knew the working world was creeping up on him rather steadily, as if it were some sort of chubby caterpillar whose two hindmost legs had been broken by the butterfly mafia because it'd refused to bend to their will, but would still eventually be forced to 'see it their way'. James would never fall prey to the butterfly mafia's evil schemes. He was the one with the magnifying glass. He was the one who got to play space laser.

"Mwahaha."

James dried his feet on his bedroom carpet and let the towel drop on the ground. It was a terrible habit he'd picked up from no one in particular. It was also probably why his room sometimes smelled like the wrong end of a public shower, even though he himself was clean as a whistle. His mom had to constantly remind him that mildew was not an air freshener.

James always argued that mildew was more of a natural odor than deodorant was, and while she couldn't beat his overwhelming logic, he always lost the argument. And always ended up having to scrub and vacuum whenever the smell became unbearable to his mother's most sensitive of mom noses. Every single time. His mom's nose could pick up on the slightest hint of bacteria at a single whiff of a milk jug. No stink would ever be safe while she was around.

James finished getting dressed and snagged a light but balanced breakfast on his way to the bus stop. His mom had already set out a packed lunch for him, and because she knew he hated his math teacher, she'd made his favorite kind of peanut butter and jelly for him; the right balance of crunchy peanut butter and grape jelly sliced into rectangles without the crusts. To James, crusts were gross, and the kind of bread his mother typically bought didn't allow for perfectly shaped triangles.

James hadn't thought about what he'd do concerning the girls at the bus stop. Was he supposed to approach them? Or was he supposed to wait for them to notice him first? He wasn't in the habit of making friends here, and seeing that he hadn't made any for a very long time, still quite rusty at it. It was a conundrum of epic proportions.

He sat near the back of the bus on the left and waited. His nerves won out over his ever astounding friend making skills. She was so beautiful; he didn't want to lose her because he'd been awkward talking with her on day one.

"Get yourself together man," James muttered, reassuring himself.

There she was. Same seat on the right with her friend, just like last week. He wondered what she'd think about his idea for a film series about the man and his pet sloth. He decided she wouldn't be worth being friends with if she didn't like sloths. James knew his concern was petty, but he wasn't wrong. And it was okay if she liked unicorns; unicorns were right up there on his list of magical and mystical creatures worth befriending, right behind sloths and dragons.

She caught James looking at her. Staring would've probably been the better term. And while it may have appeared that he was staring her, James had already begun imagining what it'd be like to have a sloth with a unicorn horn.

"There wouldn't be any reason to have a unicorn at that point."

He laughed at his unicorn horn-point pun. A unicorn without its horn would be unspeakable, a little hoarse so to speak, and James knew that horse people were more than weirdly obsessive about their animals.

"Unisloth has a nice ring to it," he thought. "Oh... crap..."

James locked eyes with her. Somehow, he'd succeeded in doing the one and only thing he'd been trying to avoid the entire bus ride. She blushed, hunching down below the tall seats to whisper to her friend. He'd blown it. He'd embarrassed her and now she would never talk to him again.

"Stupid… so…damn…stupid…" James angrily whispered to himself.

***

Midway through his pouting session, James was reminded of how good a fact it was that nobody really knew he was the true identity behind 'Knockout'. No one congratulated him on his apparently overwhelming victory because no one had put two and two together as to what Knockout looked like without a black eye. Despite his achievement sending ripples throughout the entire school and making its way up the grapevine to the authorities thanks to one select nurse. Apparently, no one had ever stood up to the bully or his henchmen or realized that the school was being terrorized by an overgrown childhood mafia. Something like that seemed outside their realm of imagination.

He'd become some sort of legend overnight. It turned out there were a lot people who'd been holding grudges against the Un'darbrids. While there'd always been a few of the more vocal students ranting about taking them out (but never to their faces), most students had been too afraid to group up and mount a counterattack.

"Who knew it'd only take one completely unknown student with no obvious motive to take down an entire criminal organization? Total plot twist right there."

James figured that the most powerful sway for this 'Knockout' character was because almost nobody actually knew who Knockout was. Knockout was simply the type of nobody everyone seemed to be able to relate to on a personal level. More importantly, he'd done what everyone wanted to do but actually followed through with it. And, since nobody knew Knockout's real identity, no one could try claiming fame. Nor would anyone want to, for fear of the Un'darbrids return was still relatively strong. Knockout's real power was that they were truly anonymous; they could be any single student in the school or all of them at once. Knockout was now the banner anyone could rally to or hide behind.

James closed his locker with a slight metallic bang and locked it. He mused to himself that some kids might go as far as creating an annual school holiday tradition to remember the fall of the Un'darbrid regime at the hand of their hero.

"Perhaps it should be November fifth," he thought. "That's when I broke his face, after all. Nah... that's already been taken."

James decided it was definitely better to remain unknown and he needed to stop worrying about it. It was test-taking time.

For some mysterious reason, the school felt dimmer and colder than it'd been before. James thought it might've been because the universe hated him just as much as he hated his teacher.

"Not out of the realm of possibility. Come to think of it... Thorne's cavern was..."

He eventually decided it was a ludicrous thought, considering he'd already met the big guy in the sky on two separate occasions and he'd trapped Thorne in the abyss. God was too chill to hate him. James smirked at his 'chill' joke for a moment, but his joy ended faster than he would've liked.

"It'd be so much better if I had someone to tell..."

***

James felt the weight slide off his shoulders as he took his customary seat on the far side of the classroom. It was a pretty standard classroom as far as classrooms went; gray walls, grayer fluorescent lights, and dark gray prison bars for windows. Thankfully, the thin gray criss-cross wire pattern that strengthened the glass panels of the windows was not large enough to detract from the view outside too much. Outside was especially gray. It was always gray during school hours. Or it was perfectly perfect whenever he wanted to be outside but couldn't. There was never a happy medium. Unless it was gray. James knew it was those kinds of little details that could make or break a student, especially one who was trying to dream of a world without trigonometry or advanced calculus integrals. Granted, he was a master dreamer among dreamers, but that wasn't to say he was untouchable. James believed the system only worked to perpetuate itself; one either had to pay their dues for upwards of sixteen years to get a piece of paper that said 'You did it!' in fancy letters, or drop out at the earliest opportunity and get a job for minimum wage in a retail position or flipping burgers at McCraggle.

"Either way, kids these days are screwed," James thought. "School empties children's pockets of their money and people of their souls just so they can work in factories their whole lives."

Only a few ever made it out alive in the imaginary sense. Those people created wonderful expressions with their souls. Those expressions were a double-edged sword; on one hand, they gave hope to those fighting to save themselves from utter assimilation into the factory of life. On the other hand, those expressions continuously created the new face of society and culture. Some culture was good; James considered this to be the cream of the crop, the one percent that truly made a difference. The other ninety-nine percent was garbage, a garbage culture feeding a garbage system. James knew the only reason this 'garbage' culture was able to continue perpetuating itself was because the faint spark of life residing in its human creators allowed them to not give up the fight completely. But they always lost track of why they wanted to create something in the first place. They settled. James knew that to settle for anything less than true expression was to die and give into the beast.

Maybe it was why he had such a hard time relating to anyone here. No imaginations. Maybe he was the one genius who saw the flaws of the system and still had potential to slip through its cracks unscathed. Maybe he'd somehow make it through the hell-hole called school and the abyss called adulthood and rise to the very top. Maybe he could be odd enough, and weird enough, to retain his soul within his body and change the world just enough to give even one other person hope for a better future. James sure hoped so. It would make everything he worked so hard at worthwhile.

He hated Ms. Brigand's personal brand of human torture. She was cruel and unusual punishment in the flesh. If the system were to have a human voice of any kind, it would most certainly be her nasally death screech from the hell-fires of old.

And he hadn't even taken the test yet.

***

Ms. Brigand had at least done one thing right. Postponing the test to the next week because her 'boyfriend' had broken up with her. James knew she'd never had a boyfriend. The reality was two of her eight cats had gone missing last Sunday and she was worried sick about them. Most likely the runaway duo just wanted some alone time in the woods to cuddle up with anybody other than their crazy cat-lady master.

"Yeah, that's probably what happened," James thought.

But there was no way Ms. Brigand would've deterred from her teaching schedule, not for a day and especially not for a week. It was unheard of. Especially for a test on a Monday morning; that was her favorite kind of torture device. James was positive the lady, if she could be called that, enjoyed watching the looks of pain unfold before her. Most likely it was because the higher ups decided, for the emotional health of the school, that all testing was to be pushed back due to the unusually high emotional turmoil the student body was going though.

"That's definitely the most likely possibility," he thought. "Even worse... I'm completely sure the old geezer is a morning person."

James shuddered visibly. So much so that he was sure he was causing enough vibration to directly compete with a dog whistle.

"Morning people... gross..."

The scary part was that James was correct in his latter assumption; the scariest part was his theory about the cats running away was also accurate. Granted, the power to read people like a book was both a gift and a curse. It allowed him to stay out of trouble whereas less gifted people would stumble right into the verbal traps of the popular crowd, but it also forced him to see how desperate and ugly most people were when nobody was watching. James had only met two, scratch that, three, people who weren't awful to be around; his mom, his dad, and fairy girl. Oh, and Miss Tammy. He could never forget Miss Tammy. He still didn't know the girl's name and the thought bothered him. Not to the degree that Ms. Brigand's voice did, but it was certainly a close second on the list. Or third. The disgusting shade of gray and gloomy outside made him want to groan in distaste.

10

"Alriiiight claaaasss. Pleeease take ooouuuut your calculatooors and scratch paperrr. Weee are about tooo begin," Ms. Brigand said.

"Hate that woman," James thought.

She sounded like an owl who'd been smoking some sort of hallucinogenic for quite some time. Even the image that came to James' mind, a big barn owl with a large old-fashioned pipe, couldn't help him not hate her; he'd decided long ago that there were a few people worth having permanently on his hate list. James knew the hate list was a real thing. One, he'd created his own over the course of the past twelve years. Possibly longer, but he believed toddler years didn't count. Two, James knew he could ask any teenage girl to have ever lived whether there were people that they wished dead.

"The answer would be yes."

"Alriiiight claaaasss, settle dowwwn. We don't haaave aaaalll daaay. Iiit'sss yoooour teesst graaade."

"Shut up, woman. Nobody likes you," James thought.

It was true. She was the boring seven-eighths of school personified in the flesh.

The test was standard as far as Ms. Brigand's tests went. It may have helped that he'd had an entire extra week to prepare for her typical subpar attempts to confuse the class with awkwardly phrased word problems.

"It's not like anyone in high school never studies, right? Or am I the only one with a photographic memory?"

James handed in his exam and politely asked to be excused to the restroom. Ms. Brigand always let him leave early. It was one of the few perks of being one of the only students in the class who didn't talk behind her back. That, and he always did well on his assignments because he always turned them in on time.

"Heee's suuucch a sweeeeet young maaan," she crowed to herself as James walked out into the hallway.

"Man, she's creepy. At least I only have half a year left with her," James said.

The thick, pale wooden door swung closed slowly and James finished zipping up his backpack on the floor. The hallways seemed to have been blacked out, except for the emergency lights. James was absolutely certain that the administration would've shut those off too if they were legally allowed.

"At least it's quiet out here," he thought.

He felt the light through the classroom door hit his peripheral vision as he stood back up. It made sense; the only other sources of light came from the other classroom doors further along the hallway, and the dimly lit red signs that read "EXIT" above the emergency exits and hallway intersections. James happened to look back in the classroom to watch the rest of his peers sweat profusely.

"Was it actually that difficult? Really though..."

James decided to stand at the door for a while to watch them as he laughed to himself. Not that he really cared for any of them. It wasn't that he was mean, it was that, like all other quiet people in the world, he was curious. Curious about what it might be like to be a normal, everyday citizen. Perhaps even a little curious to know what it was like to be a part of society to begin with.

"People are weird..."

He recognized most of their faces by name. Samantha Howards and Ricky Smith took up the two seats by the window in the row up front of where he'd previously sat; they were the most popular couple at school right now. For the moment. James knew better. He knew the two of them had been arguing recently, contrary to popular belief, and by his reckoning would probably go their separate ways in approximately a week and a half. Arnold was the cool nerd, whatever that meant. He noticed Arnold was already almost done with the test as well.

"Hey Arnold, if you think hipsters are cooler than ice then you've got another thing coming. You're already a part of the system."

James thought the hipster trend was just as much of a fad as the hippie movement was from the previous generations. Even though hipsters argued they were unique and different than everybody else, most didn't have much to offer.

"If you really want to be unique and different, all you have to do is be yourself no matter what. You'll be happier that way too," James said.

James sighed.

"But at least he has friends to pretend being cool with…"

He glanced at his teacher for a moment and shuddered again. Evil. James started to turn away from the door to protect what he had left of his innocence, when a mop of messy hair sitting in the front row caught his attention.

"Wait, since when has she been in my class?" James exclaimed. "Have I really not noticed before? Or did she just show up randomly? Did she transfer in or something?"

Fairy girl, the girl he so desperately wanted to truly meet ever since bumping into her at the coffee shop, was sitting two chairs away from the door in the front row. It looked like she was struggling.

"Poor thing, I wish I could help." James thought.

The scene slowed down, sounding of heartbeats. James later decided it was one of the more surreal experiences of his life. And that coming from a guy who'd already met God twice. James found himself in frozen awe of the girl, like a deer caught in the headlights.

Amy took her hand off her forehead, leaning back in frustration. She glanced up at the exit, wondering if Ms. Brigand would notice if she slipped away again. But he was there, looking back at her, as if standing there to block out her fears. James froze, immediately losing all his cool. An eternity passed, and she smiled for a moment, turning back to her test with what looked like her version of a war face. James, as far as he knew, had only been that determined only once, maybe twice, in his entire life. He couldn't remember the first one, but the other stemmed from the frustration he'd felt when he'd been super determined to completely finish a very difficult video game. He didn't really know what he'd done to help, but whatever it was, it seemed to have helped a lot.

James left to use the bathroom before his imagination could wreak any more havoc on the normies of school-dom.

"This staring is starting to become habitual," James thought.

11

Amy Rosenbury remembered him. She didn't know his name, but she'd recognize him anywhere at this point. After all, she'd caught him staring at her more than once. Most people would consider it creepy or concerning, especially when the person in question never seemed to talk. She didn't care though. Those people didn't know he was the same guy who'd saved her from being groped. She didn't mind his oddness. He wasn't creepy, he was just quiet. Perhaps a little shy. If anything, she was more than a little curious about him too. Why'd he stand up for her of all people? She supposed it didn't hurt that he was cute.

"We've bumped into each other before he got beat up, right? Oh right, the coffee shop. Crap... I hope he doesn't hate me because Susy slammed the door in his face..."

Amy couldn't get him out of her head. He'd done so much already and she didn't even know his name. It pained her to think about what would've happened if he hadn't been there to smite the jerk face.

"I... I need to focus," she reminded herself.

Math and science had never been her strong suits. Amy knew early on that she was much better at the arts; like Drama, or English, maybe even History. But she needed to pass this test to pass the quarter.

"How the hell did he finish so fast?" she thought as James turned in his test. "We're only halfway into class."

She watched him walk out the door from underneath her sweating hand, slightly frustrated that he'd even beat the smart kids to the chase.

"Who is this guy, really?"

Amy wished she could be in Art class. Or at the very least, somewhere else; anywhere besides here, wincing at Ms. Brigand's awful test and her awful, shrieking voice anytime she suspected someone of cheating. She hated how Ms. Brigand always made the tests purposely confusing and complicated.

"Hell on earth… she's a witch…"

Amy put her chewed up mechanical pencil on the desk and leaned back in frustration. If only she could burn her at the stake for essentially being the worst person ever.

"He's still here?"

James looked out of sorts, standing on the other side of the door with the most deadpan neutral face she'd ever seen.

"Is he… teasing me? He doesn't know me… Jerk!" Amy thought.

Amy finally decided to look more intently since he'd so happily obliged to stand there and provoke her wishful thinking.

"How has nobody else noticed he's still there?" she thought. "Is he really that invisible?"

Amy stopped herself, noticing something hidden deeper the more she looked.

"He's as scared as I am."

Amy couldn't help but smile. She had her own guardian angel.

"Am I special or something?"

Amy turned to her test and picked up her pencil.

"I can do this. Random coffee shop guy believes I can do this. So I'll believe I can too."

12

James sat down on his customary bench on the far side of the school grounds, superhero lunchbox in lap, frustrated.

"I was supposed to be making friends, not freaking them out..." he muttered.

He shook his head in disgust.

"What now..."

He wasn't used to crying. He was used to reading books and walking around at night alone, singing songs about imaginary heroes of old, not getting upset about what other people thought about him. He'd always been the quiet kid in the corner. Why'd he ever attempt to be anything different?

"At least I have you Mr. P.B. and J," he said.

James opened his lunchbox. He wasn't so far away from the rest of the students that he couldn't hear them as they chattered about worthlessly inside. The cafeteria windows were always open regardless of weather, so even when it was a day as dreary as this one he could always hear the squeals of laughter lilt over the rest of the outdoor tables. There were only a few other people outside at the moment. They sat at the other tables, bragging about their recent ski-trips to the mountainsides of Colorado. Two of them had apparently come back with a decent amount of weed.

"Not entirely that surprising," James thought.

A girl wearing knee high cold weather fuzzy boots and jeans walked up to the side of James' bench. He looked up. She also wore a rather soft and warm looking women's jacket; the white kind with a fuzzy ferret fluff on the outer edge of the hood.

"Mind if I join you?" Amy asked.

James turned his head to get a look. Opportunities with women didn't happen very often for him. He immediately recognized her. With this came the understanding that she knew him, and the feeling was wonderful. His brain exploded.

"It's her... It's her? Why the hell is she talking to me?! Doesn't matter! She wants to eat!"

"Uhh... Sure," James said, repacking his lunchbox and pulling it closer to him so she could sit down.

"He speaks! Who would've thought!?" Amy thought.

"Thanks," she said quietly, adjusting her hood and hair, hoping she looked alright.

Amy didn't know what to do or how to act after that. She hadn't thought ahead very far.

***

Neither of them knew what to do. It wasn't that there weren't things they wanted to talk about, because in reality there were plenty of things they both wanted to ask, but both of them felt that the bench was now a place of sacred peace and quiet. Or they were both quite more awkward about eating lunch together than either initially anticipated.

James opted for the quiet route, because it was right at the moment she'd asked to join him that he realized he'd actually always stayed true to himself and it was no time to change that. Even for her. He'd seen how easily friendships fell apart when people acted fake and he decided he'd never fall into that trap just to gain something temporary.

Amy, for her part, realized that he'd decided to not be awkward about it and, for some reason, the thought put her entirely at ease. They were simply two people, sitting together, eating lunch on a November afternoon. There wasn't anything awkward about it. Just peace and quiet.

But Amy got antsy.

"So uh, what's your name?" Amy asked.

"James. James Pensworth. You?"

"My name's Amy. Amy Rosenbury."

"It's a pleasure to meet you, miss." James said.

"The pleasure is mine," Amy replied. "I like your lunchbox. Superheroes are awesome."

"Thanks."

They stopped talking again. There was something in the air that made the silence more magical than trying hard to force some small-talk and fail miserably at it. They wouldn't ever admit it, but even the small-talk seemed to hold a lot more meaning than either let on. It felt different for each of them. But it was also new, perhaps even exciting, and more beautiful than anything else either had ever experienced up until that point in time, as if the stars had perfectly aligned above them on the exact moment they met; everything coming together full circle for the first time.

It started snowing, and the uproarious noises from the cafeteria became muffled. Amy looked down at the lunchbox sitting in her lap, mostly to make sure she didn't have any crumbs on her jacket. He was cute and she didn't want to lose her chance.

Amy brushed a stray hair away from her mouth with a small sound, picked up her lunch, and began eating. James noticed how the snow had started attacking her hair in droves, so he pulled out a little black umbrella from his backpack to cover her head. At first, Amy only heard the slide of the metal as it opened and got nervous because of the noise out of instinct, but once she realized what he was doing she felt at ease.

Amy felt her heart flutter slightly.

"Thanks…" she said.

"You're welcome."

"For… For everything."

James looked back at her for a moment and smiled.

"So she does know who I am."

She knew what he'd done. James felt alive. He never would've guessed in a million years that he'd ever be so grateful for getting a black eye. James felt the weight he'd unknowingly been placing on himself slide off like water flowing over a waterfall in the middle of summer. What a rush.

"Glad I could help. You… you didn't deserve all that. And, you remind me of someone."

"Would… do you want to eat lunch again tomorrow?"

James considered it for a moment. There'd be no going back. But she was worth it. And his old routines kind of stunk.

"She just needs to get to know me," he thought. "It'll take time because I'm so sophisticated."

"Sure. I…I'd like that, Amy."

Amy stood up, holding out an official mitten to shake his hand. She smiled and laughed a bit.

"Good talk."

"Yeah, let's uh… let's do it again," James said.

13

His first real interaction with her felt so much better than James could've ever imagined. Life made less sense than ever now, but for some reason the feeling of warmth inside him made it a non-issue. Amy was naturally pretty. She had light brown hair that reminded him of the color of ocean sand after a light rain, and eyes so clear and blue that they made the Caribbean Sea pale in comparison. They even had that distinct green after-hue to them so characteristic of the tropical waters.

"She'd make an amazing mermaid," James said.

The snow started falling by the inch as he shuffled down the school's main steps. James' boots crunched the powder underneath with a feather's lightness.

"Officially the beginning of winter."

The only thing that could make the day any better would be a hot cup of coffee and a good book to read. It was a good thing he was headed to his favorite place that had both.

***

"Hi James! How was school?" Mrs. Tamburton asked.

"It was good, thank you."

The little old lady shuffled over to him as he got in line. The line was longer than normal; the sudden downpour of cold weather had everyone thinking the same coffee thoughts.

"It's too bad the fall flavors won't come back until next year," James said. "They went away too quickly if you ask me."

"Ah, that's where you are wrong, my friend. Try this."

"What is it?"

"Just taste it."

James considered her demand for a moment. It wasn't as if she was a stranger. She was essentially his grandma in every way but blood relation. He eventually obliged her and took the steaming coffee cup. Not only did it smell delicious, but the steam reminded him of the beautiful, hot shower waiting for him once he got home.

"Warm is good," James thought.

"May I?" he asked.

"Please do."

James took a sip and gasped. Even a coffee connoisseur such as himself knew that the woman standing in front of him had created pure gold in drinkable form.

"Amazing!" James exclaimed.

Mrs. Tamburton adjusted her wire-rimmed glasses with a sparkle in her eye. The kid knew his way around coffee almost as much as she did.

"You like it?"

"How in the world did you make a lemon-chocolate coffee taste like a pumpkin spice?"

"Shhh! Keep your voice down!" she exclaimed as she pulled him down to her level to whisper in his ear. "It's a secret mix I don't want to give away quite yet. It's good, yes?"

"Yes it is," James whispered back.

"Would you like one?"

"Please!"

"You got it, buddy. You go back to my table. This one's on me."

"Really?"

"Go sit down."

"Thank you."

"You got it, kiddo. I'm just glad I wasn't going crazy."

James sat down next to Mrs. Tamburton's local newspaper and her other various reading material, beaming in anticipation.

"How did I forget to put her on my list? If she wasn't on it before, she's definitely on it now."

He watched as the grinning little old lady pulled the cashier up close and whispered the secret order to him so that no one else could hear.

"Maybe she should be one of the characters inside my book," James thought. "She's certainly unique enough. Reminds me of Jehu."

Mrs. Tamburton came back to the little circular table a few minutes later, heavenly ambrosia of the gods in hand.

"Thank you."

"You are very welcome," she said, easing her somewhat frail body into her seat.

"So," she continued, "anything interesting happen at school today? Meet any girls?"

James ears reddened some, but he couldn't help himself from grinning like a monkey about to throw some poop. James hated the mental image but felt it was entirely too accurate. He let loose at the fan anyway.

"You sound like my dad."

"Where do you think he got his humor from?"

He didn't have a retort. Monkey chunks sprayed all over his face. Very few people could hit back with facts he hadn't thought of before but she was one definitely one of them.

"I guess he still has a way to go."

She laughed. "They don't call me Tammy for nothing."

James knew she only gave a few select people the privilege of calling her Tammy, and his parents had earned their place on that very selective list after many years of friendship and mentoring. She picked up on his hesitation.

"It's okay if you call me Ms. Tammy. Or Nana. My granddaughter has been calling me Nana ever since she equated me with her favorite fruit as a wee lass."

James did his best to suppress the helpless giggling threatening to explode out of him.

"She's so weird. But it's the best thing ever. Who would've thought bananas are people too? Nana…"

"Thanks for the coffee… Ms. Tammy. Nana."

She leaned back her chair, newspaper in hand. After a couple moments of pretending to read it she stared James down with her glasses right at the end of her nose, the gold rims reflecting the reddish-orange hue of the light above the table.

"Is she cute?"

"Yes. Very."

"What's her name? You'll have to introduce me to her sometime."

"It's Amy. And… we'll see."

Tammy grinned as if she knew something he didn't.

"I bought you special coffee."

"You drive a hard bargain."

"You already drank your contract."

"Touché. But today was the first time we really talked... During lunch. It may be a while."

"That's fine. I'm a patient person. So what'd you two talk about?"

"Not much, but it was good. She said she likes my lunchbox."

"She's a keeper."

"That's what I'm saying."

Mrs. Tamburton smiled and went back to reading the paper.

"So, are you going to the library to work on your book-portal after you're done here?"

"Yeah. I've been thinking of making you a character in it."

"Permission granted, kiddo. It's about time someone recognized my genius."

James stood up and politely shook her hand.

"I'll be taking my leave, then," he said.

"I thought you left fifteen minutes ago."

"I'm glad you appreciate me."

"I appreciate me too."

Mrs. Tamburton was a master wordsmith. It wasn't out of the question that she'd really been the one to train James' dad in the art of dad jokes. Maybe she was the original dad joke trainer for every dad to have ever lived. James figured she probably had a vault of them casually laying around somewhere just waiting to be opened from all her free time as an old fart. Normally he'd consider the term incredibly rude and degrading but Nana had proven to him during numerous engagements and much to his mother's chagrin, that she was indeed the inventor of the sport of old-farting.

"It's a thought," James thought as he walked out the door.

14

James shivered. It was getting colder rather rapidly.

"Why on earth does it have to get dark by six?"

His boots crunched along with the enthusiasm of a little kid eating sugar cereal while watching Saturday morning cartoons.

"Not the garbage they show nowadays... nah... the garbage they used to show that was actually secretly awesome. That stuff was sweet..."

The soft white powder had blanketed everything in the entire city, everywhere downtown, and all the way into the outlying suburbs. James imagined it was as if God had dropped a big bag of flour on the ground and decided to roll around in it instead of cleaning up in a timely manner as a responsible deity should. James remembered when he used to do silly stuff like rolling around in flour; he missed those days of not getting punished for messing up.

It may have been one of his subconscious reasons for why he was so intent on escaping into the world of stories. Especially his own stories. He wasn't half bad at writing either; more than one person had told him so. Not including his mom, of course. His mom was obligated to say they were good due to the obligatory and ever secretive mom code.

Ms. Tammy loved his work too, and she counted for extra because James found she was awesome no matter what she did. She could say his book was utter garbage if she wanted to, and he would probably find himself agreeing with her.

"She's too awesome and hardcore to say no to," James thought.

James pulled on his backpack straps to redistribute the weight on his back. A couple snowflakes landed on his nose and his hood slid halfway off his hair.

"I can't not eat some," he said.

The cool snow felt magical in contrast to the still piping hot coffee he'd set on the ground. Most of the tall and skinny trees had already laid their branches bare for the season. James thought they looked dead and wiry, as if the very bones of the deceased had sprung up from the ground to begin their never ending dance of the dead once more. James picked up his half empty coffee and began walking to his other favorite place in the world, swaying in tune with the rhythm of the trees as they were buffeted by the breath of winter. One of the branches behind him broke off from the new weight of snow sitting on it, falling down with a crash.

He was his own music.

James wondered if Amy liked to dance or sing. Or even if she was talented at either of them. He'd made the mistake of not making that distinction only once; Mr. Pensworth, his dad, loved to dance and sing but was atrociously terrible at both. It was a good thing his mother had fallen for him anyway. His dad claimed it was because he'd tried so very hard to win her heart, even when it meant being awkward for her sake.

James had always kept his father's wisdom close in mind. James found it was one of the most beautiful things in the world to observe his parents whenever he happened to catch them slow-dancing around the kitchen after they'd finished the dishes. He'd learned that love didn't always appear the same way it did in the movies. Love came in all shapes and sizes.

***

James walked into the library and straight up to the third floor towards his customary desk and chair. It had taken some time for him to completely claim the prized cozy corner for himself, because for the longest time the custodial staff had habitually moved James' setup back to its original place after the library closed. Over time, the staff realized how persistent he was about his setup, and after a month of constantly rearranging the furniture he'd fully overridden their old custom. James prided himself on the knowledge.

His chair was more like a recliner that he'd repurposed from the reading corner at the far end of the hallway. He'd spent more than a year's worth of hours there, filling his head with countless stories of adventure and woe. Homework was a breeze since he had such a large mahogany desk to spread out on all at once. It was like an old pub table, deeply stained and clear-coated so as to protect from scratches and spilled drinks. At least, that's what he wanted to think. No one really knew where it originally came from. Some further delving for information might've proven that the desk was initially intended to be put in the Library of Congress but was too large to squeeze inside. He might be the only one to ever know. It was Arthrindian. And he knew that it was, by far, easily the best place in the entire building to escape from reality. If only for a while.

James carefully slid his backpack on the table so as to not damage his laptop. After adjusting the chair to his customary height, James allowed himself to sit down and snag a sip of Nana's magic concoction.

"Still hot."

Unzipping his bag, James carefully slid out his computer and opened it, plugging in his well-loved mouse. He had to be careful with it since he still needed to save enough money to pay for an external hard-drive. He was already almost a hundred and forty pages into his current piece, and there was no way it'd be possible to recover if he had to start over from scratch. He'd already written and edited his first story, hoping to publish it within the next few months. The book he was currently working on was a continuation. He felt around in his pocket to make sure the key was still inside.

But something about them weren't quite adding up. It always felt like he could change just one more word to make it perfect. And with the promise he'd made to Nana he'd given himself yet another challenge.

"How am I supposed to make her a character when she's already one?" he whispered.

It took James some time to sort through his conundrum; he was still distracted by his thoughts of Amy. Now that he'd officially introduced himself she was the only person he could think about. They'd even made future plans already.

"It's just lunch, man. Get it together. We're just friends. Or are we even friends yet? And how does she fit into all this…"

James sent his mom a quick email letting her know he'd be coming home early. He didn't want to get stuck in the snow if got too rough. She replied a few minutes later. Dinner was at eight, and if he wanted a ride he'd need to shave off fifteen minutes and be waiting by the road at seven forty-five.

"Seven forty-five it is."

***

"I got it… holy cow though, this is going to be tough…"

James had figured it out. Not only had he made Nana a character in his book, but it actually made sense within the storyline too. He felt accomplished. Once his stories started becoming reality to his readers, he would've successfully completed the single most mind-blowing, never ending, story anyone had ever seen.

"Or should I call it what it is and make it a diary?"

Now all that was left was to figure out was how he was going to talk with his new friend tomorrow. If he'd at least bought a phone by now he would've been able to call her after dinner. It was his own fault, and now he was going to have to wait until tomorrow to explain everything because of his oversight. And Tuesdays at school were almost just as awful as Mondays at school.

"Oh, the humanity."

James closed his laptop, putting it away safely to get ready to leave. He let his hand slip into his pocket again, feeling around the pendant and eventually resting on his pocket-watch. He'd always been fascinated with the idea of time, and to him, time-pieces were no different. Both were merely means to an end. Literally. James knew the idea of time was a manmade invention, a countdown to death. Age was a countdown from birth day to death day.

"Or is time a countdown to your birthday? I guess it depends on how you look at it."

15

"She must've gotten the car cleaned," James thought.

The Pensworth family van was nothing of real importance, but it did get them from point A to point B. And while it was the family car, everyone knew the Mothership had not-so-secretly claimed it for herself and was only a family car in name. James was positive she'd drive it all the way to Hawaii if it were physically possible.

"It's probably why we've never gone to Hawaii."

His dad somehow still managed to have a say on the well-being of the car. After much discussion, he'd convinced her to let him install all the random gizmos and gadgets he'd designed himself. So not only was the van extraordinarily safe, both crash proof due to the double reinforced steel frame, and bullet proof because of the military grade anti-shatter glass, but he'd also replaced the stock transmission for a manual clutch and installed a special prototype turbocharger he'd designed himself, so the thing was powerful. Extremely powerful. His dad's own car was even more amazing, but it was also his continual pet project so no one else was allowed to touch it.

Not many people could say their father designed super-cars for fun. James was a part of that list, but up until he'd met Amy he'd never had anyone to show them off to. It'd be a new experience.

Mrs. Pensworth, for some unknown reason, believed her husband's hobby suited him perfectly. James thought it was an interesting hobby to be sure, but when his dad had first begun tinkering she'd forced him to build a separate garage in the backyard to keep the noise level inside the house down. That reasoning was fine in James' book. It allowed him more space in which to think.

It was a very good thing that James' father's work could support his hobby. Materials were not cheap, and neither was the construction of an entire extra garage. They'd only just finished paying for it last year. Any average person walking by the project might have asked why it had been so expensive to fund in the first place, as the garage seemed fairly standard as far as garages go, but the true cost wasn't the shack of a building on the surface. That part of the garage was little more than storage space.

James honestly wasn't sure if his family were civilian or not. The van his dad had Frankensteined in the backyard was more like a tank with a minivan shell than a minivan. It didn't help his father's case that the extra garage had a special basement where all the real magic took place.

"It's definitely why we only just finished paying for it."

The two of them had finished the most expensive parts of the construction two summers ago. Mr. Pensworth realized that most of his research was taking place in the main house's basement since it was larger than the garage they'd built, so instead of being a normal fellow and working on the surface-world like most mechanics, he'd decided that making an underground bunker connecting the two surface buildings would be much more ideal.

***

When James learned about his father's idea over the dinner table he was un-customarily ecstatic about the project. It was exactly the kind of idea he loved tinkering with as he read books or wrote his stories. James also had an additional semi-secret motivation to help his dad. He knew in one of the alternate worlds his dad's inventions played an important role. And he asked him if it'd be possible to have his own tinkering space once it was done. Mr. Pensworth had also thought about that possibility and pulled out a couple of ideas he'd sketched out in his free time. All three eventually agreed that one hallway would not be cool enough, so Mr. Pensworth ran to the office downstairs and pulled a couple of pieces of printer paper so they could sketch more ideas.

Everyone agreed that having one giant basement connecting the two existing basements would be too difficult to hide when they had company. They weren't exactly nervous about showing anyone the finished products in the cars themselves; it was more about the experimental and prototype research his dad wanted to keep on the down low.

If his parents ever wanted to quit their work and turn their designs into a public company, they'd need to keep their progress relatively secret. It was also a reason they'd never pushed James into making friends if he didn't want to. But they weren't against him having friends, either. They simply trusted him to do what he saw fit.

The other fault with the one giant room idea was that was structurally unsound due to the layout of the house's support structure. As it stood presently, the original basement under the house was divided into two sides by a staircase and a hallway leading from it. Going down the stairs, the left door was the guest bedroom, complete with closet and guest bath. The right side held Mr. Pensworth's office, which was the same size as the guest room and bathroom combined, making the basement the same rectangular shape as the house situated above it.

***

James slapped his design down on the table with an air of authority. He'd read more about secret rooms and secret passages than anybody else. His mom and dad gingerly laid down their pencils next to their own designs in order to study his. Mrs. Pensworth crumpled up her own idea after a few moments of studying her husband's and son's designs; her boys had clearly outdone her.

"This is brilliant, son," Mr. Pensworth said.

James's design called for a secret door behind what was presumably a coat closet they'd create at the end of the existing hallway as the first passage. The closet would connect to a basement similar to the size of the current basement, perhaps a bit larger, about twenty-five feet from the base of the house, and could take up the rest of the space of the backyard, almost like a doomsday bunker.

There'd also be a second secret door in the left rear corner of Mr. Pensworth's office connected to the new space by a parallel hallway, which he could close off if he wanted privacy. His secret office door would, as it should be, be built out of a sliding bookcase.

The entire project would be topped off with a connecting hallway on the far end of the bunker, joining with the newly built garage and its subsequent basement at the front end of its left wall, as the new garage sat in the back-right corner of the backyard at the end of an extended driveway

James argued the best part of the design was it didn't interfere with the current layout of the house and structure or the new garage, as well as providing an adequate number of pathways for the new space to be breathable.

Not having to remove the hydraulic platform lift they'd installed between the basement and garage was a definite plus. Mr. Pensworth had to agree with him there. The best part of the current garage layout was the futuristic science-fiction-esque lift he'd designed and built himself, and he'd been stumped as to how to be able to keep it.

The design worked for everyone. It added more Research and Development space for the boys to play and tinker around in, as well as satisfy Mrs. Pensworth's demand that the main house remain quiet when she wanted to work, or watch a movie, or sleep. She needed her sleep, or nobody in the house was happy. Mrs. Pensworth put her seal of approval on James' plan, especially since she got an extra coat closet out of the deal.

James knew how to cater to both of their interests.

***

"I have really awesome parents," James thought as he snapped back to the present.

Mrs. Pensworth noticed James' apparent pleasure.

"Your dad finally fixed the clutch as well," she said, pointing to the floor in front of her.

"Dad cleaned the car?"

"As an apology for the late tune-up."

"He did a good job."

"On the car? Or the cleaning?"

"Both."

They laughed. He'd been incredibly busy at his job recently.

"So how did the test go?"

"I knew you'd ask that."

"It's my job."

"It went fine. I finished and got to leave early."

"How'd you do?"

"Good."

"That's such a teenage boy thing to say."

"That's because I'm a teenage boy."

Mrs. Pensworth smirked. His personality was very similar to her husband's.

"Anything else happen today?"

"Not much."

"So…" she asked, fishing for information.

"I may have a friend at school now."

"Really? That's awesome!"

James gave a half lip smile and curled up into the side of the window, closing his eyes. Mrs. Pensworth let him rest for a few minutes, giving her some time to figure him out.

"Is she cute?"

James sat up in his chair.

"How'd you know she's a girl?"

"I'm your mother. I have superpowers. And your reaction confirmed it."

James' eyes narrowed suspiciously. She had always been real adept at reading him for some reason, and he'd never been able to quite figure out how she did it.

"Maybe she does have some sort of mom superpower," he thought. "Or Tammy taught her."

James curled up into a ball and returned to his slumber.

Mrs. Pensworth glanced at her sleeping son and felt proud of him.

"My son is growing up," she thought.

16

The front door swung closed with a slight thump characteristic of many large and thick wooden doors. The door felt secure and almost medieval; when they'd first considered purchasing the home it was the first thing to catch her attention. During their family discussions it ended up being one of the many reasons they chose the home over many other perfectly suitable substitutes.

Another piece of their reasoning was that Mr. Pensworth enjoyed the idea of having a large backyard for him and his son to play around in if they so desired. Looking back on how they'd used the land over the past few years, he could honestly say that the backyard's original purpose hadn't been altered, even if they didn't rise to the surface as often as when James was younger.

James liked the house because it was only the second home he'd ever known. If he ever had the opportunity to move somewhere else he may have eventually changed his mind, as the house was relatively standard in terms of size, but with the addition of all the new laboratory and basement space, James felt it would be difficult to top the overall property in terms of sheer volume. Regardless, James still had to remind himself from time to time as to why they'd moved from their old home in the first place.

"Even without all the stuff we added... moving was worth it. I have to believe that."

Mrs. Pensworth set her purse down on the kitchen counter at the far end of the house and began washing her hands to start getting dinner ready. James noticed his father's car in the driveway. Turning away from the living room window, he leaned over the back of the couch and left his stuff on the cushion. He almost got away with it too, but his mom caught him in the act and gave him the mom look, so he rushed upstairs to drop the bag in his room before running back down and around the corners like a quiet ninja maniac. James, still in his socks, slipped on the first floor's wooden steps, almost banging his left knee on the corner of the couch.

"Careful!" she called from the kitchen.

The stairs leading to the basement were located on the right of the kitchen table and beside the door to the laundry room, underneath the second floor stairway. James' shoulder bumped into the wall on his right as he accidently overcompensated for his detour into the couch.

"Can you let your father know dinner will be ready in fifteen minutes, please?"

"Yeah," he called, dropping down the flight of steps like an awkward leprechaun.

The basement hallway still smelled somewhat of sawdust. The new light fixture in front of the coat closet screamed of recent construction. Thankfully, the carpenter smell only remained as long as sawdust littered the ground, and seeing that his mom enjoyed cleaning the downstairs more than the rest of the house for some reason, James didn't find the arrangement disagreeable.

James swore that guestroom was always spotless. Perfect sheets, completely smooth comforter, and deep, rich varnishes to the furniture were well complemented with a deep blue-gray paint. The room was his mother's baby. No one was allowed to go in there to sleep, except for guests or family when they came into town, because she hated having to wash the sheets more than she had to. The Pensworth men had learned the lesson the hard way.

"Don't touch her stuff unless you get permission. That's great life advice, actually."

The men were okay with the arrangement. After all, she'd thoroughly supported their pet project the entire way, even helping with the construction of their new play space. A few extra walls to update the bedroom space was a very small thing to give her in return, all things considered.

James let his feet slide down the last few carpeted steps, gingerly walking towards his father's office at the end of the hallway. The door was closed, which meant his dad was either deep in thought or he was further in, deep inside the mad-scientist laboratory.

James lightly tapped the door three times, then two, then one. It was a semi-secret knock they'd created to verify each other and not some strangers who'd broken into the house to try and rob them. Or a government spy trying to steal their research.

"Dad?" James asked. "You there? Mom said dinner will be done soon."

No answer. James slowly turned the golden handle, peeking his head through. Dad wasn't at his desk. James looked at the bookshelf. Half open.

"He always forgets to close it," James huffed, "makes me wonder why we even made it a secret door in the first place."

James pushed on the bookshelf and finished rolling it over to the right side. The motion activated lights powered on after a moment, and James stepped inside. He was still impressed by the fact that they'd been able to model the support columns lining the hall after the look of ancient Greco-Roman pillars. Plastering them had been a pain. The hallway, about twenty-five feet in length and seven feet in height, was lined with ten columns, with approximately five feet between each and on either side. Between each pillar was a backlit picture frame containing some of his father's original blueprints and ideas for various car parts and designs. Some of those designs had even become parts in his mother's van.

"But he closes the non-secret door. Typical."

James opened the door at the end of the hallway, the second line of defense against the smell of grease, and peeked his head through.

"Dad?"

Mr. Pensworth kicked his legs and rolled out from underneath from a sort of deep emerald metallic colored convertible. The body was part of one of the old style muscle car frames, known for reaching a hundred and sixty miles per hour without breaking a sweat.

"Hey son!" he said, wiping some black car grease off his forehead.

"New project?"

"Yeah."

"What is it this time?"

"This," he said as he slapped his hand onto the driver side door, "is the frame for a flying car."

"Really?"

"I figured a convertible would be the most stylish."

"How'd you get your hands on it?"

"Can you believe someone was parting it out because the engine and transmission were blown? The frame's still in perfect condition. So I bought the whole thing! Haha!"

"Well, most people want a running vehicle," James replied. "And you cut the roof off."

"True."

"How much did you pay for it?"

"He originally tried me at two grand," he said, "but I was able to haggle him down to fourteen hundred."

"That's awesome!"

John Pensworth picked up the rag he'd been wiping his face with, and poured a bit of gasoline on it to finish cleaning his hands.

"Is mom home? I haven't left this spot since four o'clock."

"Got off work early?"

"Yeah. Winter time is the best. Fewer orders to fill."

"Dinner's almost done."

James paused.

"You'll probably want to shower before you come up."

Mr. Pensworth briefly sniffed himself and wretched.

"Will do. Give me five."

John walked to the left corner closest to the house, around a small enclosure that served as an outdoor shower of sorts. The shower had been his wife's idea, complete with working sink and toilet. Mom didn't want the boys tracking any dirt throughout the house if she could help it.

"Good ol' mom."

Further back along the left side of the room was a trio of old sunken couches arranged in a U-shape, and sitting on top of an off-white shag rug. Behind the couches housed a space for the fridge, and a small counter that only existed to support an old toaster oven and microwave.

The setup was perfect for the all too frequent stress breaks or nap-times between projects. If James' mother didn't insist on eating meals as a family whenever possible, they'd probably never leave what had quickly become the best man-cave of all time.

James checked the secondary coat closet door that stood next to the office exit on the way out.

"At least he never really messes with the emergency exit," he thought. "Or I might as well be his only security system."

***

James walked up the basement stairs to find his mother setting a roll of paper towels on the table, tearing off a few, and folding them underneath the silverware.

"Can you grab some plates from the kitchen please?"

"Sure."

James turned, looping around the half wall connecting the kitchen to the dining area. After opening and closing each and every one of the bottom cabinets, he remembered they were actually in the upper cabinet.

James pulled out three plates and leaned on his stomach over the countertop to hand them to her. She looked at them for a less than a second and shook her head.

"Those are still dirty. Grab the nice ones."

James took them back and looked them over himself. They weren't dirty at all. But mom was always picky.

"It's her job, I suppose," James thought.

"Should I put them in the dishwasher?"

"Yes. I put the clean ones away earlier, but it seems not all of them got completely rinsed. Go ahead."

James quickly complied and walked upstairs to his room to take off his socks. The socks in question didn't exactly make it to the hamper.

"Ah that smells amazing!" he called as he tumbled back down.

"Steak night," she said monotonously.

"Really? Why?"

"Do I need a reason to tickle my sixteen year old?"

"Ah! Aha! Hehehehehee! Ahaha! Sto… sto…stop…"

"How was your test? Really answer me this time."

"It was… It… heeheehee… it was… ha… It went well."

James tried to breathe. Both laughed again. James had always been ticklish. They sat down and waited for dad.

"Is Ms. Brigand still annoying?"

"Is the grass still green?"

"Not right now it isn't."

James smirked.

"Steak sounds good," he said.

"I thought you said it smells good."

"Wrong! I said that it smells amazing."

"Are you not entertained?!"

"That line's already been used mom."

"I'm just as strong," she said, flexing her bicep.

James leaned over the table and started tickling her arm. Her skin flab jiggled.

"Stop that! I'm not flexing there!"

"Riiight..."

"Is your father coming?"

"He's showering."

"Did you see the new project?"

"Of course I did."

"Pretty neat, huh?"

"I still can't believe he was able to get it so cheap."

"You think he'll be able to do it?"

"Do what?"

"Make it fly."

"Hello, my wonderful family!"

"There's still a bit of grease behind your ear."

"Which one?"

"Left."

John walked into the kitchen to finish scrubbing.

"Now you're wet behind the ears," Mary said.

John didn't have a good retort. She was a professional puns-tress.

"Can you the toss the paper towels, please?"

"There's a rag hanging off the oven."

"Thanks. So James, is the grass green?"

"You heard that?"

"I have super dad hearing."

"So what's my superpower, then?" James asked.

Mr. Pensworth sat down next to him, and draped his meaty arm over his son's shoulder. Mary smiled from the other side of the table. Raising a son was one of the best things that'd ever happened for her. She wasn't sure if she could've handled raising a daughter.

"Too much drama," she thought.

John looked his son in the eye, and became existentially dramatic.

"What do you want your superpower to be?"

"I have to pick?" James asked.

"That's something you have to figure out for yourself."

***

James grabbed his towel and jumped into the shower before migrating back to his room for the evening. He set his laptop on the desk to charge it. He'd already come up with some new ideas for his own work during dinner, and wanted to start laying them out for himself.

James took a look at the clock.

"How is it already almost midnight?"

It wasn't enough to deter him from sitting down. His desk sat on the left side of his room walking in, next to his closet, and opposite his bed. James realized that in terms of taste in furniture he was very similar to his mom. Everything was mahogany. James liked the color because it was clean and refined, but without going so far as to be pretentious.

"No one likes pretentious wood," he thought.

After about an hour or so and twenty sketches later, James was ready to get some rest. Getting less than six hours sleep didn't sound appealing, but it was better than the alternative of no sleep at all. Putting the new ideas down on paper had been worth it, and he decided that not doing so would've been the worse decision.

James curled into bed and pressed the switch on the side of his lamp. After a few minutes of rolling around and thinking about the day, especially about meeting his friend, he flipped the pillow over, to feel the sweet relief of a firmer and cooler underside. The desired effect was instantaneous; James clocked out for the night in seconds, sleeping until morning without any more time to think about her.

17

The alarm clock went off ten minutes earlier than James expected. He hated when it did that. It always cut his dreams off right at the good part. Every single time. James wondered why everyone always seemed to want to be busy all the time. The real ideas came from walking around the world of dreams. Exploring them.

James zipped his coat and waited at the bus stop as usual. The bus had already squeaked into the stop before the usual time and many students had walked aboard.

"Maybe it's a good thing I woke up early after all," he thought.

James walked up the steps as if he owned the place, but with no actual thought in mind. Amy and Susan were already seated in their usual spots. Amy noticed his antics, and giggled.

"Hey James."

James' eyes darted to the two of them and back to the isle. Red was quickly becoming his favorite color.

"Hey."

They turned around as he walked further in, spotting only the back of his shirt. Susan put a hand on Amy's knee and whispered something in her ear. Amy nodded no.

"Be patient. He's a bit shy."

"A bit? Fine. Keeping the boyfriend from me, I see."

"He's not my boyfriend. We're just friends."

"Uh huh… riiight."

"I'm serious!"

"Whatever you say, sis."

"This is exactly why you scare people off so much."

"Ouch. So defensive. You sure you don't like him?"

"It's not like that."

"So you wouldn't mind if started dating him?"

Amy shoved her friend into the window.

"Ah, so you do like him!"

"You're mean," Amy complained.

"It's my job as your best friend to protect you."

"You don't like him too, do you?"

"Don't be such a worry wart. I'm not going to steal him."

"You'd better not."

"Relax."

Susan rotated around to the back of the bus. It looked like James was focused on some sort of paper he was drawing on.

"I approve," Susan said.

"What?"

"You have my permission to date him."

"And why would I ever need your permission to date him?"

"Because reasons."

"I don't understand you sometimes."

"Most people don't understand me at all."

"Poor you, baby."

"I know, it's sad. I need to get me a boyfriend too."

"James isn't my boyfriend!"

"That's not what I said."

Susan stood and turned around to no one in particular, raising her gaze to the starry heavens for emphasis.

"Did I say anything like that?" she asked.

A few of the students behind them wore confused looks on their faces. Amy pulled on her friend's arm until she sat back down.

"You've made your point."

Susan giggled.

"I win."

"Fine. Just stop antagonizing me."

"Yes, your highness."

***

James sat the bench and set his lunchbox down, opening it up and putting the delicious sandwich made of love in his mouth. Thankfully for him it wasn't forecasted to snow that afternoon; all the snow had already finished dumping itself on the poor little Earth the previous night. James had decided to leave his umbrella at home given the circumstances. He loved his umbrella, but without the express need for it during lunch he could use the available space for an extra snack for his newfound friend.

Ten minutes passed and James started to worry.

"Did she ditch me?"

A frog started seizing up inside his chest. He'd been so close to not only making friends, but keeping them too. James wondered why his adventure had to end as soon as it'd started. It wasn't fair. It seemed that fate was teasing him, maliciously attacking him because of his extraordinary weirdness. He knew he was weird, but he didn't think he was obnoxiously weird, nor did he believe fate should meddle with him because of his weirdness. James wondered if she'd died unexpectedly. Or worse; scared her away because he'd been too honest.

"Hey. Sorry I'm late."

"Phew," James thought.

Amy sat down and pulled her lunch out. She caught the momentary look of fear on his face and apologized.

"Sorry, my teacher held us late until we finished cleaning the lab."

"Ah. That makes sense."

"You angry?"

James shrugged. He wasn't angry.

"Nah, don't worry about it. I thought you might've ditched me but I was wrong. It's… been a while since I've talked to people my age. Still pretty new to the area and all."

Amy snuck a quick peek. She still felt bad but didn't know how to diffuse it.

"Great, just great," she thought.

"So, what were you dissecting?"

James moved on before she could panic about it.

"Uh, we were dissecting cats."

"He's not even phased," she thought.

"Nice."

James looked at the contents of Amy's lunch and found himself pleased with its contents. He'd adequately gaged her tendencies.

"Forget to pack a lunch?"

Amy looked down at her half sandwich and yellowing apple slices in embarrassment.

"How'd he know?"

"Yeah, I guess," she said, pausing. "I overslept and had to rush to the bus. Didn't have a chance to pack anything. I grabbed yesterday's lunch and ran without thinking."

"But you were on the bus before me."

"Uh…"

He had her there.

"I was still frazzled about the test yesterday. It was really hard."

James smiled. He had a friend. She hadn't changed her attitude toward him, nor had she been deterred by his overbearing bluntness.

"Nice excuse."

"I'm not making excuses."

James looked up from his lowered gaze and held his smirk. Amy's chin burrowed into the comfort of her neck.

"I'm not!"

James broke out into a smile and started unzipping his backpack. She was curious.

"What?"

"Nothing," he said.

James pulled out a gallon sized plastic bag with a paper towel covering the inside and handed it to her.

"Here."

"What is it?"

"It's yours if you want it."

Amy opened the bag.

"How... but... wha...?"

"Do... you want it?"

The bag held a gigantic lunch, full of fruit, cheese crackers, sandwiches, chocolate milk, fruit gummies, and desert pastries.

"Tha... thanks."

Amy nose and eyebrows crinkled a little. She smiled. She didn't know what else to do. She wondered if he was certifiably an angel.

"How'd you know I'd forget to pack a lunch?"

"You said it yourself. You were still frazzled about the test, miss 'how did he finish it so quickly I hate him and his large brain.'"

Amy's quizzical face turned into laugher. The kid was certainly more unique than a lot of people she'd met. Defending her honor was one thing, but the umbrella from yesterday and now a huge surprise lunch? Amy wondered why she'd never noticed him until now.

"It must be the food talking," she thought. "I'll take food over flowers any day of the week."

"I really wanted to ask you about that. How on earth did you finish that test so quick? It was insanely hard!"

"Ah," he said, "So you do want to know?"

"Yes," she said emphatically.

"Well," he continued, "I was actually in a place called Arthridall. Know of it?"

"But the test..."

"Time flows differently there."

As if that helped her make sense of him. Amy was confused.

"Arthridall?"

"It's quite nice there. If you want you can come sometime, and we can go exploring."

"Why... how does tell me anything about how you finished the test so fast?"

"Well one, time flows differently there. And that test was easy," he said.

"Wha...? No it wasn't. And what in the world is Arthridall?"

"It's not this world. Well, actually… It could be in a way if I was persuaded. It's kind of both, I guess? I well… I'd thought… nevermind."

"What?"

"Arthridall."

"You aren't making any sense."

"I'm a writer."

Amy bit into her banana.

"Oh, well that makes sense then," she said.

"Huh? What makes sense?"

Amy ripped into the fruit gummies and started sucking on a red one in the shape of an orange slice, using one of her canines to decimate its short and juicy life.

"Well, you just explained it, right?"

"But you understood it?"

Amy gathered herself and recited.

"The life lived on top of a heart of stone is smooth and impenetrable. I will break and crumble, leaving a lifeless statue of pure magnificence. But to what end? So that little children will look up at me and wonder what I did when I lived? Or will I frighten them? That the world I created, that I left behind, has hurt them beyond repair? That, when they too shall pass into the great nothingness of the infinite beyond they will stand beside me and look to the heavens, raising their hands and forgetting about the world

in front of them? What have I done with my life? It could have breathed the colors of the living. But I have chosen nothingness, and I will not pass until this world has fallen under the weight of the next."

"That was... beautiful."

"Uh, thanks," Amy said. "So... did that answer your question?"

"Uh..."

James found himself fishing for answers. She took it as a sign to return the favor and blow his mind.

"You're a writer. Arthridall is... a place in your books. Time flows differently than normal Earth time? During the test, you ended up daydreaming about Arthridall because you thought the test was easy. Time flowed into a black hole for you, compressing your test time even further... Almost like a wormhole time-space continuum or some other complicated plot device..."

"Huh..."

"How close was I?"

James considered it for a moment.

"She's good."

"Uh, ninety-percent," he said. "I remember saying that I was actually in Arthridall while taking the test."

"I'll take it, ha ha."

"How'd you figure it out so fast? I thought I was going to have to explain it piece by piece."

"Well, we're friends now, right?"

"Woo-hoo!" James thought.

"Y-yeah. I-I guess we are."

"Awesome. I was hoping you'd say that. So much less awkward eating lunch with a friend."

"Me too," James said. "I mean yeah, friends. Being friends is good."

James thought for a moment.

"But you didn't answer my question…"

Amy giggled.

"Ooohoo! But I did," she replied.

"He's cute when he's confused."

James laughed with her. She was funny. But it was also a laugh of relief for him. His gut had been right. She was the single pink pearl at the bottom of the crystal sea, resting on a bed of pure white ocean sand. She wasn't going to judge him like most people; something about her told him his instincts were right on point. It was her.

"She's just… well she's almost as weird as I am. She's alright."

"So," Amy continued, "what do you do for fun?"

James stood up and put on his most daring and adventurous archeologist face he could muster. The only thing he needed was a big boulder chasing him out of some sort of secret ancient temple. And his foot on the bench. It was a must. For good effect, of course.

"Well," he said, "come on an adventure with me and I'll show you everything."

18

"Where's your locker?" Amy asked.

The pair walked up the five concrete steps to the cafeteria doors. The doors were painted a pale shade of mint green. Black scuff marks from various types of sneakers and boots littered the bottom third of the otherwise normal steel exterior, giving anyone looking at the doors a very distinct impression of a certain flavor of ice cream. Muffled shouts arose from within.

"101-A."

"No way? That's only two away from Susan!"

"Susan?

"Oh that's right, you haven't her yet. She's the crazy one who almost smashed your face with the door."

"Her? If I remember correctly you were racing. And you were beating her."

"You're blaming me?"

James nodded his head as if to say yes.

"Ye… "

All signs pointed to Amy about to pout. James could hear the 'mayday' calls in his mind and changed his answer immediately, his voice rising about half an octave.

"Nooo? I'll go with no…"

She bounced slightly, rocking on the balls of her heels.

"I'm glad… no point in viciously attacking someone you just met, right?"

"N…Yesss?"

"I'm just yanking your chain, dude."

"Oh, thank God."

The cafeteria was a flying mess of various food stuffs. Not unlike a warzone during bunker to bunker bombing raids. James was instantly reminded why he always ate outside no matter how cold it got.

"Probably a food fight," Amy mused.

"You think?"

James tried following her line of sight as she scanned the crowd.

"You're probably right."

Amy grinned. She stopped scanning the room as she confirmed her suspicions. Susan always was in a rush and always in the thick of the action, and the afternoon didn't serve to change that habit. She palmed her forehead.

"Every freakin' time," she thought.

Amy leaned into James' line of sight and pointed to the far corner near the bars that marked the lunch line counter.

"There. That's Susan."

James followed Amy's fingertip and squinted to get a clearer picture of her friend. The only girl he saw in the direction Amy marked for him was standing on a table, a handful of green grapes in her hand and a scoop of mashed potatoes smeared into her shoulder length raven hair.

"Her?" James asked.

"Yeah. For better or worse, she's my friend. Sort of..."

James shot Amy a quizzical look, raised a single eyebrow as if to ask 'really?' and handed her his backpack.

"I'll be right back."

"Huh?" Amy exclaimed, but James had already made it halfway across the warzone unscathed before she could stop him.

"Ho...How..."

***

"Left foot past apple core, drop shoulder...Now..." James thought.

"Good, dodged that ham sandwich. It had mustard. Mom would've killed me…"

James 'C-shaped' around a full plate of cafeteria food and moonwalked behind the nearest table on the left to avoid someone's chocolate pudding. He could hear Susan's voice above the din of the room, screaming at some poor guy trying to eat his mac and cheese because he wasn't backing her up against the cafeteria tray gang.

"Get up soldier! I need you! We're losing ground here! I'm gonna rip your…"

James tugged on her arm until she hopped off the bench.

"What are you doing? There's a war going on her…"

She started to chuck her handful of grapes, but James caught her wrist before she could let fly. James cupped his hand to free her hair of the lingering potato salad, wiping it on the edge of her tray.

"Wha?! Sto… wait… you're…"

"She's waiting," he said, pointing to Amy.

Susan looked in the direction he was pointing. James stopped and loosened his grip.

"She's angry."

He let go of her arm. Susan dropped her ammo on the plate and groaned.

"She's going to roast me alive. Thanks."

"Better now than later."

"Let's get out of here."

Susan caught Amy's eye and pointed at the direction of the nearest door. Amy acknowledged and ducked under a flying chicken wing, raising her hand.

"Looks like four. Come on!"

"Four?"

"Hurry up!"

Susan had a surprisingly strong grip, or a characteristically strong grip, James wasn't sure. All he knew was that his wrist hurt like crazy as they ran along the side wall. Almost there.

"Do you play any sports?" he asked.

"Lacrosse. Why?"

"Gotcha. That explains a lot."

"What?"

Susan started shouldering the door on her right. It was usually a simple enough matter to open the doors, but due to the panicked nature of the situation she didn't hit the metal push running across the center quite right, and it stuck on the corner near the hinge.

"Aw crap! Help me out here."

James took a moment to glance back at where Amy had been standing.

"She must've taken the outside route," he said, half to himself.

"HEY!"

Susan yanked on his arm and pulled him close to her. She placed him near the problematic hinge.

"Put your hand on this. When I say three, I need you to throw all of your weight here," she said, moving his shoulder to a spot a little over half way up the door. She dodged a half-eaten pot pie as it smacked into the spot she'd been standing not a moment before. Susan kicked the offending pie out of her foot's flight path.

"Ready? THREE!"

James didn't have time to think, but he knew if they didn't get out of there right then they'd all be in trouble. And for him it would be his second time in as many weeks; certainly not something he wanted the administration to take note of on his record. So, instead of taking the time to consider the repercussions of slamming his shoulder into a solid steel mint green door, and how excruciatingly painful it would be for his poor body, he simply did it.

Susan for her part charged the other side of the door with the ferocity of a Spartan mother clobbering a bear. She had impeccable timing; the heel of her tennis shoe connected solidly just as James threw his recently rehabilitated body into a literal wall.

The simultaneous result was magical. The combined force of James' shoulder and Susan's karate kick smashed the ice cream cone so swiftly that even the magical closet door to Narnia would shudder.

They hopped into the hallway, slamming it shut as quickly as they'd opened it. Both of their hands leaned against the steel, their shoulders heaving as they both breathed sighs of relief. It felt as if their hands were the only thing capable of holding the doors up against the flurry of food on the other side. James looked at his comrade. Susan shot him a surprised look.

"Not..." she coughed, catching a couple breaths. "Not bad."

James wasn't expecting that kind of praise. Susan continued before he could say anything.

"Come on, we've got to meet up with her or we're still screwed."

19

James and Susan turned around the corner and pushed towards the gym. His hands were getting sweaty. He knew this because Susan made a comment about them while she was tearing his arm off.

"Where are we going?" James asked.

"Where we go isn't important. All that matters is that we get as far from the crime as possible."

"What's four?"

"Huh? Oh, it's part of a secret code we made up."

James offered a few hypotheses about cracking the secret girl code. He didn't receive any solid answers at first, but after some considerable pestering Susan started giving in.

"So why is she so mad at you?" James continued.

"Because she knows I started the food fight."

"What?! Why in the world would you do that?!"

"Long story," Susan said. "But lunch-lady had it coming."

Susan held a binder up to her face to hide from a passing teacher and leaned into James' ear as if to whisper a secret. Or kiss him. He wasn't sure.

"Don't say anything."

"No worries. I'm kind of invisible to most people."

James couldn't remember the last time he had to walk so fast. No sooner had they passed the teacher and rounded the corner were they running at a pace equal to the track team's past the last two sets of lockers and into the gym, finally stopping alongside the line of dilapidated navy bleachers.

"Wow, you really are invisible," she said, impressed that he hadn't lied. "We're here, Amy."

"It doesn't hurt that the halls are almost entirely dark," James replied.

"True."

The gym lights, much like the hallway lights, were also off, minus the few dull red exit signs at the four corners of the space. James wondered if there'd been a power outage in the area, but even that generous hypothesis was thrown off by the fact that the lights in the girls' locker room were completely lit. The outline of a girl cast a shadow in the doorframe.

"That was so entirely stupid of you!" Amy shouted. "Why on earth did you think it was a good idea to pick a fight during the middle of lunch?!"

Susan shrugged. A dab of potato cream landed with a soft splat against the sleek wood floors. James was glad her anger wasn't directed at him. Scary.

"It worked out, didn't it?"

"No, you're just lucky James bailed you out!"

Susan looked at the boy who had quietly taken a seat on the corner of the bottom bleacher and was pretending not to listen. Either that, or he'd already stopped paying attention. The reality was he was just hoping that they wouldn't force him to wait for them inside the locker room.

"His name is James?"

Susan walked over to him, held out her hand, and tried to catch his attention. It took her longer than she expected. Most of the time she couldn't get people to stop looking at her.

"It's nice to finally meet you, James. Beats creepily staring at me, at least."

"Uh…"

He snuck a quick look at Amy. Her wrath was still directed at Susy.

"It's uh, nice to meet you too, uh,"

James shook her hand.

"Susan. Or Susy. I'm not picky."

"Get in here! NOW!"

Susan tensed a bit and released James' hand. Amy's shouts echoed around the entire gym floor. He hoped they were the only ones who heard it, or they were entirely busted.

"Thanks man. I owe you one," Susan said, turning and walking past her friend. Amy smacked the back of Susan's head.

"Ouch!"

"You deserve a lot more than that! Get cleaned up. I left a spare change of clothes in your locker."

"You're the best."

"GET!"

Susan ran and slipped on the small, off-white square tiles that lined the girls' locker room. Amy turned to James and returned his backpack.

"I'm sorry you had to see that," she apologized.

"You have a right to be mad," he said.

Amy's shoulders slouched, her anger diffusing with the disappearing of Susan's shadow. James felt the tension in the room drain. She sighed.

"I'll make sure you get a full explanation after this."

"No worries."

"I at least owe you that much for helping her," Amy said.

"Up to you."

"But I need to go make sure she's actually doing what she's supposed to. Always on her phone. Mind waiting out here for a bit?"

James shrugged.

"Sure."

"Thank God," he thought.

"Thanks man."

"No problem."

"We'll be right back."

"Okay."

Amy walked around the corner to check on her. James kept watch for anyone who might happen to walk into the gym to find where all the noise was coming from but thankfully, no one else came. All he heard were the muffled back and forth shouts around the corner. James sat his backpack on his lap and leaned on it.

"Does this mean they're both my friends?" he thought. "Susan's certainly interesting enough. Time will tell, I guess."

20

Thorne opened his eyes to see his broken throne room crumbling on top of him. The wind was colder down here as it rushed past his face and he welcomed it; getting used to his newfound, albeit stolen powers was proving more troublesome than he'd anticipated. Dragon's blood. The power to twist and manipulate reality at his whim. It was terrifying and wonderful.

"A splintering." He thought, his anger intensifying as his shoulder collided with a hunk of falling pillar. "But these... these kids have to go and ruin... MY FUN!"

They would ruin his plans with that key if he didn't do something immediately. King would undo all his hard work. So, behind the scenes. In the rocks and caves, in dead grass and desert. In shadows. He would strike back.

Thorne's eyes flared with the fire of a dying sun as he looked up into the sky that was growing farther and smaller with every passing second. A noise far beneath him caught his attention and he snapped around to look for its source. After a moment he smiled, revealing teeth that were ready to pounce.

"Ex… cellent." He hissed.

A dark purple and black gash, or opening, swirled at the base of the abyss directly below him. A portal to where all the rumble and ruins were headed towards, as if it were sucking it all up like a vacuum.

Thorne re-spread his wings and planted his arms to his sides to gain momentum, quickly gaining speed and powering through the gateway. A loud rumble above him collapsed the rest of the remains of his now ruined abode, the smoke and debris covering the light above.

As quickly as it'd opened, it closed with a slam. He looked around as the piles of dust settled around his feet and the dark portal above his head disappeared in a sonic boom. Heaps of rubble lay strewn all about in direct opposition to the starry night sky above. His cracked stone chair sat on top of the pile, slanted to one side as if it were about to fall over from the weight.

"Earth, huh?" he mused.

Thorne waltzed over to his throne and sat down in it, clapping his hands as multiple skulls appeared throughout the pile of broken stones and columns to decorate it. He rubbed his hands on the armrests in anticipation.

"Why isn't that… so very CONVENIENT."

***

The events of the day flew by in a blur. James and Amy had math class together. Amy managed to convince the person sitting next to him to switch seats with her, especially since Shay had been jealously eyeing her seat since the beginning of the year. Most people would question her odd request. Taking someone's spot in a classroom almost always guaranteed that whoever's spot was taken would release their ultimate hatred on them in some form or fashion. Usually, it made for some interesting social media exchanges after they'd let their untamed fury reach its boiling point. But Shay got it. She wanted to be closer to the guy she liked too and was perfectly happy with the trade and Amy couldn't fault her for that.

Amy was glad she'd been able to get Susy cleaned up before lunch ended. Susan was already somewhat notorious for showing up five, sometimes ten minutes late to class. She wasn't a bad student where academics or athletics were concerned, but she did tend to lose track of time. Especially when it came to her boyfriend. Amy took a slip of paper and wrote a note to James.

"she and fred need to patch things up soon."

James lifted his elbow almost imperceptibly in order to receive the note. For having never passed notes to anyone before she noted he was a complete natural at it. James slipped the paper onto his notebook to write a reply. He glanced at Ms. Brigand, holding her attention for a full thirty seconds until she turned away after creepily smiling before he peeked at the note.

"Dang, he's good at this," she thought.

The piece of paper fluttered to the ground, landing by her backpack almost as if by accident. Even a blue butterfly or a hummingbird would be proud of its grace.

"who is fred?"

"Eyes on teacher... wait, hold gaze. She's turned around."

Amy picked up her pencil and scratched a quick reply. They had a system now.

"he's the captain of the guy's lacrosse team."

"are they... are they a thing?"

"no! they hate each other!"

"five bucks says they'll be start dating by the end of the week. by the end of week three or four they'll realize it was a mistake and they'll part ways on cordial terms."

"that's oddly specific."

"force of habit. want to bet on it?"

"you're on. want to hang out after school?"

"can't. there's something I need to discuss with my dad. it's important," James wrote.

"oh."

The two looked at each other for a moment. Amy continued.

"tomorrow then?"

"yeah."

The bell rang, and the students who'd already made the mistake of packing their bags early stood up and started ambushing the door. Ms. Brigand's shrill nasally voice choked them back.

"Thee classss is not ooover until I say that iiit is ooover."

The standing students half sat back down, groaning. Ms. Brigand looked down her nose, through her spectacles of hate, and pulled out her classic teacher death-stare. The students slid their butts all the way into their chairs and the verbal complaining ceased. Amy knew everyone's thumbs were itching to roast their teacher alive online. Ms. Brigand held them in their seats for a full twenty seconds, visually degrading each of the miscreants who had disrupted her perfect method of order.

"You may leave."

The room cleared as fast as if someone in class had passed gas. Amy crumpled the note and tossed it in the front pouch of her bag. They walked out last in no particular rush. The door closed behind them and the hallway darkened again. They looked at each other and groaned in unison.

"Typical," they said.

James said goodbye to his newfound locker buddy and Susan galloped away to her next big adventure. Seeing she'd forgotten to flip the latch to her lock all the way, he closed it for her with a small metallic click. James couldn't shake the thought that both she and Amy were possible characters in his book. They were interesting people, and he was an interesting writer. He shouldered his bag and walked toward freedom.

"I should even consider writing myself into the thing. I mean, it is journal of sorts. Now there's a thought. The author being one of the main characters in his own fiction," he thought.

James pushed on the main doors and sat on the dull concrete steps, waiting for his mom to pick him up. He'd let her know that morning he wanted her help so he could talk to dad as soon as he got home.

"I really should get a cell phone since I'll be changing my schedule all the time now."

Old spider webs from years of buildup glistened with the sprinkling of snow crystals in the looming stoop of the front entrance. James only knew there were spider-webs because he'd set his backpack down and started leaning against it and looked up columns. James decided it was as if some great mason had infused a precious crystalline glass into the upper reaches of the place.

"Certainly less of an eyesore than the rest of the architecture here," James noted, then paused. "But it reminds me of that dream…"

James pulled on the strings of his jacket until he became a clam.

"It's so cold. Hurry up mom."

James found himself spacing out, looking intently at the webs again. He wondered if they'd be considered a Halloween decoration or a Christmas miracle. He settled on Halloween decoration, since Christmas already owned the hanging lights gig and since some people considered spiders terrifying.

"It's a shame... They should make a movie with both Halloween and Christmas," James thought, "Then mom and I can watch it twice a year instead of having to choose."

Twenty minutes later his mom's tank-van rolled up to the curb and briefly honked to catch his attention. James clambered down the steps with a jitter and a shiver; he'd never had to wait this long before for a ride.

"Granted it's a new routine, but still," he moaned, popping the sides of his shoes against the side of the car door to clean them and climbed inside. "I mean really, there's no one else here anymore."

Mrs. Pensworth checked her car clock.

"I'm sorry honey. Sharon held me up at the office for an hour longer than expected. And I got stuck behind the street sweeper."

James looked at his mom and involuntarily shivered from his adjusting body temperature. She'd done her best, at least.

"Sharon's a talker, isn't she?"

"You have NO idea, son. It gets so old sometimes."

Everyone had a hate list.

"No one is safe from the menace," James thought.

"Is dad home yet?" he asked.

"He called on my way over here. He won't be back until seven."

"Oh…" James half said to himself.

"What is it, hon?"

"Not much."

"Don't lie."

James looked at the street signs; they still had about ten minutes to drive and he didn't feel like talking yet.

"I'm not. Not completely."

"What is it, then?"

James groaned in semi-frustration and started fusing himself to the side of the car.

"Jaaameess?"

"It's just guy stuff, okay?"

"Oh? Anything you can talk about with me?"

James knew he had to play his cards carefully or it could quickly become an incredibly long ten minutes. He slid his left hip down the far side of the seat in order to complete the fusion into 'Sleeping Mecha-Boy'. A dull throbbing on his left cheekbone began forming from one of the textbooks in his bag so he adjusted them around until he'd completed his nest.

"Well?" Mrs. Pensworth asked.

"Nah, it's okay. I just want to warm up and talk with dad later.

She looked back and forth between the road and her son's intense struggle for comfort. James closed his eyes, loosening his clam-jacket.

"You know I'm always here for you, right?"

"Yes, mom."

"And that I will always love you?"

"Mo-oom," James groaned.

"Alright, just so long as you remember that."

He adjusted again. Mrs. Pensworth flipped on the car's foot heater to give her son an extra boost. He grunted in typical son appreciation. She was content with the acknowledgement, so she let her son nap.

Ten minutes later, Mrs. Pensworth pulled into the driveway and an idea popped into her head. After stomping hard with her left foot on the brake, she gunned the gas pedal to the floor. James bolted awake from the noise.

"What the heck?!"

Mrs. Pensworth pulled the vehicle into the garage, set it into park, and turned off the engine.

"We're home."

"You scared me. Ha. Ha. Ha."

James wasn't amused. He was cold, and tired, and in need of a warm shower. Mrs. Pensworth laughed and messed with his hair.

"Go grab a shower. I'll see you when you're done playing caveman," she said.

James smiled despite himself. Revving the engine had been funny to say the least.

"I think I can do that," he replied.

"March. I'm not going to wait for you. As soon as dad gets home we're eating."

"Fiiinee."

"He'll be fine once he gets some food," Mrs. Pensworth thought as she watched her son meander up to his fortress of solitude. "It's written all over his face. Must've been a busy day."

21

James needed to talk with someone who might understand his dilemma. he flipped on the shower and sat down in the tub, leaning back against the obnoxiously cold tile, standing up to adjust the nozzle and sitting back down, letting the warm water soothe his shivering backside. The little pull for the tub spout jammed halfway and the shower hissed and sputtered at him like an angry teapot.

James didn't notice the hissing, nor the passage of time, or most importantly, the distinctive hum of his father's vehicle as it pulled into the driveway. All he cared about was the water streaming out of the pipe about six feet above him. He couldn't seem to be able to get the notion of having real friends off his mind, or the pressing need to talk to his dad about adding an additional space in the basement for himself so he could focus.

He was especially confused by the mixture of emotions he had to confront as new ideas for his stories in Arthridall raced across the inner workings of his mind all at once; he found himself having an increasingly difficult time separating fact from fiction and natural from supernatural. Was Arthridall more real to him because he was inserting himself and the people he knew into it? Or had Arthridall always been reality and the world he was currently residing in was a shadow? He felt like he'd been thrown into someone else's story and maybe he'd just been there so long now that he'd finally started becoming a character in it.

Was the world called Earth because he called it Earth? Was it his insertion of self into the place called Earth causing him to be unnerved, that this shadow realm had maintained a physical presence for as long as it had because he hadn't been observing it properly? Did the shadow called Earth exist outside of his interaction with it? Or had it been there all along; waiting to pull him into itself as the true reality, and away from his imagination, away from his books and his dreams and his internal meanderings?

Could he have the best of everything? Could he have what the Earthlings deemed a social life with friends and still have enough time to explore the seemingly unfathomable realm of Arthridall? Or should he bring everyone into both realms of imagination, the shadow called Earth and the light called Arthridall, so he could make a universe that perfectly reflected the intertwining of both realities? Was it possible? Or had he already set about accomplishing that very goal subconsciously without realizing what his heart was doing, and that was why his mind was so confused to begin with? If that was the case, then everything he was feeling right now would make sense. It was simply his brain's attempt to help him sort through the conundrums of this newly intertwined reality.

James hoped he could show Arthridall to those he cared about and prove that it was a very real place. But he needed to show them that Earth wasn't the only reality. Arthridall was even more real than Earth in many respects. He had to prove it. He had to prove to someone other than himself that he was telling the truth. That he wasn't going crazy. That the stories weren't just figments of his imagination.

But how could he explain to anyone, let alone Amy, that everything he wrote about actually existed? That the characters weren't just characters, but humans and creatures who lived and died, breathed and gasped, laughed and cried? He hadn't exactly chosen to become Arthridall's historian he'd one way or another been born into it. But how could he possibly explain to that to her when she had forgotten everything?

"Especially when I have to explain things as outlandish as mythical creatures and... for lack of a better term, superpowers?"

James didn't know how. He didn't understand it himself half the time and now his brain was turning to mush faster than one could say potatoes and gravy.

***

"James! Hurry up! Your father is home and dinner is on the table!"

James' eyes focused on the shower head. He'd been doing it again. Some might call it spacing-out. He knew better than to brush away what actually happened. The membrane between the realms was thinning. The space-time continuum was warping, mixing as portals and gateways were being created. Or altered.

"Time flows differently in Arthridall," he reminded himself.

James' mother banged on the bathroom door. All James heard was the drumming of war. Something large was about to take place. He could feel it in his bones. The fight wasn't over yet. He needed a secret place of his own where he wouldn't be disturbed while he wrote. The sooner, the better.

"JAMES!!!" she yelled.

It was barely enough to shake him from his trance and make him turn off the water.

"I'll be down in a minute!" he replied.

"WE HAVE BEEN WAITING FOR TWENTY MINUTES!!!"

"The jumps are getting longer," James thought.

"Sorry! Hang on, I'm drying off right now!"

It was just enough of a response to placate her. He heard her walk downstairs as he dried off and put on fresh clothes.

"That was too close. If I hadn't heard her I could've created another tear in the fabric from being in between worlds too long. My shower is last place I'd want someone to teleport to."

"Hi son. What took so long?" his mom asked somewhat angrily.

"I'm not sure you want to know," James replied.

Mrs. Pensworth raised an eyebrow.

"No! No, nothing like that!"

James looked to his father for backup. Good old dad. He'd begun explaining the Arthridall situation to him a while back, so he was somewhat on track with what was going on there.

Mr. Pensworth raised an eyebrow.

"Is it better, worse, or about the same as earlier?" he asked.

"I think it might be worse."

"I see," Mr. Pensworth said.

"Can we please not talk about this at the dinner table?"

His dad put a hand on her shoulder to calm her.

"Don't worry honey, it's not what you think."

"Well, what is it then?"

"It's just something concerning him about his book. I think."

"Yeah, it's Arthridall stuff," James said finally. "I think something happened."

"Oh. Well what does that have to do with him not answering me?"

"Apparently it's a long story. I'll let him explain it himself in his own time."

His father looked him in the eye with a face so deadpan one could cook bacon and eggs on it.

James was awestruck. He couldn't help but wonder if his own gift for hidden jokes came from him.

"Did you mean to phrase it like that?" James asked.

Mr. Pensworth met his gaze, cracked a small smile, and thanked his wife for dinner. James was puzzled yet intrigued by his father's response. It both didn't answer a single question, yet gave a stronger answer than most politicians gave in a lifetime. James was proud to be his son.

"James…" he said.

"Yes?"

"We can talk after dinner. I'm tired and I want to enjoy this first."

"Okay."

James felt relieved to hear him say that. He wasn't completely comfortable about talking about girls around his mom yet. Her constant ribbing, while gentle and playful, was still just enough to make him wary. She'd ask him questions he wasn't quite prepared to answer, and he just couldn't handle that extra pressure. James briefly looked at his father and back at his plate. He did look absolutely exhausted. His dad didn't give as much advice as his mom did, but that was okay. He wanted a place to vent more than advice at the moment.

"We could talk tomorrow if you want. I'm sure you could use some downtime too."

Mr. Pensworth stopped him short and put his silverware down.

"Listen here, son. I'll never be too tired to listen to you. I value you two's opinions more than anybody else in the world. Especially on something as important as your book."

"Thanks dad."

Mr. Pensworth picked up his fork and began eating again. Dinner was quiet until the end of the meal, but they were okay with it. It seemed like his mom was perfectly fine with not being in the loop once she realized it was something serious.

"Go downstairs. I'll be down right after I help her with the dishes."

"Okay," James said quietly.

James got up from the table and slipped on down to the basement. Walking into his father's study, James sat down in the office chair and took a few pieces of paper from the printer and a blue ink pen. It took him a moment to realize he was still sitting down. Something dug at the back of his mind and he still couldn't place what it was.

"It's never been this bad before," he thought.

He put his hands on the armrests to push himself up off the couch that was his father's office chair. The printer paper wrinkled under the weight of his grip as he stood. Seeing as the papers were now only suited for his father's random sketches, James left them on the desk after drawing a small smiley face on each piece. He turned around to grab a few more pages, bumping the chair in the process with just enough force to rotate it into the table, knocking the blue ink pen onto the floor and scattering the happily crumpled scratch paper.

"Why am I noticing all this random detail now when I didn't even hear mom hitting the door?"

James picked up everything and put it back on the desk in a haphazard heap of happy hallucinations. He didn't remember drawing those. James found himself gazing at the bookshelf. He slapped his cheek with some force to shake himself.

There was a triangle of paper sticking out from the side of one of his father's red leather notebooks. James sat back down in the chair to steady himself, fixated on the now disheveled textures arising from the face of the secret door.

"Paper..."

James wasn't sure how long he'd been staring at that notebook. Once he realized he'd zoned out for the third time that evening he stood up, paper and pen in hand, and pushed on the side of the bookcase to open the door. Luminescent white light bulbs flickered on, streaming down the line of Roman columns to the door leading into the man-cave.

"Or was that the eighth time?"

James stopped in the middle of the hallway and leaned against the wall. One of his father's framed blueprints hung opposite him. His father had impeccable skill when it came to drawing and creating blueprints; they were magnificent from an artistic and mechanical standpoint, but where his handwriting was concerned even medical doctors would feel bad and try to console him with a hand on his shoulder.

"In a manly fashion, of course."

James heard the familiar footsteps treading on the carpet down the stairs. They seemed slower and quieter than usual. He couldn't tell if it was because his father was more tired than he looked, or his mind playing tricks on him. Again.

"Probably both."

"What?" his father asked.

"Oh, did I say that out loud?" James asked.

"Yeah you did. You uh... you feeling alright?"

"Honestly?"

"Yeah."

"I don't know what's going on anymore."

James stood up with the help of his father's arm.

"When did I sit down?" James wondered.

"Huh?"

"Nothing. Just talking to myself again I guess."

"Let's go sit."

James followed him down the rest of the hall and closed the door behind them with a small creak and a thud. He sat down on the couch next to him and, leaning forward, began rubbing his temples.

"I think I'm going crazy," he said just above a whisper.

Mr. Pensworth leaned back without saying a thing and brushed his hand back and forth across his son's back.

"You and me both, kiddo."

James leaned back with a huff. His dad massaged his scalp in typical dad fashion, both lazy and comforting all at once. James scrunched his eyes and opened them again as he decided how he would approach the subject.

"Arthridall's in danger."

"Yeah. Your book, right?"

"Yeah."

James paused, lost in thought. John knew better than to interrupt. James was never not thinking, but more often than not he was thinking about a different place all together.

"Something's happening there. And I'm stuck here."

"What is?"

"Something big."

James verbally retreated again. Mr. Pensworth waited. James closed his eyes to focus his thoughts.

"I don't think it's going to be good."

"Is someone important about to die?"

"I think so. I hate to say it, but it looks like it'll be more necessary than I initially thought. People are losing memories. And I hate killing characters."

"What do you mean?"

No answer. Mr. Pensworth paused the head rub for a moment and looked at him. He looked distressed. Mr. Pensworth started massaging his head again.

"Mmmm... Okay," James said. "I explained how time flows differently there?"

"Yeah. Tell me again though."

"Well..." James said, "It's kind of hard to explain. Time doesn't flow there the way it does here."

"Try me."

"Uh... so time flows in a line here, right?"

"Yes."

"You're born, you live, and then you die, right?"

"When you boil it down to basics, yes."

"Well that's how Arthridall time works. But it's different."

"How is it different?"

"Well…"

James got lost in thought again. John waited. He could see he was having a tough time figuring out how to explain himself.

"It's…" James continued, "Earth time runs linearly. You are born, you live, and then you die. You age linearly."

"Yes you do."

"But Arthridall is different. You're born, you live, and you die. But that's where the similarities end. Aging isn't based off the linear line of time. It's based off maturity, not time."

"Wise beyond one's years?"

"Yeah. Exactly. But even within Arthrindian time there are exceptions."

"Try me. Give some examples."

"Uh…"

Mr. Pensworth patiently waited. Rubbed his son's head some more.

"Okay. Let me start from the beginning again then."

"Okay."

James pulled out a pen and began drawing some diagrams. He drew a circle on the first piece of paper.

"This is Earth."

James drew another circle on the next piece of paper.

"Arthridall."

"Got it," John said.

James wrote the word 'linear' underneath the circle representing Earth and the word 'maturity' underneath Arthridall. Mr. Pensworth nodded.

James took a third piece of paper, drawing a vague outline of a human.

"Humans are made of three governing bodies. These bodies are what make us different from other types of animals."

"Explain."

"Physical body is first. Level one. Skin and bones." James said, "Then there's the mind. Or the soul. They're... the same. That's where we get our ability to make rational decisions."

"Makes sense," he replied.

"So then there's the most important level. Spirit. Spirit is... spirit is that unexplainable part of us that separates humans from animals and makes us human. It's that part of us that keeps going after our bodies and souls die from natural aging."

"Got it."

"So…" James continued, "In Arthridall… Wait, in my books… Earth is level one, body, Arthridall is level two, or soul, and level three is what most people would call Heaven, or the afterlife. Spirit, if you will. I sometimes call it King's house. It's got a lot of names, I guess."

"King's house?"

"It's where King lives."

"Ah… that sort of makes sense, I guess. But it'll probably be easier once I read the books."

"That's what I'm trying to say, dad. We seem to be running out of time."

Mr. Pensworth stood and gestured him to follow. They walked all around the basement, finally settling on leaning against their hands on the large stainless steel table in front of them. James' dad smirked.

"Jogging the brain."

"Not helping," James replied.

"Anyhoo, even though I'm not sure why Arthridall's running out of time, do you think it might have something to do with having friends pulling you away from your free time?"

"Gah…"

James turned, huffing around the room. Even his own dad wasn't getting it.

"Bwa… ga… I don't know!" James exclaimed.

James' huffing felt annoyingly huffy. John adjusted his glasses and waited for him to calm down. James dropped the papers and they scattered like leaves along the ground of an ancient forest.

"I'm not sure if helped him or if I poked a pin into his bubble world," He thought.

"AHA!"

"What is it?"

James picked the three papers up and returned to the table.

"May I?" he said, gesturing to the massive pile of scribbles on the table waiting to be turned into basketballs.

"Sure."

After a brief flurry of falling paper, James took his papers and spread them around on the part of the table that was finally seeing light for the first time in a very long time. Taking the Earth paper and the Arthridall paper, James began tearing them into strips. James tore a few of them into confetti. Mr. Pensworth was confused but waited for his explanation.

"This is what's happening," James said. "Earth and Arthridall are tearing apart, becoming undistinguishable from each other as King and I are making portals. But something or someone is literally tearing open new ones that shouldn't exist."

His dad nodded. He was following now even though his point of view varied from his son's. It sounded like a classic case of having to face the reality of growing up. But to him it was as if the world itself was tearing apart. He put a fatherly hand on his son's shoulder.

"I got it now. Let's get ready for bed, okay?" he said.

They locked eyes as James tried to gauge what his dad now thought.

"He doesn't get it. But he's trying. And he's exhausted," James thought.

"Okay," he said.

22

James settled in under his covers. His bed was the most beckoning of beds in the entire world. There was still no question in his mind about that part of his life at least. It was so comfortable.

The wind picked up outside as the evening progressed in its dangerously relaxing manner. It was noisy, but in a cold and comforting way. Howling even.

"It was unusually cold downstairs," James thought. "Highly unusual…"

He made a mental note to double check the thermostat the next time he went down. James noted that whenever it got too cold his brain ceased functioning. Too hot and it turned to mush.

"Maybe that's partly why it was so hard to focus earlier."

A light rapping on his bedroom door caught his attention. James rolled over to show he was paying attention to the welcomed intruder. Words had already ceased leaving his mouth for the evening, so to emphasize he'd entered man-cave mode, James grunted as any cave-man ought to when acknowledging the existence of a familiar.

"Goodnight honey. Just came to wish you sweet dreams."

"Mgmgmgmm…"

"Your father thinks you're on the right track."

"Bleeurrgh…"

"He hasn't exactly told me what that means though."

"MMmmm…"

Mom walked in with a footstep only someone loving as her could make. She always walked around barefoot when she was home; she argued it was because she cleaned everything, but the men knew it was because she'd walk around the whole world barefoot if she were allowed.

Mary sat down on the corner of her child's man-cave-bed-habitat, brushing the ends of her fingers through his hair to tousle it. James grunted in quiet appreciation and rolled over so his back was facing the door. He was rewarded with a shoulder massage.

"You the best, mom," he thought.

Mrs. Pensworth leaned in to kiss him on the cheek. James remembered later how scenic that kiss was. He missed the days when she'd follow the same routine every night, but as he grew up her routine changed. Those special moments were fewer and farther in between every time they happened; the taller he got, the rarer the kiss.

He could feel her concern. He didn't know how she could have so much faith in him despite his recent withdrawal? Could love overrule worry? It certainly seemed like she'd unlocked the secret to true joy. Either that or she was the bravest person the world had ever laid eyes on. Or both.

James didn't remember her pulling up the covers to keep him warm throughout the night. Or the light flick of his lamp as he finished his final preparations for takeoff to dreamland. But he remembered the light sweetness of his mother's kiss on his cheek. Like the most delicate stroke of an artist's brush on canvas. The coolness of her breath reminded him of the warm breeze of the ocean as it buffeted the sand in a delicate game of chess. She was his mom and no one could ever take that away.

Mary got up and fairy-danced out of the room with a tiny click of the door handle. She smiled. It was a somewhat sad smile, and if one were to freeze the camera on her face there, they might conclude that she was, indeed, sad. But that was only the rainy side of the cloud. The top half shed varying shades of red and orange all across her face. Hope. And Love.

The rivers of life in the corners of her eyes did not bleed salt. They held hope for a better future for her son, cradled in the memory of the first time she'd laid eyes on him as he cried and screamed and she was the one in pain. The pain of his delivery had disappeared with his birth.

Her son was growing up. But she would always be his mommy.

James woke up to the sound of the sea. He felt the wind in his hair, and the sandpaper warmth of the minutely ground shells between his fingers. The sea salt wasn't too strong, nor were the rays of the sun harsh as they swirled around the liquid, etching themselves inside his heart strings.

He was at peace, and he had no way to explain the spontaneity of the emotions rolling inside him. It was as if the entire landscape was reacting to him; each thought, every feeling battering him like the waves of the sea and rolling of the ever-transforming clouds. It was beautiful. Inexplicable. Nature itself was crying just as he was, and the feeling that he was cared for no matter what happened comforted his aching heart.

"James."

A man approached his side and sat down. James didn't remember anybody approaching him, nor was he frightened by the sudden appearance of the fully mature man now resting next to him. They both sat in silence for a good while, with a contentedness not unlike the sense of satisfaction after a long day of work.

James took a moment to look at the person sitting next to him. He was dressed simply and cleanly in Arthrindian robes. Without a moment of hesitation, James instinctually touched the cloth, rolling it around his fingertips. It was soft and white; the whiteness was soft, and the softness seemed to exude an essence of purity. Both knew the phenomena was not the result of the fabric itself but the man wearing the fabric. Both were warm and inviting.

"Beautiful, isn't it?" the man said.

For the first time in a long time, James didn't feel compelled speak or do anything. The man sitting next to him already knew what he was thinking and how he felt. Who James was becoming was written right in front of him as the waters gently lapped against the tan hue of the shore.

James finally spoke. He found that he didn't feel any kind of nervousness talking with him as he would've had he been talking to anyone else.

"I don't get it. Why'd you chose Earth? What's Earth ever done for us?"

The man gazed at the distant horizon, watching the sunset with admiration. It occurred to James as he followed the man's gaze that there was the distinct lack of a sun gazing back. Amazingly, the colors were still just as vivid. There was simply a lack of a giant orb in the sky.

"You don't have to get it," the man finally said.

James felt comforted by the fact.

"Then why'd you choose me to do it?"

"You aren't bearing this alone."

They watched the various shades of red and orange roll across the hemisphere. They showed no signs of growing dim.

"Sure feels like it though. No one understands what's about to happen no matter how much I try to explain it. And Amy… well it's like she forgot everything."

"I get it. Just remember it wasn't that long ago you'd forgotten a lot too. It wasn't until she introduced herself that it clicked for you, right?"

James looked at the man's somewhat unkempt, brownish beard. His eyes showed no signs of hesitation. He meant what he said, and it comforted him enough to squelch the seeds of doubt that were threatening to take him out.

"She's going to need you."

"We're just friends here, though."

The man turned his head and looked at James for the first time since he'd sat down. He raised a single, quizzical eyebrow.

"But you already know you love her. Why should being on stuck Earth make that change?"

The man's statement was so calm and straightforward that James didn't feel embarrassed by him saying it.

"Yeah…"

"So tell her that."

Some deep, royal purples and blues introduced themselves into the panorama. The man smiled genuinely.

"It's not so easy to tell someone that."

"It is, though. Give her the necklace."

"But what if she ends up getting trapped?"

King rested his hands on his friend's shoulders and held James' gaze.

"Don't worry. That's why you're here. Help her remember everything and build up some portals. We're going to need them."

"But... Arthridall... they still need us right?"

"Of course they do. Even now your daughter is still trying to find out what happened."

The man spread one of his arms in an open-handed gesture to the surrounding area.

"What you see here is only one piece of the grand picture. Her diary, your books... Amy's necklace? They're all connected. And this sight alone... tells me it was worth stretching you."

James couldn't think of anything he could say to respond. Nor did he feel the need to.

"Imagine the countless, beautiful pictures out there in the grand stream of time, desperately wishing to be gazed on and told they are exactly where they're meant to be."

James said nothing.

"Everyone hears the call but so many people refuse to listen. So yeah... it hurts when someone doesn't care enough to do anything, but that doesn't mean you should refuse your place in this."

"But I'm not especially good at relating things like this to people," he said finally.

"But you are, James. Don't worry about what other people are doing. Just keep being yourself because you're... well, you. No one else can do what you can do because they aren't you."

"...I guess."

"That a boy."

"What about the books, then?"

"What about them?"

"Uh, well you told me to..."

"Write what you see, son."

"I guess. They aren't getting through, though. Aren't portals supposed to, I don't know, let people go through them?"

"That's because I've sealed them for the moment."

"Why? I thought you wanted me to get these books out to as many people as possible."

"I do."

"Then why!?"

The man wasn't surprised by his outburst. It was, in essence, the reason James felt safe enough to shout in the first place.

"I wanted to give you the first peek. It's not everyday people get to enter Arthridall through a book."

James deflated like a wet and soggy balloon.

"Oh..."

King chuckled.

"Sorry," James apologized. "I feel bad now..."

"No worries, buddy."

"Well..."

"You can do it. I'll be around whenever you want to talk. I'm closer than you think."

"Thanks... That means a lot to me."

23

James rolled around the floor in the soft and fluffy goodness known as his blanket, like a horse rolling around in grass. Or a mummy undressing itself after rising to life as an undead zombie. The ancient Egyptians would be proud. James' head popped out of the cocoon like a snow pea sprout. Two hands materialized to rub away the previous night's slumber from his eyes. Or dreams. Or whatever the heck he could call what'd happened.

"I always get one vague answer and a whole new list of unanswered questions," James muttered.

The weather outside had given his window the appearance of a snow-cone that had shown up on a missing persons list. He checked the time. It was too early to be awake, as usual.

He finally concluded that it couldn't be helped. Nor could he be bothered any more than he already was. But at least he finally knew he was getting somewhere. He could finish the portals by being himself and writing stories. Whatever that meant. And he'd help Amy in any way he could. He could do that much at least. She was important somehow.

"She's the key to all this. I can feel it. I don't know how she fits into this story yet, but she does."

***

James remembered the smell of wet bark as he walked along the side of the road. Surprisingly, the sun had yet to rise and he was already ready for school. And for whatever reason, he felt a brisk morning jog might help him clear his head. Except for the fact that he wasn't jogging. Some would probably consider his walking pace no different than a drunk sloshing around in a dance club where no one wanted him.

A small object fell down on the outer edge of the woods to his left. James' first thought was that it could've been a squirrel, or maybe a rabbit. If he was lucky. In reality, the object in the snow was a relatively small tree branch that'd finally snapped under the weight of the snow it had become unable to sustain. He was confused as to why the stick, of all things, had managed to capture his attention, but the more he focused on that feeling, the more he found himself staring at the stick.

Realizing he'd been staring at the stick for quite some time, James decided it was probably in his best interest that he pick up the quizzical stick. The brand-new thought made his mind wipe completely clean for a minute. Or ten. He'd spaced out for an unknown period of time. As his mind came back he thought about how much he wanted to be with his friends more than anything else in the world.

"This world? Or the other one?" James thought. "Or both…"

The stick teased around his frame of view like some sort of cobra he was supposed to tame by using a magical flute. The urge to bite off the cobra's head with a grimace and a growl overturned any notion of taming said cobra.

Somehow, the stick found a resting place between James' upturned palms. It was all very confusing to him, as what originally appeared to be a twig was in reality a six-foot-long staff, and instead of bearing a bunch of dead and slimy leaves on its numerous veins it was a fully-fledged weapon that bore the strength of the magic housed within its pores.

"Well, it's not every day that a twig turns into a magic staff."

James let the mysterious power between his hands fall into the snow. The sun rose to reveal the staff's true nature, and he was no longer interested in its magic. It was indeed, a stick.

***

"James?"

Amy waved her hand to try to attract his attention.

"Hello?"

James leaned with his arm on the desk, staring wistfully at the windows as if they could reveal some secret about the cosmos, or universe, or whatever it was he happened to be thinking about.

"Ja..." Amy began again.

Before she could finish her third attempt to bring him back to the realm of light, Susy swiped at the wrist he happened to be leaning on, simultaneously forcing life back into his lungs and rocketing the pencil he'd been using towards the trashcan so violently that it looked like a dart nailing a dartboard. It bounced off the dartboard and landed on the ground.

"Really!?" Amy exclaimed.

"Wha...? Oh, hey guys," James said.

"Don't you realize school's been over for half an hour?"

"Uh..."

James twisted in his seat to look at the classroom.

"Crap! It happened again!" he said.

"What happened?" Susan breathed in Amy's ear.

"Uh..." Amy scraped for time. "It's..."

"Time-space warping. Or continuum shift. Hard to explain."

"What he said," Amy replied, shrugging her shoulders.

"You people are weird," Susan said, preparing her escape from the hollowly lit prison.

"You almost made his pencil poke a hole through the wall!"

"He was so out of it... that Leonard's pot-smoking uncle would be proud!"

"Wha...? That doesn't even make any sense!"

"Guys?"

"IT makes PERFECT SENSE."

"UGH!! Why do I even bother with you sometimes?!"

"PEOPLE!" James yelled.

"WHAT!" they yelled in unison.

"It's my bad," James said after he'd recuperated from their violent decibels. He stood up and looked at both of them.

"Let me figure it out... I'll explain everything once I understand it myself. Promise."

James snuck a peek at the shadow that'd been lurking behind his friends the entire time they'd been arguing. Forcing the shadow into center-vision confirmed his suspicions, but before he could speak up the shadow retreated to the darkness of the hallway. It was a miracle he'd been able to calm them down enough so the thing behind them had no choice but to leave.

"It must've been influencing them somehow," James thought. "A ghost? Or something worse... Was that...? Thorne?"

"What?" Susy exclaimed.

James snapped back. When had he sat down again?

"Did I say that out loud?" James asked.

"Yes," Amy replied.

"Uh… Uh…forget I said that then… at least for now…" James gruffed. "It won't make sense until I explain… uh… some things…"

"Are you okay James? I know she smacked you pretty hard but I didn't think it was hard enough to lose your mind." Amy asked.

"I… I honestly don't know… no… it wasn't her." James muttered.

"Weeellll, it's been great and all but I think I'm gonna' go," Susan said.

Amy raised an eyebrow but didn't say anything. She had no right to make her stay after she'd gotten angry again, especially not after all James' bizarre outbursts.

"Uh… see you later I guess," James finally called as she left the room.

Amy waited for him to stand but found herself disappointed by the venture, taking an adjacent chair and turning it around to sit opposite him instead.

"James…"

"I'm sorry!"

"Don't be sorry, just tell me what's going on."

"I… Uh… Uh… I think it's starting to happen."

"What is?"

James gripped his hair and leaned his elbows on the desk, finally leaning back in frustration.

"Bro?"

"Sorry!"

"What's going on?"

"I guess, for lack of a better term... the plot."

James looked her straight in the eyes without hesitating. She felt like something big was happening and he was the source. She couldn't tell whether the chill running up her spine was from fear of what he was about say or if it was her heart fluttering in anticipation of a new chapter in their friendship.

"How much time do you have?"

24

"James, wake up!" Mrs. Pensworth called from downstairs.

The distance from her call to the inside of James' room seemed much greater than it should've been. By his estimate the distance couldn't be more than thirty feet give or take a few arm-lengths, and he found it strange that her voice sounded like it was coming from the kitchen and muffled enough to be likened to shouting into a pillow.

"Coming!" James replied.

He rolled over to the side of his bed and, standing up, put a hand to his head. It felt heavier than usual, as if he were being pulled back by some sort of invisible rope. And on top of the innate feeling of tension that permeated the atmosphere, James felt like the room felt warmer than usual. Much warmer.

"Did I turn up the heat last night?" he thought, flipping his hair and stretching his back.

Nothing else seemed unusual, besides the oddly soft calling of his mother being the thing that finally woke him from his dream. James walked around, wiping the grit from his eyes. He had to alert Amy of the impending danger creeping up on her, even if it was only a dream and he was simply acting paranoid. Considering how crazy the past few days had been, crazy didn't seem so out of the ordinary. Not anymore. There was no more time for miscalculations. Thorne was coming for her. James walked over to the mirror, the back of his head weighing him down like a bag of bricks.

"...THE HECK?!" he exclaimed.

The face staring back at him wasn't his. It was a girl's face. He could tell it was a girl's face because it was much smaller than his own. James rubbed his face again, trying to make sure his eyesight from just waking up wasn't the issue, and put a hand on his check to feel around for his own face. Not surprisingly, it was still his cheek. In fact, nothing would seem odd about it given the recent events, other than the face of a girl with long hair looking back at him through the mirror and mimicking his exact movements.

James waved with his left hand and pulled on his ear with the right. The girl did the same. James put a palm on the glass. A smaller palm mirrored his. James' vision felt blurry.

"Why is this room so warm?!" he shouted.

"James, are you up yet?" his mother's voice called.

"Y...Yes mom!"

He wasn't sure if it was even his mom calling him anymore. James frantically circled the room. The girl in the mirror did the same. James had no idea as to how he was supposed to remedy it. It sat right outside his comfort level despite his normally strong ability to handle the criminally weird and obtuse.

"Why does she seem so familiar?" James thought. "She looks just like that dream… memory?"

He felt inexplicably drawn to return and to look at her more closely. If his vision would finally focus for once in this weirdness room.

"Everything about this feels odd."

He drew as close to the mirror as he could. Something inside told him that looking into her eyes was the key to solving it. James' breath clouded the part of the mirror near his mouth. The girl's breath did the same. Odd, because the room felt so warm.

James' vision came into clear focus as he and the person in the mirror locked eyes. She was pretty.

"Amy?" James said aloud.

No sooner had the name escaped his lips was he knocked back by some sort of invisible energy blast. James fell back on the floor as if he'd been electrocuted. The boy in the mirror did the same.

He couldn't tell if he'd been knocked unconscious or not by the blast, especially since he found his vision had left him. Some sort of electricity had zapped up his hand and down his spine, leaving him completely helpless and paralyzed. James couldn't even lift his head to check if she'd been knocked back too in her weird alternative nightmare world. All he knew was his whole body felt like it was on fire and even though he couldn't move, the pain was excruciatingly unbearable.

"My back?!" he thought.

The shock continued racing around his spine even after the initial impact of the invisible energy blast, causing all sort of bone-cracking sounds not unlike those arising from a torture chamber. James couldn't tell if he were dead or not. It did feel like he was being electrocuted for no apparent reason. He couldn't tell if he should be scared out of his mind or grateful for the free back crack. Or both. James granted himself some relief for a moment, allowing himself the time to think that, whatever the feeling was, the experience was electrifying.

"Is this how I die? This has to be a dream."

No sooner had it started did the sensation stop. James found himself standing upright with his feet planted on the ground and with perfect visual clarity. James instantly walked back over to the mirror to see if Amy was alright. But it wasn't Amy staring back at him. It was him staring back at him. Somehow, everything had turned back to normal. James breathed a sigh of relief.

James looked up at himself in the mirror to check for any signs of injury or burn marks on his clothing. Anything that might give him some sort of clue as to what was happening in this house of horrors or what he was supposed to do to get out. But nothing seemed unusual other than that he was looking up at the mirror.

"Did the dresser get taller? Or did I get shorter..."

A pit knotted itself in his stomach. He tentatively lifted a hand to his face. The James in the mirror did the same. It felt softer. And rounder. His hand felt tiny. James brought his hand down and looked at it. It was definitely smaller.

James covered his mouth and let out a small gasp. The owner of the gasp sounded like Amy. James looked back at the mirror. He was still there, covering up his mouth. It looked super odd to him as he almost never made wild poses in the mirror like this. It felt childish. He scratched the idea, searching for a better term.

"The word isn't 'childish'... Ahah! It's girly!"

His lips felt different. They were smaller, and felt fuller. The James in the mirror licked the back of his hand and smelled it. Even his breath smelled different. The thought of what might've happened from looking in the mirror in this haunting-house finally dawned on him and he gulped palpably. James touched his throat, hoping his horrible conclusion was wrong and he would wake up from the nightmare as soon as possible. James looked to his mirror-self, hoping for any sort of ray or glimmer of understanding, and after a moment looked down at himself. And shrieked like a girl.

"WHAT KIND OF SICK JOKE IS THIS?!" James exclaimed.

His mom's muted voice called from downstairs.

"James? Is there someone up there with you?"

James almost replied without thinking but stopped himself. He looked at the mirror, but the reflection was gone. He reminded himself that he'd have to answer soon or he'd be in trouble anyway.

"Nah, just me," James said finally, hoping for the best.

He hoped his voice hadn't actually switched with hers and that, per the rule of the haunting-house, as long as he decided it was his voice speaking and not hers, that the dream would respect it. That, if it was only a strange dream, he might alter said dream to help himself out. But he wasn't so lucky, catching her voice just in time, shutting his mouth as quickly as possible to prevent any more unnecessary chaos.

"Okay! Just checking! Mmmph... I thought I heard someone," came the muffled voice.

"Phew, that was close," James thought.

Maybe it had worked. Still no reflection though. James felt his body again. He was still 'Amy'. He realized he had no choice but to go along with it for now.

"If this wasn't so weird and freaky this would be hilarious... Imagine how much trouble I could get her into since I'm apparently her... conscious?" James said, finding it hilarious that he was plotting Amy's humorous demise with her own voice. "I'm really not sure what I am... Oooo

Amy….. This is your conscious! Let's get oooooouut of heeeeree!"

He stopped talking immediately, trying to cover up his plans so he wouldn't get busted. Or have his mom bust him for having a girl in the house without permission. He waited for another call from downstairs, but nothing happened. James walked around his room, trying to get a feel for her body.

"Really not too much different than me. Shorter step, different balance," James said.

He paused. Amy's voice again.

"But honestly though, this has got to be a sick joke."

He hopped around the room a little, testing various menial actions and stretches to try to laugh away his fear. He found it surprising how similar their actions were. Not that women were aliens, but he always figured they were an entirely different species.

"Apparently not that different… Seriously though… how in the world can she deal with this pressure? It's all… this is… so weird. How does she not notice this feeling? Like she's being slowly suffocated… I need to get out of here."

He opened the door and began his descent, finding the house oddly quiet. No replies from mom. James walked to the stairway, immediately noticing the typical portraits had been replaced by mirrors and were emptily staring back at him. At least at first. Once he started walking past them the pictures changed. Every time Amy looked into one of them, his own reflection would stare back at her, and after a moment or two would run down to the next mirror, beckoning her to follow. James didn't realize how long the staircase was until he'd reached the bottom was looking back up. He couldn't even see the top of it, or the light from his room he should've been able to see even if it were a nightmare.

"So freaking weird."

James felt the sudden pressing need to search the house for at least one of his parents. It felt like someone was watching him. Or her. Or whoever he currently was. James touched his face again. He was still Amy.

The silence was deafening and the threat felt increasingly close. The silence was only broken by the sound of her voice.

"Seriously. Of all the times…"

James opened the front door and ran outside, trying to rid himself of the suffocating feeling.

"This isn't… This isn't what I imagined when I wanted to hang out with her."

James' peripheral vision picked up some movement arising from a nearby snowbank.

"I think I just want to date her. Eventually though… Not actually be her…" he said.

James spoke aloud, hoping there was no one around to hear him. And in Amy's voice.

But someone else was there. Standing on the snowbank. He could feel it, and he shivered. The body he was trapped in shivered more than he was used to in his own body, and he found some comfort by it.

"No wonder they always complain about the cold," he thought.

His thoughts sounded like his voice. So it really was just a dream.

"So I'm literally her?" he wondered. "Or am I glimpsing Amy's future or something? Possible future maybe? That seems more likely…"

He didn't know if it was his thoughts that scared him or if it was due to their mutual predator getting closer, ready to spring the trap. What if his mind never made it back to his own body? He mentally shivered.

"So weird…" Amy thought.

She wiped away a tear she hadn't previously realized was forming. Gritting her teeth and pursing her lip, Amy whipped around to look at the snowbank, trying to nail down the predator's hiding spot.

Nothing.

But the sensation of hairs rising on the back of her neck heightened her suspicions that something was, indeed, watching her. Someone was watching her intently. Waiting. Watching for an opening to attack. Silence rested on the snow. The invisible hum of the stalker's presence continued to raise the creep factor. Something told her the beast was after her for some reason and not James, but she couldn't figure out why.

"Is this in Amy's future?" James thought. "Am I dreaming about the future? That still seems to be the only explanation."

There was no way for the beast to know he was there with her. Everything James thought to do seemed to resonate with her actions; it was as if his mind was trapped in Amy's body, aware of the real Amy's mind and her decisions but unable to change her movements. He was just being allowed to see things from her point of view. He was, for all intents and purposes, one and the same person as Amy for now, at least until he could escape from the nightmare and return to his own life.

"I can feel her conscious... and I can't get her to do anything she doesn't want to do... that's a huge relief I guess... But why couldn't I see my bedroom light? Wait... this all started happening because of mirrors... mirrors... why mirrors? They've got to be the key."

The silence itself gave away the stalker's position. There, down the road, or the field, it didn't matter, stood a figure about a hundred yards away. Amy blinked. First mistake.

"Mirrors? What do they do? They... they reflect what they see within view... they let us see our faces... eyes? Gateways to the soul... portals... no wait... that's true but it's off-track, I can feel it. What is it?"

The figure closed the gap between him and Amy from a hundred yards to fifty. Blink. Twenty. Amy gulped. Ten feet.

Her feet felt glued down and sluggish, as if she were treading on a swimming pool filled with honey. James could feel the frustration and fear rising in her mind.

"I can't help but feel this is all my own fault somehow. Mirrors! Gah! What... what are they there for?!"

A feeling of helplessness overwhelmed her and the coldness started eating at her from the outside in. James knew. They were Amy's real emotions. Why he could recognize it he would never know. It was as if his conscious had been allowed to enter her dreams and was watching from her point of view like some sort of ephemeral movie screen.

"Think! They reflect! They... they reveal... no no no that isn't it! Aha! Mirrors compare, but not completely accurately! The left and rights are switched all around! I was comparing myself to her? And it... And it was stifling both of us... And I wasn't even being accurate... because it had to come from her point of view... That must be it! But why was I comparing? It's not like I've known her very long here..."

Amy raised a hand to stifle her scream. The figure stopped moving towards her now, his shadow casting a muted gray smokescreen in a small circle around him, melding into some sort of steam rising from his feet and covering him up to the knees.

James felt helpless to warn her. Had he told her yet, or was he somehow able to feed her the information in here? There was no way to tell; it was all happening too quickly for any real deduction on his part.

The figure was tall. Extremely tall. James knew that the demon could transform into whatever form he wished now, whenever he wished. It was one of the numerous pieces of information he'd gathered and spread throughout Arthridall. But was it really Thorne? There was only one way to tell. But why come to Earth?

"Does she already know all this? Or am I telling her?" James thought. "Wait... she's making all her own decisions... And I know she learns everything on her own here as well... which means that she's... oooohhh... well duh, it all makes sense now... That'd be just like King to pull a fast one like that and give me a warning in a dream... This isn't a nightmare, this is a possible future."

The man wore a long, black leather trench coat that appeared both highly fashionable and eminently practical. Six silver metallic buckles lined one side of the coat, glimmering and bobbing slowly, as if he'd broken free of a psych-ward and his coat was a crazy-vest.

Amy finally brought herself to look up at the man's head. A strange hat covered his face. It was a shade of black not unlike the rest of his style choices, with a large and wide brim. The brim was completely flat, except for the squared off central part that rested perfectly centered on top of his head. Like a giant pancake topped off with a shortcake. Except black. And sinister. If the man weren't exuding such an air of death around him Amy might've actually laughed at how absurd the hat was. As it stood, he was terrifying.

Amy tried to scream again but her voice caught in her throat as he reached inside one of his coat pockets and pulled out an ancient looking silver gun. The gun itself was terrifying enough in of itself, let alone the man holding it. The gun looked like an old-style revolver with a modern silencer on the barrel, except far larger than a typical handgun and covered in all sorts of ancient and evil runes. Even James wouldn't have ordinarily picked up on that kind of detail so quickly, and he doubted Amy would've either, even if his hypothesis about her did prove correct. But as it stood, the details etched into the sides of Thorne's instrument of death were being raised towards her face in a surreal and slow-motion instant.

"Is this what it's like to have your life flash before your eyes?" James wondered.

Amy felt her body go limp from the stress. She stood still opposite the gunman, thankful that the paralyzing part of her stress had finally released its grip. The only thing keeping her upright was muscle memory. She'd used up all her adrenaline in the time it had taken to simply blink three times. Three measly time and space-warped seconds and she was as good as dead.

James felt the despair rising from her heart. He also felt powerless to stop the figure in black and prepared for the worst. Amy gasped.

The man finally raised his head to look at his prey.

"It's him!" James screamed, hoping she could hear him somehow. "Thorne!"

It was him. The great and terrible demon of old, come to reap the head of his best friend in the entire world. The dark one. Thorne.

James knew it was Thorne. His eyes were the only thing capable of revealing the demon's true nature no matter what form he took, man or beast. They were the eyes of a dying star, a damned firestorm burning eternally with the colors of malice and hatred. And they were fixated on his best friend. On him.

The demon made as if to smile, but didn't. Instead, his mouth dropped slightly, revealing two rows of teeth filed into sharp points, dripping of unspeakable filth. The darkness was palpable. Amy struggled for air. She was going to die.

His mouth fell loose, as if he'd been socked in the jaw so hard it'd been dislocated. He grinned like a shark with bloodlust and swung the revolver's inner chamber out, showing Amy the bullets within, taking a single bullet out and dropping it onto the snow. He spun the remainder of the bullets back into the gun like some sort of twisted game of Russian roulette.

Thorne turned sideways, tilting his hat-topped head at a bone-crunching angle, and pointed the ancient firearm at Amy's forehead with an evil glee.

"Die."

Thorne used his gruesome thumb to pull on the hammer.

He pulled the trigger and she screamed. The gun clicked with a distinctly quiet snap, telling her he'd missed.

Amy started to breathe a sigh of relief when the unthinkable happened. The demon smiled, actually smiled, his head snapping sideways with a deafening sound of broken bone to his other shoulder.

"Give me the key."

Pulled the hammer, pointed the gun, and fired the bullet before she finished inhaling.

***

James shot awake in his bed mid-breath as if he'd been revived with defibrillator paddles. He'd been right, after all. It was a dream. It was all a dream. A warning.

"The ice is growing thin… he's… he's coming for us."

25

James blinked his eyes, rubbing the sand from them. He was pretty shaken. The dream had been way too realistic to ignore.

"Or was there more than one dream?" he thought.

Were those dreams real life, or were they simply realistic dreams? Were they more premonitions of the future? Or memories of the past? Was waking up here another dream? Part three? Or four? If real life, then what was the dream, and what happened outside while he'd been asleep?

James looked at his bedroom window, grateful to find he could see through it. Instead of frosted death it was remarkably sunny. He felt his heart pound. He knew for a fact it was still winter on Earth, and having real sunshine in this part of the country during winter was as rare as a unisloth refusing to eat its cinnamon-sugar infused oatmeal.

"Not saying it's impossible, but all things considered it's highly unusual," he mumbled.

Mary called from the kitchen downstairs.

"James? Are you up yet? It's almost time to catch the bus."

James' heart pounded a bit and then relaxed. It sounded like his real mom's voice. He put on some clothes and brushed his hair in front of the mirror.

"So far, so good," he mumbled. "I'm not stuck in her skin anymore. Or whatever the hell happened. That... that dream was way too strange."

"James!"

James tied his shoes one at a time by propping them on top of his mattress. He scanned the room. Seemed normal enough. It wasn't enough to convince him yet. At least he wasn't a girl anymore. Or getting shot at by a character from his books.

"Coming!" he called, opening the door.

His mom started vacuuming around the kitchen table. James noticed there were only two soiled plates. He watched her as she reached underneath to pick up a used paper towel.

"She seems real to me," he thought.

Mrs. Pensworth noticed him as she started wrapping up the vacuum cord.

"Better hurry. The bus is about to get here."

James blinked.

"Are you alright?"

"Uh... yeah..."

"What's wrong?" she asked.

"Uh… it… just a real strange dream last night I guess."

She noticed him staring at the previous night's dinner.

"You fell asleep last night before dad got home so we ate with just the two of us."

"Oh…"

She continued, seeing his apparent confusion.

"You're probably pretty hungry."

His stomach growled as if to respond in its master's stead.

"I was going to wake you up for dinner but when I came in your room you were already passed out. I figured you'd rather sleep than be too tired to eat or talk with dad after we ate, so I kissed you goodnight and turned your lamp off for you."

James nodded. So even spilling the beans to his dad last night had been a dream. The dimension mixing at school and the ghost preying on his weirdly behaving friends. A dream. Amy getting murdered by the demon, a dream. Three dreams, all night long.

"Thank goodness," he thought.

"James?"

"Yeah."

He snapped back to the present.

"You okay now?"

"Yeah."

"Really weird dream, huh?"

"Yeah."

Mrs. Pensworth stashed the vacuum in the storage closet, grabbed yesterday's dinner plates, and set them in the sink. James blinked, sitting down on the living room couch.

"Buh buh buh! No time to dawdle! The bus will be here soon."

Mom picked up a few shopping bags and handed them to him.

"Thanks."

"You're welcome. I packed three lunches with extra snacks for the ride there and for whenever you get the munchies."

"You're actually the best mom ever."

"I know. Now get going or I'm gonna' tan you real good."

"Yes please, I need to tan."

"Git..." she said, smiling despite herself.

James took the bags and slipped them into his backpack. The front door clicked shut behind him and he was off on another adventure.

"It was all a dream," he mumbled. "I still haven't told even a single person anything here... or everything... well Amy might know a bit about that last one now I suppose… I'll have to ask."

***

The sunshine felt warm on James' face even as the rest of his body was left to thaw underneath his swelteringly warm coat. James wondered if the sudden heat was an indication that spring was right around the corner. It didn't take him long to remember that the full brutality of winter had yet to arrive at his doorstep. James consoled himself with the fact that he was at least back in reality again, and while the heat from the sun would soon disappear again for the rest of winter, facing that reality helped him cope with the thoughts of his impending and blindingly long and cold winter's walks home immensely.

"It must've been a combination of something," he thought as the bus approached.

James heard the crunch of melting snow under foot and the cheerful murmurings of his school-mates as they chattered about the sunshine bringing back the warm weather for a bit. It was noticeably warmer than the previous day. Yesterday had been awfully miserable. He would know, considering he was one of the few people who actually went outside at lunch.

"That's right. There was a food fight and I officially met Susy for the first time," he thought.

"Hey dude!"

James turned and saw Susan waving at him some distance away. Amy was there as well, knees bent as she attempted to re-buckle her snow boots.

"I have to tell her about the dreams..." James thought.

He thought better of it. He needed to sort through it all himself first before he could explain it to anyone else.

The girls walked over to him and Susy gave him a great big bear hug. James felt a little uncomfortable being the one to receive such a warm welcome, but she was not to be denied her chosen form of affection.

"How you doin' ol' buddy ol' pal?"

James couldn't help but break into a small smile. He'd been too wrapped up in his thoughts. Susan didn't notice the hesitation, instead releasing him to pat her friend on the shoulder.

"This one here almost made us late for the bus," she said. "Sleeping in late and what not!"

"I already said I was sorry!" Amy interjected.

The bus pulled into the stop right on time. James allowed himself to break into a larger smile. He was back. He noticed she didn't say anything after her apology. The buses' brakes screeched to a halt and the students started piling into their respective rows. He filed the mental note away for later. He just needed to make it clear she could always talk to him whenever she wanted.

"We're friends here now," he thought. "That's what friends do."

The trio walked up to take their customary seats, which they'd finally settled on after lots of dispute as being right behind the bus driver and the adjacent row for Susy. James allowed Amy the distinct privilege of taking the window seat and sat down next to her.

Amy held her backpack in her lap as if it held something far more important than her homework assignments. Before he could ask her about it, Amy tucked her feet up next to her jean pockets and leaned against the window with her eyes shut. James looked to Susan for support. She shrugged.

"She's been like this all morning. It's not like her to really pout about anything, not even grades."

James nodded to affirm Susan's suspicions, then looked back to Amy, trying not to shrug. She was wrong. Amy definitely pouted about grades.

"Was the test really that difficult for her?" he asked himself.

The rest of the bus ride seemed relatively quiet for the most part, other than the occasional bleeding through of their fellow classmates' humming. Susy left the two of them to play cards with the upperclassmen in the back. James looked at Amy, finding himself empathizing with her more so than his usual stoic and quirky self was used to. James wondered if it was something as simple as her test result eating away at her, or if it was something else, something far worse that she couldn't bring herself to speak about.

"Did something happen to her last night?" he thought.

The bus pulled into the school, dropped most of its passengers off, and impatiently waited as the stragglers got off so it could speed away to its next round of victims. James tapped on her shoulder to wake her up from her mid-morning nap. Susan had already left to go inside with her newfound poker buddies.

"Amy?"

James tentatively tapped on her shoulder again.

"I'm not asleep," she said without turning.

"Oh..."

James didn't know what to say.

"Well... we're here. We need to get off."

Amy didn't say anything and instead stood up to follow him down the steps. The little yellow terror behind them spun its wheels in the snow, taking off with an angry hiss of doors. Amy stood in place, her chin hugging her binders.

"James..."

James didn't know what to say that wasn't going to make her upset. Didn't want to blow his chance with his newfound friend.

"Yeah?" he finally said.

Amy sighed heavily, finally looking up after a moment. Something told him it wasn't going to be good news.

"I had a dream last night. I saw this beautiful sunless sunset. An amazing man in this white robe showed it to me on this... perfect beach I felt like I'd been to before. And... another dream... I... I died."

James was frozen in time. No amount of sunshine could've thawed him from his spot. She searched his eyes for any sign of hope, an involuntary tear dripping down her face onto the snow-slushed pavement.

"James?" she asked, her voice catching in her throat.

James took a slow breath, doing what he could to snap back to the present.

"Yeah..."

"That sunset was you... wasn't it? Can we talk?"

James didn't know whether to wrap his friend into the biggest bear-hug he could muster or run away from embarrassment. He finally found himself strong enough to choose the middle ground and reply. With words.

"Yeah..."

Word.

It was all she needed to hear. Before he realized it, James was embraced by one of the most terrified friends he'd ever known. James let his initial shock and embarrassment wear off, finally allowing himself to lower his arms around her and hug her back.

"She's shivering," James thought.

James wasn't wrong, but not because of the cold. She was scared. Sad. Exhausted. James didn't know what to say. He'd never really given anyone his age a hug before. At least not here. Not on Earth. He didn't know why. He just hadn't seen any reason to until he'd found her.

His heart broke for her. He didn't know what to say, so he said nothing. He too, was scared out of his mind. He had to stay strong. If not for himself than for the both of them. As a team.

They could talk later. But they both already knew that.

26

Amy would look back on that day and remember that he felt much warmer than he looked. She knew it wasn't because of the coat he was wearing either; she knew what winter coats felt like. Up until he'd hugged her back they'd been one of her only sources of warmth. Coats and blankets and showers. Her childhood friend. And now him.

She didn't know if the warmth came from the combination of things, or from the single person standing in front of her. Warming her. Her heart began beating again, feeling like it was the first time it had beat in a long time. It beat to the tune of a high-pitched, squealing locomotive, running along the tracks at full force.

Amy found herself shivering; whether from the sudden release of fear or from pure happiness she wasn't sure.

"Probably both…"

***

Amy knew he didn't know much about her, but her gut told her she'd made the right choice in opening up to him. Most people burned her almost immediately, especially if they took the extra leap to get to know her. And her past. But he was different. It was like he knew what she needed before she did sometimes.

"She's weird!" the kids used to say behind her back. "Gross!"

"Crazy!"

"Psycho!"

It hurt deeply, cutting her to ribbons and leading her to stop caring. She never thought she'd done anything wrong by telling them about her life, but experience told her most people didn't have the capacity to handle her. Or they didn't care enough to help even when they could.

One time, when she was a kid, Amy found a squirrel sprawled out on the sidewalk that wasn't doing too well, probably from eating something bad or poisonous. So, like anyone her age, she called to the neighborhood for support. And they came, asking her what they could do.

The problem was, she didn't know the first thing about first aid for squirrels and she was at a loss for words because of it. The other children eventually lost interest; there wasn't anything fun there to do anymore, so they left her behind and returned to their games.

Amy's concern for the squirrel overrode her feelings of isolation. She tried everything she could think of to revive the poor thing, even going so far as to gently poke it with a twig. Nothing worked.

Finally, after much deliberation and against her better judgement, Amy decided to pick up the squirrel.

"Kissing the frog turned it into a prince, maybe kissing the little guy will bring it back to life."

Little Amy knelt down, gingerly scooping the poor animal into her tiny left palm to get a better look. Its eyes were closed, and it felt cold and soft in her hand. After much deliberation, little Amy decided to kiss the squirrel on the forehead the in case that it did wake and decide her lip was its next nut to bite down on.

The squirrel didn't squirm as she brought it close. Although she was relieved that she wouldn't get scratched, the squirrel's lack of movement was unnerving. Amy placed a gentle kiss between its ears, on its beautifully soft fur, waiting. Nothing happened, and it made her sad.

Little Amy knelt down, gingerly replacing the dead animal where she'd found it, closer to the grass in the hope no one would step on it and make the poor thing's pain any worse. As she began grieving, a miraculous thing occurred.

Amy watched in amazement as one of the ears twitched briefly. Even as the tears continued welling in the corners of her eyes, the squirrel opened its own. It eventually stood up on its hind legs as if nothing had happened and, looking around his surroundings, noticed Amy standing nearby. He moved his head as if to acknowledge her help in rescuing him, afterwards scampering up the nearest tree to be with his fellow squirrel-mates in their lofty and well-groomed forest.

Amy was excited about the miracle. So much so that she ran all around the neighborhood telling her friends how her kiss had brought the dead squirrel back to life. Everyone seemed excited to share in the victory with her, even though they hadn't had anything to do with the squirrel's rescue. She hoped they'd finally accept her as one of them because of it.

When she went to play the next day, and join her new friends and their games, they avoided her like the plague more than ever. It wasn't until later that she found out someone had spread a rumor about her, saying she'd killed and eaten the squirrel herself since no one else had seen her so called miracle.

It was one minor story out of hundreds. Thousands, if she ever took the time to remember them all.

***

Amy had been betrayed more than once. Secretly, or not-so-secretly beaten by her long deceased, alcoholic father. Verbally abused by her poor mother until fourteen when she'd passed away from cancer. The neighborhood basically crucified her when they found out and she'd been raised by her grandmother ever since. She called her Nana, and Nana was her fortress. Amy wouldn't know how she would've coped without Nana.

James had saved her from so much more than Astwin's clutches that day. It felt like he'd stood up to her father too. She was always more concerned about saving others even if she got hurt in the meantime, especially since it always seemed she got burned no matter what she did to help.

He'd jostled her out of her own tormented mind somehow and brought her back to the land of the living. A mind with plenty of time to mull over each and every time she'd been hurt. And betrayed. And beaten. Over, and over, and over. From the pain of an ever-caring, tender-hearted little girl whose parents had abused and left abandoned to the world.

She couldn't bring herself to tell him how much he meant to her. She was freezer-burnt.

At least, not yet. Not that she didn't want to tell him now. She wanted to remember this moment standing in front of her before he too would leave along with the rest. A single, magical spark of warmth to keep her alive in an otherwise cold and dreary world. She'd given up on too many memories, but she didn't want to lose another one. Not him. She couldn't give up this time. She couldn't give in.

***

"I can hear his heartbeat."

"It goes thump… thump… thump... So familiar…"

***

She would've accepted the fact that it was his singular word of encouragement that gave her any hope at all. She didn't know why she felt compelled to stay there in his embrace, or maybe she did but felt free enough to give in to the urge anyway. Amy stayed where she was; head on his chest, arms clutching his back.

She felt the strong tenderness of his hug. She didn't know if he'd hugged her out of obligation or his own willingness, but it didn't really matter. His hug felt warm.

"Confident even?"

She couldn't place the sensation. It was similar to some sort of warmly welcomed dream, whose memory comes and goes like a treasured childhood fantasy. She doubted he really had any idea about what she'd been rambling about, with sunsets and death and the like, but she knew now she'd be able tell him eventually; he'd somehow understand because that's what he did better than anyone else she'd ever met. He was her friend. Even though she didn't think he understood her yet didn't matter; he'd returned her embrace with his own instead of running away. He'd given her heart to her, packaged up in a single beautiful shape and added his own to it. He'd put it on the line for her, instead of crushing hers to pieces as so many others had.

When he was around she felt free to be herself. When he was around her tormented past felt more like a distant nightmare than a constant companion.

"Please don't leave me too," she thought.

"Hmmm?" James asked.

"Uh...Uh..." she said, struggling to back-pedal.

She released her hands from his back.

"Crap!" she thought. "I had to open my mouth... Of all the times..."

"I uh... thank you. Really... I needed that... you... I mean this." she said.

James slid a hand into his pocket and scratched his head with the other.

"I uh... sure thing. Let's... I uh... we can talk about your dream at lunch okay?"

"Yeah," Amy finally said. "That'd be nice."

She felt her heart flutter as she watched him walk past and go up the stairs.

"He hugged me. I mean I guess I kinda stole it... but he didn't pull away."

***

Susan walked over to him as he neared the door. She'd already decided she wasn't a huge fan of poker anymore and had turned back to meet back up with her real friends, only to witness them hugging it out in the middle of the schoolyard.

"James?"

He blushed. If he'd gotten his hand stuck in the cookie jar twice in the same day, he would've looked less guilty.

"Yeah?"

"I don't know if you know if you know but, Amy's not much the huggable type. She has good reasons not to be."

"I..."

James looked for the right words.

"I didn't know. Sorry," he said.

"Amy felt extremely huggable though..." he thought. "She's wrong."

Susan snatched his chin to emphasize her point. He reddened more deeply.

"Don't be sorry," she said, squeezing his jaw. "Just man up and don't screw it up."

She let him go and walked inside as if it were no more than a routine checkup. James massaged his aching jaw, following her example. He shook his head.

"Thanks, I guess."

27

James sat at his customary bench in the courtyard outside the cafeteria. The mint green doors swung open more than usual. He figured it was probably due to the sudden change in weather. It was warmer for sure. Perhaps not warm enough to sustain the popular girls awkwardly conglomerated all too nearby, as they were currently shivering together like a single, terrified ice-pop. They'd made a poor life choice and now they had to live with it. Choosing to wear cute clothing instead of warm, marshmallow-stuffed coats had been their mistake to make. Every time the cafeteria doors swung open and another one came out they found they'd been tricked into being sacrificed to the desolate wasteland. A collective conniption fit by the rest of the squeak-squad still inside and the slamming doors told James the unusual outdoor activity was the result of a poorly thought out prank. Their boy-friends had already decided to stay inside in order to 'protect' the rest. What the pranksters were protecting the shrieking squeakers inside from remained to be seen.

If he hadn't been concerned about Amy's state of mind, he may have been somewhat gleeful by the sudden consternation of his classmates. The looks of terror besetting their faces could've fooled anyone observing the scene into believing that being exiled from the warm gooey center of the school was infinitely worse than enduring the second apocalypse. It may have also been the fact that they were all huddled together for warmth on the same single bench and the picture was hilarious.

Hilariously enough, James found he was the only male presence in the immediate vicinity. Fate was mocking him, mocking the torment of his impatience. He hoped Amy would eventually come out of the belly of the beast by her own volition. He didn't expect Susy to abandon her food-kingdom in its greatest hour of need, but he did hope Amy would find a way to escape.

"Nothing's ever set in stone with her…"

She'd hugged him. Him, of all people. Her embrace had been too real to be another dream. As sweet as his mother's rare goodnight kiss. A beam of light from a lighthouse to chase away a lingering mental fog. Did she remember Arthridall? Remember him? Or was it love? He certainly still felt something and that something was strong enough to keep him from going clinical again. But his impatience was quickly making up for lost time.

"She's late," James mumbled. "Again."

He hoped she would emerge from the cozy den of wonders like some sort of glowing virgin sacrifice. That she might do something so amazing it'd take his breath away and she'd put it back in his lungs before he could ask. A girl who made everything she wore look as beautiful as her wedding dress. But for who? Him? Had she remembered her daughter? James secretly hoped it was for him.

"I need to write," he thought. "All men need to understand these things… Things… heck… what am I saying? It'd be a big fat lie to say I understand women… dang it Amy… where are you?"

He had to remain calm for fear of getting laughed at by the popsicle conglomerate. It wasn't the first time she'd been late. But he was worried. His dreams had shaken him to the core and it'd be unfair to assume her dream hadn't shaken her at least as much. It hadn't escaped his notice that her dream sounded exactly like his own, as if they'd somehow shared them through some connected dream reality. He'd already had some time to process it. She hadn't. Plus, he'd already had some experience in bending realities. Amy hadn't, at least not as she stood now, nor had she ever been immersed in the bizarreness he seemed to make his continual abode in.

"Well… actually… maybe she remembers more than she's letting on… No… I'm positive she isn't telling me something…"

James reminded himself that it might be possible she was worried about something entirely different. Just because he'd experienced nightmare-ville didn't mean she'd had.

"But… There's no way it's not the same. She was too specific."

The thought embarrassed him. If she really had seen his sunless sunset then she'd seen the real him; the good, the bad, and the ugly. She wouldn't need him anymore. She'd already understand him entirely and wouldn't be interested in sticking around anymore. The thought cut like a knife. She'd be holding his heart and could do anything she wanted with it.

"Not that she doesn't already," James mumbled.

"What's that?" Amy asked.

"WHH? HO!! You startled me!"

"Sorry..."

"How long have you been here?"

"Long enough."

"You... uh... well... uh... you seem to be doing better," James said.

"Uh... yeah. I am..."

Neither bundle of joy knew how to get the fun train rolling. They hated awkward silences. The kind of silence even crickets shy from. Amy cleared her throat.

"Thanks for earlier."

"You were scaring me for a moment there."

"Sorry."

"Not your fault."

"Sorry for being late again."

"It's okay."

Amy shifted uncomfortably.

"I forgot my lun…"

He handed her one of his lunch-bags mid-sentence.

"Thanks."

"Welcome."

"I promise it's not a habit."

"Honestly, it's okay."

The truth was, she could count on one hand how many times she'd eaten a full-sized lunch at school in recent memory. All made with love, courtesy of James' mom. But he didn't need to know that yet.

"So… uh… do you, want to talk? I can wait… if you need to…"

"No!" Amy exclaimed.

The collective gaze of the courtyard gaggle snapped towards them instantly, immediately turning to whisper among themselves. The other girls flustered her. A quick glance in their direction gave her away.

"I mean…" she said, looking up at him. "Sorry… I…"

Amy let out her pent up air with a sigh.

"I want to talk," she finally said. "I just…they're… they're all so merciless and I'm tired of it."

James looked at the gossipers. He could feel it too. The accusatory stares drilling the back of his head when he wasn't looking. Their maniacal laughter echoing against the dull concrete bricks.

It was an unusual experience for him, being the center of attention and all that, and the experience made him squirm. Being a bookworm and author and avoiding people usually solved the issue, but the sudden attention of the crowd reminded him he'd already left his safety-zone a while ago. Amy waited for him. At least they were clear on one thing; they needed to get out of there.

"Let's go." James said without second thought.

She was confused.

"It's still school though."

James' eyebrows furrowed. He did have a perfect attendance record.

"Other than the fist fight, of course," James thought. "But this is important. I need to give her the necklace."

"Yeah, I know," he said.

"Then we have to stay away till school gets out."

"Do we?"

He'd already decided it was for the best. Amy searched his eyes for any signs of betrayal. She was all too familiar with that look guys used to give her when they used to say that. She found herself meeting his gaze with an intensity most unlike her.

"He's actually concerned," she thought.

James waited for her to respond. He'd already decided what to do for himself.

"He's not accusing me…"

The feeling of being genuinely concerned for by a guy was certainly unusual. But it felt safe. She felt safe for once, shying away to blink away a tear and gain some space. She let it wash away, shivering.

"I almost forgot how to feel anything anymore… damn…"

She considered his proposal to skip class, glancing back at the others. She made up her mind. It wasn't the first time she'd run away from somewhere.

"Let's go then," she said.

"Are you sure?"

"Whoa don't go backing out! I just made up my mind!"

"I won't," he said.

Amy half smiled and stood up, turning towards the edge of the school grounds and blinding him to the fact she was crying. Again.

"He wants… He actually wants me… not Susan."

She grabbed his hand, pulling him off his chair.

"Let's… Let's go somewhere else."

James slipped the other lunches back in his backpack.

"Lead the way."

28

Running away from the school they both hated was both exhilarating and exhausting all at once. It was an utterly terrifying feeling; they needed to time their escape perfectly or they might as well not bother trying. Not only did they have the popular crowd breathing down their necks, but there were also all the random students meandering around the front lawn, trying to use the unique winter wonderland slush to their collective romantic or social life advantage. There were simply too many people capable of spotting and reporting them. Or worse, spreading all sorts of rumors to the circulatory system of the student body, beginning with the neurotic hubs that played the status game slightly better everyone else.

Amy figured it was the end of the line for their little game of espionage before it'd really started. The front entrance was packed with too much hubbub and insincerity. It wasn't exactly the first time she'd run away to the woods to escape. Usually, she'd feign illness with Ms. Oranorth and, as she was quite the skilled actress, found she could always manage to get a sick note.

But she didn't have her mom's sickness around as a reason to give up on school anymore. She'd already sown and reaped from that harvest too many times. And even if she still had that trump card there was no way she'd be able to convince Ms. Oranorth to let her so obviously run away with a boy.

James had other ideas.

"There's no way this will work," she finally said.

He stopped her.

"It'll work."

"Can't we just wait a few hours until after school?"

James huffed slightly, peering around the corner.

"Too many people," he thought.

"I mean, want to talk."

"I do too. But..."

James breathed.

"Something's about to happen here and we need to figure it out, and I mean everything, before it's too late. You had the same dream I did, right? Don't lie. I don't think it's a coincidence! Thorne's..."

Amy stomped her foot.

"You don't think I didn't know that?! There's just no way though. We need to wait. Plain and simple."

"There's always a way," he said shakily. "Thorne... I don't think it was just a dream. It was a warning! I... I'm not going to let you die."

Amy shook her head. He kept talking.

"Waiting at school will be the death of us if we don't take the future in our own hands. Let's go."

"Tho... Thorne?" she asked, suddenly feeling chilled. "You saw... Wait... But... wai... where are we going?"

"Nurse's office."

"It won't work."

"It has to work because we don't have any other choice."

"I... James, I admire your enthusiasm but your logic is horrendous."

"It makes perfect sense if you're as insane as me. I have a plan."

"What?"

"Never mind. Coast is clear. Let's go."

Amy forced him to stop halfway down the sidewalk in plain sight of anyone who cared to look. James fidgeted uncomfortably.

"It's crazy and you know it," she said.

"Yeah..."

"What?"

"Affirmative?"

"Stop."

"No."

"Why won't you listen to me for once?!"

James stopped. She was seriously shaken up. He wanted to comfort her again, but they weren't safe out in the open. He did what he could.

"Do you trust me?"

"Yeah, but..."

He looked at her emphatically.

"Amy, do you actually trust me?"

Everything inside her screamed to say no, to turn around, to run into the school she hated and hide in her favorite bathroom stall and cry. To forget all of it, forget everything, go back to the raw fear, the blistering pain. The numbness. She'd die if one more person betrayed her. Or worse. If she betrayed him.

She couldn't go through that again. She couldn't betray her one childhood friend no matter how great James was. Was it even still love? Or was she just trying to hold on to those few precious memories? She'd love being alone again. Then she wouldn't have to face giving them up.

But she knew if she left now, after all James had done for her, there would be no turning back from the shadow of oblivion. The oblivion of not feeling anything; the oblivion of living and breathing but not being alive. But she would still have her memories.

Could she live with the idea of pure chance and breathe the smell of adventure again, or had she already suffocated? That she'd simply drifted along, avoiding life, just to prove to herself that her friend wouldn't be mad when she returned to her old home? It was all very confusing. Crazy, even. She made up her mind. She snapped back to the present.

"Amy?"

"Yeah."

"Yeah?"

"Just...yeah..."

Amy looked at him, holding his gaze. He found himself entranced but not embarrassed. Reality snapped him back. It wasn't safe to be out in the open. They needed to escape from school. He was sure of it. Thorne had been tracking her all day long. He hadn't been sure about it until he'd seen her pouting on the bus, but even the weather was more surreal than normal, and he was sure it was because they were being manipulated into a corner. Being observed.

"All for a damn necklace she doesn't even have at this point in time." he thought.

"Good." James said. "He's been watching us all day. Since at least this morning. He may have started earlier than that. I don't know."

"What? You mean Thorne?"

"Shhhh! We need to come up with something to kick him back to Arthridall or it's going to get worse. Much worse. I don't think it'll get better until we finish what we started. We've done gone too deep down the rabbit hole to try climbing back up now."

She raised an eyebrow. He'd inadvertently referenced one of her favorite books. James took note and continued.

"See? That's exactly what I am talking about. Books, books, books."

"But... what... how did you know that..."

"I dreamed last night too. Three actually. I think mine are all related somehow. And I think you had the same dream. Right?"

"Wha...? So what would that have to do with me? Just because I was upset this morning doesn't mean you need mock me!"

"I was watching you in one of them."

"Oh WERE YOU?"

"Sorry... that came out wrong."

"You think?!"

"It was like... I saw and felt everything you saw and felt. And there were these mirrors all over the place... And one minute I was you and after that it was like I was watching your future from your point of view… And if you saw the beach then that means you're starting to remember even without the necklace…"

"What?!"

James checked his pocket-watch.

"We're running out of time. He's coming to kill you."

"Just… why?"

"Because of the necklace. Do you trust me?"

"Trust? Yeah, stop asking me that!"

"I'll figure out something better once we escape."

"Fine… Let's go. You said you had a plan, right?"

"This actually works to our advantage."

Amy didn't speak. She was done.

"Do… do you hate me?" he asked.

"No…"

"Then why are you sulking?"

"I'm not angry. I just… I hate sometimes how you always think you're right," she said. "You didn't wait for me…"

"I waited!" James interjected. "You just didn't show on time!"

"…to finish."

He stopped. She smiled mischievously.

"So… are we good?"

Amy grabbed the nurse's office door, noting the time on his pocket-watch and motioning him inside.

"Of course not," she said, smiling. "Ladies first."

***

"You have to understand," James said.

"No. I absolutely don't, young man," Ms. Oranorth retorted.

James' face contorted in frustration as he sat on the bench. Amy stood up to make her plea.

"I kept telling him you wouldn't let us," she said.

"And why would I? I run a clinic, not some store that buys you out of school!"

"But…" James said.

"No!"

James started to speak again. She cut him off.

"Absolutely not."

"I wouldn't even be asking if I didn't think it was important! You know me better than that!"

Ms. Oranorth sighed heavily. He had a point, if only a weak one. He never asked for favors. They usually just arrived at his feet wrapped up in some sort of gift-basket. But they were both out of sorts. She made up her mind.

"So why, exactly, should I believe you?"

"Because," James said, "It's about life or death."

"About what?" she asked, finally growing curious.

James sighed.

"It's… complicated."

"Try me. I've seen people die right in front of me. People I still love."

He remembered. There was no way he could forget her background. It was too powerful.

"I, I uh… sorry."

"It's not your fault."

"But it could be. That's part of what I'm trying to figure out," James said.

His answer surprised her. She started to ask another question when Amy chimed in.

"It's more than if my mom was sick, Ms. Oranorth."

"Well…what is it then?" she asked.

Amy decided to be blunt.

"He said there's an ancient demon that's been stalking me all day long. Maybe even longer than that."

"And you believe him?!" she asked incredulously.

"It makes as much sense as everything else I've gone through! And the dreams too? Somehow… It fits. And I hate it…"

Amy sat next to him, huffing. They were steaming. Ms. Oranorth was taken back by their united determination. She'd never seen her so animated about anything before; not when she'd fume about her father, and certainly not when she'd asked for counseling about her mother.

"A demon? You sure it's not just another bully picking on you?"

"Yeah I'm sure… From his books."

"I'm giving up my attendance record for this," James said.

The nurse sighed. She gave them a stern look. Neither showed any sign of backing down.

"They're serious about… whatever this is," she thought.

Ms. Oranorth reached into one her desk drawers, pulling out two orange slips of paper, filling them out with date and signature, and slid them across the desk.

"Sign them. At least do the paperwork so you won't get in trouble. Figure out your demons, I guess."

James looked at the paper with a sigh of relief and reached into his backpack for a pen. Amy snatched her favorite one from Ms. Oranorth's collection without asking. The nurse pursed her lip.

"Where… do I sign?" James asked.

"There," Amy pointed without hesitation.

The nurse raised a quizzical eyebrow, stamping Amy's pass and putting it in her file. Even not counting all the times she'd run from school through the office she still had the largest file in the cabinet. Ms. Oranorth couldn't help but see some of herself in her.

"Poor thing," she thought. "I hope this time's different."

James lifted his pen and put it away, handing his family friend the pass. She tore off the staple and handed him his copy, finally allowing herself to show concern.

"Please, be safe... I still don't really know what you're doing but I know you two enough to know it ain't dirty. Just don't do anything stupid," she pleaded.

"I can't promise that," James said.

Amy grabbed her hand, cusping the other one between her mouth and the nurse's ear.

"I think... I think it might be him? I... I'm sure of it..." she whispered.

The nurse was flabbergasted. She pulled her away.

"Really?!"

Amy felt embarrassed and pulled the nurse close again. Her voice was softer than before, little more than a song on the wind from a land on a distant shore.

"I... I think I like him."

The nurse pulled back.

"You sure?" she asked, holding her arms. "You know that means you'd be…"

Amy looked at her friend while he wasn't looking. She whispered as softly as a baby's first hairs.

"I… I've got to move on at some point, right? Got to grow up. And he… at least he makes me feel wanted. It's nice… He… I… can't tell him yet. It's too soon. But I want to… I want to show him he… I… uh… am I the right choice?"

The nurse pulled her close and hugged tightly, congratulating her.

"You two… you are perfect together. Couldn't ask for a better fairytale. He believes in you. I can see it in his eyes every time he looks over here. I get the sense he's known you a long time."

"I'm… scared… What if he doesn't… love me back? I… I just don't know if I could… I wouldn't ever be able to go home."

"Amy… my sweet. The past is the past and love is always a risk. I know he's weird… eccentric even… But he's always honest… and he's… He's intentional. Believe it or not."

"But…"

Amy sneaked a glance at her friend. James bent over to zip his backpack. Her heart raced. Everything he did was adorable.

Ms. Oranorth watched her and lightly pinched her cheek between her fingers. James slid the straps around his shoulders and stood up.

"He always makes a choice," she whispered. "It might take him time... But when he does make a choice... It's always the best one. He chose you to be his first friend here, right?"

"What?"

"Swear I'm not lying... you share a lot in common. Good luck."

Ms. Oranorth released her from the hug.

"Ready?" James asked.

"...Yeah," she replied.

Amy turned to the nurse, who was barely holding back her own tears now, instead facing a cabinet and pretending to be filing something or another. Both knew she was faking it.

"Thank you," Amy said, walking towards the front door.

"It's why I'm here."

The two ran towards their freedom. James couldn't help but be curious about what they'd said behind his back. He thought he was the only one from school who knew the nurse but apparently that wasn't the case.

"So, uh... you okay? What happened back there? How do you know Ms. Oranorth?"

"None of your beeswax."

"Oh come on," James implored.

"No. It's personal. She helped me get through a lot."

"Well, fine then. Where do want to go?"

"I'll show you."

"Lead the way, leader."

The two ran down the sidewalk as Amy struggled to make up her mind. She already had a place in the woods she could go to but letting anyone follow was an important decision. It was her special place. A place only she knew. The place she'd run to when things took a turn for the worse. He'd be the first person to lay eyes on it. But he was the first person she trusted enough to show.

They neared the entrance to the woods between her section of the neighborhood and the school in undeterred silence.

"James?"

"Yeah...?"

"I'll tell you everything. Eventually."

James eyes softened. He looked back, smiling.

"Can't ask for more than that."

29

The first thing James noticed following Amy into the woods was that it was significantly cooler, albeit quieter. It was cooler not for lack of sunlight, as it was the warmest part of the day, but it was something he'd always noticed about travelling though secret places in the past; they were always so nice and peaceful. And not freezing cold like the school. The large trees surrounding them both kept her secrets hidden and held the sunshine tightly and just out of reach. He wasn't allowed to show anyone else her secret spot. Just because she was allowing him along for the ride didn't mean he could stomp all over it.

"Where are you taking me?" he asked.

She didn't answer, instead grabbing his hand. It was an unwritten sense of unity and they were both perfectly okay with it. She allowed herself to awkwardly lean into his shoulder for a moment, pulling the tip of her nose and forehead after a brief connection.

Their hands remained loosely tied together, but strong. She felt his pulse racing back and forth like some sort of relay race with no end goal in mind.

"He feels so warm… I say that a lot now… ha…"

She made sure to gain his attention. It was easy to get lost in the woods, so much so that she was positive without her knowhow he'd get lost and be unable to get back in time for dinner. It was exactly why she'd been able to keep it secret for so long. Amy placed her palm on a nearby tree, waiting for him to notice. It took him time to pick up on the gesture. Amy removed her hand to reveal a symbol she'd carefully carved into the bark. And, while James was quite familiar with symbols, hers felt new. Try as he might he couldn't figure out what she meant by it.

"What is it?" James finally asked.

Amy traced the symbol's outline with her finger.

"This…" she said, "This is what has kept me going when nothing else has. I think it's a reminder to me of some sort."

"I don't get it," he said to himself.

"Have you ever had those times when it just seems like everything comes crashing down around you and you wonder what hell the point of it all is?"

"Yeah…"

"But you know that somewhere out there, there might be something more? Something wonderful? Waiting for you to find and explore it because no one else is willing to?"

"Yeah," James said. "It's why I write in this book. I want to help others find those special places they didn't know existed."

"But..."

James waited.

"It's more than just an adventure. It's... finding yourself. Looking back from the other side and realizing that you're different... from your old self... and from everybody else."

The symbol's meaning finally snapped together like two interlocking pieces of a wonderful puzzle. James couldn't help but feel like he'd always known the symbol's meaning now, even if he couldn't explain it. Before, it was just a key. But now, it was familiar. Dream-like. A gateway back to the lands of beyond the beyond. Amy smiled as he spoke.

"It's a bridge, isn't it?"

"Yeah. An infinite bridge."

***

Amy and James meandered along the path she'd carefully carved through the shaded trees. James paused every time he spotted one of the bridge symbols, admiring each and every one. Each was exactly the same in form and function, but each one stirred him in a different way; one might be nicked a little more on the left side, or the right. The shape was circular but not a perfect circle. But it wasn't due to her lack of effort; every stroke of her knife was pristine and clear cut, hot as fire and cold as ice.

It reminded him of The Book of Kells; how it seemed to twist and spin into itself the more one looked at it. It befuddled him even while providing limitless delight. He couldn't quite place how it the symbol made him feel; the bridge had taken him captive and he was perfectly fine with it. It wasn't stealing his emotions, but he found himself willingly drawn close to it, each piece spinning magnificently to reveal another hidden facet within her personality that, until that point in time, he'd never seen before.

James was tentative to touch the carvings as he passed them. The ephemeral light they exuded was alluring and innocent. It was perhaps the most beautiful thing in the world, untainted by the trees' rough bark.

"The path of one is loneliness. The path of two, divine romance," Amy said. "Most search for that real spark in perversity… All over the world if need be… but… they never find it. Not until they look at the life unfolding right in front of them and play their part to the fullest… even if it means getting hurt."

James didn't know what she meant by it, but somewhere deep down he understood. He felt like he'd heard it before.

"A bridge attached at one place hangs on the edge of abyss until it's picked up by another," he replied.

"Two hands, one heart," Amy whispered.

"A bridge between worlds," he said.

"Life and death," she said. "No… wait… that's not it. Life and living… yes… Death is…"

"Death doesn't matter if the bridge is connected."

"…Because you can walk right over it. Stomp death with your heel… wouldn't that make life heel-ing?"

"My puns are contagious."

"Please… I've been cracking eggs since I was a little kid. Me and my friend, we would…"

"You'd what?"

"Nothing…"

"What? Oh come on, I'm your friend now too, right?"

"Don't worry about it. It doesn't matter anymore. He's gone. I moved away. End of story."

"Well then…"

James shrugged, brushing it off with a half-smile. Even with her being upset there was something about this forest that reminded him of being a kid again. Peaceful? Yes, that was it. He felt safe here, unable to be chased away from its sanctity. Without the glow on each tree guiding them each step, that simple carving of undeterred hope, there was no path.

"James?"

"Yeah?"

"Are you sure you want to listen? Are you sure you want me to...? I can't take them back. If you don't want to listen to... I'll lead you back the way you came and we can pretend this never happened."

"You mean... pretend we never knew each other?"

"It might stop Thorne from reaching his goal any further than he already has," she said.

"Amy?" James asked.

"What...?"

"If I cared more about stopping Thorne than I did about knowing you, then I'd..."

"Then you... what...?"

"I... I think I would've stopped writing a long time ago," he said. "Before... well, before... damn this is hard."

"But... You said so yourself. You wouldn't know what to do with yourself without them."

"......"

"James?"

"Yeah... I... uh... I started it to... I wanted to..."

The sky released the beginning mist of a sun shower, slowly drifting between the trees, thankfully masking the pale blush as it appeared on their faces, tears creating channels through their twisting emotions.

"What... did you want to do?" she hesitated.

"I only started writing after I met you, okay? You left me behind and it's all I had left! There, I said it. Happy?"

"Then all this? This is... I'm just another story to you? Another one of your characters?"

"No! It's...!!! It's more than a story, alright?'

"What is this to you, then? Another one of your sadistic jokes?!"

"FINE! I started writing everything for you! Because of you... This place, the school, Thorne, Arthridall, all of it. I... It was so you wouldn't miss anything when you came back..."

"You've been doing all this... for me..."

"Yes!" James exclaimed.

"Then why? Why do it? Any of it?"

Amy stormed deeper into the forest. The greenery darkened, her pace gaining traction. James struggled to keep up with her.

"Amy! If I knew a better way to tell you everything, I would. Please stop running!"

Amy refused. It was all he could do not to lose her in the thick and interwoven patterns of her forest. James stopped to lean against one of the trees, trying desperately to catch his breath before he lost sight of her again. She was as fleeting as candle flame struggling against a harmful puff of wind. The wind stilled.

"Amy… please… come back…I wouldn't know what to do without… without… this is the best idea I've got left."

He climbed over the final hill, finding her standing in the light of the clearing. Crying. But he was there now, the tears no longer bitter or cold. She could cry on his shoulder. She could even ruin his sleeve and he'd be okay with it. That's why he came.

The trees hummed with the sound of an eternal song. It was sweet, and sad, and so incredibly vivid that anyone who dared to brave the danger would find their hearts bursting. The song, the bridge… the eternality and finality in that moment of timelessness, that thought… feeling…

Neither of them could explain it, nor cared to. To explain the mystery was to lose the wonder forever. They both knew it. The symbol she'd carved. His following her here after all this time. Him following her into the woods just like their first. That symbol, that gift. It'd finally begun revealing its true nature and the earth was rejoicing.

A never-ending cycle within a circle. The inner ring joined the sun and the moon, the seven posts of the eternal bridge spinning around in time with its own heavenly frequency. The seven stars of old watching on in admiration, grateful to look upon the king and queen's endless dance.

"Amy?"

"Hmmm?"

"We're going to make it, aren't we?" he said.

"Yeah."

"Amy?"

"Yeah?"

"I got you."

"I...I'm counting on it."

They smelled the air before they saw it. Sweet and flowery. The floral scent was otherworldly, fully bodied with strong notes and succulent tones. Like a perfect cup of coffee when needed most. The aroma invaded the upper reaches of their noses, and the fact they were experiencing the sensation together was almost completely overwhelming.

"Magnolia blossoms?" James asked.

"Yes."

"Why magnolia blossoms?"

"Shhh..." she said. "Open your eyes. Hopefully it'll explain some stuff."

James couldn't remember having closed his eyes. It must've been to balance the sensory overload.

"That smell... it's so sweet," he thought. "But it's that good kind of sweet... the kind you can't ever seem to get enough of no matter how hard you try..."

"James? You still here?" she asked.

"Yes, yes. Of course," he said.

"Then open your eyes, silly."

James blinked, allowing his eyes to adjust to the brightness of the sunlight. The clearing was blanketed in soft green grass, with a single great oak tree on a hill in the center from which one was free overlook the entirety of the surrounding forest. James couldn't help but speak.

"We're in a big circle, aren't we?"

"James, just stop talking," she chided. "This is important."

She let him off a bit.

"Yeah, it's a circle. Don't make this weird."

"No promises," he replied, grinning childishly.

"James…"

"Shhh… we got to enjoy these times when we can. Who knows what tomorrow will bring?"

"I…!!! Yeah…yeah, you're right."

The notes of the magnolia blossoms echoed and spun within themselves, the streams of wind passing through, lifting and lowering each flower according to their unique tone. Some echoed and vibrated where they were placed, remaining behind for the sake of the song; others allowing themselves to be lifted to higher levels for the sake of being marveled at by whoever cared to pay attention.

James once again held his friend's hand. She didn't pull away. They were enraptured by the experience and the mystery of the place, too energized by the quiet vibrations of the other's life to care about mutual embarrassment. They had no reason to leave, nor did they want to destroy the song they'd decided to sing.

Twelve great trees surrounded the great oak, tall and strong. Magnolia trees, with deep green leaves, wide and supple, emblematic of the unyielding nature of Amy's mysterious past that she'd led her friend to come see, held within their grasp an abundance of strong, yet delicate white flowers. He was breathless.

"Why now, of all times? Why'd she have to show me this? This was her sanctuary of sorts, and now I know how to get here… Have I stolen something? I can't give it back now, can I?"

"James, look at me," Amy said.

He did as he was told. Amy sat down, leaning back against the tree. He laid himself down on the grass next to its roots, knees pointing to the sky. He found the position surprisingly comfortable. Amy watched him intently as he adjusted, deciding to do the same.

"Ooofff…"

James felt the back of Amy's head as it squeezed a bit of air from his stomach. Amy laughed silently as James rested the side of his hand on her the top of her nose, gently prodding between the bone and cartilage. His second knuckle weighed against her cheekbone, putting a little bit of pressure near her eye, but she didn't mind. It didn't hurt. It was nice. James felt the weight of her laughter as her shoulders crested and crashed. He laughed a sigh of relief too. They were safe here.

Her laughter didn't last as long as either wanted.

"James…"

"Yeah?"

"I uh… you're the only friend I have left."

"Huh? What… what about Susan? She cares about you too, right?"

"She doesn't…"

"What?"

"She sees me as her project."

"What?"

"I uh… I'm an orphan…"

"What?"

"I live with my grandma."

"Yeah? So?"

"It's not so pretty."

James noticed some of the blossoms had fallen and already rotted from the cold.

"But I'm here now, right? Here to help."

"Well, I… I uh… Where should I start? So, I guess… My mom and I ran away from home when we couldn't take dad's abuse any longer. My dad he… he lost his job… and he… and he… I'm so sorry dumping this on you… I…"

"Amy…"

He didn't know what to say. Her tears washed into his shirt, wet with painful memories hidden deep within her heart. He forced himself to breathe slowly, trying to be strong with her. James offered his hand. She squeezed it tightly, her knuckles turning white.

"My dad… he took… he drank a lot… He blamed… he blamed us for losing his job because of it… It was his own fault but he blamed us… He blamed me for everything!"

James didn't know what to say. He hadn't heard her side of the story before, only what he'd been told by his parents after she'd moved.

"He cheated on my mom… and the other wife… she was younger and prettier… but my mom had me… and he couldn't… choose? Somehow my mom's coworker found out and told…"

"Shu sh shu shh… Amy, you need to breathe. Remember where we are. I'm still here. We have time."

It took some time for him to get through, but she eventually managed, even if she was only haphazardly gasping at first. It was as if she'd finally reached the surface of the ocean after drowning in it for far too long. She sat up to calm down, one short coughy-breath at a time. James waited patiently. She'd hinted at her rough home life before, but nothing so terrifying as this.

"Amy..." he whispered. "I'm so, so sorry."

She shuddered violently, finally managing to grasp hold of the deepest breath she could manage.

"It's... not your fault."

She curled into a ball, wrapping her arms around her legs to calm herself.

"James I... okay... I told myself today was the day to... finally tell... someone... I've been... I've been wanting to tell you ever since you punched him and... Okay... okay... so we ran away. Holidays, family, friends, you name it... We moved in with a friend until we could find a place we could afford."

"How uh... how old were you?"

"...I was nine."

"Oh my God..."

"She would've filed for divorce. But... we didn't have any money to fight the court case since everything we had was in his name. But... well we were saved, somehow. My dad had spent all the money we had... we didn't ever have much but what we had was nice. But even with all that... One night he spent it all on booze again, took too much painkiller... and in a moment of rare sobriety between vomiting he made a noose… and kicked the chair out…"

Amy choked. James rubbed her shoulders. Normally he knew better than to hug someone in pain, but she'd already buried her head in his chest an was all but begging for some human comfort. He eventually obliged. His friend was in pain. She needed help. He was here. And the only one she trusted.

"At… at least that's what the police told us. We ran away by then cause it wasn't safe. I'd like to hope that somewhere… deep down… that my real daddy was still there… That he made mistakes… yeah… but that he was sorry for everything in the end… He was the only one there so… we'll never know… But I can still hope… right?"

"There's… there's always hope."

James knew he was telling the truth, but it was hard. He knew it was right, but it didn't feel as strong as before. He spoke to reassure himself as much as for her.

"James… There's more."

"Yeah…" he said, bracing himself.

"A lot of people know about my dad. It was all over the news. But my mom… she… sh…"

"sh sh sh sh… it's okay, it's okay, 's okay. You're okay, you're safe. Sh sh sh sh…"

Amy sobbed. It was the hardest part, and the most recent.

"She got cancer four... four years ago... When the doctors told her it was terminal....... She changed. James? We used to be so happy! To have her home torn from her and told she had less than fourteen months? It's not fair! It's not fair! IT'S NOT!"

He gripped her, holding her close and shivering all at once. The poor, poor girl. He didn't know how to help.

"James... okay... okay... my mom she, she had to quit her job once it spread to her abdomen. Bedridden. They put her in a hospital bed on undetermined leave. Life insurance even covered a lot of the bills. At first she was hopeful; she decided she was going to do everything to fight it... for me. People had miraculously survived it before... Right? But she developed sores from being in bed so long...two and a half months... and... they... they got infected. Developed into small mounds... Like what?! How the hell... she was rushed into the E.R. wing to have them cut... and they were successful."

"......"

"But that surgery crushed any last hope she had. I was so excited when they told me the operation was successful... but when she came back... and she was so cold. To everyone really... She turned on me... Told me all of it... daddy... cancer... all of it... my fault. It hurt..." she cried, clutching her heart.

"But I still loved her... even as she started losing her mind. She'd lost her will to... stay alive... be with me. Ten months later, I get a call to the principal's office. Nana... drove me to the hospital to say goodbye. I walked in..."

Amy's tears fell on her coat.

"It was the first time it'd been quiet since she'd first got there... James? She spoke... barely more than a whisper but I heard it. Nana did too... Her sanity... it came back... even as... too weak to fight any...more... James? ... she said..."

Amy apologized profusely, trying to center herself. James managed a sad smile.

"I'm sorry... for lying to you... hurting you... baby... I love you... I love you...I'll always... love you. James I... I watched her die in my arms... No one knows what that feels like... that unfair... hopeless... ripping despair..."

James wiped his nose and offered her a paper-towel.

"I... I... felt the last bit of warmth leave her... like a black hole James... Nana did her best but... she wasn't momma... I was completely cold to everyone after that... even Susy..."

She finally looked into James' face and managed a feeble, whole-hearted smile, tears sliding down her cheeks.

"Until I met you... I didn't know why I wasn't taken with them when they were... well... But I know now... and... I get to keep living. For them. And for myself."

"And that's why no one's allowed here..." he said.

"Yeah..."

The sun-shower rose into more than a mist. The mist was almost pleasant, one of the best sensations either had experienced in a long time. As it was, the mist turned into a cool rain, filling the clearing with perfectly round and perfectly small drops of liquid, if such a thing were possible. They were enraptured by the almost instantaneous change. The change was energizing and they welcomed it warmly.

"And now we've come full circle," James said.

There were no words in the human language to describe it; tiny magnifying glasses, brilliantly and effortlessly dividing and combining into trails of color and awe. The rain, if it could ever truly be called that, was carried by the wind in tune with the symphony of smells from the magnolia blossoms. The place was special.

"It really is magic," Amy said. "I can't explain it... but I feel better now."

"Amy?"

"Yeah?"

"No matter what happens, I'm gonna keep you safe."

"...Really?"

"I want to... You... you've been a mystery to me ever since we met... I don't think that'll ever change. If you think I'll leave you too... well, as long as you want me around you've got me."

"James, I think... I think I love you."

James didn't have time to think. He didn't know what to think. Sure, he'd thought of telling her the very same thing over and over; it was the only thing he'd been wanting say for ages. And she'd gone and said it first.

"Have I finally found her again?"

Love. Her love for him. His love for her. Unshakeable, unchanging, staggeringly potent, indescribably wonderful. James had his answer. He'd found the passage across the chasm he'd been searching for so long, and she'd told him how to find it. She was it.

They watched the flowers rise from the grass they'd been resting on not a moment before. And, in some mysterious and magical way the soft, white petals began to take on a vivid pink hue to their edges; whether from the sunlight or by magic they didn't know. But the how of the matter didn't actually, in fact, matter. It happened, and it was beautiful. That was all they cared about. It was the first time in either of their lives that something happened and they found themselves unconcerned with how something was accomplished.

"Amy…"

She stopped him short and stood there with him, hugging him as if she were about to lose him and couldn't bear it.

"Don't say it. Every time someone says that it's because I'm about to lose them," she said calmly. "James… I'm really unsure about a lot of things… but I'm completely sure I don't to lose you too."

He so very desperately wanted to say it, to shout it out to her. They both knew he meant what he wanted to say dearly. He'd sung to her and she'd responded to his never-ending call. The wordless song, brilliantly colored and endlessly alluring. It was safety; a winter coat he'd offered her without expecting it back. It warmed her as she put the coat on, and it warmed him as she received it.

The wordless song. The sunless sunset. They were one and the same.

"Amy?"

"Yeah?"

"About everything you said earlier… on the bus… was it a dream, or was it something else?"

"I'll tell you. I'll tell you when we get back. When we're back in time. But let's enjoy eternity if only for a glimpse."

"That sounds like a wonderful idea. May I write it down?"

"Because of those silly books? Yes, yes, you may. Don't ever stop," she said, half-laughing.

"Okay. Well then… I have to tell you something very important, but I suspect somewhere deep down you already know."

"What is it?"

"If something happens... if anything ever happens to me... you know where to find me?"

"James... You mean Thor...?"

"I mean it... Here. This belongs to you."

Amy sighed. He was only trying to protect her. And protect her from Thorne.

"If anything happens... I'll come back here. No one else knows the place, but now you know the keys are the same."

"Good... Good... This, this was worth it. Let's... I hope we can run away again sometime. Never turn back or something like that. I dunno, you with me?" James asked.

"Yeah..."

"Hey Amy?"

"Yeah?"

"Wanna dance?"

"It depends."

"Depends on what?"

"It depends on how long you want to dance. It's getting late. We need to get home so our families don't start worrying."

"Amy... please... May I have this dance?"

"It depends..."

"Depends on what?"

"How long do you want to dance with me?"

"I don't want to stop. I don't ever want to stop."

"Well then," she said, pausing to offer her hand. "We should dance."

30

James looked up from his laptop as he heard an uncharacteristic thumping noise coming from one of the lower floors. He couldn't tell whether it was from the first or second floor, but it sounded very much like a book had fallen off a shelf a counter.

"Yeah, it must've been the checkout counter," James thought. "For some reason it's the only time people aren't careful handling books."

James knew it wasn't one of the librarians who'd dropped it. They treated books like most people treated their phones. It may have been a different story during the summer; they'd hired some crazy college kid who didn't know the difference between the Dewey Decimal and Metric system.

James never really understood why they'd hired him, and when he'd finally decided he cared enough about the other library patrons' sanity he asked the senior staff why the kid was still around. They told him he was a summer-intern. Whatever that was.

James stood up from his magnificent desk and walked a few feet to the balcony. He'd been right; he could hear the mother of a little child apologizing and nearby line-waiters cooing as she picked up a plethora of picture books and scoop up the ever-curious infant at the same time. The sight didn't bother him in the slightest. The kid was adorable. And it was nice to get a bit of sound inside the building every now and then; it let him know there was still life and adventure to be had both inside and outside of books.

James pulled out his pocket-watch. It was getting close to his self-designated finishing time. Quarter to eight. He had fifteen minutes left if he wanted to add any last thoughts to the book. He walked back to his throne of a chair and sat at his laptop again, seeing if he could squeeze out anything else, but nothing came.

"It's not writer's block at least. I know that much. It's just up to her to help me now. It's not a one-man operation anymore."

James had never experienced writer's block, but just because he hadn't come across it himself didn't mean he didn't know what it might feel like; he'd seen most, if not all, of his schoolmates lose out on a passing grade or two because of the disease.

James already knew the cure to the plague should he ever find himself in that most unfortunate of positions. It was easy; instead of looking within to find the answer, one had to look outside of one's self. After all, a person could only write what they knew based on past experience or research. Once a person reached the extent of their knowledge they were screwed if they refused to change and grow. The only other alternative was to imagine the future and write about that, but with that came an entirely different set of rules.

"All the what-ifs and what-nots; the possibilities of endless possibility. It only takes one fact, or even a reasonable theory, to completely change the outcome of any kind of scenario, fictitious or otherwise," James finally wrote.

It wasn't writer's block and he knew it. If he had to give it a name he'd probably call it 'being overwhelmed' with the magnitude of what he'd written.

"Or emotionally moved."

James sat in silence, gazing at his work absent-mindedly on the screen in his word processor. It was a weird feeling, looking at a screen and having his life looking back at him in the face.

"It's like talking to my inner self, but my inner self is a piece of paper," he thought. "Really is sorta-kinda like a diary, I guess."

James knew his story understood him; that it understood how he felt as he poured his heart out to Amy in his extended love-letter. It was rough around the edges to be sure, but even that fact comforted him, to the extent that the stuff he'd written was raw and real. He could edit and re-edit later and, if he were to continue his analogy, could perfect his inner man with a few clicks on the keyboard. But for the moment, the raw-ness was exactly what he wanted to show her.

"After all, she's the one who showed me what that means…"

He'd been given a great gift; to display his heart to the world if they ever chose to look. James knew his story was multilayered, as it often was. He could feel his emotion bubbling up like a spring even as his characterization of himself allowed him to feel his emotions again. The entire experience of putting it into words was overtly surreal; it was majestic. Addicting even.

It was why he kept writing even when he didn't feel like he could keep it up any longer. To stop writing about himself, what his friend meant to him, meant stopping his interaction with that part of him that struggled to speak up. He knew he was only a small character when it came to the big scheme of things. A mere speck or collection of thoughts in the entire story of eternity. But if he could help her by speaking his heart it'd all be worth it.

He was simply an Arthrindian, and he was okay with that. He was just glad he'd been allowed to glimpse that truth before his time ran out for good and his part in the mortal dimension of the tale came to an end.

He felt that her characterization was accurate as well. He felt it within himself, to the very core of his being. His friend. His existence brought her story to life. But she needed to tell it.

"It's not her reality though. It might be accurate but it's not real."

That thought had been bottled up inside for so long, desperately waiting to be revealed. For the moment his reality, the reality of his story, and his characters solely belonged to him.

"Only for the moment, I hope."

Sure, he'd shown his family bits and pieces of it along the way. He'd even shown Ms. Tammy some of it for her input on her character, but none of them had all the pieces yet. He didn't even have all of them yet, so there was no way he'd be willing to push something like that on his audience even if they were rooting for him. He knew the rest of the pieces were there, waiting to be revealed by his best friend.

Bottled up somewhere deep, the full story waited to be unburied by his insatiably curious audience; shown to the face of the world in an epic parable, but only revealed to the people who looked within with their hearts and ignored their minds.

"They won't get it, I'm sure. They can try, but then again I can only reveal so much without losing everything."

He knew it in his heart. His story wouldn't be complete without her. Now that she was in the picture again he couldn't imagine a world, or any number of worlds, or stories, or adventures, or anything, without her there to explore with him. Even if he could, he didn't want to. He only wanted to write because of her. Arthridall, because of her.

If James didn't need his friend to help him finish the book might've simply been a story about Amy and her trials and over-comings. He wouldn't need to be there in her story, really. If anything, he was no more than a guardian angel. She was the real main attraction, and she'd always been the main attraction. He was little more than a spring-board for her to bounce her thoughts back and forth on. A fire starter for the main events to follow when he was no longer around. Or a chronicler looking within, writing, creating, his story as best he could. At least until she could stand up and they could combine as one, single story.

"That's it!" He exclaimed.

James hunkered down at the flurry of irritated hushing's from the library patrons a few floors below.

"Oh, so cute kid gets a free pass and I get torches and pitch-forks. Figures." He whispered.

But he didn't really care about their anger. He'd finally put together some of the most important pieces.

"The reason I started writing in the first place. The portals to Arthridall. For Amy."

It only made sense to share with her. But now, not after he'd finished it. It was just like in the book; it wouldn't be complete if she didn't have a say as it was being made.

"That's what it was lacking," James thought. "I guess I don't have a choice. I need to show her if it's going to be finished, and she has to co-write it. That's the only way it'll make sense, now that I think about it. It's only half a story without her."

James felt the electricity of the ramifications race up and down his back, finally turning off his laptop and packing his belongings as he got ready for his mom to pick him up. It was time to leave, after all.

"This is only one side of the bridge," he thought, "and she's on the other side. It's up to her what happens next. And I'll be waiting."

***

"Hi, honey! You must be hungry," Mary said as her son shut the door behind him with a metallic click.

"Yeah, starving," he replied.

"Anything exiting happen today?"

James fastened his seatbelt, feeling quite contemplative. Mrs. Pensworth eyed her son, checking for any sign of distress. She didn't note any; as far as she could tell he was surprisingly relaxed.

"James?"

"Yeah... I, Uh... I made a friend today, if that's what you mean."

His mom smiled.

"Is she cute?"

"What? There's no way it was that obvious! There's no way you could've known my friend's a girl!"

Mrs. Pensworth smirked and refused to say anything, letting her son stew over his statement. She waited.

"Well if you didn't know before... you know for certain now, don't you?"

"Bingo."

"Well... yeah... I have a friend now I guess. Maybe two, but it seems to me that I'm going to have to choose."

"They're not fighting over you, are they?"

"What?! No way! Susan's too into lacrosse to be into guys right now. I don't know about Amy yet."

"Her name's Amy? How adorable!"

"What?! Oh, for crying out loud..."

"Does she like you yet?"

"Uh... she sat down with me at lunch today. She liked my lunchbox... and we've been talking a little, so I guess we get along, I suppose. Her liking me... well... who knows?"

"She's a keeper."

"That's what Ms. Tammy said when I was getting coffee. I know she's a keeper, and I've been doing everything I can to convince her of that. It's complicated..."

"Have you told her you how you feel yet?" she asked.

"No. What? Wait! I didn't tell you anything about me liking her!"

"Relax, I'm not going to spill the beans before you do."

"What?"

"You are going to tell her, right?"

"Tell her what?"

"That you like her."

"We're only friends!"

"Oooo... kay... if you say so. I'm just having fun being your mom. No need to get defensive."

"I'm not...!"

James stopped himself before falling into another trick question.

"I'll tell her eventually... It's going to be a shock though."

"Good man. I believe it. Let's celebrate with some pizza."

"Really? I haven't really done anything yet."

"Doesn't matter, my treat. You deserve it. And don't sell yourself short. You finally found your friend again, right? I know it wasn't easy, but you persevered and finally got social."

Mrs. Pensworth grinned.

"It's about time someone pulled you out of your turtle-shell. I was getting worried you'd made yourself a permanent isolation chamber."

"What? I wasn't isolating myself! People are just... I wasn't! Well fine! If you insist."

She sighed, smiling knowingly as they pulled up into the driveway. James shook his head; he hadn't been isolating himself. He'd just been waiting for some solid quality people.

"It took way too long... yeah I guess it might seem like... No, I wasn't! Other people just weren't quite sincere enough," he thought.

"You still ordering pizza? Because I'm still eating the pizza." he said finally.

"I insist."

"Ahhh! Mom, stop it."

"No. I'm your mom. It never stops. I'm too proud of you."

31

James blinked. Last night's pizza was delicious and he couldn't wait to dig into the leftovers.

James waited, sitting at his favorite bench in the school courtyard, patiently staring at the heavy, mint green doors that led to the warm, gooey interior. He congratulated himself for his work regarding the mental promotion for the recently discovered species of unisloth. He'd already decided the unisloth was originally endangered and by his efforts alone had managed to save the new emerging breed.

"Of course they're endangered. All the cool and exotic animals always are. It's the only way to get any sort of real publicity anymore for support. Hardly anyone looks up from their phones anymore to help."

He'd start by selling tee-shirts with baby unisloths on the front and a catchy phrase on the back so they could start trending. Tee-shirts were easy enough to make, and once he'd made enough money off those he could expand the line-up to stuffed animals, jewelry, ring-tones, documentaries, comic books, children's television shows, theme parks; the possibilities were endless.

"All so we can support healthy breeding programs and help them survive again in the wild."

James knew the plan was surefire because people liked to help cute animals and be stylish at the same time. And he could use his power as a writer for a good cause and be the guy who got to create the slogans and catch-phrases. It was a foolproof plan.

James opened his lunch and examined its contents. It wasn't anything special other than his couple slices of leftover pizza. The ones he'd purposely saved for the purpose of eating today. The ones he was thinking about so lovingly that he'd already finished them and had gone on to eat his 'real-fruit' cup.

"Dang."

***

Amy walked out through the main entrance to scout the courtyard ahead of time. As luck would have it, she 'forgot her coat', having left it inside her locker for 'mysterious reasons' known only to the world of girl minds. Amy peeked around the corner; He was there, absentmindedly pondering the meaning of life, or some other existential something-rather she had no possible frame of reference for.

"Or he's not thinking about anything at all," she thought. "No matter, he's got a coat. And I want."

James juiced down on a bite of 'real-pineapple', blinking for a second or two, apparently staring into space, or the mint-green steel doors sitting some distance away across the courtyard, whichever was closer.

"He's probably waiting for me to come through there to meet him. Yeah, that's got to be it," Amy thought.

She watched James as he carefully set his 'fruit-stabber' down and leaned back against the bench, arms spread wide along the bench's length. Amy sighed wistfully. She had so much she wanted to tell him. She wanted to ask him what he liked and disliked, what he wanted to do with his life, where he wanted to travel and see. He was innocent, curious, and full of life, and for some reason he'd decided to protect her from being bullied when no one else had stepped in to help.

"I need to know why. I don't want to find out that he's actually just crazy."

Before she had the chance to ponder the thought, James looked directly at her from her hiding spot, and winked. Amy pulled back into the corner, heart beating heavily. Whether from fear or exhilaration she wasn't sure.

"He's crazy. I knew it. There's no way he could've seen me... I was hiding!" she thought, then wondered.

"Did he really just wink at me? That's so cheeky!"

Amy peeked around the corner to spy again. James was leaning over his lunchbox, apparently munching on his crust-less sandwich in four-fourths time, trying to keep the crumbs from spilling in his lap due to his two-hundred forty beats-per-minute tempo.

"He eats like a rabbit! Adorable!"

She laughed. Other than his atrocious eating habits when she wasn't around, nothing about his demeanor gave any reason for suspicion.

"Did I just imagine it?"

She calmed down. He wasn't the one acting crazy, she was. Amy took a deep breath, holding and releasing it slowly to steady her heart while peeking the corner again. He was happily crunching on a bag of potato chips without a care in the world.

"Why am snooping around when we could already be talking? I'm getting ahead of myself. I'm overthinking it."

Amy picked up her bag and walked over, nervous with anticipation.

"Hey friend. Want a seat?"

"Hey James. Sure."

Amy sat down and began eating. She'd made sure to make one the night before so she wouldn't be a burden. They sat quietly, soaking in the pleasant vibes and wishing one of them knew how to swing an ice pick. The only sound they heard came from the distant sound of laughter from inside.

They both looked up. James smiled.

"Sounds like Susy's leading another food fight."

"Yeah... wait, you know Susy?"

James pushed down on the metal clip on his lunchbox.

"How do you know Susy? I'm serious. We haven't been friends all that long, James."

James leaned back and looked up at the overcast sky.

"I can't tell if it's going to snow or rain tonight."

"Hello?"

"It'll snow. It's getting too cold for rain now."

"James?" Amy asked. "Please?"

James turned his attention back to his friend and smiled slightly. And a bit sadly.

"Long story."

Amy furrowed her brow as she pondered his answer.

"What do you mean?"

"If you want to know anything about me... all you have to do is ask," he said finally. "There's no reason to spy. It proves lack of trust."

She didn't know what to say. He was right. Amy felt guilty. A knot formed in her stomach, quickly diminishing as her curiosity returned. He wasn't condemning her; he was simply stating facts. For all she knew he was only talking about his connection to her friend.

"Maybe he met her when I wasn't around or something. I don't know," she thought. "But he's not really the type of guy she hangs out with."

"Amy?"

Amy startled, returning to the conversation.

"Yeah, sorry. I'm fine. Didn't mean to pry."

"You're really cute when you spy around corners."

"Thanks, I was just curious how you knew her and…."

She stopped.

"You saw that, huh?"

James nodded.

"I… Oh… this is embarrassing."

"Amy…"

"I'm so sorry…I…"

"What would you have done about Astwin?"

"I, uh… what? If you hadn't punched him? I don't know. I don't know if I could've done anything else if you hadn't showed up. I didn't want to get hurt but I didn't see any other way to save that girl… I can't remember her name."

"I see… Then are… we only friends because I saved you?"

"I'm terrible with names… Oh! Uh…"

She didn't know what to say. Sure, it meant a lot that he'd stepped in for her, but was that the only reason she was sitting with him? He seemed to be putting a bunch of weight on the question. She didn't know.

"I... well... That's pretty loaded, bro..."

She couldn't remember having known him before the past few days. He didn't know about her, or her past, or her family, or anything really, so that was out as well. But something, something deep inside, told her it wasn't anything she'd done wrong. He was struggling with something.

"That has to be it, and for some reason I'm the only one he wants help from," she thought.

"I know I haven't known you that long, but also feel like I've known you my entire life..."

He watched her intently. Silently brooding on something important.

"I... I mean... sorry...Gosh... that sounds weird. I don't know... It just feels right being here... You're my friend. No no no... I think that fight was just the beginning... but I think we were meant to be friends regardless."

James smiled.

"I was hoping you would say that."

"Why?"

"Because that was my thought as well."

"Do you really think I'm cute?"

"Amy…"

He paused, sighing.

"I need to ask you something important."

"I…I uh… that's okay… Yeah, fire away."

"Would you let me protect you if someone worse than Astwin were to try to hurt you?"

Amy looked at him, confused, wondering what he meant by it.

"Is he about to cry?" she thought.

"Well… I'm not sure you really know me since we haven't known each other long… but, well you see, I'm not entirely unused to getting hurt… I… I'm actually quite used to getting hurt… and when you stepped in I felt human again for the first time since I moved from my old neighborhood."

"I see… That may be true, but it's not what I asked… Would you let me protect you again if it were to happen?"

"I… uh…"

Amy felt flustered. And confused.

"What's he trying to say?"

"Well…" she said finally. "You've got my permission if that were the case. But… it's ultimately your choice whether you protect me."

"Well, in that case," he said, "I want you to have this."

James reached into his pocket, and after opening her palm, placed a small, silver piece of jewelry into it, closing her fingers around it.

"Don't ever lose it," he said.

Amy opened her hand, puzzled by the strangely wonderful gift.

"What is it?" she asked. "I feel like I've seen…"

"It's a piece of jewelry. Something I made a while back for someone special," James replied.

"Ah, wait… No, I mean… what is it? It seems… familiar somehow. Does it mean something?"

James finally allowed himself to smile.

"It means a lot of things. Hopefully we'll be able to figure it out together. But for now," he said standing up and brushing off the crumbs, "call it my promise to keep you safe."

"Oh…"

"I uh… well, may I help you put it on?"

Amy considered his proposal for what seemed like an eternity.

"Of course. It's your promise. I guess it's my job now to make sure I don't lose it."

She smiled. James took the necklace and unclasped the latch gently. She lifted her hair so it wouldn't catch.

"I won't lose it. Not now, not ever. You made your promise," she said, letting it rest in her hand again. "And I get the privilege to decipher it with you as long as I don't lose it, right?"

James stepped back after he finished closing it. Amy let her hair down and smiled at him

"I promise you've put it in good hands."

"I know," James replied. "It's why you're the one I made it for."

32

James plopped down in front of the bench and crossed his legs, supporting himself with his palms.

"So, tell me about yourself. I want to make sure I get to write you in properly," he said.

Amy wiped a drop of juice from the corner of her mouth with a napkin and moved her lunchbox to the recently vacated space on the bench. James couldn't stop grinning.

"What?"

"I'm glad you're my friend."

"Oh... Ha! Well, uh, what do you want to know?" she asked.

He laughed.

"You are so weird."

"Of course I am. I'm a guy so by definition..."

"That's not what I meant."

He raised an eyebrow.

"Maybe I should talk first then, seeing as I'm apparently the weird one."

Amy pulled out her pack of 'real fruit gummies', beginning to eat them all at once.

"I can be weird too!" she exclaimed through the chewy cacophony.

James made a funny face to get her to laugh. She almost choked, but didn't. She kept chewing with a pout. He pretended to stop laughing but his body language gave him away.

"I could've died! Don't do that!"

"But you didn't die, did you?"

Amy huffed. He wasn't wrong. She waited for him to speak. James didn't answer and instead pulled out his pocket-watch, looked at it, and put it away again. He grabbed the backpack sitting on the ground next to him and, after leaning against it, closed his eyes and began dozing off. She was semi-mad but decided against giving into it.

"Probably another ploy to antagonize me," she thought.

She turned to her lunch and started eating again with the precious time she wasn't getting pestered. It was a nice feeling, being with a guy who didn't seem to have a care in the world. She decided against her better judgement to sneak a glance lest he catch her with some sort of prank.

"How is he actually sleeping already? Holy cow," Amy thought. "That's impressive."

James hadn't moved and was snoring lightly as far as she was could tell. James half opened an eye when she wasn't looking. It was a nice feeling, being with a girl who wasn't afraid of him, or his weirdness for that matter. He closed his eye again and soaked it in; it was nice.

"I'm not alone anymore. Maybe I have been isolating myself all this time. Maybe that's what Thorne's been after all along."

James allowed his thoughts to wander as he began falling asleep. A couple minutes later he heard her lunchbox zipper. He wondered if she was going to leave since he was napping, but decided it wasn't something he could see her doing. A rustling sound accompanied by the soft thump of her lunchbox hitting the pavement confirmed it. James put his hand behind his head and patted her head softly. Amy giggled as her hair tickled her nose.

"I was right," he thought. "After all this time, I've finally found you."

James felt his heart swell with emotion. He didn't know what to think or say anymore, but at the same time it didn't matter. After a while she spoke up.

"It's funny," she said.

"What is?"

"This actually isn't the first time I've laid on the ground with someone like this. Isn't that weird?"

"Nah."

"It was a long time ago… before I moved from my old house. I was really young then… And I guess I didn't think about what other people thought about me all that much."

"What changed?"

Amy paused, considering how to break into it without scaring him off. She'd scared so many people off.

"I don't know. Wait, well…some uh, real hard family stuff started happening…"

"Ah…"

"Long story short… I had to run away with my mom… my mom passed away, and here I am."

"Got it."

Amy sat upright from the shared backpack and looked at him.

"What? You don't want to know all the crazy details?"

"Not if you aren't comfortable telling."

"I don't think I'll ever be comfortable talking about it."

"Then tell me when you're ready."

"Uh… yeah… I'll tell you when I'm good and ready, then."

"Glad to hear it," James said, standing up and offering his hand.

She gladly took it.

"We're gonna be late for class."

"Yeah…"

James walked toward the cafeteria.

"Hey."

"Yeah?"

"Could… would you mind walking me home from school? Same neighborhood, right? I don't want to take the bus…"

"It would be my privilege."

"Really? I mean awesome… Thanks."

33

James sat on the front steps of the school waiting for her, wondering how he was going to break into the tougher subjects without causing harm. He knew she was so close to breaking into new territory, rather, his fictionalized version of her character. It wasn't to say that his characterization of her wasn't inaccurate. He felt like he was staying pretty accurate, even though he knew deep down he could only tell their story from his point of view.

"But what she said at lunch... I remember laying down like that too. Maybe the necklace will help jog her memory."

His characterization of himself in his story was also fully aware of the fact. There was James, the author in the real world trying to write a book to win the heart of a fair maiden, and there was James, the fictional version he'd created to win the fictional Amy's heart.

"But if my fictional-self is actually me in every aspect just on paper and makes all the same decisions I would... because I write it like that... man! Why does it have to be this complicated?!"

"You okay?" Amy asked.

"WHOA! Hah… you startled me."

"Sorry. I ended up spending a little too long fiddling with my locker combo. Stupid thing kept jamming up on the seven. Wai… I was saying… Are you okay?"

"Yeah… Long story."

"Well, we could take the long route home so you can tell me all about it. I usually understand… complicated."

James stood up, sliding a shoulder under one of the straps.

"Yeah… I believe it."

"Your zipper's open."

She grabbed the corner of his backpack and carefully pulled it shut. He thanked her, raising his hand against the surprisingly bright rays of the late afternoon sun.

"The sun peaked after all," James said.

"Yeah… I guess it di…"

James sneezed violently, spraying a fine mist of bodily fluids all over the place.

"Oh man, that hur…"

He stopped, realizing he'd misted her right in the face. Amy blinked, wiping from cheek to chin with the side of her sleeve without a word.

"I am so, so, sorry," James said, flustered.

Amy grabbed her backpack.

"Ah crap," James thought.

"Here," she said, handing him a tissue travel-pack.

"Oh uh… thanks."

"No problem."

They started walking to the street. He tried thinking of some possible way to break the silence. Some way to apologize that might dampen the grossness he'd inflicted. No relief.

"I… Uh…" he started. "I…"

Amy turned, shielding herself as James violently sneezed again in her direction, which also happened to be the direction of the sun. She laughed.

"Photosensitive much?"

"Yeah, very." he replied, grateful she didn't seem angry.

"I almost lost it laughing when you sneezed the first time, but I figured you needed to suffer a bit first. Let you stew in your failure and all that."

"You aren't mad?"

"It takes a lot more than a sneeze to phase me. Please."

"Well, I gue…"

"Don't… ever do it again. Got it?"

James immediately started apologizing again but the sight of her super-serious face barely hiding a grin gave her away.

So he didn't say anything. He picked up a stick laying on the side of the road, raking it along the fence-line and hoping to break the silence with it.

"Even after a warning... I can't tell if she's serious. She's good."

They decided to stop in the park on their way after realizing neither had any important commitments that needed immediate attention. By some mysterious reasoning, premeditated or not, it was how they convinced themselves to stop and actually hang out for a while.

He climbed the slippery monkey bars as she looked on but ran over to the swing set and sat down as soon as his attention was drawn to it. Amy joined in on his child-like joy-parade. Neither had much to say, nor did they want to for the moment, instead climbing to the furthest height the swing-set chains allowed. The connections on the ends of the swings squeaked in perfect sync until James finally tired out from his forced and apparent over-excitement. Amy soon let her energy divert as well, her victory finally on the swings allowing her to slow down too.

"Where do I begin?" James started, the chains slowly swaying in the late autumn breeze.

She sighed.

"I guess you should start from the beginning."

"Yeah, that's a good starting place I guess..."

Amy ran her fingers through her hair to detangle the ferocious beast. James watched, eyes glazing over but snapping back whenever she looked at him expectantly.

"Okay, the beginning. So... I'm a writer. Not that it means much, but well, uh... you know. It's something I like to do, I guess."

"Oh! Nice."

James laughed even though he was already embarrassed.

"Right now... I'm in a conundrum... I have a bunch of parts that make sense on their own but every time I try putting them together... well, I know they're going to fit somehow, but for whatever reason they don't quite seem to click."

"Well, explain the pieces first then. Maybe I can help figure out how they fit or at least give some suggestions."

"Ironically that's exactly why I wanted to talk. I need your help."

"Really?"

"Yeah. Anyways..."

James took another breath.

"I don't know, it's just... every time I try telling it to myself it makes perfect sense and I get really excited, you know? But whenever I try to put it on paper it gets super confusing."

"Sounds like you have too many pieces then. Or they need a common theme. Sorry, keep going."

"So, I guess I'll start with the first parts and build off of those..."

Amy nodded.

"Okay. So I'm a writer, historian... I like to write about worlds. You could say I live in them. Wait that's getting ahead of myself. I'm an author. That's the first piece. I've always loved reading, but it wasn't until a few years ago that I got the idea to start writing my own. It came from the desire to make something better than the ones I was reading. I always wanted to change things and make the plot flow better... add important details, change the endings, settings, times... anything really. I wanted to write my own stories because I felt I could make better ones."

"I get that! It's like... it's exactly like all the stuff in movies or performances that's not scripted but ends up making the entire show that much better."

"Yeah! Exactly that! I know, right? So, after lots of brainstorming and daydreaming I started writing ideas down for stories all over the place... sticky notes, random papers, my computer... you name it, I've done it."

"Niiice..." Amy said.

"So," James continued, "My first idea was for a trilogy. It'd be in a different place than earth and have all the things a good story needs; strong underdog heroes, villains, action, adventure, romance, you name it... it had it in there somewhere."

"So what happened? Start changing your mind?"

"No... not that at all... I guess... after a while I realized the stuff in the trilogy started looking a lot like stuff I'd read or seen before. I was having a real hard time trying to figure out how to be new and different."

"Not just for the sake of being different, I hope."

"No, no... I don't know. I just... I knew I could make it better. Yeah, So I wanted to write so I could be true to myself. And... the trilogy... after a lot of work I started figuring it out. It revolves around the idea that there's more to life than meets the eye. Parallel worlds, or dimensions, or something like that... And portals that go between them."

"How many worlds?"

"A lot. As many as I wanted to. But the trilogy made sense to keep it at three since there'd be three worlds."

"Got it. That's actually clever!"

"What? Of course it's clever. The first realm was Earth. The second Arthridall. And King's home of course. And each realm represents a piece of a human."

"You lost me."

"Oh, sorry. The parts of a human: physical body, the mind and its emotions, and the spirit?"

"Oh."

"Earth is body, Arthridall, the battle of the mind, and the spirit is the king's realm. King's House."

"Ah…"

"I'm sorry, I know it's a lot. Unfortunately that's not even the tip of the iceberg."

"It kind of makes sense… a little… Maybe."

"Yeah… so after a while of entering the world of my stories, I realized it would actually be impossible to fully explain it to an audience in a way it could really make sense. Or, at least, making those worlds as real and vivid for them as they were for me, being a historian of sorts in those worlds if you will."

"It makes sense if you're the one bringing them to life, I guess."

"Yes!"

"Yes?"

"Hmm… It was as if… I wanted the people who read the books to live in the worlds I'd created alongside me. I don't know how else to explain it."

"You wanted the places you made to be just as real as this world for someone other than you?"

"Yes! Exactly!"

James swung around on his swing, excited someone was finally starting to understand.

"Anyways... Long story short, I created the universe of those books, and found myself constantly thinking about things I could fix in them, and change them, or add onto if I wanted to tweak it."

"That's understandable. You should see me put on all those different masks in my rehearsals. Or all the lines we end up switching! It's a lot of work, sure, but it usually tends to pay off."

"It felt like I was living in this imaginary universe I'd made more often than living in the real world. My universe was just as real to me as living here."

"Did he listen to anything I just said?" she thought.

"But that's good, right?" Amy asked. "It means the places you create are believable. People can relate to that."

"Well, that's where it gets tricky. I made a huge mistake in judgement."

Amy leaned back in her rubber swing-seat, letting her hair brush against the dirty mulch underneath.

"How so?" she asked.

James furrowed his brow, trying to figure out how to explain it without losing her again. He found the idea almost insurmountable, and he couldn't think of anything other than explaining the entire truth all at once and hoping for the best. Amy sat back up in her swing, watching him.

"He looks confused."

"Alright… okay, here goes," James said.

"Ready."

"So, in order to fix the problems I'd made for myself in the trilogy universe I started writing another book."

"Without finishing your trilogy first?"

"Yeah."

"But why?"

"Let me finish," James said, his eyes squinting against the slowly dimming rays of sunshine that raced across the horizon like a field of racehorses.

"So this book is before the other ones, and a completely separate storyline I think… but it has crossovers so the readers can follow what was going on in any of the books. Primarily…"

"Because people love crossovers?"

"Well, the new book is an origin story about us written by my daughter in Arthridall. In a future part of time, of course."

"I… What?!"

"But it's completely separate from her part in the trilogy of books I'll be writing since I'm only sixteen."

"James!"

"Yeah?"

"Let me answer you."

"Sorry," James said. "I tend to get carried away."

"I noticed you looked at m... anyways, I think I get what you mean," She said, putting on the jacket she'd refused to wear earlier. "This new book... it's like a bridge to the other ones... a book someone can read if they want so the universe of your other books can be as real to them as it is to you."

"Yeah, when you put it that way."

James laughed. Amy shook her head.

"I don't see how it's actually that complicated James. Aren't origin stories a bit cliché?"

"YES! Yes! Exactly! So now, here's the kicker."

She sat back down and rocked back and forth as the early-evening wind died down.

"Lay it on me, bro."

James leaned in while remaining on his swing, like some sort of side-to-side 'swing-chariot'.

"That book, my daughter's diary so-to speak, is written about the universe... of this world..." he said, stamping his foot on the ground.

"Explain."

"The real world. This world. I made myself the main character in my fictional world, which is actually this world… and it's written from the perspective of my daughter."

"So… the fictional you is actually the real you? Then this is…" Amy asked. "That sounds like a cliché cloning thing though…"

James started to speak but she kept going.

"OH! I get it! Hee hee hee! I get it. Then you could interact with the other fictional worlds that you, the writer you, eventually finish making, both in this real world… and in the fictional, real world…"

"Yeah… I…"

"Literally pulling your readers into the other universes because the book is based in the fictional Earth, so to speak…. Which is entirely based off of…"she stomped her foot.

"But… I…"

"This world. Then they enter your universe completely because they exist in this world. Earth."

"Yeah… I guess so. You got it right on the mark…"

"What's wrong?"

"I…"

James shrugged.

"I wanted to finish so I could understand it for myself too. It's just so complicated. Or at least… it was complicated until you explained everything."

"Oh…"

Amy sighed. She'd jumped the gun.

"But it's nice to have someone to talk with again," she thought.

"Sorry… I guess I got excited."

"It's fine."

"No, I'm serious James."

"I know. Not your fault. It's crazy cool stuff. And that's not even all of it."

"Seriously?

He grinned.

"I'll get to it eventually. I leave it at this… the other universes, or realms, or whatever I made… I didn't actually make them myself. King showed them to me and asked if I wanted to write about them as if they were fictions."

"Who?"

"King."

"His name is King?"

"You could say that."

"What?"

"Only his friends call him that. A nickname of sorts… but not really. Most people here call him something else."

"Ah… Sounds like Thorne, or whatever he's called."

"Eh… Not really. Thorne stole King's idea and twisted it."

"Even so, it seems absolutely brilliant!"

"I know."

"I'm serious, man! I don't think it's ever been attempted before. It's exactly what you were wanting to do, right?"

She stood, pacing around in excitement. James shrugged.

"I guess so. I mean, pretty much all my ideas for the stories come from King. He's the mastermind, I guess.

"But you transport readers into the books by making them a part of the stories? By writing an entire story about real life… whatever that really means… just as a book, right? So the books can interact with other fictional realms? I'm serious, James. That's amazing. Even if they aren't all your ideas."

"Thanks Amy."

"Yup!"

James rolled around.

"Because of her diary, my diary, I can make everything or anything I experience on real Earth just as real to someone else as to me, simply because they both actually exist here…" he said, "and in the fictional real world. Which is connected to the other worlds, or books. Especially Arthridall."

"Hey, it's getting dark now. We should start walking."

"But I..."

"You can explain it more later. Come on."

"But..."

"Come on, man."

"Fine... You're right.... as usual... Let's go."

They began walking to the sidewalk. A long line of short, dark-green hedges lined the space between the park and the path before them. Amy squeezed through one of the few gaps that'd worn down over time. James followed her lead.

"Hmph..."

"What?" Amy asked.

"Nah, don't worry about it. I never noticed how many trees this park had until now. It reminds me of another place."

"Ah," she said. "Hey James..."

"Yeah?"

"I don't understand why you're having so much trouble with it all. I mean yeah, you haven't finished your other stories so yeah... It'd make sense this one wouldn't have quite the full effect you want yet."

"I know that."

"Until you fully address the connections between the crossovers... But the new book has an entire storyline of its own, right?"

"Yes..."

"So what's the problem?"

"Well... that book isn't quite finished yet..."

"Oh... well... why not?"

"How do I say it... um... well, it used to progress exactly how I wanted it to. I'd go to the library after school for hours and, I mean... I made that place my second home mind you... and wrote a lot. But then I introduced the fiction version of myself to someone... and, well..."

"Well what?"

"It started out great. At first it was awkward. But eventually we both decided it was nice being friends."

"What does that have to do with it?"

"Well, eventually my friend... well... she started opening up about her past, and I realized I'd been there... the places she kept talking about with fond memories... That I was the friend she'd left behind... And my daughter was..."

"Hey, what's wrong?"

James shrugged. He was tired from being unused to talking so much.

"It's uh... well... We eventually figured out we'd been friends when we were kids and got separated when she had to move away for... a lot of reasons. So I decided... even as a little kid... I'd chase after her somehow."

"James... that sounds like..."

"That somehow... I'd convince my parents we needed to move, or something... anything..."

"Come on. Keep walking, buddy. It's already pretty much dark."

"I needed to do everything to find her again. She was my friend... and got stolen from me for reasons I didn't understand at the time... until she told me about her parents..."

"James, please."

James stumbled haphazardly, still lost in thought.

"I knew... I knew I had to protect her from getting hurt any more... It was killing me... And the only way I knew how to cheer her up was making stories about fantastical worlds where good triumphs over evil... just like we used to before she left."

"James... please keep walking... I don't want to see you cry..."

"So I told her told her those stories... Amazing worlds we could go to whenever we wanted to escape... And we could fight evil there... and we were good so we'd always win..."

"JAMES!!!"

Her shouting shook him from his sob fest. She grabbed hold and hugged him tightly, head buried in his arms. He pulled away.

"Please… Not you too… not you too… Every damn time I open up to someone even a little… they either run away or I make them cry or they turn it on themselves… I hate it! I hate my life! Stop!"

"The evil I'd written about tore open portals to the real world… twisting and manipulating the connections between his universe and ours… even breaking some of them… perhaps beyond repair…"

"James, stop! I need you to calm down. Please! Those are just stories. This is real… right?"

"And… that evil tried destroying me in order to take over my world too… by making me choose…"

Amy sighed, seeing he wasn't listening. She released her embrace.

"Dare I ask? Will you listen then?"

He rubbed his forehead.

"I decided… no, that's not it. Thorne decided to go after my only friend and kill her to steal her power… I had shown her the paths to the other universes so she could explore with me… because I'd made her my co-author… she had power…

to rewrite the entire universe we'd made together if she wanted to..."

"Walk with me."

He stopped walking. Amy didn't notice until she turned around.

"So I had to make a choice... a choice that would determine everything that would happen from that point on..."

Amy walked back and grabbed his hands.

"Whether to let Thorne murder my friend and lose the only reason I'd started writing to begin with... or join the ranks of people who'd broken her heart... and trust my sacrifice would give her enough strength to power it all the way through to the end..."

She wiped away a tear. He was obviously distressed about the choices he had to make if he wanted to progress. She didn't quite understand why he was making all the fuss about a book, but she figured it probably had something to do with the bizarre meta-world he was making.

She understood where he was coming from. But still, it was unnerving how emotional he was being about it. The strangest part was she couldn't help but feel a bit emotional too. Amy gathered the courage to speak, hoping her words would somehow help him make up his mind.

"I'll help you see it through to the end if you'll let me..."

James finally looked up. Amy took it as a good sign.

"What?" he asked.

She handed him a tissue.

"I want to see the choices you end up making."

"Oh… I see…"

"You alright now?"

James looked at her.

"Do you mean what you say?"

She forced a smile, hoping to cheer him up from his emotional slump.

"I always mean what I say," she said finally.

"…… I… I know you do…"

James tried returning a half-hearted smile.

"Thanks Amy… look at me… ha ha… making all the hard life-choices…"

"You can do it."

"Only if you help."

"Deal," she said, patting him on the back.

They began walking again, the cold setting into their bones deeply as the sun's last rays shed their final light over the little slice of Earth they'd made their friendship on. He asked if he could hold her hand again. Amy gladly complied, taking it a step further and cuddling into the jacket she'd been longing to sneak into all day.

"He feels so warm…"

Amy blushed, glad he wasn't aware of how enraptured she was by him and his story-stuff. She'd found someone truly special and was glad her input was wanted for once. She was wanted. It was nice.

"It's okay. At the end of it all those are just stories, right? Fictional characters can only die fictional deaths. Saving real people from real death is way more important than saving characters from fictional fates. It'll be okay. You'll find a way to make it work. I know you will."

34

James could feel the weight of his decision weighing him down like a millstone crushing grain. It was heavy, impossibly heavy. But there wasn't any other way he could see.

"Even she agrees," he thought. "And she doesn't even know the story is all for her."

He looked over to his friend who, upon further inspection was lost deep in thought about one thing or another. Amy's complete lack of concern about anything threatening her anymore was written all over her demeanor, and it had the wonderful effect of allowing him to escape his own fear if only for a moment.

Somehow, he felt deep down her feelings were generally more elevated than his somehow, and after some intense inward reasoning decided it was because she was the pretty one. Hence the need to compete with the queen to regain his crown.

James shook his hair as if he'd gotten cobwebs in his face.

"You okay there, buddy?" she asked.

"Jealous?"

"All you did was flip your hair. I didn't even know we were competing."

"Bite me. I'm the prettiest."

"Oh yeah?"

Amy let her hair down and whipped him with the brunt of it, catching his face with her vastly superior hair products. She laughed. James didn't care that she'd beat him, allowing himself instead to be transported away by how good the air now smelled. Something about a little competition made him feel comfortable again.

He needed to make sure she was unaware of the choice he still needed to follow through on. Even with calmer nerves, every time he looked ahead the choice was still there, like some steaming pile of refuse with a mind of its own. It wanted to swallow him whole every time he braved a glance in its direction.

"I need time to think! Crap... I need to think..."

James knew. He already knew he had the answer he'd been searching for. He'd known the answer ever since he'd witnessed the future in those dreams. He'd known what his answer would always be ever since he'd met her all those years ago; ever since they played together in the old forest behind their houses. Or when they used to push each other on the swings at the park. And every time he came back to this time and place the answer broke him.

"If I tell her I love her she'll hate me just like everyone else. This'll just have to do."

Amy shivered. The sun had already set, leaving only the street lamps to light the road and the shop signs across the street to keep them from slipping on the pavement. She asked if they could cross to get out from underneath the trees. James agreed, still hesitating. They waited for the sign at the crosswalk.

"It's strange," Amy said. "I know it's late, but it's not that late. Where are all the cars?"

"It is odd, now that you mention it."

James already knew why.

"James? Are we the only ones here?"

"No, we aren't."

"What... what do you mean?"

"Amy... I made a promise..."

"I know," she said. "It's right here, right?"

Amy lifted the necklace up to the street light, the silver glistening brilliantly against the yellow hue. A large shadow darted around the far side of the park, just outside his peripheral vision. He needed to hurry her out of here.

"Yeah... And I still plan on protecting you."

Amy shook her head. He hadn't answered her question. Again.

"What does that have to do with there not being any cars? I said I'd keep the necklace safe, didn't I? So why do you have to be so… Ughh! Stop being so cryptic… I already said I want to help."

"I'm sorry… It's not your fault really. I don't know about the cars. And every… Everything you had to go through with them… If you… If you were literally anyone else all this would be so much easier! But I need you to leave for now."

The shadow reached the next cluster of trees, its presence looming. Closer, and closer.

"What the hell, man? What's your deal? I didn't do anything wrong!"

She retreated, hurt and confused.

"I… what? I didn't mean it like that. Please…Amy… it's important… I've got to protect you like I promised. You haven't remembered."

"What? What? That's all you have to say? I thought we were friends, man! I even opened up to you! I haven't done that in ages!"

She started running away from him, but not out of fear. The shadow reached its tentacles over the hedge and across the road, inch by inch. James knew he was there. Every time he looked the shadow was conveniently out of sight.

"Right outside my sight," he thought. "All this… it's damn Thorne's fault…"

"I keep the promises I make… I always keep them no matter what…"

"I want to believe you're just keeping your promise." she said, pausing. "Trust me… I really, really want to believe you. But I've been told that crap all my life."

The shadow dipped up and down under the ground and hovered above the asphalt. She held up the necklace.

"People make me promises and break them all the time! Every time! They say we're friends and leave… they always leave! They say they love me! And they never come back! I'M SICK OF BEING LEFT BEHIND!!! ……I'm so tired of being let down… every time… every damn time…"

James' face contorted with sadness. She turned and walked away.

"Amy… please… You've got to believe me…"

The shadow reared his ugly head behind him, preparing to strike. James took a deep breath. She paused again, briefly looking over her shoulder.

"If you can't even explain all your book crap… or your life… there's no way I could ever really open up to you. Or feel like you'd understand even if I did…"

It was time.

"Amy… I keep my promises. I'll tell you everything. I'm going to prove everything even if it kills me. Just… don't lose that key."

"Bye James. Maybe in another life."

Her words cut deep. He knew there wasn't another way, but it still didn't ease the cold and bitter sting racing to his heart as she ran home to safety. He resisted the torment as best he could.

"I broke her heart..." he said. "I'm no better than anyone else... I couldn't tell her that... I love her."

James turned to face the demon he'd described over and over throughout his stories. He stood in front of him, motionless, exactly as he'd appeared during the dream. Hatred and pain burned within the beast's eyes, ready to rip into his failing hope and drown it in the abyss.

"I did everything I could to protect her... and in the end she wasn't allowed to see it..."

"Hello James!"

The demon was oddly cheerful, like a gambler bragging about his ill-gotten winnings. He took his hat and blew on it lightly to dust it off and placed it back on his head.

"Sooooo... I see you gave up the necklace. Giving up on Arthridall now too, aren't we?"

The demon danced around, his glee rising, his eyes flaring. James stood still, patiently waiting for him to finish gloating.

"You decided to sacrifice yourself to save her? How very kind of you! But, you see..."

He disappeared, reappearing behind his shoulder and placing an appendage on the side of his neck. James' skin crawled but he stood firm. He'd made his choice, and his resolution to follow through with it infuriated the beast.

"IT'S CLICHÉ'!" the demon whispered.

Thorne reappeared in front of him and began to walk back and forth, apparently contemplating how James' choice would ultimately benefit him. He began cackling at the fruitlessness of it until he started coughing up blood, which dripped slowly and loudly from his ever widening array of teeth.

"IT DOES YOU NO GOOD! EHHEHEHEHHEH!! I'm gonna kill you! I'm gonna kill her! I'm gonna TAKE the necklace. And I'm gonna make its powers mine!"

James didn't speak. The demon reached into his dark leather coat, pulling out his gun and waving it around nonchalantly as if he had all the time in the world.

"You think she wants to read about how I killed you? You think a little story-weaving is going to save her?! I thought you wanted to help! You heard her, right? She's been told that all her life! She just finally had the guts to spit it back in your face!"

James took a deep breath as if to speak, sighing uninterestedly instead.

"She doesn't remember Arthridall! She doesn't remember you! You lose! Hehheheh… you lose! Your plan backfired!

You thought she understood you and ya lost her! Again! And Again! Hehehehehehehe!!! And now your damn fake stories will die with you, never to see the light of day! I tell this world's tale!"

The demon became serious, opening the ancient revolver's chamber and relieving it of a single bullet.

"You played the game, James."

The demon aimed and fired the gun. It clicked with a metallic snap.

"And you lost the bet."

The gun fired. James' world went black.

35

Amy sat in her bedroom and cried alone in her bed. Nana had already gone over to the Pensworth's for the evening to eat and catch up with them since it'd been a while since they'd last met. Nana had asked if she wanted to come, hoping she might want to meet their son since he was about her age and seemed to be the right kind of person for her.

At least, that's what the text said. She set her phone on vibrate and tossed it to the edge of her bed.

"I thought I'd finally met someone I could be around, too. But that was a joke."

She wiped her eye with her stuffed bear's ear, hugging him close.

"At least I have you, Mr. Snuggles. It was so much better back then..."

She remembered the boy who'd given her the gift all those years ago. Before her dad started hurting her. Before her mom had passed away.

"Now he was such a good friend… and we went on so many amazing adventures together… But I lost him when we ran away…"

She cried and cried.

"Mr. Snuggles…"

He'd given it to her as a birthday present. Her only present that year as she recalled, with a big red bow on top. She'd invited everyone she knew in the neighborhood and he was the only one who'd shown up and spent time with her.

"He even brought a cake…"

She hated James. He'd somehow brought those memories back up without her even realizing it.

"James wasn't paying attention at all."

She could never get her old friend back. She'd moved, leaving him behind without a single explanation as to why. The house she'd grown up in was no longer hers. She'd never forgiven herself for it.

"But he deserved better anyway… I wonder if he still lives there if I went back sometime. Not that he'd remember me… the girl that deserted him…"

Amy couldn't shake the remorse. She could handle her mom and her dad now, but not him. She rolled over and dried her tears on her pillowcase.

"It's not my fault though… There wasn't any time to say goodbye. I had to run… It's not my fault!"

Her phone vibrated softly at the end of her bed and the screen briefly lit up but she didn't care. She didn't want to see him anymore.

"Why'd he need to blow it? I thought we were getting somewhere. He was so nice... protected me even! And then he wouldn't listen when I finally tried helping!"

Her phone buzzed again. Amy laid on her back, slamming her palm on the bed.

"He was actually real nice... If he hadn't kept going on and on and on about his book... Blah... Everything in it was so much like my own story. I wanted to run."

Her phone vibrated yet again so she used her foot to push it to the ground alongside one of the offending blankets.

"If he would've just listened! I told him I was interested! I wanted to... Damn it... why did I get in the way again?"

Amy slid under the covers to try to warm up. She was freezing so she only let her head peak through and wrapped the other end of the blanket around her feet.

"I said I'd help, didn't I? Am I... Promises?! I already broke one person's heart. I can do it again..."

She realized she might need to respond to Nana if she didn't want her to worry.

"I don't really mean that, do I? I hope not... I... I hope he's not angry..."

She fumbled for the phone, but it was trapped somewhere inside the blanket she'd thrown off the bed. It only served to make her more upset.

"I hope he can somehow forgive me... I mean I was pretty rude just leaving him standing there like that..."

Amy finally gathered enough strength to get up out of bed and pick up the blanket. Her phone dropped quietly to the floor.

"I... I hope we can still be friends. It was just too quick, I think. I... I don't want to lose another... Not again... It was too much the first time..."

Amy pressed a button and curled herself into the blanket like a cat.

"Five unread messages..."

From: Nana

Hey sweet, I'm not sure if you got my first one, but I'm over at the Pensworth's house eating lasagna. You're still welcome to come over but it might be a bit boring for you

From: Nana

They said their son isn't home. His name is James if you meet him. Goes to the same school as you. Maybe you can find there sometime

From: Nana

He's a nice kid, if a little quiet. I see him at the coffee shop from time to time when he's people watching. Says he's getting inspiration for a book he's working on. Pretty neat, huh? If you become friends maybe you can get him to show it to you sometime. He said he was going to make me a character in it so make sure he gets my good side will ya?

From: Nana

I asked them where he went. They said they didn't know, but he's probably at the library working on his book as late as possible. He told them it's for a friend of his who's   been going through a rough patch. Pretty cool, huh? I think it's nice to have someone looking out for them like that. It's super cute

Amy smiled through her tears in spite of being upset and scrolled to the next message.

"I didn't know he had other friends. So that book is to help someone out? No wonder he was having such a hard time with it. It's a lot more than writing a book then… But I guess he did make that pretty clear."

From: Nana

We're almost done eating. Do you want to come watch a movie with us? They expect he'll be back in the next hour or two so you could meet him then if you want. Or not, it's up to you sweet. Are you at home yet?

"So, he's at the library…"

Amy typed a reply.

To: Nana

Hey sorry I'm home. It's okay, start the movie without me. Long day. Tell you later. I actually already know him. Remember the guy who saved my butt at school the other day? Well… yeah… we're friends now. Or, at least I hope we're still friends. It's complicated…

She sent the message. Three seconds later Nana's chat bubble began to reply.

"She's fast at responding… wow… way to go Nana."

From: Nana

Oh! So you do know him? How neat! You'll have to tell me what you think when I get back. Isn't he a cutie? Okay, we'll watch the movie without you then. Enjoy your alone time. I'll tell him you said hello if he gets back while I'm still here

To: Nana

Thanks nana. You're the best

From: Nana

I know

Amy grinned and set her phone to silent. So he was off saving the world for someone. All she had to do was apologize next time. It was going to work out. The thought warmed her heart. She shivered.

"I'm gonna take a shower," she said. "It's too cold."

36

Amy couldn't believe how cold it was getting outside. Her blankets were poor excuses for warmth; they were more like crutches, meant to protect her until she shambled to the warmth of the shower that awaited her. Seeing she was still shivering inside her cocoon only served to improve her suspicions.

"Knowing me I wouldn't get warm even with the shower."

She always felt cold in the house, especially when she was the only one around. Nana's thermometer was always set to the most random temperatures of chilliness. It didn't matter what time of the year it was; the inside of the house was always ice-cold regardless of the weather.

The reasoning behind Nana's strange habit stemmed from her desire to cuddle while piecing together the puzzle they were working on, clad in warm fuzzy socks and oversized sweaters by a roaring fire. It was an odd tradition to say the least, but they were some of her most treasured memories in recent years.

She remembered how excited she'd been when she'd finally connected her first two puzzle pieces. It was the first time she'd genuinely smiled since moving in Nana after her mother's passing. It was also the first time in a long time that she'd felt like she still had family.

"This stinks."

Amy grabbed the towel hanging on the hook on her door and walked down the hall, shivering the entire way.

"Every time… Every time I try getting close to someone I care about… I mess it up."

She rubbed her puffy eyes, yawning like a lioness. After the magnificent display she turned to the sink, grabbing a small makeup remover and wiping off the day's traumatic events. She hated wearing makeup of any kind, but time after time she purposely fell into the ruse. It was easier to simply deal with it rather than looking gross all the time.

"But it even if it makes me pretty… well, I still feel gross, that's for sure."

She sat down in the tub, the shower raining down wave after wave of bliss. Amy snagged her phone off the bath-mat, careful to keep water from leaking on it. She knew she needed a waterproof case. Leaning over the edge of the tub to browse the internet was one of her more common habits.

But she couldn't bring herself to buy one; even though money wasn't terribly tight it still felt like a waste of resources. And at the end of the day she didn't care too much about it. She didn't live her life on social media. She preferred looking up gaming guides. Or rehearsing her lines for an upcoming play.

"Or singing, maybe... Most the social media stuff is fake. Sure, there's a lot of information, but most of it is put in the best light and I hate when people lie about themselves."

Amy scrolled down her photo feed absentmindedly, pausing only to give her approval on a beautiful wedding dress adorned with an intricately interwoven silver lining along the waist and a beautiful photo someone had taken and edited to look like a fairy's forest.

"I wonder if he's still working. He seemed awfully sad about his book... I hope he doesn't give up on it even though I kind of told him to stop for now."

To: Nana

Is he back home yet? I want to see if he wants to meet up tomorrow

Amy dropped her phone on the ground after a quiet click and waited. She retreated into the warm puddle of water that'd become her bath and let the back of her head sink down into its warm embrace, even though it meant the ordeal of drying and untangling it later.

"Must be a good part of the movie or something..."

If anyone besides Amy had, by some random chance, happened to be walking around inside the house during those late hours of the night, they would've heard a sound not unlike the moaning of a ghost-whale as the impatient bath taker waited for what she hoped was good news. She didn't care whether the news was even beneficial. Anything was better than being left in the dark.

The sound of rushing water sloshing excitedly accompanied the distinctive ring of her phone and hopefully a decent piece of news.

From: Nana

How's your bath?

It was a good thing her phone didn't crack as it violently slammed into the side of the sink and landed in the trashcan with a thud. And that the bath-tub was on the first floor. Otherwise Nana would've had to call a repairman to fix the hole in the floor her tsunami of frustration had carved into the poor little bathmat.

It was a travesty of enormous proportion. But not really. What it meant was that she had to get out and walk to the trashcan to grab her phone before retreating back to warmth. And more importantly, hope to the powers that be that her attempt at pulling information from Nana wouldn't electrocute her.

To: Nana

Where is he then?

In a fashion more characteristic of Nana than her, the reply was instant. She fought long and hard to suffocate the imp of anger threatening to bubble over the safety wall of the tub again.

"Not the time for jokes Nana! I love her... I love her... I love her... Oh, how I love my Nana... Nana, Nana, Nana..."

From: Nana

How is bath

Amy grabbed the nearby bottle of bubbles, squeezing more than a generous portion at the shower nozzle. Despite her annoyance, the bottle made a funny noise, ruining her internal imp's chances for total annihilation of the entire universe. She almost forgot why she was angry in the first place.

To: Nana

Good I guess... Where's James

From: Nana

Not here

"That's it! I'm done!"

Amy flipped the shower off and got out, grabbing her towel and letting the tub drain.

"I waaaaas going to have a nice relaxing bubble bath! But noooooo, I'm apparently not allowed to have nice things!"

She snagged her phone from the toilet bowl lid.

"What a waste... Whatever... I'll figure it out tomorrow."

37

Amy flipped her bed-side lamp on and closed her door, almost making it back to the sweet warmth of her bed waiting amidst her collection of pillows and blankets, but the distinct glow emanating from her computer caused her to alter course.

Amy sighed and turned it off, meandering back to the safety of her bed. Not many people knew she was a part time gamer, full-time winner. She liked to think it was because she was good at keeping secrets. But she knew better. She didn't have friends.

"Well, I might have two... Nah... One... well maybe even then... crap... I won't tell... I hate when people stereotype. Generally speaking, of course."

Amy rolled around to get comfortable and stared at the lamp's yellow light until her eyes grew heavy.

"I mean sure... I get all the perks whenever I talk online but that's stupid. It wouldn't be a challenge if they just gave me everything."

Amy smiled as her eyelids closed.

"Plus, if they found out they'd get all butt-hurt since I'm better than most of them."

And with her distracting, wondrous thoughts rolling around her mind like a happy carnival, Amy's thoughts finally slowed as her dreams called her.

***

"Amy…"

Amy opened her eyes, finding herself standing on the sidewalk where she'd been earlier that evening.

"James? What's going on?"

James didn't respond, instead gesturing with a hand in the direction of their neighborhood.

"You want me to go home?"

Again, James didn't respond, instead gazing intently at the necklace around her neck. She didn't remember putting it on, or of being aware of it until his gaze pierced her. No sooner did she look at it did she feel the weight of the gift.

"It's heavy… but comforting…" she thought.

"Please don't lose that… no matter what. It only gets harder from here Amy but that's why I need you. Do you remember anything? Please… Please remember…"

Amy gazed at the pendant. A comforting hand supported hers. A vibrant series of images flashed and swirled around her like reels of movie film.

"Are... are these memories? James, what? How are you doing that? How..."

He smiled and turned to fade into the shadows, stopping for a moment to look over his shoulder before disappearing into the dark. Somehow, she didn't know how, but she could hear him. It was as if he was whispering to her soul.

"Amy... Don't give up... You know where to go. What to do. Find the portals again. I'll be there... On the other side. Don't forget... no matter what... Don't forget the promise we made..."

"James? Where are you goi... James! Come back! Please... I don't know what you mean. I need your help..."

Amy shot awake in her bed, shaken. Something had happened that evening. Something horrible. She knew it. She didn't know how she knew, but she knew James had something to do with it. She looked at the clock; three-thirty-four. A.M.

"Just a dream..."

She struggled with her racing thoughts again, rolling around, trying to somehow calm the heartbeat threatening to burst out of her chest. She couldn't help but feel like his no-show at home last night was her fault.

"Just a dream though... Everything's fine. I'll talk with him and we'll be good."

The light from her computer screen sprung to life and the shocking brightness it almost killed her. Almost, but thankfully, not quite. A small, metallic object laying on her desk reflected rays of light onto the ceiling.

Amy refused to move. The teddy bear she so desperately loved was splayed on its side in the far corner, looking sad. She wanted to comfort him; to bring him up into her arms and give him the attention he deserved. Mr. Snuggles gazed at what appeared to be the edge of her bedframe, eyes cold and dead.

"He looks so sad..." she thought.

Amy didn't remember leaving him there. She'd never treat him like a piece of trash and yet there he was, admiring the quality of the patterned comforter that was washed up and twisted across the mattress like a patch of earth torn up by grenade blasts.

"Mr. Snuggles..."

Amy rolled off her bed and stood up shakily. Her eyes dilated as they absorbed the light particles off her screensaver, the bubbles bouncing off each other like giant marbles. She picked up the bear, tossing him back to the comfort of her pillow-fortress. Amy turned her attention to the desk.

"That's right... he gave me this necklace. Said it was important... Then was it James...?"

Amy set the necklace down with a small metallic clink, pressing the power button on the bottom corner of the monitor and rolling back into the safety of her bed. Everything was alright. She had the necklace, Mr. Snuggles was safe, and she was going to make it up to him during lunch.

"So why does something feel so... off?"

The thought ate at the back of her skull as she tried doing everything in her power to lay still long enough to fall asleep again. The monitor had woken her, nothing more. Nothing was wrong.

"It'll make sense in the morning. I'll make it make sense."

***

Amy woke up to the sound of Nana stomping around upstairs. She rubbed her eyes, finding there was a surprising amount of grit in them. She had an odd grandma; she didn't know any other old lady around who'd be doing an entire cardio workout at the unreasonable time of seven A.M. Ordinarily she'd be stomping around even earlier, but Amy chalked it up to the fact that she'd stayed longer than anticipated for movie night.

"Must've been a really good movie if she gave up her morning routine for it," Amy thought, stretching her arms above her head and killing the whale with a massive moan.

Amy wouldn't have normally noticed the disruption in time. She usually slept through Nana's daily ordeal from force of habit. She chalked it up to her lack of sleep.

"I need to fix whatever this is so it doesn't happen again. Me needs my sleep... I need to stay awake so I can get that armor tonight..."

The face in her mirror grunted in agreement. The whale screamed its dying breath as Amy cracked her back like the master chiropractor she was. She opened the door, hearing a call from upstairs as Nana paused her workout video so she could say good morning.

Amy spat out the mouthwash she'd painfully held in for two minutes from the bottle that said nine out of ten dentists recommended it for stronger enamel daily. She swished multiple mouthfuls of water to dampen the pain and grinned, checking for any missed spots. There weren't any.

"It's because I'm perfect… But that tenth dentist may have the right idea because I'm really feeling it."

The smell of a beautiful eggs-benedict arose from the kitchen as a beautiful virgin sacrifice for her stomach monster. Amy knew her belly was a monster and not a fairy because it growled constantly.

"Fairies don't growl…" she thought.

Amy walked around the corner.

"Unless they're hungry for eggs benedict."

"Did you save some?"

"Hello! Well good morning to you too, oh miss beautiful wonderful sweet pea of mine!"

"Did you?" Amy said, bypassing the obviously friendly sarcasm.

"Yes," Nana said, scooting her chair up to the table. "There's still some in the pan."

"Thanks…" Amy said, grabbing a plate. "How was movie night?"

"I enjoyed it very much."

"What was it about?"

"Oh, you know. The tortured long-distance romance spiel where the pair gets separated early on so they do everything they can to reunite by the end."

"Ah."

"It was super sad, but I suppose it had a sweet ending."

"How'd it end?" Amy asked, cutting into the second half of her meal.

"Can't tell you, or I'd ruin it."

"No it wouldn't!" Amy exclaimed. "You know I don't watch many movies anyway."

"That's true… All those video games."

"So will you tell me?"

"Nope."

"Why?"

"Because it's fun. Not very often I get to interact with my baby this early and she actually wants to listen. It's refreshing."

"Please?"

"Hahaha nope," Nana said, standing up and walking to the sink to scrape her plate.

Amy finished her last bite and followed her.

"Will you at least tell me if James made it back safely?"

Mrs. Tamburton put her plate in the dishwasher with her fork and knife.

"Who?"

"James?"

"James who?"

"James Pensworth? You know, the place you watched your amazing movie at last night? Ring any bells?"

"The Pensworths don't have any children. Must be thinking of someone else."

Amy felt her stomach sink sharply.

"James Pensworth? Really? You were talking all about him last night!"

"Sorry sweet-pea, you must've been talking with someone else. As far as I know, the Pensworth's have never had any children. They'd have told me if they did, wouldn't they?"

"No… No… no no no… that can't be right," she mumbled.

"Hm? Did you say something? Here, let me take that," Nana said, sticking Amy's dishware next to her own.

"Huh?! Oh yeah, thanks. I'll see you tonight Nana." she said, rushing back to her room.

"Okay honey!" she called behind her. "Stay safe and send a message if you need anything! Stranger danger and all that!"

38

Amy closed her door with a thud and slid down in disbelief. It didn't make sense; unless Nana had contracted a mental disorder overnight there shouldn't be a way on Earth that she'd forgotten James. And she knew she wasn't joking; their occasional bickering made had made it clear that making friends was still a sore spot for her, and while Nana liked to joke around she knew of more wholesome ways to go about ribbing her than pretending one of her friends had suddenly ceased existing.

"It's got to be something related to that dream. Yeah, that's got to be it."

Amy briefly glanced at her desk to make sure she wasn't going crazy. The necklace was there, gazing back as if waiting for her to decide what to do. She needed to think. It was still possible that everything could still be a fluke.

"He didn't just cease existing. She's pulling my chain or I'm still dreaming somehow. It wouldn't be the first time either's happened."

Amy looked closely at the symbol on the necklace and, not surprisingly, her heart skipped a beat. Something strange was happening and she wasn't about to sit back and let things pass her by.

"I need to find him. Somehow it's all connected and he's the only one who had at least some semblance of an answer. And... that cave..."

Amy picked up the necklace and fastened it gently around her neck. After tucking the small pendant under her shirt, she grabbed her backpack and ran out the front door before she had a chance to overthink it.

"That cave has something to do with his book, I think. And... this symbol, as he called it. He said it was a promise. A key."

Amy wiped the stray hairs from her face with a flurry of lip-spits as she stood on the steps of the front porch.

"Sun and moon... that seems easy enough... the stars too... Support for the sun and moon? But what are these things on the outside?"

Amy zipped her winter coat and shivered as the outside air attempted to find an opening in her defense. She expected the necklace to be ice-cold on her skin, but it surprisingly wasn't.

"I'd say lamp-posts or gate-posts... Hmm... seven of them huh? Just like the stars... obviously connected somehow..."

She pulled the necklace out to look at it again, trying to figure what he'd meant by it. She knew it wouldn't be as meaningful if she had to ask about every detail. It was a puzzle.

"He'd never let me live it down if he had to explain every little detail. Hold on... maybe..."

Amy pulled on the chain, careful not to tug on it too tightly. The pendant sat perfectly balanced on the piece of silver connecting the sun and moon.

"If I spin it? Mmm... worth a shot."

She used her index finger to get it spinning, and after a few moments turned it sideways to get a better view. Amy watched in amazement as the necklace gave off some sort of light, as if she was catching a glimpse of the invisible connections between the planets.

"Wow... This is amazing James!" she said, looking up.

He wasn't there. Amy felt her heart sink. It'd felt like he was there for a moment.

"But... the light-posts... they're connected and everything! The heck, man? I thought this would summon you or something! Like a dog-whistle. Oh..."

Amy smacked her forehead with a mitten.

"Duh... they aren't just light poles... They're the supports for a bridge, right? I couldn't see that until they were moving though... Almost as if I had to start driving to watch them pass behind me? Hmmm... like a never-ending bridge..."

She began walking slowly down the sidewalk to the road.

"I think I'm starting to get it... Hold on! Then that guy, Cifer? James... No one knows you exist? I can't believe that... No! You're alive... You... you're waiting for me to start walking? I... I'll do it."

She shivered in anticipation. She knew it in her heart. He was waiting for her. Somewhere. But she needed to move before it was too late.

"We can do this... We're going to beat him... no matter what. I'll find you and... We'll win... we'll win and we can... we'll go on an adventure. No matter how many steps I need to take, I'll keep walking. I'll find you no matter what, James Pensworth! I promise."

***

There was a sudden lack of temperature change and a sudden lack of light. It was interesting and not interesting at the same time, nor it wasn't scary. Or sad. It wasn't warm or cold either as he originally anticipated. James found himself in an endless expanse of what he could later only describe as nothingness.

It was odd for him to be in a location that, by definition, was impossible to exist. Or to be described for that matter.

"So... nothingness exists? Somehow nothing can be defined by... something... A word? Ah!"

James wasn't floating around as he imagined a person would if they were to encounter what he termed existing within the void. His hypothesis that space was equivalent to nothingness was blown out of the water. And yet somehow, by his guess, due to the nature of his existing in the void, he didn't feel upset by the fact.

"I guess what's done is done. There's no logical reason to beat myself up about it."

James sat cross-legged on some sort of surface, or more precisely, the void's version of a surface. Whatever the surface in question was made of apparently didn't matter very much, because it acted just like any normal floor. Looked like any normal floor would too, if the floor were in the middle of space and was pitch black and endless. James likened the sensation to sitting on a crystal glass floor he couldn't see through, especially since there were no lights around to make the distinction between floor materials. Oddly enough the floor lacked temperature too, and while it had solidity it lacked the sensation of touch.

"It's weird, and I don't really care that it's weird."

He opened his eyes, finding he was exactly where he imagined himself to be, if that place he imagined was non-existence, and if it was actually possible for him to exist within non-existence.

"The same view eyes opened or closed... Hah! I guess I'm not very surprised I'm not weirded out by the weirdness. Somehow... my personality is still the same, even here."

James tried standing in order to explore the place, or void, or whatever term the non-descript existence preferred to be described by, be it named or un-nameable. Somehow, he was able to do so. It made sense to him that he could too; if he was only dead in the fictional sense, but not in the real-reality as he self-described it.

And if, by standing up and walking, he meant that he was actually sitting down cross-legged and staring into the limitless void regardless of the signals firing from his brain to his spine, he may have been correct.

"Maybe I am moving," James said.

Or thought.

He didn't remember opening his mouth to speak, but then again he very well could have, and the nature of the void had caused him to forget before he could bring the action of speaking to fruition. It was a very annoying sensation, and he found himself not caring about it in the slightest.

Apparently getting annoyed in the void was also impossible, since the void itself didn't actually exist. The fact didn't the hurt James' hypothesis that his fictional-self was paused in the fictional reality of his story; one that he had conjured up on his computer screen to be a place holder for his story until his co-author answered his call for aid. The real Amy.

"If that's the case… then I've taken a break from writing… and want Amy to finish writing it with me… which is what I… I'm fictional? I also wanted to do that… because we're the same. I'm real, then…right? Or the imaginary me? The one the real me wrote about and because of that I'm real?"

James tried standing and walking around again and achieved the same non-existent results.

"This is so weird... It's like I'm just a copy of the real James... It makes sense since I wrote me exactly like I would... but this place feels just as real to me just as if I were the real me in a void-space I couldn't explain... myself."

James sat down.

"So... are we the same person? Just with two separate... actual, real, timelines that exist simultaneously, combining into one completely original reality? One that... only the fictional me... Me? And the real me could only comprehend completely if we were a single person?"

James' head would've literally exploded if it were possible to feel pain in the void.

"Well... I... let's see, after Amy left... right! Thorne put a gun to my head and shot me! Made my head explode? Probably... Hah! Hilarious! Boom! Head-shot! Right on my pimple too!"

James shook his non-existent head, rolling his eyes.

"The humanity! How was that a good idea again? Poop... Oh wait! No! That's right! I meant for him to do that... because then... Ah yes! I remember... What? Does that include the fictional and real realities for everybody else too? What the heck... What the heck! Even for the real me this is complicated!"

James paused as another realization struck him, or would've struck him if realizations could exist in the void.

"If I assume that I'm the fictional one... and he's real... But my feelings feel real... does that mean his feelings feel fake or fictional? Are they real and superficial at the same time because we're the same person? Or both not real and superficial precisely because we're the same person? What's to say we aren't both completely real? Or both imaginary?"

A projector screen, or what appeared to be a projector screen, appeared in front of the semblance of the character, whether fictional or real, of James. It was large and incredibly so; almost as if whoever overseeing the entire mental fiasco had finally decided that he, or she, or whoever was writing the story at the time, needed to push their plot forward and see it to completion using something both relatable and interesting to their audience. If indeed the James in question, the one in the void, was the fictional one. And, if the James in question was the real James, a real, actual projector appeared in front of him as both he, and the projector screen, meandered around the nothingness of the void.

"At the very least... if I'm the fictional James... and someone is reading about me right now because I finished the book... Well... hopefully they'd at least be able take away the fact that this entire part of whatever or wherever I'm playing a part in is supposed to be entirely confusing so as to bend the fabric between reality and imagination."

James sighed in relief, thankful he'd finally sorted out the puzzle. It'd been a problem he, the author James, had been struggling with since he'd introduced Amy into his story at precisely the same time he'd met the real Amy. James wondered if his now solved problem was also why the real James had decided it necessary to kill himself off in his book. Only one needed to exist because they were the same.

"Hmm... anyways... it'll drive my fan-base bonkers as to who I am... or who I'm not... I guess that's one thing accomplished!"

James raised his arms high above his head and grinned knowingly, addressing his imaginary audience as if he was cool enough to have one.

"Bring it on fan base! Tell me who I am so I can light-heartedly mock you! Hah! You're wrong! Just kidding! Not actually kidding... Nah, I'll totally play along if you're right!"

A man dressed in old-fashioned robes quietly sat down next to him, watching the large white screen as it flickered slightly. By James' reckoning, the void wasn't any different now than if he were sitting in an empty movie theater with his old friend.

"Hey, King. Long time no see..."

The man put a hand on his shoulder and started to talk. James couldn't tell if he was physically speaking or if his words simply penetrated his mind the way his own thoughts seemed to physically materialize. Whichever the case, King spoke softly. But James heard him as clearly as ever, and he missed these times a lot. His dream about the beach seemed like ages ago. It had been too long.

"So, you figured it out then?" he said.

James didn't feel pressured to look his way, instead continuing to watch the movie screen in front of them as it flickered blankly.

"Yeah, more or less," James replied.

"It's pretty genius, you know."

"What is?"

"Well, you are figured out how to tell her you love her despite her barriers and still be yourself."

"I didn't get to tell her though. She didn't want me to even though... I was more than willing to... Am! I just hope I did enough to prove it somehow. If all this meant... meant even a little to her... It'd mean the world to me."

"Ah, but you did tell her. Yeah, everything you've done so far has proven it... even though she hasn't got it all together yet. She's... well, she takes a bit of time to complete puzzles."

"Yeah, I know."

King laughed.

"James... you... you little genius! You got around all those barriers, man. Talk about love? You showed her you love her, using all the words you could possibly want to and then some! Look above you. Hopefully it'll clear up some of your confusion about this place."

James looked at the ceiling, which had suddenly appeared thanks to King's pointing it out, the dark emptiness above giving way to a beautiful, somewhat yellowed paper ceiling lined with calligraphy ink and letters.

"So we're...? No... Yes?"

"Totally."

We're inside her diary? Wait... so it's... Oh... then..."

King smiled. James was dumbstruck.

"All those words up there... Then it's finished?"

He nodded. James grinned and King patted his back.

"Yep. Great job. Once we're done here... may I have a copy for my place?"

"I guess it explains why I've continued existing even through my apparent death... What a weird portal."

"James?"

"Huh?"

"May I keep one?"

"Ha!" James said. "It's so funny when you're like... my place..."

"James..."

"A lot of people would murder to get there and you're all like... Yo it's my crib! It's pretty awesome! Come on in!"

"James... please stay focused."

"Well... not murder? That was a poor word choice. You know what I mean? We're in her book you know? So I guess it's changeable... supposedly?"

King firmly grasped his shoulders, finally catching his attention. James grinned goofily and King did his best not to laugh from James' crazy antics. James giggled childishly.

"You already know what I'm going to say though!"

"Please?"

James sat upright, his head and shoulders swaying slightly.

"Of course you may. You orchestrated pretty much all of it, after all."

"Thank you," King said, letting go of his shoulders. "That means a lot."

"King?"

"Yes?"

"So... yeah... was it all worth it, then?"

"Of course, James. There's more to this particular episode than your death. It's kind of why you sacrificed yourself there in the first place. Look at the screen."

"Is... the screen another portal?"

"Well, yes. It's more like a projection of that story. A mirror of sorts. Mirror worlds, if you will. Want to watch her?"

"That's not even a question. I'm came here because I love her and that's that."

39

Amy dug a circular trench in the snow waiting for the bus. It was getting colder rather than warmer as the day progressed and the thought bothered her. She hated being cold, and it was only possible to care more when it came to winter fashion. The only benefit to cold weather was no one questioned why she wore jeans.

"I don't have to shave if I don't feel like it. That's literally the only plus," she thought.

Amy found it surprisingly sunny considering the snow the night before, meaning that even though James had been right about the incoming storm, he hadn't called how long it would last.

"Suck it, bro. You aren't always right."

A few other neighborhood kids started gathering and chattering about all the latest school gossip. The head cafeteria lady had apparently been fired yesterday due to spitting a wad of tobacco into a kid's chicken noodle soup because he was, in her words, 'acting out of line', and 'the tobacco had run its course' and it was 'spittin-time' and she quote 'needed a bucket'.

She needed to find James. He'd understand why she felt uneasy about last night after she apologized. Just being here with her would help soothe the paranoia scratching at the back of her skull. She distracted herself by watching Susan waltz up to the stop-sign at the corner and slap her hand on it to support herself against the onslaught of her countless admirers.

"Please, please! One at a time!" Susan shouted, grinning wildly.

Amy finished the other half of her figure eight in the snow, doing everything within her power not to steal the spot light with an uproarious emotional outburst that would threaten to steal Susan's crown for being the most obnoxious and interesting morning attraction.

"Susy! Susan! Is it true you organized the maniacal lunch lady's demise?" one asked.

Susan smirked, motioning to the guy who'd asked the question to get on his hands and knees so she could stand on his back. He happily obliged, quickly dropping to the ground to become the mastermind's soapbox; she was the hottest thing on campus right now. And also pretty. And talented. Amy got distracted by her acquaintances' antics in spite of her growing anxiety.

"Well! Well! Well! You heard about that, did you?" Susan shouted as they surrounded her. "AH HAH! HAH! OOH!"

For a lacrosse player she was incredibly dainty, hopping on the boy's back without so much as a pause. The boy grunted slightly under weight. Amy noticed that his grunt of pain had a distinct note of satisfaction in it. Susan leaned over them to build up the suspense. The crowd ate it up faster than hot-cakes.

"Was it me?"

The crowd huddled together, full of anticipation. Susan stepped between the kid's shoulder blades and he started shaking under the rapid weight redistribution. Without missing a beat, Susan hopped. Amy couldn't believe it; she literally hopped, landing on the kid's butt as light as a feather.

"There's no way she didn't plan that," Amy thought bitterly.

"Was it you?" someone in the crowd finally asked.

Susan leaned back, spreading her arms as wide as if she'd just won an Olympic gold in Gymnastics.

"Yes, my friend! It was me! And I covered it up perfectly too! Want to know how?"

The crowd unanimously shouted.

"Yes! What'd you do?"

"I... my friends, started the classic tradition of... Drumroll please!"

The crowd rapidly slapped their hands against their legs, raising the noise to a fever pitch.

"An All-American!"

The drumroll intensified.

"One-hundred-percent! Bona-fide!"

Everyone gave into the frenzy.

"FOOD! FIGHT!"

Everyone whooped and hollered as she jumped off her soapbox and onto the flurry of arms raised to catch her. Even the late arrivals upon seeing the spectacle as they gathered at the edge of the neighborhood joined in on the fun. Amy checked her watch, feeling the weight of her necklace against her skin. The bus was at least fifteen minutes away.

"No sign of him," she thought. "And there's no way I'm dealing with her groupies this long. I can only take so much."

Amy walked away from the crowd and down the sidewalk leading towards the school. It wasn't the longest walk imaginable; the only reason people didn't take the path was because they wanted to be a part of the party bus.

"It's always the biggest bus because of her," Amy thought. "I'd never use it if she didn't push me in first. She hardly ever sits with me anymore though... Not since middle school."

Amy found the sound of fresh powder crunching under her feet to be a very enjoyable noise. After about ten minutes of running from Susan's shenanigans she bent down, making herself a very large, veritable snowball; one even James would be proud of getting smacked by if he dared show his face.

She stopped walking.

"Why would I do that? I want to apologize, not destroy his face, right? Well... not with a snowball..."

She blushed, finding her gaze fixated on a stick on the side of the road. It wasn't a very interesting stick, other than the fact that her imagination had been fixated on it for some time now. She dropped the snowball on the road where it made a crunchy snow-puff sound upon landing and looked back to the fallen branch.

"Walking stick..."

***

James looked up from the screen.

"It's just like her to pick up on the most uninteresting part of the book."

King looked at him intently. He furrowed his brow into a quizzically and somewhat humorous look that said everything from 'Really?' to 'After all this time you get hung up on the fact she got hung up on the same stick you did?' James made a gesture to prepare his defense but was cut short.

"Shhh..."

The sound was so perfect, and the shushing, so perfectly teethy, that James found himself bereft of words. They went back to watching the screen, doing everything they could to stifle their laughter, struggling to succeed behind two sets of clenched and ever-widening lips that threatened to break into smiles. It'd been a while since they just got to hang out like this.

James remembered his days of note-passing with her fondly. While hopeful for the future, his heart burned for the present to come to fruition like an islandic volcano threatening to erupt. King looked on knowingly.

"Patience. Soon. Very soon. She's got one more battle to fight."

James nodded in acknowledgement. He'd waited this long. He could wait a little longer.

***

Amy looked away from the forest towards the school, her sandy-blond hair whispering gently behind her. The building gleamed dully in the morning air, the large tree in the front grounds swaying slightly in the morning breeze. She found the sight oddly beautiful. It was mesmerizing to watch the scene unfold, in the romantic sense, as no one else had arrived yet to spoil the memory for her. It was a bittersweet feeling; one that sprung up on rare occasions from the top of her chest and into her head from somewhere deep within.

She loved finding secret gems like the view that lay in front of her. Places that ordinarily housed the hopes and dreams of many; places where many people would gather to express themselves and their ideas. To her, school was only one of those gems, even when she didn't like school-work. It didn't really matter where she was. The romantic feeling stemmed from being in public places when no one else was around to steal the serenity of them from her. Part of why she didn't want to be around people all the time.

Amy knew if she told most people about her odd likings of things and places that they'd simply attribute it to her introversion. And she'd disagree, then run away to some far off, wonderful place within herself so she couldn't be disturbed.

"It's a sad feeling," she said, gazing at the portrait of the school-grounds, "being alone in a place that should be filled with people. But it's nice at the same time..."

Amy picked up the stick and stuck it into the snow. She didn't know how to feel about it. Longingly looked at the building again.

"It's like... I can take the time to truly feel everything that goes on there... all the energy... and the conflicting, tumultuous emotions... without getting distracted for once... wrapped up in the insanity of it all."

***

James watched the movie screen intently as she spoke, shifting around in his seat but not saying a word. King noticed James' barely contained excitement again and threatened to reveal a proud grin under his wide-lipped smile.

"The love the kid has got in him... wow," King thought, scratching his head. "Color me impressed. He's been taking notes the entire time."

40

Amy sat at her desk, slouching under the tabletop because she could. James hadn't shown up to class, and with him her only reason to make herself presentable.

"James, why aren't you showing?" she thought.

The nasally voice of the teacher she so desperately hated, now more than ever, echoed across the chasm of the classroom like some sort of malfunctioning blender trying to learn to yodel.

"No one likes you," she grumbled.

Ms. Brigand loomed over the inmates, sweeping over them like some sort of ugly sorceress.

"Riicky!? See me aaafter claasss please!"

Amy watched the poor guy frantically flipping through the pages of his test to confirm his poor arithmetical sentence. She wondered if he'd really failed the test; he was typically one of the more mathematically astute and it'd be a bad sign if he was dejected by his grade. She heard the audible sigh, watching on empathetically as Samantha carefully consoled him.

It was true, then. She felt her heart reach out to him, only to sink as the crazy cat lady with a voice made of wormwood waltzed into her line of sight, slapping down her own judgement with only a hint of crazy.

Amy looked at the large number circled in red ink and looked up at her teacher in disbelief. Ms. Brigand leaned over with a noticeable creak and smiled genuinely, but the experience of her teacher's expression of pleasure was so unnerving that Ms. Brigand might've as well had extreme gingivitis. Or straight-up scurvy.

"Weeellll donnne, honeeeypottt!"

Ms. Brigand turned to the rest of the class. Amy hunkered down in her seat by another 0.523599 radians, embarrassed by the sudden attention. Every pair of eyes in the room drilled into her skull like jealous meat spikes.

"Miiiss Rooooseenbury recieeeeved one of only twooooo aaaaaceptablee grades this tessst!"

Still, it was a relief for her. Amy looked at her score again to make sure she wasn't dreaming.

"It's still there... That means I passed the class," she thought.

The ninety-one which determined her immediate future grinned back at her as she imagined James would've if he'd been watching the scene unfold from outside the classroom door again. She instinctively looked over to check and instantly regretted her decision as a pang of remorse stormed over her like a tidal wave.

"James... would you please show up... I did it somehow!" she thought. "And it's all thanks to you..."

***

James hadn't shown at their usual spot during lunch. When she asked Susan if she'd seen him at her locker she didn't have a clue who she was referring to. The endless thoughts tore at her relentlessly. She needed to talk; to let them all out at once. Venting to anybody would be better than bottling it up anymore.

"James... why doesn't anyone remember you? It doesn't make sense. Not at all..." she said, packing up her belongings from her locker and zipping her backpack.

"Were you always this invisible..."

Amy shuffled down the hallway to the sidewalk, beginning her migration home after sending Nana a message about the good news. Happy and elated as she was, without James on the bus she didn't have a reason to ride it anymore. She'd given up on the idea that she could steal any significant amount of time from the lunch queen there too; her buzzing bees making her buzz off every time she attempted to shorten the distance between them.

Her resignation to the thought hurt. If she'd at least had a bit of time to talk to somebody, even Susan, the entire heartbreak thing would've been much easier. As it stood,

Amy found herself struggling to stand as winter's signature attack continued to melt under the pressure of her boots.

Amy took the long route home. The swings that'd been so full of energy the evening before were cold and lifeless now, creaking like old bones tend to when they need to be greased.

"Is he really that mad? I know he was upset and I blew up in his face… but even with that none of it makes any sense… It's like he's completely disappeared from the face of the earth and I'm the only one who knows…"

Amy wiped a tear from her cheek, eventually lifting the pendant from under her jacket.

"Is this why?"

She shivered. The sun did little to warm her, quickly retreating behind the darkening clouds as swiftly as it had arrived that morning. Moments later, the snow began falling again, topping off the seats of the swings with powdered sugar. She sighed as she watched the scene change; it was everything she wanted in an empty park. At least, it was what she used to want. Her memories from yesterday were still as fresh as the snow falling from the sky.

"It's not fair… I'm supposed to be the one everybody forgets. I'm more used to it. James… I'd rather be forgotten instead and still have you here somehow! You… you don't deserve to be forgotten…"

***

The look in James' eyes pleaded with King; pleading to go back to the way it was before he'd left. Being with her. Showing her he was never going to leave through the simple things. Not being able to tell her he loved her was still better than not being able to do anything at all.

"You've got to be patient. You of all people knew this was going to be the most difficult part of the journey."

James winced and turned back to the projector, hoping against the odds that his friend would have the tenacity to stay strong until the end. As it stood, she was wavering. Shivering. Afraid. Hurt.

Alone.

The hardest part was he knew all his friend's current hardships were a direct result of his choices. He knew the alternatives, and even though he knew that there weren't better ones it didn't help his demeanor. The pain of separation from her was the same.

***

Amy closed the door behind her, taking the fluffy beanie off her head and placing it on one of the hat hooks. It fell off as she walked to the kitchen, but she didn't care. She found herself caring about trivial matters less and less.

"I wouldn't have noticed if I weren't planning on going out again," she thought.

"Nana!" she called. "I'm home!"

She heard the thumping of her beneficiary upstairs as she gracefully dropped what sounded like a heavy dumbbell or a heifer onto one of her specially designed workout mats.

"Coming!"

Ms. Tamburton danced into the kitchen before Amy could bat an eye, snagging the hand towel hanging from the oven handle to wipe her face.

"You have a tough grandma, you know that?"

"Apparently. Two workouts in the same day? If I had a pair of sunglasses, I'd rip them off and call it insanity."

"Why would you need sunglasses?"

Amy groaned and tried explaining to her indefatigable grandma what she was referring to.

"It's a double entendre Nana. I was referring to a workout routine and a television show... You know what? Never mind."

Ms. Tamburton pulled their meal out of the freezer to de-thaw it, sitting down at the table and dropping her sweat-drenched towel on it.

"Hey now, don't be grouchy. But I fail to see your double meaning, kid. I probably don't even want to know what you mean by sunglasses. I definitely don't want to know what you mean by insanity."

"Wait... What? Eww! Gross! I wasn't talking about anything nasty!"

"What do you think a double entendre means, sweet?"

"It just means a double meaning, right? Cause that's how I was using it."

Grandma shook her head, snickering politely. Amy started walking to her room in frustration. She'd had enough annoyances for the day.

"Yeah," Nana finally managed to squeeze out in between wheezes. "It means a double meaning. But not the way you think."

Amy turned sarcastically. Nana put a hand up to her ear, whispering the meaning in her ear. Amy stopped.

"Oh… well I won't use that phase anymore, then."

"It's an innocent mistake, as far as mistakes are concerned."

"Still," Amy said, going to her room. "I'd rather not use it anymore."

Nana chuckled like an old man with the voice-box of a heavy smoker.

"I'll have dinner ready in about an hour, sweet."

Amy replied from the other side of the door, walked over to her desk, and sat down after turning on her computer. She watched the loading screen for her favorite game absentmindedly.

"Geeez, I haven't been this flustered in a long time," she thought.

A couple clicks later, MasterOfChaos404 charged her sword with electricity from the sky to summon the god of thunder and appeal to him for an armor upgrade.

"Hopefully something a little more modest with some extra hit-points, or at least an overall defense boost."

Amy liked the new gift, quickly equipping it on her avatar right away. The two weeks of grinding for experience points had been worth it; she now bore the extremely strong and lightweight scales of the blue sky dragon.

"Short of the Shining White Plates of Plantou'f, I now have the best armor available for my class. Awesome sauce."

Amy wasn't too worried about getting the best stuff in the game yet, as she'd been playing for just under a year and still had lots to explore. She knew people in game who'd been playing for over three years and would kill for something as specialized as her new upgrade, so their misery at her benefit was enough for the moment.

"And now I'm too strong for them to even try," she grinned, chuckling maniacally. "It doesn't hurt that the back-swing on my sword gets a 3.7% damage boost on people weak to electricity. This is awesome…"

Nana called from the kitchen to let her know dinner was done and ready to eat. Amy locked in her equipment and exited from her moment of escapism.

"Coming!" she called.

41

Mrs. Tamburton finished her last bite and, leaning back, sighed heavily, rubbing her stomach so much even an old man toting a massive beer belly and greying foot-long beard would mutter in appreciation. She smirked; something was bothering her granddaughter and she was going to bait it out and trap it so it wouldn't be allowed to torment her anymore.

Amy watched her with a grossed-out face laced with notes of secret appreciation. Nana readjusted her glasses, pretending to finally notice she was being observed. For the first few moments, she froze as if she were a kid with her hand in the cookie jar. The kid face didn't last very long, but rapidly devolved into a baby face that spoke volumes about her innocently sinister plan she was going to enact soon.

"I'm gonna do it..." she said, the rims of her glasses gleaming from the light of the dark forces she was about to release.

Amy quickly rose from the table, grabbing her boots and coat to run away from the impending monstrosities of the grandmother variety. In particular, her grandmother's variety.

"I'll be back later," Amy called, lacing up her second boot and opening the front door.

"Ohoho! This is only phase one! Heeheehee!"

Amy closed the door as quickly as she'd opened it, pulling her hood closer to her face to retain what little heat she could. She heard her grandmother cackling up a haunted-house-esque storm inside. Rumblings within ensued.

"Children have died in there," Amy thought, striking out onto the dimly lit path to the neighborhood streets, destroying all hope for every snow-ant that evening by stomping their igloos underneath her boot.

"I'm the only survivor," she mumbled, stomping on the ants' icy homes, one snowball at a time.

Meanwhile Tammy decided, for her own sake, to open the window above the kitchen sink.

"And the porch while I'm at it," she thought while walking outside, relishing the chill of the open air and deciding to drink something warm.

Tammy looked at the night sky, admiring the crescent moon as it shone brilliantly against the backdrop of the stars, as if it were hanging onto every lumen of light being generated for the evening. It was breathtaking.

"Well... that's not the only thing that's breathtaking. Hah!" she laughed, putting the coffee pot on to boil. "Hopefully whatever she's going through won't stink so badly when she gets back."

***

Amy wanted to walk to the entrance of the neighborhood. She wanted to believe James was home somehow, sitting in his room and working on his book, his desk lamp barely providing enough light to prevent his eyesight from degenerating. She wanted to see a light in his bedroom window; to sit out in the cold of winter's eve and shiver for her own reasons. She wanted to wait outside his house, on the sidewalk at the edge of his yard, and watch him turn off his lights as he crawled into bed for the night.

Instead, Amy found herself shivering from the blistering cold. She wouldn't have minded it if he were there with her, holding her hand delicately, as one would a beautiful and delicate rose. Then it'd be possible to console herself instead of running from her predicament, perhaps even enough to steel herself for the next onslaught. If only she'd at least had the chance to see any sign of life from him. Any sign would've sufficed. As it stood, Amy stood at the edge of her yard, unsure of what she should do. Unsure of where to go. Feeling as trampled on as the miniature snow houses she'd left in the yard. As stone cold as a statue in a graveyard during the midnight shift, as the wind created its impression of a wolf's howl, careening into the dark and dangerous woods beyond.

Amy stood still. Cold. Numb. Not knowing if she'd ever be able to leave the chilling reality of her total isolation in the world. Or if, after running to the far ends of the universe and having the grandest adventures, nothing would change. No one wanted to listen because they'd never be ready for her.

She gazed down the sidewalk leading to the Pensworth's house.

But she did care. A lot. Every little word James spoke, even when he wasn't listening, because he was the first person who'd cared about the little words in life as much as she did.

"James would've named all these awful feelings... all of them... what would he call it... But would he even be able to help if he were here? Or am I assuming? No... he'd be able to feel it too. He could put a name to it..."

A gust of wind echoed its lonely howl down the road as she stood there, pondering, wondering what it might've been like if she hadn't missed her chance to really vent instead of bury herself under a couple of rehearsed catch-phrases as she'd done with every other opportunity in her miserable life. Amy pulled her hood tight to her face, the brown and grey furs tickling her forehead, teasing her for warmth.

"It's just not the same without him... Damn..."

Amy turned her head away from the entrance, protecting herself from the wolf's howl as it threatened to tear away at her coat.

"He would have called this... ice-olation..."

Amy walked opposite his house towards the back of the neighborhood, for no reason in mind other than to search for answers.

"Answers so complex and convoluted only he could've created the questions for..."

***

James sat in the theater, watching his friend's performance on the screen in front of him.

"She's not wrong," he said, stretching his arms behind him. "I would've totally called it that."

King watched his young companion as he stretched but he didn't speak. James continued.

"Although… I probably wouldn't have used as much buildup as she did for it. Even if it were clever, which I fully admit it was, I know I'd complain if there weren't more to it than that. Multiple meanings and whatnot."

"Well, she's writing her story, not you," King said. "And if you'd actually paid attention to everything she said instead of being so cold about not being in the spotlight you'd have realized that the ramifications are actually tremendous."

James pouted. King wasn't wrong. He was never wrong. It seemed like it was impossible for King to ever be wrong. But it bugged him because he hadn't figured out what he meant yet.

"It is okay, James. All of the pieces are there, even if it takes you a bit of time to put it together."

"Probably. Well, definitely, if you said so…" James said somewhat dejectedly. "It always feels like I haven't seen all the other sides of all the pieces yet. They're all scattered and upside down."

"And that's why she's there, James. You made the pieces whether you were aware of them or not, and now she gets to put them together. Come on. There's someone you need to meet."

***

Amy walked. Further into the neighborhood she walked. It grew colder, the snow seeming to sprout up from the ground more often than it fell from the sky. It was as if the snow on the ground was emanating the cold weather, even though somewhere deep in her mind she knew it was scientifically impossible for snow to emanate cold. Amy didn't know how she knew, since she hated science, and cold weather in general, but she knew.

"Cold is just the absence of heat... right? It can't emanate cold, it just steals heat. And darkness merely the absence of light..."

Amy didn't know what to call her travels in the night. There were light-posts lining the street on both sides, but they flickered from time to time, effectively removing any sense of security she might've received as she passed them one by one.

"Why didn't I just stay in my room? Just play games until I passed out? James... this is all your fault! Not that I hate you... But I wish I could punch you in the face right now!"

Amy stumbled on a patch of broken concrete, almost turning her ankle in the process. She wanted to cry out in pain. To cry about every time she'd ever been abused.

"So! So stupid!" she thought, crouching down and massaging her tender tendons, wincing inwardly as she pinpointed the offending nerves.

There was no one around to call to for help. Alone again. After sucking it up and taking her boot off, sock and all, she jammed her bare foot deep into the snow.

"It's not so bad this time," she mumbled, half smiling, half wincing.

Amy pulled out the necklace to reassure herself. Her dad wasn't around anymore.

"Good news is, it isn't permanent. The pain passes once the swelling goes down. It always does," she said, shakily putting her shoe on and ever so slowly readjusting her weight.

It took a good while, but eventually she could put some weight on it. Something about her late friend's desire to help her in his own way kept her pressing on. The pain was excruciating at first but, as she anticipated, the swelling went down as quickly as it began.

"Short and sweet... Alright James," she grimaced, determined to pursue her instinct. "Let's see what's in store, right? I have a feeling it's about to get worse before it gets better... for both of us."

42

The sidewalk continued further into the neighborhood. Deeper and deeper it went, winding around the corners of countless trees, leafless and lifeless and covered in snow. Blankets of snow were piled up between the houses, many of which looked to be geared up for Thanksgiving, but she was confused. Many homes seemed to be gearing up for Christmas and Halloween too.

She figured her reasoning wasn't even the odd part. It might make sense in a weird way that a family might prefer to celebrate one holiday over another. But that wasn't the piece that didn't make sense. What didn't make sense was she'd never seen any of these houses in the neighborhood before. And while they initially appeared festive and inviting, like everyone was getting ready for a carnival, the decorations were cold and dark, like an abandoned amusement park.

"They're lifeless," she thought. "They're eerie, like... the night before Halloween... not Halloween... Halloween's obviously eerie. It's more like... that dream... no... That nightmare."

A distinct noise similar to an owl's hoot echoed through the neighborhood as she carefully limped further on and around the corner. Into the carnival of evilly intrepid houses.

She braced herself to turn around, preparing to shout into the expanse of the frigid evening air. All the familiar homes had disappeared. The atmosphere was markedly quiet. Something was there. Something sinister.

"It's like… Like… SOMEONE'S TRYING TO SELL ME SOMETHING!!"

Amy scanned the area behind her with the eye of someone who'd been burned too many times by false advertising.

"Nothing? Huh…"

She shrugged, finally turning after noting every possible place a sneak attack could come from. Late-night snowball fights were commonplace in the winter. She knew it wasn't one of the dweebs though. James had proven otherwise that day at school. That a lot of those times she'd felt afraid weren't because of a person. There were sinister forces at play.

"Again? Geez… but I thought we ditched him a long time ago. Would make sense why I can't find James though… Audible sigh…" She thought. She turned around again, shouting. "The dread before the demon arrives! Is that what you want?!"

The dastardly demon of the hellions materialized out of the shadow of the house in front of her, hop-skipping with glee to the snow bank on the left. He lifted a beautifully clawed hand to the brim of his now obnoxiously large hat, tilting it on its side as his eyes rolled up into his skull, his neck snapping ninety degrees in the opposite direction.

"Who?" he said, sticking his sickeningly yellowed tongue out to taste the air, his teeth squared into perfectly spaced rows of tombstones.

Amy stood her ground, giving the beast a fierce look of determination. The demon pretended to shake in his boots, grinning wildly, mocking her.

"What do you want?!" she exclaimed, putting on her brave face.

The master of chaos waltzed with one foot in front of the other towards the poor, shivering girl as she did everything in her power to stay standing in the face of incarnate terror. He looked stronger and angrier than ever. The beast stretched his hand towards her, changing the direction of the wind, effectively blowing Amy's fuzzy hood off and wildly tangling her windswept hair.

"I killed him," he said. "I killed him with this gun! Damn easy after you left him!"

The demon, while within talking distance, leaned to and fro to emphasize his point. And, even though she could see how far away he was standing she could still feel the odor of his breath on her nostrils, as his deathly cackle licked the inside of her ear from behind her neck.

Amy felt his vileness oozing around her, as if his very presence were a sludge of misery. She started to crumple beneath the impending weight of her doom but snuck a quick glance to her left on the chance he'd overlooked something. At first, she thought her entire left side had gone pitch-black because of his shadow. But upon further inspection she could see the bases of the trees behind him, and the light of the brilliant moon above.

"So he's not as all-encompassing as he'd like me to think," she thought. "Good to know…"

The demon stood upright again, his shadow wrapping around her back, his head retreating with him.

"What do I want? Didn't you hear me?! HE'S GONE! NADA! DEAD!!!" The demon coughed wildly. "No one knows he ever existed! What I want… Is that key."

Amy ignored him and walked deeper into the maze with fierce determination. She'd spotted a park at the end she'd never seen before and her curiosity started overcoming her raw fear of the devil.

"He can't touch me unless I let him… Right?" she thought with each step. "James let Thorne kill him on purpose… If he tries killing me here… he kills himself too."

She looked him in the eye, grinning at the ludicrous-ness of her friend's ingenuity, which only served to fuel the demon's hatred.

"You're wrong, though! He's alive! They'll learn about your plans because I'm still here! And I'm going to tell them all how he beat you at your own game!"

Thorne hissed at her. He knew she was right. Amy kept walking. There was something important waiting for her at the other end of the park, something hidden deep in the woods. Something very near and dear to her heart. Something James had started writing because of her. Writing for her.

"A very long, and very detailed love letter… I'm starting to remember."

Thorne pulled out his ancient, silver colored weapon of death and pointed it at her chest, every fiber of his being wanting to fire it and end her. Amy pulled the amulet from underneath her coat. She found herself almost tempted to tease the demon at his utter failure but thought better of it, instead letting the necklace hang on her heart between her hands.

"This is the key you want?" she asked. "The defense of surrendering… of perfect surrender that'll never give up hope? I can't give up on him. Or myself. He gave his life to protect mine!"

She kept walking, walking past the carnival of empty shells of entrapments and fake loves to the edge of the park.

"Sacrificing yourself to give me a chance? That's the perfect defense now that I think about it. You kept your promise, James. Just like you said you would… But I've got to stand up for myself this time."

Amy turned to face him and saw her old neighborhood burning up by fire like dried cardboard being whisked into the sky, turned to ashes by winter's flame. Thorne's coat smoked from the heat of his rage.

"You… You think?! You think I would just LET you GO?! You're naïve! You will DO as I say!"

Amy's determination turned to horror as she watched his face radically transform, morphing into that of her deceased father's. Thorne noticed her hesitation.

"Thaaat's right… you can't do anything that I can't. I will have that amulet because you don't have a choice."

"N…No!"

Amy felt the tears well up in her eyes. He'd even gotten his voice to sound like her dad's. Personality and everything.

"James isn't going to come for you. Your mom isn't going to fight me. You certainly aren't strong enough to do anything… Just… give up. This can all just… go away. You can be… numb again. No more pain… no one gets hurt."

An unusual thing happened in Amy's heart. Despite her father berating her and tormenting her and abusing her, there was something there. And that something, she suspected, had been there all along. But that something didn't come from him. It had been hidden inside her, buried beneath the frozen tundra of numbing herself to those memories all these years.

Power.

"You're wrong."

Amy opened her eyes to face him. The wind picked up around her as she redirected it, the fire behind Thorne hissing at the sudden influx of air. Her hair whipped around her face and Thorne's coat flew behind him like a cape. He shook his head, his face returning to his own.

"Tsk... Tsk... you're really starting to piss me off, ya know? All I'm ask for is a little trinket that doesn't matter to you and you've gotta go and stand up to your dear ol' dad!"

Thorne cocked his revolver angrily and shook it at her.

"I think you're bluffing. I killed James, so if I kill you the story's dead! Easiest steal of my life."

Amy smiled, and the wind around her instantly snuffed the fire and blew the remaining ashes away. Her hair rested on her shoulders.

"I don't remember everything yet," she said, holding the necklace close. "But I'm not going to let that stop me."

She held the necklace up the same way she'd seen James do it in her dream and it began to glow brilliantly. Thorne snarled and dropped his weapon to allow his arms to twist into claws, his coat morphing in a fearsome set of leathery wings as he rushed toward her to slice her throat. Amy wagged a finger at him.

"It didn't work then, and it won't work now!" she quipped. "Life is uncertain, but love... Love is."

The night sky in the sphere around her exploded with the light of a thousand suns and Thorne in his fearful fury shrieked as the energy of the blast vaporized his partially unfurled wings. Rings the color of haloes rippled through the newly formed valley like ripples on a pond, and what was left of the snow was instantly blasted away with the demon who had haunted her for far too long.

The light from the necklace receded, the smoke cleared, and the night sky returned to its original hue to reveal a blanket of beautiful stars. Amy breathed a sigh of relief, her chest feeling lighter than it had for as long as she could remember.

"I... I did it. I faced down my demons."

She didn't feel cold in that moment, her excitement overriding her need to feel warm. Her real home had already reappeared fifty yards away, covered in snow, and replacing the old neighborhood that'd clouded her vision for so long. Nana had turned on the front porch light for her, not knowing when she'd return from her midnight adventuring. She put her hands on her hips.

"I don't know when either, Nana," she said, somewhat elated by the thought. "I may not ever return at all. I need to figure out what's real. I need to recover the real me..."

Amy zipped up her jacket and put on the straps of her backpack, which had magically appeared beside her during her home's reappearance. The bag's weight pushed down on her ankle but for once, it was a good kind of weight.

"There are lots of adventures I still have to go on, Nana. I'd forgotten all about them till now."

Amy smiled, feeling completely unprepared but perfectly fine with it.

"It's simple, though. I'll figure it out when I get there. Hold on, James! I'm on my way!"

43

"This way, James. He's waiting for you on the other side," King said.

"Who is? What? No! I told you I need to keep an eye on her!" he said, glancing at the paused movie screen.

King raised his arm and grinned, causing a doorway made of pure light to materialize next to him. James decided it was more portal-esque than doorway-esque. One could never always tell these days.

"Do you trust me?"

"Well, yeah."

"Go. I'm doing both of you a favor. Trust me on this one. It might not make sense now, but it definitely will later. He's waiting. I'll even keep an eye on her for you."

James sighed.

"But…"

"No buts about it, young man. This is more important for you."

"How on earth is meeting a complete stranger more important than helping her?!"

"Calm down. You might end up surprising yourself."

James shook his head.

"Fine. But I'm only going because you asked."

"That's all I'm asking. I'll see you soon."

***

The snow piled down on Earth in droves. Most of her inhabitants had already bunkered down for the evening, lighting fires in their communal hearths and sipping hot cocoa topped with miniature marshmallows. Well, almost everyone.

Amy put her arms above her head to shield her face from the wind, which had returned to its prior course. The impending blizzard pushed back, each wave stronger than the last, buffeting her so badly at times that she was physically forced to bend her knee to keep from going airborne. She couldn't remember how many waves had hit her over the past few minutes, but her soaking wet pant-legs from her knees down sent shocks of cold so chillingly vitriolic that they threatened to snap her bones in two.

"I don't remember a park ever being this large," She coughed, the icy air sapping every bit of remaining moisture from her lungs. "Then again, I don't remember there ever being a park in my neighborhood. Or seeing the sky during a blizzard."

Amy tried scoping for any sort of landmark available to her tightly squinted eyesight. From what she could tell, the park wasn't really that large; if anything it was average or quite small depending on how she squinted. She decided it was probably average, but on account of the wall of icicles bombarding her from every which way the park truly only existed in the form of whatever piece of playground equipment lay immediately in front of her.

After what seemed to be an eternity of intense blast-backs and shiverings, Amy found herself at the swing-set, gripping one of the steel support structures with every ounce of energy she had left after her recent battle. At least she knew she could always go back home to warmth and safety. But it wouldn't mean anything if she turned back now. Home meant nothing if she couldn't be with everyone she cared about.

"If I didn't have to find him first… I'd force his tongue to touch this pole so it'd stick and he couldn't keep running! Crap, man! Why's it always got to be like this?!"

Amy watched the swings flail wildly above her, as if they were sails trying to catch the northern wind. She felt like they were important somehow, but quickly remembered that these swings weren't the ones they'd played on before he'd left for wherever it was he was going after he'd sprung his trap on Thorne.

A thought ruminated relentlessly in her mind the more she tried to ignore it. Not the swing-seats, or what she first believed was a passing thought, but a memory. A memory she'd long forgotten; one of the good ones from before she'd been forced to run away.

"Well, at least until he jumped too far and hurt himself. The silly kid trying to show off… Typical James… wait… Oh my God… How could I have not seen that?! He was the kid!"

Amy let go of the pole before her hand would stick, glad to see she was remembering the good times too but anxious that she couldn't experience more of them until she brought him back. The need to press on to the woods was way more important now. She could feel it.

"I'm getting close."

No sooner had she made it past the black plastic of the playground's mulch liner did she experience the cessation of the blizzard's grasp. Looking back, she remembered it clearly now; it was the playground they used to play on as children.

"The same merry-go-round, the same jungle-gym, the same swings… It's all here."

Amy smiled. It was as if she'd trekked through every danger from her childhood in mere minutes. She looked past the sidewalk leading to the entrance, down the street, brushing off the loose snow still stuck on her back.

"Can't believe it... And my house is right there. This is crazy."

Amy walked to the edge of the forest, her shoes barely scraping the top edge of the snow. Everything was quiet save for the soft crunch of snow at her feet, but now it was the peaceful sort of quiet. Amy wondered if the feeling was akin to what normal people felt like all the time.

"Instead of fighting demons and reliving brutal and haunted childhoods they're becoming peaceful and productive members of society..."

She shrugged.

"Meh... probably not. Most people just don't feel like changing to begin with."

Amy skirted the tree-line, searching for any sort of clue James might've left behind. She pulled out the necklace he'd given her from what seemed like ages ago.

"Unless... No... it couldn't be that simple. Could it?"

The necklace didn't feel warm in her hand anymore. She was a little saddened by it, as it had provided a great deal of comfort since she'd last seen him. And, even though she'd literally blasted demons away with it, Amy found herself missing the little bit of heat it produced more than any amount of power it might still contain.

"James... You don't make any sense... you know that?!"

Amy squeezed her hand as if she were about to suffer a heart attack. Instead, it was the first time in a very long time that she felt her heart beating on its own, supplying some warmly-welcomed heat to her shivering body.

"What..."

She dropped like a rock, giggling helplessly. It quickly became a sort of belly laugh; one that shook her entire body so thoroughly that it hurt. She didn't care that her entire backside had made the snow beneath look like dry ice.

"Is this what it's like ti be alive?! HEEHEEHEE... Oh wait... Christmas miracle? A girl be warm when it be cold? Heresy!"

Amy shook her head and stood back on her feet after exerting a tremendous amount of effort.

"When did I turn into a pirate? I hope he didn't see that."

Amy brushed her jacket off for the umpteenth time that evening, slipping the necklace back under her coat.

"I guess... Ha! Ha! Very funny man... It's not that odd for a girl to go crazy over a guy, you know? What am I looking for here, Bro?"

One of the neighborhood lights at the end of the street flickered as if to reply.

"Wait..." she said.

Amy pulled out the necklace and looked at it again, then at one of the trees at the edge of the park, and back to the necklace.

"You've got to be kidding me... James! Why didn't you just tell me you like me?!"

There was no more doubt in her mind; she'd really entered inside the world her friend had made. Before her stood a tree with the very same symbol carved into it as her necklace. It was beautiful to see the gothic piece in another medium, especially one as natural as a living, breathing tree.

"I expect you'll want me to follow the trail, then?" she asked, expecting her friend to be watching her every move.

"Kind of difficult if there's no light to follow…"

***

James tentatively walked through the opening King had made. Brilliant flashes of concentrated energy spiraled around him in infinite swirls made from the briefest moments of happiness. He didn't know what to expect from the person waiting for him on the other side.

"Sure, I know he's had me do a lot of bizarre things in the past but he should know better. I'm finally getting through to her, aren't I? This is stupid… I shouldn't… If anyone else had told me to leave I would've smacked them."

He found it convenient that the portal he'd entered was moving around him, pushing him forward while only taking a step here or there rather than some of the more violent ones he'd encountered in the past. It reminded him of waiting on an escalator versus being strapped to a rocket.

"Either King's being super generous, this place is close, or he remembers that one time I got stuck in that desert for four months. Was it four months? Eh… who cares, it was hot… Glad I wasn't alone on that one… Or I'd be… Toast? Totally toast…"

The vacuum of the light-portal released him with a light pop, and James found himself looking at a familiar scene. A light breeze sent shivers up his jaw and down his spine. James looked anywhere for a coat he could put on, but was quickly distracted again by the newness of the place.

"I give up watching my friend on the big screen for... going back to school? You've got to be kidding me! And of all places! Really? The practice fields? You know I'm not a sports guy!"

"You never were."

James startled visibly. It wasn't very often someone could get the drop on him. James scanned the area for the intruder but didn't spot anything out of the ordinary. The baseball field on the left was empty and the soccer team's practice field was mostly muddy from the thin layer of snow that'd already melted.

James shivered again but smiled slightly once he spotted a brown-hooded figure sitting at an old and rusty white metal-wire table and chair, waiting for him to join about twenty feet away on the path between the fields. James shuffled towards him, hands tightly dug into his pockets to retain body heat. Even the late afternoon sun wasn't enough to warm his fingers.

"So, you're the guy King said I needed to see?"

"I am."

The man stood up to greet him, and James realized that he was a giant, broad-shouldered man's man. James shook his hand and sat down in the other chair.

"So, why do you think you're here?"

"No idea."

"Do you know why you're here?"

"King told me to go, so I did."

The man breathed, laughing to himself. He pulled back his simple and worn brown-leather cloak, revealing a war weathered face and a slightly graying beard. James was surprised that he didn't have any noticeable scars to speak of.

"You must be cold still. Here, take this."

James wrapped himself inside the warm material, finding it oddly familiar and comforting.

"This man is a friend for sure," James thought. "He gives me warm things."

"Ha!" the man chuckled, watching the look of relief spread on James' face. "I still remember when I was given that cloak many years ago. It's served me well over countless winters."

"I can see why. It's super warm," James said.

The man scratched his head.

"So," James said, "I take it you're from Arthridall?"

"I guess you could say that. In a way."

"So… do you know why I was sent here?"

"Yeah, I do. I asked him to send you here. As a favor."

James shrugged, shaking his head.

"James, look at me. If we don't fix this it might spell disaster for everyone we care about."

"You pulled me away from someone important to me…"

The man sighed, doing everything in his power to stay calm. The window was running out.

"I could say the same to you."

"Yeah right! I don't even know who you are! All I know is you're technically my ally but you're pissing me off! So, hurry up and tell me your name so we can both go back to our lives."

"Does it matter?" the man asked.

James jumped from his chair, knocking it over violently and shaking the table's edge with the side of his fist.

"Doesn't matter? Doesn't matter? Names are everything!"

James was quickly shushed by the man's commanding stare. Something about him seemed familiar and it bothered him greatly that he couldn't nail it on the head.

"Calm down, buddy. I… I know Amy too. She's a wonderful lady and you should be proud of her, and proud of the person she'll become. That alone should be more than enough for you to trust me."

James sat back down in a huff, the hood of the cloak draping lightly around the back of his neck.

"But… but… fine… what do you want to say, if it's that important?"

"James… did you notice you misheard me when I replied to you?"

"No…"

"That's why I'm here. You actually know me quite well, believe it or not."

"I probably do…"

"Well, listening properly isn't your strong skill yet. And you have a very strong tendency to force your own opinion even when it's not the only one."

"Can you prove that?"

"I don't have time to, James. But you could ask anyone who really knows you and if they care enough, they'll tell you bluntly."

James shivered again under the cloak. The sun had begun its descent, and he was still somewhat seething.

"James, I'm serious. If you really believe I'm an Arthrindian and I know your friend, then you should listen to me."

Both sighed. Neither of them wanted to be at the school any longer.

"Fine," James said finally. "I trust you. Shoot."

The man chuckled despite himself. James almost got angry again but decided against it. The man was laughing at one of his own inside jokes, nothing more. He was sure.

"Listen to your friends. Make sure you actually understand them," the man began. "It could save your life."

"Got it."

"Don't cut them short. Ponder their advice, accept their wisdom, and most importantly…"

"Is?"

"Listen to your wife. She's smarter than you. And prettier."

"My wife? You mean Amy?"

"For now, I'm going to leave that cloak with you. I don't need it anymore. Besides, it fits you."

"Wait! Wait… wait… hold on man… my wife?!"

"Yep. Believe it or not, she's the one who sent me back here to knock some sense into you. Glad I did, too. Totally worth visiting again. It really does bring back memories. I'll see you on the flip side, kid."

James blinked, and the man disappeared. James blinked again, and he found himself inside the portal of light on the return flight. James blinked a third time and found himself back on the other side where King was still sitting, waiting to hear how it went.

"How'd it go? You weren't gone very long, but I suppose it's for the best. See? Amy's right where you left her. Just like pausing a movie. This place is a nifty little invention. Nice work."

James sat down next to him, dumbfounded. King looked at him quizzically, wondering why he looked bothered.

"I... Uh... I have no idea what just happened."

"That's a start, I suppose. Did you learn anything?"

"I... uh... I think so... I got the guy's cloak? Gave it to me after telling me a bunch of mumbo-jumbo..."

King smiled.

"Ah, I see. Good for him. Good for you."

"What?"

"I'll show you eventually."

"I see... you don't make any sense either. But at least you aren't acting so weird about it. That other guy now let me tell you... He was the weirdest guy I've ever met. And here I thought I was the most complicated person around..."

"I see."

King smirked. Time travel had always been and continued to be a wonderful thing. James continued.

"I sure wouldn't want to pick a fight with him, though. I've met a bunch of Arthrindians in my time and he was by far one of the scariest. I'm glad he's on our side. For sure."

"Me too," King replied, smiling, turning back to the screen. "I've trusted him for many years. I trust him even more now, thanks to your meeting with him."

"Glad I could help, then. But can we please get back to the real show?"

"Sure."

King waved his hand and they began watching again. Less than a minute later James smacked his forehead, remembering his mistake.

"Oh, crap. She's right," James said. "I didn't leave her with anything to go on, did I?"

He looked at the man. King shrugged, as if asking 'what're you going to do about it?'.

"Do you have a pen I could borrow?" James asked.

"Yes."

"Can I use it?"

"Yes."

"Well where is it?"

"He's right in front me."

James cocked his head to the side. He raised an eyebrow and, after some serious consternation, decided to take a stab in the dark.

"You're not serious?"

King shrugged.

"Nope," he said. "I'm just a guy in some robes."

"Really... You're going to use dad puns? I forgot something and I gotta put it in!"

King shrugged again.

"Yup," he said, after considering it. "I guess that'll work."

"What will?"

"Ha... I've got to hand it to you, Mr. Pensworth..."

James sighed heavily. He used to think his dad had bad taste in humor, but King's wit was of an entirely different caliber.

"So... I... I'm literally?"

"Yep. Go for it. Be the pen."

James stood up almost in disbelief, raised his hand and, after a bit of concentration and focus, pulled a page of the book down from the ceiling until it stood next to them like a wall of graffiti. He paused, looking confused.

"What are all these stains and smudges doing here?" James asked.

King looked at him as if James already knew the answer, but he answered anyway.

"Those are the stains Thorne's already made on the Earth, the fruit of the innocent being tricked into giving up something precious."

James nodded, then shrugged, then turned the pages and got back to work. King sometimes made things so official sounding.

"Mmmmm? Get it?" James asked after some time.

"Writing on the wall? That's a good one. At least you won't get expelled for doing that here."

"Dang, I was hoping to stump you a little longer."

"Tough."

James shrugged, turning back to the page. After a bit of thought, he made a space for the new section, using the motion of his hands to craft the new golden glowing letters.

"There," he said, sitting back down. "That should help."

***

A paper fluttered from the sky and landed on her head briefly before she brushed it off violently, thinking it was some sort of ice-bat raining small-animal-hell from above. Realizing her error Amy picked it up from the snow, careful not to smudge the ink.

"What the…" Amy said, confused.

She held it up closer, trying to make it out in the varying degrees of available light.

"Amy, I'm not who you might think I am. But neither are you. I need your help. And in case I can't get back…"

Amy looked up at the night sky again, surprised to find it overflowing with starlight now. Most of the time the city lights ruled the night sky and it bothered her. She sighed, grateful for the change.

"Listen, we may be stuck on Earth for a while longer. I'm not sure how long. But we've got to get back home and warn the others. Although we managed to keep him busy… Good job by the way with the necklace. But I think all it's done is made him angrier. But at least you seem to have started remembering. I accidently forgot to add in a piece of the puzzle."

Amy blinked, almost at a loss for words.

"James? Wait, are you watching me? Really… you… You can't break the fourth wall if you want me to take it seriously! That's like… rule one of storytelling!"

She looked back at the paper to finish reading and found the words had been replaced. She shook her head, squinting to make out his obvious scribbles.

"Haven't you noticed the little kid that's been watching you from his window ever since you walked outside?"

Amy quickly turned around, suddenly paranoid there was someone other than a phantom James snooping around from the beyond. The message changed again.

"There's no one there now. He already left for his next mission."

Amy sat down and pouted. She hated being teased. And she wasn't even sure it was James on the other side of the note.

"I'm in a book though, that I do know. Otherwise Thorne couldn't attack. And the kid? No idea."

"You need a light through the forest, right? Use the necklace. I promise it'll work now."

Amy coughed and stopped short, looking at the tree and back to the note.

"As if I'd ever put up with more of this. Well, I guess… I'm still stuck here if I don't move forward. But there's more to this though, isn't there... Has this happened before?"

The note changed.

"I'll see you soon, I hope. Until then, be careful. This story isn't finished yet and Thorne's doing everything he can to stop it. King showed me the stains he's already made. Stay the course and try to find Jehu. He'll know what to do."

The ink on the note disappeared. She blinked, and the page burst into little ashes of light, leaving her holding nothing but air. If she didn't know better, she could've sworn the entire thing had been her imagination.

"I guess that settles it, then. Go find Jehu, whatever that means."

***

James looked over at King. The man shook his head, feeling sorry for the girl.

"How else were we supposed to fix it? The whole fiasco was spiraling out of control. At least she has a shot at remembering everything now," James said. "I don't know if she could ever forget Jehu."

"James…"

James shrugged.

"What you did was fine. But you didn't need to antagonize her with extra details. It was rude."

"What? Not really. I got the job done, didn't I? It's not so bad."

King raised an eyebrow.

"It's your funeral. Way to get some points, buddy."

"You probably aren't wrong," James said, getting up and offering his hand. "I tend to be decently blunt most the time."

The projector turned off and disappeared back into the earlier pages of the book as King stood up. James nodded his approval.

"James?"

"Yeah?"

"Do you remember when I told you writing on the walls won't get you expelled?"

James searched the ceiling of the seemingly infinite expanse of the book they were standing inside, turned a few of the pages, and brought one down to eye level to examine it.

"Yeah. It's right here. Wrote it myself."

"Well, the thing is, I might've been only partially correct. Writing here might also get you expelled."

"You mean, write myself back into the story?"

"Yes."

"Then... would it be possible to forget all the weird stuff that dude said at the practice fields?"

"If you wanted to. I suppose that's not technically impossible. I wouldn't suggest it though. That's a part of the scene now."

"Sir?"

"What is it?"

"See you back in Arthridall?"

"You can count on it. See you there, my friend."

***

Amy held the necklace up to the tree carving. It seemed like the thing to do now. Even if it was cliché.

She wasn't sure what to expect. Thorne could've made it back already and be lurking nearby for all she knew, waiting to pounce at her again. But she was confident in her friend's judgement, despite her minor annoyance with what was obviously a stop-gap measure. The pendant fit perfectly into the carving, as if by magic.

"I'm on my way, James."

After a moment, the symbol in the tree began to glow brilliantly. She put the necklace away, certain it was doing exactly what James intended it to do.

"If my guess is correct, he gave me this thing so I could remember our time as kids before he knew everything else it needed to do in the story. Well played, friend. Well played."

Amy got caught up in the spectacle, brimming with excitement as the tree's carving shot what looked like a silver beam of light into the forest. Leading her on the path to Arthridall.

"He figured it out, somehow," she thought, taking her first step in. "The genius. He trusted me to figure it out, too."

44

Amy couldn't help but feel like she'd seen the carvings in the trees before. It was an odd sensation to follow the path, but she found herself growing more and more comfortable with it the further up and further in she walked, like a familiar story one reads over and over every night before peacefully falling asleep. The forest smelled rich and earthy and inviting, rather than the frozen wasteland she'd endured what now seemed like ages ago.

"That's right! There was another forest when we were... I showed him... Oh my... how did he remember that?"

The petrichor permeated the atmosphere, as if her being there had caused the wondrous forest smells to increase their vivacity in response to her presence. There was no guide other than the light emanating from each of the carvings. The stars that'd peaked out in the night sky after her encounter with Thorne were being choked out by the immense size of the trees all around her. She was somewhat disappointed by that particular aspect in the change of scenery, but felt it was also probably somewhat safer.

"Dragons hunt at night. And after all, the starlight might interfere with the clarity of the path," Amy whispered. "Man... He remembered that... All this time... I thought no one understood..."

Deeper and deeper she went, stopping at each of the carvings her friend had made before he'd left. It was as if they stared straight into her soul, like an all-seeing eye making a bee-line to her inner mind. Amy found the thought almost too revealing, but at the same time it was one of the most enlightening experiences in her life.

"It's like he wanted to show me my past... But the good parts... As if he already knew me and all this is just for my benefit."

Amy giggled softly and wiped away a tear.

"Typical James, always looking out for me. Probably watching me when I least expect him, too. The creep. Ha!"

The feeling that someone as amazing as James wanted to help her that much stabbed to her core. She looked around. Every single cut into each one of the trees was an unbreakable, unyielding, eternal bond that could not be undone. The trees would bear those cuts as long as they lived. Frozen in ice, burning with fire.

"You can't unhurt someone, I suppose," Amy said, approaching what appeared to be the last of the carvings. "But you can always show someone love... even when the one you love isn't always looking..."

Amy smelled the wonderful aroma of the magnolia trees before she saw their blossoms. The stage before her was an amazing sight to see; the trees bursting with visual fragrance from every limb as if it were already the height of spring. She almost cried right then and there. But it wasn't until she felt the warmth of the summer breeze on her face and the gaze of the stars above as they gently breathed on her like a lover's kiss that she finally allowed herself to break down.

She walked up the hill to the center of the clearing. There was a large oak tree waiting for her there with her name on it. She was sure of it.

"The memories of getting hurt will always remain… but the pain from them can always be healed. The past only tells you how you survived to get where you are now… but the future shows you your opportunities to grow. Sleep is for the dead… Right, James? Got to wake up and grow if you want to live life and go on adventures."

Amy drew near the oak tree and began examining it for any sort of clue he may have left. It was an accurate assessment.

"Is that what you've been trying to say all along? You could've written everything differently if you'd wanted… You could've made everything as if it'd never happened or something… But it wouldn't have changed the feelings we had to work through… Back then… and now. After all, most battles are in our heads, not our hearts."

Amy lifted her index finger and traced along the light-posts of the picture they'd drawn as children, etched into the solid wooden bark of that great and mighty tree they'd found all those years ago. She smiled warmly as another bitter piece of her past released its hold on her and floated away.

Her parents were gone. But she was not alone.

"Minds battle for minds. That's easy to figure out. Our minds can only make forests to protect our hearts for so long… before they crumble to dust like statues in the wind, baring our hearts for the entire world to see."

The symbol began glowing brilliantly, rapidly becoming one of the brightest lights she'd ever seen. In fact, the more she looked at the carving, the more she wanted to jump on top of the bridge and never leave. She wanted to live on the edge again.

The thought struck her that, knowing her friend, she'd never been allowed to leave. The bridge wasn't just a simple song her friend used to sing to distract her from her terrifying home life. It was an eternal song; one that sang the continuous melody of their time together.

"Simply complex. Wonderful! Just wonderful!"

Theirs was the story they'd made as children, to show the world who they truly were inside and out. They were destroyers of death, freely walking across the bridge of love, closing the despair of separation for good.

"We make our own adventure. What we do with our breath depends on when we take the leap."

Amy turned around upon hearing an approaching footstep. She wasn't alarmed by the sound, instead choosing to stay entranced by the peacefulness of the circular clearing. The memories binding her to her old self continued colliding with her present self, seamlessly connecting and leaving only harmony, as if it'd been beautifully orchestrated to happen that way from the very beginning.

The approaching footstep only served to solidify her sense that everything she'd gone through until then was all for leading up to the now. There was nothing James could've done to prepare her for the majesty of the man that sat down on the grass nearby, motioning to her to sit with him.

Everything about him was entirely simple, but his presence spoke volumes. He wore plain white robes, but they were clean, pure as freshly fallen snow in the most frigid of winters and glowing brilliantly, akin to the symbol she'd traced not moments before. Amy didn't know what to say. She also didn't feel pressured to say anything either, so she sat down and joined him, content to simply be with him.

After a while the man leaned on his hands to support himself, suddenly wincing in pain as if he'd been pierced by something sharp.

"I thought James made this place just for me..." she thought.

She tried to ease his discomfort in any way she could, but he stopped her.

Amy sat in front of him. Tears streamed down her face. She didn't know how to explain it, but she could feel it. The man in front of her carried the largest burden out of anyone she'd ever met. She couldn't help but feel like it was entirely her fault and felt ashamed for having ever pitied herself.

"He's actually gone through hell and back... He can stay... I... I like him."

He finally looked up, gazing at the stars through the branches and to the moon, and finally, down to the little girl sitting at his feet. She finally noticed that he wore a simple crown of gold encrusted with many precious gems.

"Was that there before?" She wondered.

He smiled genuinely, and she felt warm again. He spoke tenderly, but with authority. And humility.

"It takes a heart, to have a heart. It takes a heart to break a heart. It takes a heart to fight a heart. It takes a heart, to heal a heart. It takes a heart, to win a heart. It takes a heart to keep a heart. And it takes a heart, to give a heart. You can't give what you don't have. Do you understand?"

"You're King, aren't you?" Amy finally said, awe-struck by the realization.

The pieces were finally coming together. King laughed.

"What gave it away? Welcome back to Arthridall, one of the many lands I rule."

Amy got flustered, quickly trying to make herself presentable since she knew who he was now.

"I... I... I... Oh my God, this is embarrassing... Please forgive me... for... for... Oh God James was right... I... I... I..."

King chuckled heartily, standing up and pulling her up in his arms with a giant bear hug.

"Nice to meet you."

"He's so warm," Amy thought, melting into his embrace.

"Why, thank you," King said.

"YOU HEARD THAT?!" Amy exclaimed.

She found herself unsurprised by the fact. The man chuckled.

"Amy, I've waited a long time to personally meet you. Welcome."

Amy pulled away.

"I... Uh... Thank you... for... uh... allowing me... to uh... be here. I guess."

Amy felt ashamed that he valued her as much as he did. Before she could think about it, she was retreating backwards towards the edge of the clearing. She needed to leave the place. She needed to run.

"He doesn't deserve someone still as messed up as me," she thought.

The man called from the tree on the hill.

"You're wrong, little one! Where do you think we are right now? Arthridall, yes, but we're also inside your heart. Why'd you think it felt so good to be back? It took a while," he said, walking toward her, "but I knew you could do it."

His words reached her, and she crumpled. Amy began crying again and slumped to her knees, first in misery, then relief. She didn't really want to leave. He fell on his knees too and began weeping loudly. His wailing echoed, the magnolia trees shaking violently as the flowers surrendered to the ground's embrace. The noise finally reached her, and she noticed he was crying too.

"Mr. King... sir? Why are you crying?"

He wiped his face. She found even watching him wipe snot from his nose was glorious.

"I'm cry because my friends are crying... and it breaks my heart. I hate everything that hurts them and makes them cry!"

"King..."

Amy didn't know how to comfort him.

"King, are you crying... because Thorne murdered James... and... he's crying... for me? Am... Am I the one he's been searching for all these years?"

The pieces clicked together.

"I'm the one he's been searching for… right? For……. Me? Me… right?"

King gestured for her to sit with him. He sighed, pulling himself together for her sake.

"Yeah… he was there. He was there on your birthday when no one else came. He watched, helplessly, when your father tortured you and forced you and your mother to run. He got left behind… all alone… helpless… not able to keep his promise to you… too young to stand against your father and fight him."

"What?"

"He wanted to beat some sense into him because of what he did to you and your mother…"

"He wanted to…? But we were only nine!"

"After you left… He tried talking to him first to speak some sense into him. It didn't work…"

"What?!"

"James got socked in the face."

"My dad punched a kid?!"'

"He got back up… and kept trying to reason with him."

"Moron!"

"He took at least six punches before someone saw it. Your dad was obviously… well, you know…"

"Yeah…"

"The first thing James did when he woke up was tell his parents why he'd gone over there in the first place."

"But… James?"

"I've restarted his heart more times than you'd ever want to hear."

"Wha…?"

"What does do when I'm not around?" she thought.

"His act of bravery convinced his parents to help him find where you and your mom ran to and move to the area once they found out. So, once he was strong enough, he could protect you the way he wanted to… They admired his courage."

"Then all this…"

"They found your city through an old family friend. Years passed… He didn't know exactly where you lived… but he knew you were out there somewhere… so he wrote about his countless adventures for you so you could read them when you reunited and catch up…"

"Because we used to play pretend…"

"Then your mom died and you moved in with your grandmother… see the connection?"

"Nana… she was their family friend, so when… they moved to the city they naturally moved into the same neighborhood… Oh… wow… so he's… he really is the boy from… right? That wasn't just my imagination. Where is he now?"

"He's waiting. You ran all the way to the ends of Earth and he pursued you every step of the way so he could protect you like he promised. All because you're his best friend. All because he…"

"He really loves me…"

Amy looked at King with a miserably pleading look.

"And I wouldn't let him tell me… because I'd been hurt so much and wasn't listening to anyone… Oh… James I'm so sorry! Please… Tell me… tell me where he went!"

King rested his hand on her shoulder, smiling until she got it. He chuckled. Amy shook her head.

"Then all this is part of the real world and his… his interpretation of it? And you orchestrated all the events so they'd work out in both?! You really did help him write everything, didn't you?"

"I may have given him some pointers…"

Amy crossed her arms, waiting for him to speak up and defend himself.

"What? It's my duty to protect my friend's personal interests!"

Amy raised an eyebrow and tried holding back her smile, finally losing it completely.

"I like you, King. You're the real deal."

King walked back to the oak tree. Amy followed. She couldn't help but feel like he was already more of a dad to her than hers ever was.

"Just remember," King said, holding her close, "you aren't just my subject here."

Everything in sight went blindingly white as King revealed the true scope of his nature. The girl shivered violently from the joy emanating out of him, and it was the most magical feeling she'd ever felt. The epitome of true love in an instant. It was warm and it left her speechless.

King spoke.

"You are my friend!"

45

Amy found herself standing in the middle of a large field at the height of day. Sunshine shone on the scene sprawling before her, as if the light itself were a solid substance similar to honey. Everywhere the light touched flowers bloomed in all shapes and sizes and colors, as if the light itself was responsible for the transformation.

Amy turned to look behind. Her grove was there, hiding secretly in the forest and awaiting her return. She could see the edge of one of the magnolias when she looked far enough up the path. It was an odd sensation to be able to see a place that was over a mile away. She felt special, as if she was one of the few people who'd ever been allowed to explore that special place.

"Or even see it, for that matter," she remarked, turning back to the new place in front of her.

On either side of the field stood two ridges of mountains. The end of the field gave rise to the valley country below.

"If only they had hover-boards we could surf around with here! It's so smooth and colorful!"

She could already smell the collective culinary efforts in the town nestled between the mountains far away. Someone was baking fresh bread and the smell was altogether intoxicating. Amy smelled the bread when she focused her nose towards it, but whenever she looked in any other direction the smell of the flowers quickly replaced it. She couldn't decide which one she liked most; every time she focused on a different kind of flower, the smell changed. Despite the wonderful flower smells, the lure of freshly baking bread reminded her it'd been at least an hour since she'd eaten dinner with Nana back on Earth. She was famished.

"Well... I'd typically say it's because I like food too much. But didn't James say time flows differently here? Who knows? Maybe it's already been a week travelling here! In that case I need to eat again!"

Amy waltzed through the field without a care in the world. She figured King helping her get here might've had something to do with it.

"Totally not justifying being a fatty or anything... I know he'd laugh if he found out my weakness is food... mmm... food... Do I really care? Nah... I don't care... He probably already knows."

She felt tempted to start singing and dancing to her personal 'about-to-eat-some-food-and-it's-mine-all-mine' song. Realizing the flowers were literally throwing themselves at her feet and clearing a path for her down the hillside she decided the land itself was even begging her to go eat.

"Arthidall is awesome!"

Amy sang her heart out for food. For some reason she rose into the sky the more she sang, not unlike the rising of yeast working itself through raw dough. She found the sensation both amazing and exhilarating as a combination of weightlessness and secureness lifted her up, twirling and spinning her along the currents of the wind.

"I'm flying for food?" Amy giggled. "HA! Flying to get food! I'm can fly here? What in the world? Just…"

She threw her arms out to her sides to stabilize herself with her human airplane wings.

"Why though?" she wondered. "Not complaining! Just, Hee-Hee… Why?"

Amy couldn't help but wonder what else was possible here. She drew close to the town, the smell of bread growing invariably more powerful and aromatic. She was pleased to experience an entire host of extra delightful smells.

"That ain't no ordinary bread!"

Amy laughed so hard she snorted. Realizing snot was gushing out her face like Niagara Falls she made a motion with her hand to wipe it off, and a handkerchief materialized out of thin air to calm the offending waterfall.

"Handkerchief? What... That's garlic bread! How'd they know? I love garlic bread!"

Amy heard someone calling out to her from down below. She scanned the town carefully until she spotted an elderly, bald-headed man eagerly waving his arms above his head.

"He saw me? All the way down there? Got to hand it to him, he's got amazing eyesight. I guess the cats are out of the bag."

A dull red and brown-checkered carpetbag materialized in front of her, seemingly held in place by the weight of the summer breeze. It startled her so much she almost fell straight out of her flight path but was held up in the same manner she'd gotten up there. She almost didn't know what to make of it.

"Wait... Oh No... There's no way... No... Nah..."

Amy air-walked to the bag, unlatching the brass clasp on top to examine its contents. Thousands of cats and kittens exploded out in a flurry of paws and fur. Amy watched in horror as they started raining down from the sky. There was nothing she could do to help them and, as they began dropping like rocks, she couldn't help but feel like it was entirely her fault.

"Cats out of the bag..."

Just as quickly as the feline nightmare began, the most unusual thing happened. The cats fell into the shape of a perfect spiral staircase leading back to the ground, with the last of the kittens landing right at her feet, their tiny kitten paws linked together in some sort of menagerie of limbs.

"Oh no...NO no NO no NO no NO! THAT is literally terrible! Animal cruelty, I say! JAMES!!!"

It was dead silence, save the slight whistling of wind beneath her and the exasperated shouting of the old man calling below.

"Actually... I guess this would be... PURRfect..."

Amy shook her head in disgust. Cat puns were not her favorite.

"How else was I supposed to get down though? WHEN I'M FLYING AND I DON'T KNOW HOW?! Geez... I'm a terrible human being. I don't deserve to live on this planet anymore."

In spite of her rant, Amy placed a tentative foot on the first kitten's back and it mewed pitiably. And, despite her animal rights speech, she snorted helplessly at the kitten's antics.

"I... I hope I didn't hurt you, little guy. Are you alright?"

The kitten looked up and opened its mouth as if to meow again. Amy leaned in close to hear its cuteness. The kitten licked the tip of her ear and she almost died from squealing.

"NAH GIRL, YOU GOOD," the kitten replied with the deep vocal capacity of a fully large and grown man-cat-thing.

"EEEEEEK!!! YOU CAN TALK?!"

Amy freaked out. She didn't have the chance to respond to the otherwise perfectly reasonable looking kitten. The successive meows from the other cats as she stepped on their bellies and backs resounded though the entire valley, drawing every set of eyes from the town below straight to her. The old man patted her back after the shaky landing. She kissed the solid ground with the enthusiasm of an actress who'd finally escaped the paparazzi long enough to gain ten minutes of blissful solitude. The rest of the townsfolk shook their heads grudgingly and returned to their daily duties as if those kinds of events occurred frequently.

"What were you doing?!" the man exclaimed. "It's dangerous to fly when the dragon is around! You should know better!"

Amy finally caught her breath and stood up to get a decent look at the man. And, even though she was average height for her age, found he was three inches shorter.

"Cats… They can taaalk!"

"Well of course they can! At least when someone isn't stomping on their faces," he said, gesturing for her to follow him inside his home.

Amy complied willingly. Her adventures in wonderland were driving her a bit insane and a hot meal with someone who seemed to understand things around these parts sounded amazing.

The elderly man's home was both plain and simple, but it smelled like garlic bread and he seemed friendly and unassuming. He gestured her to sit at the table situated in the middle of the cramped but tidy living room. She gratefully accepted, pulling in the well-worn wooden chair with a scoot.

"The name's Jehu. I was told you'd get back today. Good thing I saw you when I did too, before he smelled ya. He must be off bothering someone somewhere else. Nasty beast keeps snatching everyone up and taking 'em to its lair to torture them with his nasty habits before murdering them for sport."

"Dragon?"

"Yes. Nasty thing keeps trying to destroy the world and whatnot. Goes by the name Thorne. You might know 'im I hope. Terrible creature, he is."

"Th... Thorne!?"

"Calm down. Most people even here don't really know what he's really planning. They don't care, either. And!" Jehu exclaimed grimly, "If we don't stop him he's going to rain hell on all of us."

Amy scooted back from the table, her wooden chair scooting now seeming obnoxiously obnoxious. Jehu pulled the garlic bread out of the hearth along with a pot of what he self-deemed the world's best spaghetti.

"I... I already faced him... Back... on Earth. This is Arthridall, right? Not some alternate dimension James cooked up?"

"No," Jehu replied, scooping out a massive heap of pasta and meatballs onto her plate. "It's definitely Arthridall. Last time I checked. Here you go. Dig in."

***

Amy tried to take in the new information all at once, but it didn't seem to matter how she tried going about it. Solving what appeared to be yet another one of her friend's ridiculous riddles was proving to be both bothersome and aggravating. She was stumped. Jehu noticed her consternation as she ripped somewhat angrily into the bread he'd so carefully prepared.

"I'm glad you like it," he said, reaching into the red and white cloth checkered basket sitting on the table. "It takes quite a bit of time to let the yeast work all the way through. It's got to be long enough to get it as fluffy as I like."

He stroked his beard softly and waited for a response, chuckling appropriately. The glazed look in Amy's eyes disappeared.

"So... Thorne... so he really can change forms? I wasn't just going crazy then..."

Jehu nodded his head in agreement, setting the hunk of bread that wasn't stuffed in his mouth back on the plate. Amy watched his every movement and waited for him to finish. Much to his chagrin, he decided it better to talk with his face full of half chewed mush. It was as if he'd subconsciously decided his embarrassment was overshadowed by the immediate necessity to answer his guest's questions. Jehu picked up a napkin, politely covering his mouth in order to keep speaking.

"In layman's terms, well, yes, he even goes by different names when he needs to," he said, swallowing. "And yes, he can turn into all sorts of creatures. Even people. In your world too… he and his cohorts have also been known to take possession of people if they don't defend themselves…"

Jehu dropped his plate in the wash-basin on the far side of the Arthrindian equivalent of a kitchen. Most homes, as far as she could tell, were more like small cottages; everything in the home was part of the same room, so Amy couldn't quite bring herself to call it a kitchen.

"It's more of a… kitchen space," she thought.

The plate clattered and crashed on top of the massive pile of older dishes, almost causing everything to spill over the sink and break into thousands of tiny pieces on the floor. Amy shrieked briefly in anticipation of the impending destruction, not unlike whenever she spotted a roach or some other creepy-crawly insect back home.

Amy blinked, then blinked again. The entire kitchen, no, the entire cottage, was spotless.

"Uh… ah, Jehu? How'd you do that? Is everything in Arthridall magic? Is that why that note said for me to find you?"

Jehu didn't answer, instead scooting back to the table, propping his elbows up and stroking his long greying beard, watching his guest eat with awkward intensity. Considering everything she'd recently gone through she didn't find his mannerisms all that strange. If he'd done the same thing back when she was eating with Nana it would've been terrifying in the 'socially-awkward-but-well-meaning-stalker' sense.

"I'm his guest though… and it's probably some sort of polite courtesy here," she thought, twirling the next bite of pasta on her fork and stabbing the other half of her meatball to top it off.

"Anything to do with Thorne is a nasty business. You best not interact with him if at all possible."

Amy looked at her host, trying to decide how to tell him about her recent experiences. She decided he was definitely, at the very least, a little crazy in the head. Either that, or he hadn't been listening to begin with.

"Sir, you haven't even asked me my name yet."

Jehu grinned toothily, his jaw slightly ajar as if he was a heavy smoker on pain-killers, or a baby who'd recently soiled his diaper.

"It doesn't matter what your name is because you'll eventually tell me, right? All that matters to me is your friend told me to expect you on this day and at this time and have one of your favorite meals ready and waiting when you got here."

"About that," Amy said, leaning back from the table. "Thanks for the meal. It was delicious."

"Quite welcome. Are you finished eating, then?"

"Yes."

Jehu reached for her plate, flinging it like a discus into the sink without missing a beat or moving from his chair. It landed without a noise. Amy was startled by the lack broken china.

"That should've been super loud!" she exclaimed.

"Well obviously," Jehu replied.

"What happened to it then?"

"Isn't it obvious?"

"No!"

"Calm down, miss. Everything's back in the cabinet safe and sound."

"What?"

"Dishes are Ay-okay."

"But you... you threw it! The dirt! The..."

"Ah, but Arthridall has different rules than Earth. You should've learned that by now. Right?"

"Riiight... Even still..." Amy petered off.

Jehu grinned again, glancing out the back window and briskly standing up, frolicking out the back door and up the small hill in his backyard to get a better view of the flowers. Amy, not knowing what else to do, followed him until they reached the top. Jehu dropped to the ground like a rock, laying on his back and gazing at the late-afternoon sky to study the cloud patterns. After some consideration, Amy quietly seated herself a few feet away so as not to disturb him.

Amy leaned her hand against her forehead, muttering under her breath.

"James, what have I gotten myself into? And Jehu? This place is complete bonkers... where are you hiding?"

Amy leaned back and closed her eyes, shifting to her side after a few moments to get more comfortable. After a while, Amy heard what sounded like Jehu's slight snoring. It was of the old-man variety, the kind that comes after a heavy Thanksgiving meal. Half-opening one her eyes to confirm her hypothesis, she shrieked in the old man's face before cutting herself short.

"You... you were awake?"

Jehu revealed his old-man chompers once again. If she hadn't been so startled by his antics, she probably would've found his stupid grinning for her enjoyment to be on the side of hilarity. As it stood, Amy backed away involuntarily to make some space. Jehu rolled to his side, propping himself up with an elbow.

"So how do you know James? Almost nobody knows about him nowadays."

Amy cleared her throat. Jehu was weird, but he was harmless enough.

"And he did feed me…" she thought.

"Well?" Jehu asked.

"Uh… Well I… He's uh… He's my friend. That's how I know him. And it's why I came here in the first place. I think… I need to find him so we can go home and be together again and go on adventures and lo…"

"Ooohooo miss! Slow down."

He stood up, his back cracking in what sounded like eight different places all at once. She didn't know whether to be impressed or be creeped out. Jehu's face lit up with glee.

"That sounds like something he would do."

"What is… wait, how do you know him, then? Was he here? Did he tell you to make spaghetti? Where did he run to? Did he say where I should meet him?"

Jehu helped her stand to her feet, completely ignoring her questions.

"Shush. No, he wasn't here. At least, not the James you know. I haven't seen your James in ages. Age? It's been a while at the very least. Your James said he had a project he needed to finish back home before he could return again. Whatever that means."

Amy forced herself to calm down and contain her excitement.

"How do you know… my James, then?"

"That's an easy one, miss. He's a friend. And," he continued, "He's one of the historians of Arthridall. King personally commissioned him. Pretty important stuff, mind you. Those historians are a strange bunch though. How on earth did you meet someone as crazy as him and not immediately run?"

"You're one to talk," she whispered under her breath.

"EH?! What was that? I didn't hear it."

"I said that… he's a writer. Not a historian."

Jehu nodded his head as if the fact meant something to him. He raised his bushy eyebrows, causing the skin on his forehead to fold until it looked like the roof of one's mouth.

"Oh… well, he's a writer back on Earth at least," Amy said, defending herself.

"Naturally."

Amy sighed inwardly. It seemed like everyone was a critic or an atrocious pun maker; so much so that she wondered if it were one of the necessary traits to be a citizen.

"By your logic I guess that makes me a historian then, too," she said.

"You're a writer?" he exclaimed.

"I…" she paused. "I guess so. He made me his co-author to protect me from Thorne. Honestly though… I'm more poet than author… maybe an actress at times… Not that I'm any good at acting… or dancing… oh, and gaming… But now I can't seem to find him anywhere and as per usual he's being an ass about it."

"Well that part of it is obvious, miss. He already tagged you and now you're it. Don't you know how to play games anymore?"

"Oh…"

"And miss, since you're not a man… You're a woman… person… You're you!" Jehu exclaimed, trying to explain himself. "So the correct term for you here is not a historian. You are a herstorian."

She shook her head at the terrible joke, still trying to salvage what was left of the conversation to get what she needed.

"You knew? Oh yes! Of course! Of course. I'm a herstorian. You caught me."

"Now you get it, miss!"

She walked around, stretching her arms in the anticipation that her James was going to jump out of one of the nearby bushes to surprise her. She was determined to be ready to punch him in the face and catch him before he ran away again.

"My name's Amy by the way," she said, offering her hand for a handshake.

"I know," Jehu replied, using his fingertips to tickle her hand.

"You. Are. A. Total. Child!" she thought.

"How'd you know?" she said sarcastically. "Who told you?"

Jehu pointed at her.

"You did. Silly."

46

Amy huffed and walked back to the entrance of the hidden grove. She couldn't handle him any longer. Jehu, for his part, buzzed around tirelessly like a fly begging to be swatted from the sky with a newspaper.

"How does he have this much energy? I've never been as excited as him about anything in my entire life!" she thought.

Jehu waved his arms even more rapidly, doing everything he could to catch her attention. Amy could've sworn every time she tried listening to him it was similar to trying to converse with a hive of bees that'd been poked one too many times with a stick.

"WHAT!" she shouted angrily.

Amy spun around angrily, prepared to yell in his face if need be, fully expecting him to be twiddling his thumbs or blowing snot bubbles that would magically explode into confetti. Whatever it was, it would be childish and irritating beyond belief. Instead, she found the buzzing of Jehu's increasingly hyper voice to have disappeared. He was nowhere to be found. She allowed herself to sigh in relief, finally turning back to continue her quest to find James at their designated meeting place.

"AY! You found me!" Jehu exclaimed.

Amy fell back on her rump. Jehu chuckled heartily, rubbing the crown of his head as if he were trying to get his wishes granted.

"Ow... that hurt..."

"Are you okay?" Jehu asked, inching up to her and acting like a concerned grandfather.

Amy pretended to cry to draw him in, then grabbed him by the scruff of his shirt without thinking twice. Amy felt a brief moment of concern as he seemed to grunt in pain from her surprise attack.

"Oh my! I wasn't thinking! I'm sorr... Seriously? Wipe that stupid grin off your face!"

Jehu stood up, brushing the loose dirt off of his clothing and offering a hand to help her stand up. Amy sighed angrily, but after a moment of watching him grin innocently she unwillingly obliged.

"What do you want?"

"Where are you going, Amy?"

"Home. I'm going to find James a different way. I'm tired of dealing with you! I'm tired of dealing with all the weird garbage that happens here! I'm tired of dealing with..."

"School?"

"Not school! I'm tired of dealing with you! Your childish pranks! Yes, school! Wait, how'd you know about school?"

"James told me."

Jehu made a gesture with his hand and a large, pointed hat with an obnoxiously floppy brim suiting his personality appeared in his hand. He gently put it on his head, finally deciding it would fit better if he pulled it over his genie-lamp like a sweater.

"James told you... James? Wait I thought... Which James? How in the world did? Where did? Hat?"

Jehu raised his right hand to point to the countryside in the distance, his staff appearing from thin air to rest in his palm.

"I bought it at a market somewhere over that way a number of years ago. Good quality stuff is hard to find nowadays. So sorry! You can't have mine! Otherwise we could match. Maybe one day, honey."

Jehu pirouetted like a ballerina and chuckled like a bear.

"It'd be so neat if we matched!" he said excitedly.

Amy blinked, trying to think of a response.

"And... where did the staff come from?"

"Oh… This? Uh… I'm not really sure. I know I punched one out of a tree just like this one way back when, but I lost it soon after."

Jehu sighed.

"It was a good stick too. Real hardy. Great for bashing bad-guy heads! We were pretending to fight cave monsters in the glow-wormy cave… In a cave… Oh is that where you're going? I can help since I have a war stick again!"

"Uh…Well then… Wait, you said we?"

"One of my grandaughters… you'd love her. I miss her so much! But she said she needed some space for a while. Says she's learning Cry… Cryo…"

"Cryogenics?"

"AH! YES! Cryogenics! Wart removers or something."

"Actually, Cryogenics is the study of producing materials at very low temperatures and how those materials behave in those freezing conditions."

"PIT PAT! I KNEW THAT!"

"Then why wart remove…."

"Come to think of it this could be the same stick… Or its cousin or something! An Earth stick! Ooohooo! This is exciting!"

"He jumps around way too much," Amy thought.

"Are… Are you a wizard? Is that why you know about the field in this forest?"

"Absolutely not! Not a wizard!" he exclaimed, pointing his staff past the town behind them. "Being a wizard implies a false sense of superiority! Narcissism! They think they're the real deal! As if using dark magic makes them big shots! Well! It doesn't!"

"Do you understa…"

Jehu cut her off.

"Plus their hats are obnoxiously floppy. Ridiculous! And don't even get me started about how bad they are when it comes to interpersonal timing! They think they can channel power through wands! Or staffs! Or whatever! Twigs!"

Jehu launched a volley of various power-blasts as if he were raining down a hailstorm of fiery meteorites on an army somewhere far off in the distance.

"I wouldn't be surprised if he were, honestly…" she thought. "James… you seem more normal than I first thought… Jehu… He's bonkers!"

Amy couldn't help but be excited and terrified by the man in front of her. He seemed harmless enough, even if he seemed mostly crazy. Launching fireballs the size of meteors was definitely crazy. She was at a loss for words.

"Hate them wizards! They never do anything for anyone else! They think they're more powerful than everybody else since they think they can channel real power? Through twigs? Amy!?"

"Ye... Yeah?"

"Wizards are counterfeits! Purveyors of darkness and death! They need a weapon to be useful in any capacity... and... well..." he said, leaning in close, "If you want true strength all you got to do is be one of the good guys. Everything else is a reflection of that, or a revealing, if you will."

"Huh?"

"True power comes from strong relationships and intimate brotherhoods. And in here..." he said, pumping his chest. "You've got to know who you are if you're ever going to be able to fight. King's really good at rallying people to him too, so yeah... GOOD STUFF!"

She still didn't know what to say but she could tell that he was right somehow, even if he was a complete wacko. And the feat of strength he'd performed for her seemed very much like King's light. Or hers in her battle against Thorne. Both experiences were unmistakable.

"So you know King, then? Uh... I uh... is that his real name? I mean... is that his real name, or just a title?"

"Amy?"

"Yeah?"

"He's King."

"What? That doesn't answer anything."

"Amy?"

"What?"

"That answers everything."

Jehu smiled warmly, his eyes carrying a beautiful shine to them. Amy believed him. He revealed his real personality for the first time; the senile old man-child routine was an act he'd put on for her benefit. She found herself completely at ease after that.

"Do you see how old and wise I am, Amy? My voice is raspy too, like I've been smoking for my entire life."

"Have you?"

"Never! Well actually there was this one time I was relaxing at the beach with a beautiful young lady much like yourself, and I thought to myself 'Man, it'd be hilarious to blow her mind by smoking this pipe and self-fulfill part of a future that I made up on the spot.'"

"That's not very nice. Why on earth would you do that?"

"Because she told me that I was crotchety old fart, that's why. So I played the part. She told me she liked to act, so I did too! Relationships!"

"What? You aren't a crotchety old fart!"

Jehu smiled.

"The answer to your question is yes. I do know King very well. He's my friend... I've known him for a very long time... Like... Longer than you've been alive! He's the only man I'd ever give my allegiance to, and his mission to protect this world is my mission too."

"Hhmmmm..." Amy said, trying to process it all. "Then the reason I flew earlier was... because I met King... he showed me why I needed to be here and..."

"Answer my question, miss!"

"What?"

"Where are you going?"

"The forest."

"Why?"

"To get back to Earth and find James."

"How?"

"What?" Amy asked.

"How does a forest help you accomplish that? You trying to run away? There's a glow-worm cave in that forest, you know? But watch out for imaginary cave monsters."

Amy shook her head.

"But it's how I got transported to Arthridall, right?"

"I don't know your life! You tell me."

Amy considered it. She didn't actually remember whether she'd arrived in Arthridall through the forest, now that she thought about it. For all she knew James could've made up some other mechanism to protect his writing, if only to mess up any theory she may have made while she was inside it. Or King, since he'd apparently played such a big part in it. For all she knew she could've been in the real world the entire time.

"I... I actually don't know... exactly. For all I know, I could've been in Arthridall the entire time and not known it. It would certainly explain how you know about my hating school. Or..."

"Actually, my James told me that one. Or maybe my Amy... Heh... poor old man brain..."

"It'd be just like him tell you, if only to shoot down my theory. Well, wait... then maybe Earth is the fiction, and Arthridall is real... I... It's a thought. Wait... You said your Amy?!"

"I said it would be something my James or Amy would do," Jehu replied. "But let me ask you this. James made you his co-author, right?"

"I... think so?"

"It's a yes or no question, honey."

She found that she didn't mind Jehu's gruffness anymore. If anything, it was endearing.

"Well… Then… I'd say yes. But he only did it to keep Thorne from getting to me too, right? Like a 'kill me too the story ends and so do you' thing?"

"Meh… Wrong. Try again."

"Huh? But that's exactly why he did it!"

"That's not the only reason. You of all people should know it was a more important reason."

"And how would you know? If I might be so bold as to ask."

Jehu waited for her to answer her own question.

"Your James told you. Or mine… he could've written it that way so that you already knew. So, there's a physical book."

"Technically, it may be a yes on both accounts."

"Wa… I just thought of something."

"Yes?" Jehu asked.

"Just how old is your James? Or your Amy?"

"Huh?"

"How old are they?"

"They… uh… well you see age is kind of a weird phenomenon here compared to Earth… kind of a maturity is age thing… but if I had to guess…"

"Yes?"

"My James and Amy are married. They had a child... a beautiful baby girl. And she's actually..."

"So we... we... Oh my... We're married here..." Amy was dumbstruck.

It was finally making sense. In a very odd, bubbly, wild, endearing sort of way. She was a mother to a beautiful baby girl.

"I have a child... I have... with James... married..." She whispered.

Amy's heart swelled, her face blushing deeply from the ramifications of her imagination. It made sense though. All of the oddities and ins and outs of his stories made sense now; she couldn't explain it, but she no longer felt like anything he'd ever done was wrong now. It was adorable.

"Jehu... What's my baby girl's name?"

"I don't know. They... couldn't bring themselves to tell me... To keep her identity safe until she was old enough to have it."

"What?!"

"That's what I'm saying. Right? It sucks... Not that they didn't trust me or anything silly like that. No... it's because of one of Arthridall's oldest prophesies... they think their daughter might be... Well it's a long story..."

"Oh, I totally see where this is going."

"You do?"

"Thorne's hunting down the chosen one. He wants to murder her to claim her power for himself and steal King's throne. It would explain James' entire book. And why he was after us. It's actually a pr..."

Jehu was surprised.

"How on earth could anything this remote possibly bring you to that conclusion?"

"Uh..." Amy shrugged. "I think... call it a mother's instinct. Or... well, it would explain why he's been hunting us this long. He's searching for power but doesn't know who or what carries it. So, he goes after anyone who seems to have it... Or at least be making headway in getting it."

"Your deductive skills are astounding. No wonder my Amy had her James meet up with his younger self... they had to... He needed to clear up some misconceptions with his younger self."

"Younger self?"

"Whoops! I spoke too much! ZIP!"

"What?"

"PREQUELS!"

"Uh... Well then... I... uh... I'll drop it for now then..."

"GOOD!"

"Good?"

Jehu nodded his head in agreement, clearly wanting to change the subject.

"Prequels…"

"Anyways…" Amy said, returning to the earlier topic. "More stuff up his sleeve… James wanted me to be a part of something near and dear to him. Yes… Right, his books. His stories… our story… And knowing him, there are even more worlds and dimensions than those somehow."

Jehu sighed, apparently tired from her seemingly endless and circular reasoning.

"Do you still really not get it? He wanted you to be his co-author from the very beginning. He didn't have the heart to finish making anything without you, so he tried asking you in his own way for help. You're his reason he creates stories. Right? Didn't he tell you that? Or did he forget… James… Oh bless his heart he's so forgetful…"

"No! N… Yes… he did. I… threw it in his face. That's why I need to find him again. To apologize… For everything."

"Wake up! Wouldn't you think he'd already forgiven you? He's your husba… friend, for crying aloud! Isn't that why you came here? You're here, right? Does it matter? Amy! Stop believing he's the only culprit in your wacky little adventures. For crying aloud…"

Jehu sighed. Amy was shocked.

"…"

Jehu continued.

"You're both equally important in Arthridall and on Earth! Way more than I have time to explain right now. It doesn't matter where you are. You two will always be together no matter what. Riiight? And," he continued, "for all you know... anything I'm saying here has an equal chance of being put in a book by either of you, if indeed this were part of your story. But that's apparently only one of the options!"

"James? Or me?"

"Does it matter?!"

"Yes! It does!"

"Hmmm... Or both of you writing at the same time. HAH! It doesn't matter who writes it down... or when it's written... you both have similar skills... no... similar interests and styles... Yeah, that's more like it. In fact," Jehu said, "Your writing styles are so similar... I wouldn't be surprised to learn that your daughter is the author. If or when all this is written down, of course."

"Huh?"

"May I help you?"

"Uh..."

"Yeeees?"

"But... that... could possibly mean that all this... It's simply the result of her overly elaborate imagination!"

"Wouldn't James have already told you that? Correct. Or it could also be real, like she's making a diary to try tracking you two down. I mean, ya'll do hop around quite a wee-bit. Or both if you got super existential. Hah! You make me laugh! Such a cute married couple… friends! Daughter!"

"But… Why would either of us ever do anything something that horrid to a kid? And why do you keep bringing that up?!"

"What's your heart telling you?"

Amy searched deep within herself. Everything was both shouting and staying quiet at the same time, and in the in-between of it she found herself. She didn't know whether to cry, or simply cry a lot. None of it made sense and all of it was driving her crazy.

"For all I know," she said, choosing her words carefully, "I could be speaking to myself right now through you, if you were just a character… I could also be speaking to James. Or… someone entirely different altogether. Like a daughter. Or even a completely different author. You did mention something about your James… and your Amy… Right?"

"All are possibilities," Jehu said, smiling. "And I'll throw another wrench in every one your theories by clearly stating that I'm entirely real. In no way am I fictional character, nor am I the product of ya'll's wacky imaginations. I refuse. I'm already wacky enough as it is."

"But…"

"AH BUH BUH BUH! No! Stop. If this were a book your audience would hate you. You're making it too confusing, girl!"

He took his hat off and dropped it on the ground where it disappeared altogether.

"I..." she began.

"I saaaiiid... stop it."

"No, not that. How on earth did you do that?" Amy asked again, this time more concerned about figuring out how he so seemingly and effortlessly pulled objects out of nowhere.

Jehu returned to his goofy grinning again. Amy couldn't decide if she liked that part of his personality yet.

"I don't know, Amy. You. Tell. Me."

"This is frustrating."

"Why is that?" Jehu asked. "Maybe I'll teach the future you how I do down the road... Who knows...?"

"Because... I could literally be talking to myself through you; speaking to my older self, which I guess... has to be me... because I'm in Arthridall... and have no idea how long I've been here. Or if I ever even left..."

Jehu laughed, putting a hand on her shoulder.

"I'm so sorry. I know it's confusing. But it's exactly the right amount of confusing the entire shindig needs to be, right? If there wasn't any mystery to living... or... if we are indeed in a book... it wouldn't be interesting, right?"

"I suppose so," Amy said, after some thought. "I'd like to think that... well... that my life could just make sense somehow. Even just once."

"You and everyone else. Ha! Are you ready for another piece of the puzzle?"

Amy began to sit, only to find that they'd both sat down in rocking chairs. And if the random appearance of rocking chairs weren't odd enough by itself, Amy also found the ocean waves lapping the sandy shore at their feet entirely lovely.

"I love watching the ocean as the sun sets," he said. "Especially when the colors in the clouds change. It's so pretty. It's like King's painting one massive picture for the entire world all at once. They're never the same, either. All different. Unique. Every time I look, I find something new."

Amy found herself agreeing completely with the little odd man. She loved painting, even though she didn't believe herself to be very good at it. She rocked back and forth in her chair, swaying with the salt air. Eventually, her curiosity got the best of her.

"Jehu?"

"Yes?"

"How did we get here? Weren't we just at your cabin a moment ago? Or at least... in the field out back?"

"I don't know. You tell me."

"But… Is this how you've been able to change things around whenever you feel like it?"

"Imagination certainly plays a part, I would imagine."

"That's something James would say."

"It's possible. But it may also be something you would say. Or me. Because I'm a real person too."

Amy thought about it. He wasn't wrong. It was something she'd say even if James didn't exist in her life. But it was also something that Jehu might say as well.

"Or if James never existed at all, now that I think about it," Amy thought.

Jehu smiled briefly and closed his eyes, puffing on what appeared to be a long, old-fashioned pipe. Amy chose to not begin the circular argument again, instead just letting him be. After a while, Jehu coughed on the smoke slightly as old men do. If she didn't know any better, she could've sworn he'd fallen asleep on her again. Even the snoring was a near-perfect replica of what she imagined Jehu's real snore to sound like.

She couldn't blame him for wanting to rest a bit.

"He's an old man, after all…" she thought, starting to grow drowsy, her eyelids drooping under their own weight. "Wait! No! This is exactly what he did last time! Crotchety old fart!"

Amy shook herself awake. He was still sitting in his own chair, snoring. Not rocking, which was a clear indicator that he hadn't moved since he'd fallen asleep.

"But that's just what he wants me to think," she whispered, half to herself. "Lulls me into a false sense of security, then wham!"

"Amy?" Jehu asked.

"I knew you were faking it!" she exclaimed.

Jehu continued snoring as if he'd been asleep the entire time.

"Stop faking it!"

"Faking what?"

Jehu smoked on the pipe.

"THE FAKE DREAMING!"

Jehu half-opened an eye, then closed it again.

"Who's to say all of this isn't just a dream?" he said. "Wonderland calls to those who dream in color. Neverland calls to those who run from reality. Arthridall? Well… we haven't quite decided… but we're way better than those places when you give us a shot… maybe? That's up to you to decide. Arthridall is the land of what you make of it."

Amy seethed with anger. The rings of smoke emanating from his pipe only served to add fuel to the fire, as if the smoke itself was the physical embodiment of Jehu's ridiculous answers.

"JEHU!"

"What?"

"Stop!"

Jehu leaned back into his chair too far and fell out of it, rolling into a reverse somersault and standing up no worse for the wear. Amy noticed that he didn't open his eyes for the entire performance. He spoke.

"Who's to say that we haven't just been in a dream the entire time? Who's to say Arthridall isn't just as real a place as Earth? Who's to say whether Earth is imaginary and Arthridall is the real world? Where's the line, Amy? Who's to say I'm not the author and you and James are my characters?"

"I... I don't know! I DON'T KNOW!!!"

Amy clutched her head and felt the cool rush of the waves at her feet. She found herself standing on the sea about thirty yards from shore.

"It would sure make sense if it's all a dream!" Jehu called from shore. "And you and James made this place from your combined dreams! The result of your combined aspirations! Think about it, Amy!"

"I AM THINKING! I'VE BEEN THINKING!" Amy called back, cupping her hands so he could hear her over the sound of the waves. "NONE OF IT MAKES SENSE! I'M TIRED OF THINKING!"

"It never did, Amy! And it never will! It's impossible to explain love! No matter how long you try! You can't reason it away! You've got to feel it! YOU'VE GOT TO EXPERIENCE IT TO UNDERSTAND!"

Amy walked back to the sand, still trying to understand how she'd been able to walk on the water in the first place. Jehu opened his eyes, chuckling as Amy imagined a little kid would while trying to imitate their father.

"A very long, and very detailed love letter..." she said.

"But of course. It doesn't matter where you are. It doesn't matter what you're doing. All that matters is who you're with and why you're together. That is the reality. That is the truth. And that my friend, is the story."

"Reality... Reality is what we make of it. Reality... It's what we make it to be. That's Arthridall."

Jehu smiled.

"James chose the right gal."

"I thought... I thought he was writing in order to help his friend out... And I wasn't wrong. I just didn't stop to think that the friend he was writing for was me."

"Do you want to go back now? To go back home?" Jehu asked.

"I'm already home," she said, finally returning his smile. "Home's where the heart is. And my heart's always with James. It's pretty simple now that I think about it."

"Ooohoo!" Jehu exclaimed. "Is that so? I suppose you've finally made the connections then!"

"It's more than just connections, I think..." Amy said, watching the ocean as the sun began its descent. "It's a path I have to take as well... a choice to make? Ha, that rhymes! One wrong step on the bridge means death. And a right step... means life."

"To love is to live," Jehu said. "All the world's a stage, created for this task."

"Jehu..."

"That stage can be anything or anywhere, but it must be built, and it must be built on love for it to be alive. Love is the very fabric of every reality."

"Oh Jehu..."

Amy cried. But they were the good kind of tears. Tears that continued to heal the deepest wounds; hurts that threatened to drown her in the deepest of seas. She felt like she was back on top of the ocean again, floating on the deep blue-green waves. Flying into the sky to be embraced by the warmth of the summer sun.

"James... he built a stage... a whole universe... for me to stand on. He used to be my only audience member... But that's not really true, right? All these people... but for some reason he's the only one I wanted to watch me this entire time."

Jehu gave her a great big hug.

"That's called love, my sweet baby girl. The real stuff, not the shim-sham-flim-flam most people call attraction. Go on. The portal you need to reach your man is drawing near. But if you don't start getting a move on, you'll miss it entirely. It's all about the timing, if you catch my drift. Man, I love sea puns..."

Amy scanned the sky as it continued changing hues, trying to figure out what he meant by it.

"Portal? Is that why we were on Earth?"

"The green flash? No?"

Amy shook her head. Jehu clarified.

"It's an old seafaring legend that's stood the test of time," he said. "Right as the last ray of the sun sets over the horizon, the entire sky glows green."

"I... what..."

"What people don't know... is that the flash is actually one of the portals between Earth and Arthridall. Rather, the green flash occurs because someone uses the portal. It's probably why most people have never heard of it, let alone seen it. Takes a bit of imagination, you see? Most people never imagine that there's tons of portals hidden beyond the ends of their world, even though they're always right in front of them when they need them most."

"Waiting for them to take the plunge…" Amy said. "Kind of like letting myself fall in love."

"Exactly."

"So how do I reach this one?"

Jehu hugged her again and let her go, smiling through his tears.

"Faith, trust, hope, and love." Jehu nodded. "And a little bit of risk and adventure never killed ya. Till we meet again, my friend!"

47

Amy walked to the edge of the sea, the seafoam reflecting the changing light-show in the sky. Everything was color. She wondered if it was King's way of showing his friends there would always be hope no matter what. To follow him to the ends of the earth. To chase after love. One giant game of chase and be chased.

"Till we meet again Jehu…"

Her whisper disappeared on the currents of the wind, riding along them like the trailing mist of a dolphin in mid-flight. She finally understood what he'd been trying to show her all along, the reason why she needed to meet Jehu, and it was beautiful.

Amy didn't look back because she knew in her heart the only way to see Jehu again was to look to the future. He'd be there, waiting to tease her as if he were her own grandfather. For as much as he'd annoyed her, she had inadvertently shown him her heart and he would always have a place in it now. Of that, she was certain.

Amy braced herself to walk across the water. The land, her land, was across the sea. It awaited her return and she, for her part, was eager to return to her friend.

"James…"

Amy walked towards the sun, finding her eyes growing accustomed to what seemed to be an ever-increasing brightness. She felt her heart rise and fall with the motion of the waves, her toes touching the surface of the sea with the grace of a royal princess walking down the aisle to her beloved prince.

She wanted to run. She wanted to dance and sing and be with him again. He called to her; shouting her name to the ends of the universe for everyone to hear. For everyone to be amazed by his unyielding love for her.

"And I'll chase you, James. You don't need to worry anymore. We're in this together no matter what we have to face. I'll make sure of it."

Amy watched the stars fly to her aid. One after another, after another they flew with increasing precision, mixing together with the light of the sunset and the clouds below. The wind picked up around her, almost as a cyclone would, and she gave in to it, allowing herself to be lifted into the sky.

The sun became a pillar of light, drawing all other sources of joy to it. Amy watched the moon traverse from one side of the sky to the other, dancing its way to the beacon of light the sun had made for her. Pink and purple sunset colors blended seamlessly with the stars on either side.

"It's like the entire sky is held within two pages of a book…"

Amy smiled, glowing from the significance of the remark.

"And the sun and the moon bind it all together…"

Amy's heart burst with joy.

And the entire sky burst with green.

***

"AMY!"

James woke from his nap, breathing heavily from the end of the nightmare. Leaning up against the oak tree, he rested his chin on his chest. The place was peaceful, as he expected it should be. It was his resting place, and she'd soon be here too.

He hoped.

"It was so… weird… what do I even call that?"

He closed his eyes, brushing his somewhat messy hair to the side. He slipped the hood off his jacket and chuckled to himself because he knew she'd insist on fixing his hair once she arrived.

He could feel it in his heart.

"She's going to get here soon."

***

Amy watched her life pass by in a blur. She felt nervous that she wouldn't be worth it to him. She dismissed the fear with the understanding that her new reality was looking up for the better. All her memories, some remembered and many forgotten until now, flashed past her face in increasing fashion. A cinema, once appearing like film snippets stretched together across the screen for all they were worth like a seamless masterpiece and, at another glance an orchestra, a beautiful symphony of sorrow and joy.

"It all fits together so well now…"

Everything went white.

***

Amy slowly opened her eyes, her ears pricking up on a sound and feeling the weight of something weighty sitting on her lap. A slightly uncomfortable hardness supported her back, and at a touch she remembered the large oak tree. She didn't remember when she'd fallen asleep.

She allowed her eyes to focus on the object as it came into view, the sunshine filtering down through the tree limbs above. She found the scene entirely pleasant as the cover of the object sitting on her lap reflected the sun's rays.

"It's a book…?" she asked.

The object slipped off her lap as she adjusted her position. A small, brown-leather bound book lay there on the grass, a familiar and metallic looking symbol embossed into the front cover. She looked at it in disbelief for a moment, then frantically felt around for the necklace James had given her to compare them.

"It's gone? Where'd it go? He's going to freak!" she exclaimed.

"Don't worry. It's in there. Or out here too, if you were wondering." he said.

"J...Ja….. James? JAMES!"

"Welcome back."

"JAMES! I thought you were dead!"

"In the flesh?"

Amy almost punched him, but her happiness overtook her.

"You're alive! Wha… I thought he'd killed yo… James…"

James smiled warmly, giving up on the charade. He stood up and offered his hand. She gladly accepted.

"I'm glad I made it too. I was getting worried neither of us were going to make it this far."

Amy looked into her friend's eyes, noticing they held what seemed like an infinite expanse of joy in them. He happily returned her dumbfounded gaze.

"See something you like?"

Amy felt the blood rush to her face, but in a good way. It was different now. She found herself not caring about her embarrassment, instead choosing to embrace him with her entire heart.

"I see myself. And I see someone that I like. Someone I like quite a lot, actually."

He winked. A pair of doves flew out of the magnolia trees behind them, but neither was startled by them because they knew that wasn't what was important.

"You got that way faster than me and I even had a dream about it! But... once I realized you reflect me it finally made sense." he said, smiling. "You found me and pulled me back... kept me from drowning again. But I knew you would. I could feel it... you were right there with me. Right there... all along."

Amy held his hand and leaned back, supported by his strength.

"James... I'm sor... I'm so, so sorr... sorry... I..."

"No worries. I wasn't angry. All I ever wanted was to make sure you knew that. Even as kids I knew I was different... Everyone was so one-dimensional... But you weren't. You spent time with me and listened... And I knew our adventures... We'd make the best stories the world had ever seen!"

"James..."

"Hmm?"

"Did you spend all this time with me just to write this?" she asked, picking up the book. "Am... am I just another character to play around with?"

James pulled her close. Amy felt the rush of his soft breath as it brushed the top of her nose.

"No. I wrote that so that I could say this. I love you. I always have. And I will always love you, to the end of time."

Her lips parted ever so slightly and she smiled. Their eyes locked, infinitely reflecting the other's gaze. His face reddened.

"Everything I've ever done... I wanted to tell you that. I really wanted you to understand that even when I couldn't say it. That I could tell you... I..."

"I believe you." She said.

She leaned in.

"I'm my own person again... I have you to thank for that."

"Amy..."

"You saw who I wanted to be... or try becoming... Before I saw it myself. I... I love you, too."

Time stood still. Space ceased to exist. Love blossomed as their entwined destiny sang. The distance between their lips disappeared, leaving a soft and sweet aroma in its wake. They lost track of who they were and let their lips do the talking. They didn't know where they were, or where they were going. And they found themselves not caring about it. It didn't matter where they were. It didn't matter where they were going.

They'd cross that bridge together when they got there.

****

And so it goes…

Heroes of old and new…

Begin their parts in the story…

But it is only a beginning…

A single passing thought among friends…

A single glance beyond the mirror…

The Peacemakers reign.

I couldn't remember who I was

I wandered this Earth

In the shadows

In the night

My voice swept by the storm.

A boy like me stood on the shore

Just as sad

His tears freely flowing

I asked him why

He told me

"No one listens to

My call across the world

There's more to me than meets the eye

There's more to this than we see."

I grabbed his hand

It felt so warm

And spoke to him

"Please tell me more."

He smiled sadly

And gazed around

Then spoke so quiet

He made no sound

"Friend...

I live to tell the tales of others

The stories

Of heroes old and new

Those times don't matter though

When I'm standing here with you."

With that he turned the page

And walked towards the light.

My heart sank beneath the waves

While I watched him walk above

To tread the places I hadn't seen

To see with eyes I'd never have.

I wept

For the things I'd never known I'd wanted

The things

I didn't know I needed

I missed my friend.

His tears

Fell

From the sky like rain

I knew he missed me too

His tears

Smelled of flowers

And all I could do

Was drown in them

Beneath the waves

The darkest shadows

Shades of sorrow

And guilt.

I heard his voice call out to me

Breathe life into the air

And it was warm

His hand reached out to me

Pulled me up

Brushed me off

I found myself wearing white robes

Just as his

They were soft

Familiar

And wrapped between his arms

He spoke

My heart sang to the tune

"I need you

You're the only one who understands

The things I'm trying to do

Everything is real

All I do

Is reflect what I see

The worlds beyond call out our name

Limitless

Infinite

Adventure

Love."

We kissed

We ran across the bridge together

Went a little crazy

And let our hearts explore

The true reality.

"The strongest bridges build the greatest stories."

-Jamey

Epilogue

Jamey readjusted her shoulder in the tree-hammock she'd made for herself out of various woven cloths, the breeze from the nearby field lulling her gently towards the most wonderful of naps. It had been a long and arduous journey for everyone to be sure. Especially for her tired little feet. She found solace in the fact that she wasn't alone anymore; she had friends now, and one of them was actually her age for once.

She liked it here. It was quiet, but not lonely. It was cooler up in the trees but not cold, thanks in part to the sunshine just peaking though the branches. It reminded her of the knight's academy in the good old days, before Thorne and his army resurfaced. Or of Jehu's cabin, with the view of the mountains and the sea.

She missed being there. But it reminded her of why they were journeying, and why times like these were so precious.

It reminded her of Jehu's wonderful tales about Earth, and of her parents. She hated the cold. But if she could go there even once, and finish figuring out what happened to them, she would brave the worst to find even a single clue. Hence her diary. Someone needed to piece together Jehu's stories about her parents, and she figured it might as well be her.

"Jay! Sweet? You up there somewhere? We need help prepping supper."

Jamey peeked over the checkered brown and green hammock. Jehu was walking down below on the worn grass and dirt, happy as a rooster when the magical ball in the sky returned each morning just to bring wonderful food to it. She stifled a giggle and hid again, hoping the minor noise hadn't alerted him. Her great-grandad was the best at hide and seek.

It was quiet again. But no longer peaceful. Jamey finally decided to sneak a peek over the lip of her blanket again, hoping against hope that he'd gone on to another part of the woods to search for her.

He wasn't there.

"Not exactly comforting," she whispered under breath.

"Oohoo! Did you finish it? Lemme see!"

"Eeek! Why!?"

"More like, HOW? And I'm glad you asked kiddo. But sorry, I'm not going to tell you yet. When you're older mayhaps."

Jamey's ghost returned to her body as quickly as it'd left, her initial peace and quiet tranquility having been replaced by ultimate disgruntled-ness.

"My my, you look just like your mother sometimes."

"You scared me. Again. And you invaded my nest," she said in monotone. "My nest."

"Well next time just answer me instead of trying to hide," Jehu replied, feeling perfectly justified.

Jamey huffed and gave up, handing him the well-worn, leather bound diary. Jehu accepted it and briefly flipped forwards to the last few pages.

"Couldn't figure out how to finish, huh?"

"Well, sort of... for now, I guess. It's hard to finish putting it all together when you only give me bits and pieces to work with. And when it's all outta order."

"No, no, no! It's because there are more stories yet to tell. And the ordering isn't my fault, it's yours. Oh, there's so much more to tell you! And I never said they were dead, so stop moping! Just uh.... Keep it as a journal or something. I do like how you portrayed me though. So incredibly manly!"

Jamey sighed. Her grandad would forever be unflappable.

"But... how do you know my parents aren't trapped there in..."

"Two reasons, sweet. One, I'm THE Jehu, and I know more things than I let on. And two, there's more than one way to cross between worlds. Your research right here is living proof there's more than one way to make a portal. Many more! Many more! Now climb back down to this one for the night. The others are waiting."

www.ingramcontent.com/pod-product-compliance
Lightning Source LLC
Chambersburg PA
CBHW030924020726
47498CB00001B/100